MADE IN CHINA

LEON G. CHABOT

PAGE PUBLISHING, INC.
Conneaut Lake, PA

First originally published by Page Publishing 2020

"Made in China" is a work of fiction, and though some of the places and events depicted in the story are real world, all characters are purely fictitious. Any resemblance to real world persons is coincidental.

Preliminary Cover Design by Neil McGonagle

ISBN 978-1-64628-601-0 (pbk)
ISBN 978-1-66243-610-9 (hc)
ISBN 978-1-64628-602-7 (digital)

Printed in the United States of America

For Susan

I only miss you in the morning

For that's when I remember you most,
in the morning rush as you made ready your day
and I made the coffee and toast.
Yet I must admit just after noon
as the sun climbs high in the sky,
I will think of you and the promise of us,
and I'll sometimes start to cry.
But I know soon the evening comes
and with it some blessed relief.
Then I see you sitting, awaiting my return,
you rise to kiss my cheek.
We sit and talk, recall the day,
remembering things we'd said.
Then night would fall, sleep would call,
and off we'd go to bed.
And now, in the wee small hours of night,
as I lie alone, you taken without warning.
I know by the morrow's midday, I'll be okay,
for I only miss you in the morning.

L.G.C.

Special thanks to all those who lent a supporting hand:

Leo and Irene, Rene and Jack, Robin and Eric, Rob
and Dana, Erin and Cory, Brian and Stan, Craig
and Sue, Chris, Anne Marie, Debby, Susan P.

Chapter 1

*T*he little Asian man walked down the brightly lit corridor for the last time he knew. The pristine tile floor mirrored his reflection as he stepped briskly to his task. He had always marveled at the cleanliness. Because of the sensitive nature of much of the work done here, a sterile environment had been created and maintained throughout the facility.

Reaching one of the many inner-level security doors, he stopped and lowered the parcel he'd been carrying to the floor. He pressed the intercom and waited. The building housed a number of top-secret government research projects, and consequently, there were multiple security checks to pass. He did not mind. He was a patient man by nature.

After a few seconds, a monotone voice asked, "Identification, please."

"Henry Wong. HAMTIN Corporation. Scheduled maintenance," he said. After another short wait, the voice said, "Enter your passcode, please."

Always so polite, he thought, smiling wryly to himself as he punched a six-digit number into the keypad. Instantly the heavy metal fire doors slid open with a hiss. Henry Wong again hefted his parcel to his shoulder and walked the remaining nineteen steps to the end of the corridor. Here the hallway split left and right, leading to various research labs and offices. Located in the center of the end wall was one of the many fire-fighting stations that could be found throughout the building.

HAMTIN is an acronym for Hazard Management and Technologies International, an Arizona-based company that designed, installed, and maintained fire control systems in many of the newer government facilities. Henry Wong is one of the company's senior inspectors. A chemical engineer with a degree from Caltech, he had personally supervised the *development of a new chemical fire extinguisher, the prototype of which he was placing into service today.*

He hefted the unit off his shoulder and gently lowered it to the floor. Alone in the corridor, he removed the existing extinguisher from its cradle and set it next to the larger prototype. From his shirt pocket, he took a small, specially designed screwdriver and removed a three-inch faceplate from the rear of the larger red cylinder exposing an assembly of computer circuit boards and fine electrical wiring. He reached inside and turned a small switch to a position marked "armed." He set a second switch to "receive," then replaced the faceplate. On the front of the unit near the top were two indicator lamps. The one marked "charged" was now lit. The one marked "needs service" was a dummy, never meant to come on. The engineer secured the unit to the wall hanger, where it had been designed to fit perfectly. With the special tool back in his shirt pocket, he threw the old extinguisher over his shoulder and headed out of the building.

"No problems, Henry?" asked the Marine sergeant sitting behind the main security desk at the front entrance as he slid some paperwork in front of the engineer.

"Everything is perfect," he said with a grin, signing the papers. "I am done for the day."

"Lucky you," said the armed Marine guard standing by the door.

"You're all set, Mr. Wong," the sergeant said after casting a hard look at the guard. "Have a nice day, sir."

"Thank you, I will," he said, and with the extinguisher over his shoulder, he left the facility.

"It ain't right, Sarge," the sentry complained. "Fuckin' foreigners are gettin' all the tit jobs."

"Stow it, Kehoe!" the sergeant commanded. "You don't have near enough brains to do that man's job."

Outside, at the bottom of the steep stone steps, Henry Wong paused to set down his load. Behind him, inscribed in large letters into the stone facing over the entrance to the building, were the words "Dahlgren Marine Laboratory." As Wong bent down to lift the extinguisher, a sparkle of light caught his eye. On the side of the unit near the bottom was a small silver nameplate. He knew what the inscription said. He broke into a broad smile that soon turned to a chuckle and then into a deep, uncon-

trollable belly laugh. Passersby stopped to stare at the little man laughing hysterically, wondering what could be wrong with him. Suddenly there was a blinding flash of light, and the lab and everything around it disappeared, vaporized in a millisecond to be sucked skyward by the monstrous atomic cloud rising higher and higher.

*****

"Noooooooooo!"

Sam Mason bolted straight up in his bed, screaming. He was bathed in sweat.

"Good God Almighty!" he exclaimed. He rubbed his face and shook his head, trying to clear the grogginess. *Christ, that felt real,* he thought to himself as he swung his feet to the floor and shuffled into his bathroom. He splashed some water on his face and, leaning tiredly on the countertop, lifted his head to look in the mirror. His bedside clock said 3:47 a.m.

"You've got to stop eating Chinese before you go to bed," Sam mumbled to his reflection through sleepy eyes. He started to lower his face for more water when he suddenly stood straight, eyes wide open, staring incredulously at himself.

"Fire extinguishers!" he said out loud, grinning like a fool. "Goddamn fire extinguishers!"

Sam Mason flipped on his bedroom lights and, with a half-dozen fleet steps, was seated in front of his computer, waiting for the screen to light.

"Damn, this thing is slow," he said impatiently to no one. Sam always worked on a laptop because, as a writer, he needed the portability when doing research. His IBM ThinkPad was getting old he knew, but he'd put off upgrading for no other reason other than he tended to procrastinate about such things. Sam had produced four best sellers on the little machine, and he'd developed somewhat of a sentimental attachment to it. So for now, at least, he tolerated the lack of speed.

The bedside clock now read 3:51 a.m., and from the next room, a perky little schnauzer ran in to look at Sam, her paws clicking on the hardwood floor. She stopped to cock her head and lift her ears as if to say, *What's goin' on? Why're you up so early? Where's my treat?*

"Morning, Annie," Sam said, reaching into the basket of dog biscuits he kept on his desk. He tossed her one, which she snatched in midair.

"Did I wake you?" he said to the pup as his word program came on screen. "Sorry, girl, but this couldn't wait."

Sam started to type when a thought occurred. He looked at Annie.

"Too early to call Irene, you think?"

If Annie thought so, she kept it to herself.

*****

Irene Leslie-Taylor was Sam's publisher. A woman of great esteem and remarkable energy, she'd taken over the family-owned firm from her retiring father over twenty-five years prior. With an extraordinary eye for new talent, she had continued to build the business into one of the most successful and well-respected publishing firms in New York. Now in her midsixties, Ms. Leslie-Taylor was enjoying her semiretirement, choosing to work with but a few of her top authors. Sam Mason was her favorite. He'd become the son she'd never had, and though it was often her job to be demanding and critical, all Sam ever needed to do was to smile warmly at Irene and then watch as the hard edges softened, her heart melting. With his parents long dead, Sam enjoyed a special rapport with this woman and often sought her out for guidance. Both being highly intelligent people and of the same moral fortitude, great mutual respect existed between them—which is not to say they never disagreed. On the contrary, they loved to argue and did so often, but the exchanges were always playful and marked by their most endearing quality, an equally sharp sense of humor. Seldom did either miss a chance to poke fun at the other's expense.

Four a.m., Sam mused. "She ought to be real happy to hear from me," he said as he pressed a number on his speed dialer.

"This had better be good," came a whispery voice after the fourth ring.

"Fire extinguishers, Irene!" Sam said excitedly into the speaker-phone. "That's it, that's the answer!"

"Mr. Mason, it is four o'clock in the morning," Irene said, more than a bit annoyed. "Have you taken complete leave of your senses?"

Sam ignored her mood. "I knew you'd want to be the first to know," he said. "I've solved the problem with the bombs!"

"What, pray tell, could you possibly be talking about?"

"Now, Irene," Sam teased, "did we forget to take our ginkgo biloba last night?"

"Okay, smart guy," she said, sitting up, turning on the night table lamp, "now that you have me awake, why don't you refresh my memory?"

"You remember our lunch last week when I flew down for that signing?"

"Vaguely," she fibbed, feigning disinterest.

"I picked up the tab, remember that?"

"Ahh, but of course. Such rare events do tend to jog one's memory."

"Good." She was awake now; he could tell. "Anyway, I told you all about my idea for a book on Red China, remember? Their development of nuclear weapons. Their inability to compete through the Cold War. Drug smuggling. Any of this ring a bell with you?"

"Of course," Irene said, now serious, "I told you the concept had merit, but that I didn't think one could just go about burying atomic bombs in the ground, and how would these people gain access to all the high-level security bases and facilities you talked about?"

"Exactly!" Sam said, excited again. "And that was my problem."

"And you seem to be mine at the moment. Sam, would you please make some sense."

"Don't you see?" he explained. "Every military building, every air base, every missile silo, every top-secret government lab, even our submarines. They all have fire control systems, right? In case a fire breaks out. Alarms, sprinkler systems, fire hoses, firefighting equipment, and of course—"

"Fire extinguishers," Irene said, finishing his sentence. "Interesting. I like it. Yes, I like it, Sam."

"Think about it, Irene. They're the perfect size. From what I understand, we can now make tactical nuclear weapons small enough to be fired from a handheld rocket launcher. Plenty small enough to be built into a dummy fire extinguisher."

"My guess is you're right about that, but you still have the problem of getting them onto the bases, or wherever."

Sam's mind was racing now. "I'm working on that. Who would you think handles the installation and maintenance of systems at high-security government facilities?"

"No idea," she answered.

"Me either."

"The Army Corps of Engineers, perhaps?" Irene offered. "It would be some military organization I should think."

"Yeah, you're probably right," Sam said. "Do me a favor? Find out for me? And seeing as how you have so much spare time on your hands these days, could you also find out who is the largest manufacturer of firefighting equipment in the US? Could you do that for me? Please?"

"Oh, you are such a charmer, but yes, I suppose I can do a bit of research for you," Irene said with a sigh. "And what avenues of interest are you to pursue?"

"Right now, I'm going to get some ideas down on paper while they're still fresh in my head, and then I think I'll head down to DC for a few days to get the skinny on government overspending."

Irene Leslie-Taylor smiled to herself at the other end of the line. "I think I know where you're going with this," she said. "Have fun, Sam, but be careful. Some of those 'good ol' boys' down in Washington do not much care to have their laundry aired publicly. Give my love to my niece and call me at my office when you get to DC. Goodbye, Sam."

"Good night, Irene."

Chapter 2

Sam Mason lives with his dog, Annie, in an oversized cottage on Cape Cod, Massachusetts. Perched on a hill high above the bay, overlooking Nantucket Sound and the little beach houses nestled in the sand, the big white house has high ceilings, wide hardwood floors, and a white picket fence enshrouded in beach roses. The old cottage is pure Cape Cod enchantment, and it was from here that Sam had penned his first four novels. The views of the tranquil harbor below and the vast ocean, spreading beyond afforded him the serenity in which he liked to write. Not always so peaceful, his life was about to change once again.

Having grown up in Sandwich, Massachusetts, a quaint little coastal town that sits just east of the Cape Cod Canal on the inner bay, Sam had lived by the water since he was a young child. Tragedy had first come to the boy all too early in life when, at the age of twelve, he lost both his parents in a plane crash. His father, an aeronautical engineer by trade, had also been a private pilot, and he'd shared his great love of flying with his family, teaching Sam to fly at a very young age. On one fateful weekend, Sam's mom and dad had flown over to Nantucket for an anniversary celebration. They never made it back. The plane was lost at sea, the bodies never found.

Sam was devastated. An only child, he was then raised by his paternal uncle, a first mate in the Merchant Marine. The uncle was often away on long cruises to faraway ports, leaving Sam alone to fend for himself. Not surprisingly, the boy ran wild for a time, desperately trying to vent the anger he felt at the loss of his parents. He became a loner, unable or unwilling to establish an intimacy with anyone. Sam's only interest seemed to be for the ocean. Those who tried to maintain a closeness to the boy secretly figured that it must have been his parents' loss at sea that drew Sam so forcefully to it, for he was drawn to the ocean like the tide to the shore. With time, the boy's grief subsided somewhat, yet Sam remained curious about the vast waters that surrounded him, and as a young teen, he developed a deep love and respect for the sea.

Sam would spend entire summers on the water. Whenever possible, he could be found on a boat, either working or playing. He made his spending money as a stern man, hauling lobster traps for the local fishermen. On his days off, Sam and his buddies would chase the big game fish that ran in the Cape waters. Blues and stripers were always plentiful if you knew where to find them, and late in the season, when the Gulf Stream's warm currents flowed further north and closer to shore, the boys would venture out to deeper water after tuna or swordfish. It was a rare thing to land one of these monsters, but on the few occasions that they did, their day at sea would prove to be quite profitable.

On one hot, late August afternoon, on a shifting tide, Sam hooked into an 850-pound bluefin tuna. Neither he nor his friends had much money back then to spend on expensive gear, so they'd been hand-lining off one of their father's boats, an eighteen-foot Boston Whaler. For four hours, they fought the giant tuna as it dragged them out to sea. Three different times the boys thought they would run out of line when the big fish went deep in its effort to lose the hook.

"This is just like 'The Old Man and the Sea'!" Sam had yelled to his young friends as he wrestled the giant beast in close, only to have it run again, taking line so fast it would burn through his gloves. By the end of the third run, the boys had long since lost sight of land, and Sam's friends were getting scared. They pleaded with Sam to cut the fish loose. It was just too big; they argued. But Sam would not relent and threatened to throw his two friends overboard if they so much as even touched the line.

Finally, the big fish started to tire, and as the sky was starting to lose light, the boys pulled the tuna alongside. All three stood silent, the two friends awestruck by the size of the massive beast. Sam too exhausted to speak. They managed to get a rope around the tail, and with Sam at the wheel, they towed their prize back to safe harbor. The biggest fish caught on the Cape that summer, it dressed out at almost seven hundred pounds and at $3.50 per pound, their catch netted them over twenty-five hundred dollars. The boys were rich, and Sam had started to earn the reputation as one very tough and slightly crazy young man.

He had no way of knowing it at the time, but future years would prove the reputation to be well deserved. Sam Mason was an enigma. A freak of nature, he was a perfect physical specimen blessed with the physique and conditioning of a professional boxer. That, plus the skill and agility normally gifted to a circus acrobat, easily made Sam his school's best athlete. Incredibly tough and durable, he was just one of those people who never got sick or hurt. Academically he was in the top percentile in his class and upon graduation could have secured a full scholarship to any school in the country. To no surprise to those who knew him, however, Sam chose instead to join the Coast Guard.

For the next two years, Sam Mason spent many of his days and nights jumping out of helicopters on search and rescue missions. An incredibly strong swimmer, Sam proved to be fearless, often plunging into seas that had been determined to be too rough to attempt a rescue. He saved many lives, and his unit became the pride of the service. His commanding officers took note, and something very unusual happened. In his third year with the Coast Guard, Sam was offered a lateral transfer to the Navy and an invitation to the Navy SEAL School. He accepted.

The Navy SEAL (sea, air, and land) program is known to be the most torturously demanding military training in the world, both physically and mentally, and only one in ten thousand seamen are recruited for it. Of those selected, only three in ten make it through hell week and go on to complete the training. A Navy SEAL graduates with the gratification of knowing he is one of the smartest, toughest, and most skillful fighters in the world. Sam Mason graduated as a team leader and was quickly pressed into service in the Gulf War.

Three years and several covert operations later, Sam asked out. His stomach had suddenly soured to the brutality of the job when, on a black op in South America, things went very bad. Mason had been part of an insertion team sent in to take out a drug lord, one of the heads of the Colombian cartel. Professional soldiers, the SEALs never concerned themselves with the politics of a mission, but on this op, Sam felt like nothing more than a paid assassin. He'd had a bad feeling about it from the start.

Three sniper teams of two men each went into the jungle. They were to make their way to three different high grounds overlooking one of the target's known base of operations. Sam's job was to give fire support to the shooter—to watch his back in effect. His sniper's name was Mickey Neally, and he was the closest thing Sam had to a best friend. The two had gone through SEAL school together and had served on the same team ever since. Smart and tough, Mickey was perhaps the craziest, most affable person Sam had ever met. Inherent of a quick Irish wit and a penchant for mischief, Mickey had led Sam on numerous adventures. They trusted each other implicitly, and Neally seemed to understand Mason better than most. The Irishman had a curious way of getting into Sam's head, and the two just liked being around one another. Together now in the jungle, neither man was happy with the dirty job at hand.

The first team to reach their high ground, Sam and Mickey both lay dead still, Sam fifty yards behind his friend, watching and waiting. Somehow, one of the sniper teams was compromised, and the quiet, steamy jungle air was suddenly filled with the sound of small-weapons fire. Firefights seemed to break out all over, and Sam knew the mission was a bust. He radioed for immediate evacuation and signaled for Mickey to withdraw to the designated extraction point, but as the two SEALs started to make their way through the heavy undergrowth, they found their retreat blocked. A dozen men with machetes and machine guns were cutting their way up the hill that Sam and Mickey were trying to get down. Sam devised a quick ambush, and with the element of surprise and their superior skills and armament, the fight was soon over—but Mickey had been badly wounded. He had taken two hits, left shoulder and left thigh. Sam applied quick field dressings to the wounds, and with Mickey slung over his shoulder, he headed for the extraction point.

Arriving at the clearing, Sam found only one other member of the mission team and no chopper. Still en route, the gunship would be late because the op had been aborted so soon after insertion. Heavily outnumbered and with Mickey lying unconscious, the SEALs dug in to make their stand. Once the fighting started it quickly grew fierce, and though many of the Colombian mercenaries were dying, Mason knew that by sheer numbers alone they would soon be overrun. As the enemy steadily closed in, Sam fully expected to die, in a fight no one would ever know about, in a place they were not supposed to be in. The young man wondered for who's bullshit political agenda was he about to give his life, and why.

At the last minute, just as the two SEALs were being flanked, the chopper swooped in, laying down suppressing cover fire. This was the first time Sam could ever remember being scared, within seconds of that rescue. Carrying Mickey over his shoulder, he sprinted to the hovering craft while the other SEAL sprayed cover fire into the jungle. Once Mickey was safely onboard, Sam yelled 'One more!' to the flight crew, then dropped to the ground to give cover to his teammate who ran zigzag across the clearing, diving over Sam into the chopper amid a hail of bullets.

Thinking all three remaining SEALs were safely aboard, the pilot started to take off. Sam was barely able to grab hold of a rising strut as the gunship started to climb. Dangling helplessly, he desperately tried to pull himself up as the craft gyrated violently, avoiding enemy fire. Just as he was about to lose his grip, a single strong arm reached down, grabbed Sam by the wrist, and hauled him into the chopper. To Sam's surprise and complete amazement, the arm that had saved him belonged to Mickey. The other SEAL had also been hit and lay unconscious on the floor. Mickey had come to, and though weakened by his wounds, he'd somehow summoned the strength to save his friend.

"You're supposed to ride these things on the inside," Mickey quipped through a pained smile. And for the first time in a long while, Mason felt glad to be alive. Perhaps it was the near escape from what seemed to be certain death. Sam didn't give it much thought—he only knew he wanted out of the killing business.

Sam Mason finished his service time back with the Coast Guard, stationed right at home in a small base at the east end of the Cape Cod Canal, and it was here that he fell in love.

Chapter 3

O pen a history book and turn to the chapter that talks about the Chinese Civil War, and you should find this event placed as the greatest threat to the future of modern democracy. After a short cease-fire during World War II, the already long-running battle renewed with fierce intensity. The American people, however, were mostly in the dark regarding the actions and consequences of a war fought in a country on the other side of the world. The people were thoroughly tired of war, having just lost over four hundred thousand young soldiers fighting prolonged campaigns on both European and Pacific fronts. There was little concern in postwar USA for the happenings in the Chinese Civil War. Few at home cared that the rebel movement was being orchestrated by the Chinese Communist Party (CCP) under the name of the People's Liberation Army (PLA), and though these developments were certainly distressing to both military and political leaders alike, no other option was offered by the US to the Chinese people to help them emerge from thousands of years of unfathomable poverty and oppression to a more democratic, noncommunist way of life. History shows us that the only US course of action would be to continue to support the corrupt, immoral dictatorship of Chiang Kai-shek's Nationalist Party, right up until the party's exile and then years beyond. This action was an important undertone throughout the civil war and contributed greatly to the vicious resentment and mistrust the Chinese would harbor for the Western world, a hatred that would persist throughout the following decades.

So when on October 16, 1964, near Lop Nor in the central Asian province of Xinjiang, China detonated her first atomic bomb, celebration among military and party commission heads was tempered by the split that existed as to how China's newfound power should be put to use. The reigning top command chose to shun *Star Wars*-type fantasies and avoid arms races. Modernization would continue, but the PRC would display little sign of developing a high seas naval fleet or of sending expeditionary forces abroad as in the style of the British or Japanese empires. As in ancient times, when the great wall was built, the giant would remain at rest.

This philosophy would persist much to the chagrin of many of the top right-wing military leaders who feared an impending doom of the fledgling Chinese nation. By the end of the decade, Vietnam was in full battle, again bringing Western interference onto Asian soil. It would only be a matter of time, the right wing argued, until Western oppression would come to bear on their very homeland.

Having politically alienated herself from Russia, China had thereby forsaken the Soviet protective shield, and what could the PLA alone do, the dissident right wing wondered aloud, to deter an all-out nuclear attack? By the early seventies, at the height of the Cold War, the PRC had amassed only a token arsenal of nuclear weapons—less than 300 compared to the 8,900 warheads the United States boasted and an estimated 3,500 the Soviets could deploy. Worse still, their missile program was almost nonexistent. China had obtained none of the German scientists at the end of World War II. These 'spoils of war' were divided solely between the US and the USSR, leaving China far behind in the modern arms race. Due to the focus given to modernizing the Chinese workforce and to industrial growth in general, military technology had lagged severely. New developments would come slowly. The Chinese had only medium-range ballistic missiles which would be rendered useless against the far superior, more advanced weaponry both the US and USSR could bring to bear. The younger aggressive right-wing leaders knew there must be a better way of securing their nation, their very race, in fact, from annihilation at the hands of the decadent Western barbarians. And a movement ensued.

The most vocal and powerful of this contingent was General Wu Xun, the head of the National Defense Scientific and Technological

Commission. A brilliant scientist and tactician, Wu's rise through party ranks had been meteoric. One of the youngest generals in the PLA, he was revered for having the best mind of the new generation of Chinese leaders. Wu Xun had the good fortune to have been born into a rich family, and it had become obvious at an early age that the boy was special. The father arranged for Wu's education abroad in schools in France and England, then later in the United States. His experiences overseas gave Wu an insight into the ways of the Western world that few of his contemporaries could lay claim to. An advantage he felt over other leaders, men such as Lin Biao, who had never set foot outside of China's borders and knew nothing of the outside world.

Very charismatic and persuasive, Wu Xun garnered many friends and loyal allies throughout the upper echelon of the CCP. He had followers even among the Military Commission itself, whose members ranked higher on the party ladder, such was the esteem in which this man was held. One such commission member was Ch'en Li, a well-respected former naval hero who had evolved into one of Red China's greatest tacticians. Serving also as head of the PLA's Board of Military Academies, Commissar Ch'en was a senior party member and, as such, answered only to Chairman Mao himself.

Ch'en Li shared the experience with Wu Xun of having also been schooled abroad. The two often spent long hours together in deep discussion over the philosophies of Western cultures and the threats posed to the Chinese way of life. Ch'en shared Wu's fears and beliefs that, given the chance, the opportunistic, exploitive machine that was the ever-expanding Western economy, would one day not hesitate to snuff out their emerging nation. They understood China's place in the great scheme of world politics. They understood the delicate balance of power. It was only by luck, they agreed, that Adolf Hitler had not developed the atomic bomb first, or by now the world's population, or that which would be left of it, would all be speaking German. As Hitler had tried with the Jews, it would only be a matter of time, they both believed, until a similar *tsi sing gweilo* (crazy white barbarian) came to power and chose to systematically purge the world of the superior yellow race. Such prejudices were ancient and irrefutable, and they would persist as their own sacred religion taught, well into the centuries ahead. Wu Xun and Ch'en Li believed with every fiber of their being, that fate had indeed cast them as the saviors of not only their nation but of their very race.

In May 1973, in an attempt to educate their peers to the seriousness of the Chinese nation's vulnerability to Western attack, Wu and Ch'en together petitioned the government to appoint a special commission tasked only with devising a plan of action that would take the PRC out of its defensive mode and place her into a position of offensive capability with true power and threat. Only then they claimed, when their military could strike fear into the hearts of their enemy, would China come to be respected. Only then would they enjoy a security that could not be denied.

A hearing was granted, and two months later on July 15, the chairman of the CCP sat with the CCP Military Commission, the premier of State Council, the Ministry of Defense, representatives of the National Defense Scientific and Technological Commission, members of the National Defense Industries Office, the General Political Bureau, and of course the highest-ranking officers of the general staff of all the armed forces. Virtually every important party member was present.

On the surface, it would seem that the CCP was being receptive to the proposal, paying tribute as it were, by bringing such a large contingency together. But it was merely a ruse, and Wu Xun knew it. The chairman realized that in a smaller group, party members would be more open to discussion and possibly more receptive to any variance to the existing military doctrine. The more voices present, the greater the chance of objections and argument, ruling out any real chance of convincing a majority to adopt a more immediate, aggressive course of action.

And so it went. Rather than a presentation of new hope and new direction for the PRC, the huge assembly turned from a political debate to a political debacle. Though Wu and Ch'en spoke eloquently of the dangers of the growing threat of Western supremacy, their words fell on deaf ears. The great majority of those present, out of fear of being tagged disloyal to the party, predictably fell into the conservative line of power under the chairman.

There would be no change. Not now. Not in the foreseeable future.

Perceptively angry and frustrated, Wu left the assembly disheartened but with no less resolve. His supporters expected he would step down in protest, but he would not. He could not. Wu would need to remain in a position of power if he were to affect what he knew to be the only course of action that could ensure his nation's survival through the centuries ahead. Wu Xun knew what had to be done, and only one with a mind as brilliant as his would dare to undertake the scheme he had devised.

Wu stormed down the steps to his waiting car with his executive officer close behind. Major Hu Shi stepped aside when they reached the general's limousine, allowing his superior to enter first. "The old ones are weak, my general," the major said when they were both seated in the rear of the bulletproof car. "Their ignorance will lead us all to annihilation!"

Hu Shi was Wu's most loyal and trusted supporter, having worked under the brilliant man for the past nine years. "No one will blame you for leaving the commission," he said angrily. "Let them try to replace you! They will see what fools they are when progress grinds steadily to—"

"I will not be resigning," Wu interrupted solemnly. "Not now. Not ever."

Hu Shi sat quietly, for he knew the tone of his general's words meant there was much left unsaid.

"Do you trust me, Hu Shi?" Wu Xun asked, staring straight ahead.

"With my very life, my general!"

Wu turned to face his comrade. It had to start somewhere he knew.

"Hu Shi," the general asked, his voice grave, "can I count on your complete loyalty? An unconditional commitment to myself alone?"

"We are of the same mind, Wu Xun. Say the word, and I will die for you!"

"Good, Hu Shi!"

Wu beamed at his subordinate, inspiring great pride in the younger man.

"Listen carefully," he said. "Write nothing down."

The general turned to face forward again.

"In one week," he said, "contact Ch'en Li and set a meeting for him and me alone at my country house on Hainan. You also will be there, no one else. No others may know of this meeting. I will leave it to you to handle the details."

"Consider it done, Wu Xun," the major said with certainty, hiding the excitement he felt at the sudden intrigue.

Wu took a single piece of paper from inside his coat and handed it to his executive officer. "Contact the five men on this list personally. Arrange meetings they can all attend. In the fall, when the rains come. These meetings will also take place on Hainan. These men are to come alone or not at all. They must all be unaware of each other's invitation. Tell them that it is at my personal request. They must speak of this to no one. Memorize the list, then destroy it. Never put these names together again. Not even in conversation!"

The major's eyebrows lifted as he scanned the opened paper. He looked up at Wu Xun, his mouth agape, the question obvious in his eyes.

Wu smiled. "You will learn soon enough, my friend."

Chapter 4

"I 'll be right back, Annie," Sam said to his pup through the front porch screen. The faithful little schnauzer had trotted to the door on Sam's heels, hoping as always to go along with him. Realizing it wasn't happening this time, she settled for lying with her nose to the screen, poised to patiently await her master's return.

"You be a good dog and stay out of the trash," Sam warned, "or no treat for you when I get back!"

Who me? What trash? I don't know what you're talking about, was what Annie's expression seemed to say as she lifted and tilted her head.

"Yeah, you. Be good!" Sam commanded as he turned to head down the walk and through his front gate to start his daily five-mile run.

Mason had just finished a marathon session working on his new book, and he looked forward to the exercise. A nice brisk jog was just what the ex-SEAL needed to loosen the aching muscles that always came when he sat at his computer for long stretches at a time. After his early morning conversation with Irene, Sam had put in nearly ten hours, breaking only twice to feed and walk Annie. Almost six in the evening now, the night air was cooling nicely as the sun fell toward the horizon. This was always Sam's favorite time of the day to run, with the heat of the late May day gone by and the normally crowded seaside route nearly deserted.

The ex-SEAL set a quick pace as he jogged down from the Heights to the seashore and the miles of panoramic oceanfront road-ways that define the Cape's seaside charm and aesthetic allure. The ever-present smell of clean salt-sea air coupled with the beautiful ocean vistas has drawn runners, cyclists, and in-line skaters to its roadsides for years. The Falmouth Road Race in fact, a one-time local 10-K affair, had grown in popularity so much so that it was now an international event, drawing world-class athletes from around the globe.

Sam just found the run relaxing. As he shuffled along past the dunes and the tall beach grasses, he could let his mind wander, his thoughts free to drift off to faraway places, his imagination free to go to work. Some of Sam's most creative thoughts would come to him as he went chugging through the wet sand, playing tag with the ebb and flow of the ocean's waves as they lapped at the cooling beach flats. Oftentimes he'd find himself picking up the pace as he got excited about a new idea forming in his head, and soon he'd be racing home to get his thoughts on paper.

Sam owed a lot to this little stretch of shore. For some, it was the mountains; for others, the wide-open spaces of the western plains. For Sam, it was the ocean. It was his inspiration. His church. His temple of inner peace. Whatever label one might choose to put on it, this was the one place where Sam could come to search out his most inner truths. Here alone, he found sanity, or that which would pass for it. Here he found the patience that led to understanding. Here, the compromises made between birth and death seemed less harsh, allowing the ex-SEAL to find peace in his life, not such an easy feat for most in this ever-confusing existence we call life.

And here was where Sam came to be with Michelle.

Louise Michelle White was the first and only woman Sam had ever loved. She'd been a graduate student studying marine biology at the Woods Hole Oceanographic Institute during Sam's final month with the Coast Guard. As fate would have it, the two were destined to meet.

Michelle had summered on the Cape with her family since as long as she could remember. As a kid, she'd spent endless hours on the beach splashing in the surf and romping through the hot sands, basking in the glorious summer sunshine with her childhood buddies. Michelle had absolutely loved the ocean and everything about it. Her father had been a surgeon and a man who enjoyed the finer things in life. The good doctor owned his share of expensive, shiny sea toys, and Michelle's favorite was a twenty-six-foot catamaran. She could be found aboard the sleek sailboat whenever she could charm dear old Dad into taking her along, which was almost always. The young girl was totally at home on the water and, by her early teens, had become an accomplished sailor. Her love of sailing had persisted through her high school and college years, right up until the day Sam fished her out of the stormy, choppy waters of Nantucket Sound, seconds from drowning.

The day had started out harmlessly enough. Michelle had been sailing her fourteen-foot sunfish up the Falmouth seacoast, venturing in and out of the endless inlets and coves that characterize the southeast stretch of the Cape coastline known as the Fingers. It was a Saturday morning with no classes, and when her girlfriend had canceled their planned day of shopping without warning, Michelle didn't hesitate to drive straight to the docks, happily seizing the chance to go sailing for the day. But this being a last-minute opportunity, she had made the cardinal sin of heading out to sea without checking the weather forecast. Ordinarily, this would bring no great danger for she always kept the little sailboat in close to shore. In fact, that was exactly what she had done throughout the first hour of her morning sail. But this particular day seemed to be growing exceptionally clear and calm, and Michelle had grown tired of the same old length of seacoast she'd been sailing for so many years. So on a whim, she decided to take the little sunfish over to the Vineyard for a quick lunch. It was a decision she would soon regret.

Only four miles off the mainland, the big island appears much closer, especially on exceptionally clear days, and while Michelle had made the crossing to the Vineyard dozens of times, she'd never done it alone, and never in anything so small as the sunfish. But what the heck she told herself, she'd seen guys on jet-skis zip back and forth lots of times, and they'd never had a problem, so why worry. What the young woman had failed to consider was the great advantage of speed, which would allow a jet-skier to race to shore within a few minutes, should bad weather suddenly threaten.

On this splendid, early September day, however, there was not a cloud to be found in the sky. A pleasant, gentle breeze was blowing out of the southwest, which would allow Michelle to tack east for about an hour and a half, then turn with the wind and ride it straight into Vineyard Haven. Perfect. Two hours across, an hour or so for lunch, two hours back. She'd be sailing back into Woods Hole by four or five at the latest. Michelle had wanted to make this sail for some time now and she figured she'd never get a calmer day. What she did not realize was that the placid weather pattern she was feeling that morning was the proverbial "calm before the storm."

A fast-moving squall had been moving up the coastline from Long Island Sound, and when Michelle was about two miles out and just about to change course, the breeze suddenly stiffened and shifted—to northeast. Any good sailor in these waters knows a northeast wind can mean big trouble, and Michelle was immediately concerned. The young woman didn't panic, but she decided it best to turn back and make a run for the mainland. She was already midway across the sound now and about an hour and a half northwest of the island—the worse possible position. A southwest heading back to Woods Hole would take her right into the teeth of the gale!

Seemingly without warning, the sky darkened dramatically as the heavy thunderheads rolled up the coast. Fueled by the warmer Gulf Stream waters, the early Nor'easter moved at incredible speed. The ocean swells were building heavily under the little sunfish and white caps appeared in ever greater numbers as the stiffening wind blew the tops off the rising waves.

Alone and scared, Michelle started her run for the mainland, but the quartering chop quickly became too much for the little boat, and she had no choice but to turn head-on into the building seas to avoid being capsized. She started the electric motor she kept secured to the transom for emergencies, praying the little engine would give her enough power to keep the bow headed into the growing swells. With the little sunfish tossing in the heavy chop, Michelle gathered in the sail, gathered her courage, and with no other choice, steered straight into the raging storm.

Within minutes the squall was directly over her, the full force of the gale whipping the ocean around her into a boiling frenzy. The rain came down in torrents, blinding what little vision Michelle had of the darkened waters ahead. The little wooden sunfish bobbed up and down like a cork, riding up a cresting wave then crashing down the other side only to rise up again on the next swell. With the storm intensifying, it would just be a matter of time she knew until a rogue wave swamped the little craft, plunging Michelle into the violent sea.

Fighting her fear, the young woman battled desperately to keep her boat afloat as long as she could. She knew that even with her life vest on, she would probably not survive a prolonged pounding in seas this rough. With each wave she crested, she had but a few brief seconds to scan the darkening horizon for signs of another boat, but visibility was already less than a few hundred yards, and there was no help in sight.

Michelle was tiring. The pounding was increasing, and it was becoming near impossible to keep the bow into the wind. She knew she had but minutes left. A deep sadness swept over her as she realized she would never see her family again. She would not get to finish her schooling. How ironic she thought to be lost at sea, for the ocean was her first love, her passion, the very subject of her studies, and now she seemed doomed to a watery grave. And suddenly there it was! And no sooner did she see it, then it disappeared behind a wall of water. Had she really seen it? Was there really a light? The little sunfish fought its way to the top of the next giant wave as the wind howled in Michelle's ears. Yes! A light! A boat! There was a boat making its way toward her! And then it was gone again. But she had seen it! On top of the next wave, she caught a glimpse of the angled, orange stripe on the bow of the white vessel. A Coast Guard boat!

"Smitty, hold her steady as you can. Just off her starboard beam!"

Sam Mason had a hand on his helmsman's shoulder, his mouth less than six inches from the man's ear. Still he had to yell to be heard in the screaming wind.

"Dylan," he shouted to a young seaman, "you're with me on the bow. We're gonna try to get a line across her."

By sheer luck, the forty-one-foot patrol boat had been racing in from a training mission off the outer Cape when the new cadet had thought he'd seen a mast bobbing in the chop off their port bow. Sure enough, Sam saw it too, and the three-man crew swung into action.

Mason made his way easily along the side rail and up onto the open bow of the 41. He seemed to be as one with the deck as he rode the swells, seemingly unaware of the violent heaving the boat was enduring. The new cadet was having a much tougher go of it, losing his footing several times and finally scrambling on hands and knees to the harpoon gun where Sam was making ready the rescue line.

"Hook yourself to the gun," Sam yelled to the prone cadet. "I'm gonna fire a line across her beam. As soon as she gets the harness around her, we pull her in. I'll be on the rail, you anchor me. Got it?"

"Got it!" If Dylan was scared, he hid it well.

"Good, you'll do fine!" Sam yelled. "Just hang on to that line!"

When Sam had the line ready, he paused to smile at the novice seaman. "If I get swept over the side and you don't pull me in, I'll fail your rookie ass!"

"Don't worry about me!" the young cadet shouted over the howling gale. "I'll do my job!"

Sam nodded. *Baptism under fire.*

Smitty brought the 41 around so the bow was heading into the waves. Working the throttles on the twin props, he maneuvered in as close as he dared, keeping the little sunfish about forty feet off his port beam. The two boats rode the swells together, rising and falling in unison. Sam allowed for the wind and the rolling deck as best he could, then fired the lifeline at the little sailboat. His aim was true, and the line fell across the bow, just forward of the mast. Her spirits renewed by the prospect of rescue, Michelle scampered forward to grab hold of the rope, but in doing so she had to let go the tiller on the electric motor causing the sunfish to pitch to starboard just as a huge wave was rising under her. The little boat was tossed on its side, spilling Michelle into the swirling sea. Sam watched the whole thing as if it were happening in slow motion. By the time Michelle had hit the water, he was already at the railing signaling for Smitty to come about.

"Hold that line!" he yelled to Dylan. "Bring in the slack as fast as you can!"

Mason searched the dark waters behind the overturned boat until he caught a glimpse of Michelle as she bobbed to the surface in her orange life-vest. He took a quick bearing on her and, without hesitation, jumped into the water feet first—arms and legs extended so as to minimize his immersion. Sam timed his dive to catch the top of a swell, snagging hold of the lifeline as he went in. Riding the swells, then sprint-swimming in the troughs, he closed the distance to the drowning woman in under a minute. Upon reaching her, he found the young woman unconscious, apparently having hit her head when she was thrown into the water. Mason managed to work the line around her while at the same time keeping his own head above water. With one arm around Michelle's limp body and the other holding the lifeline, he fought to keep their heads above water as Dylan pulled them toward the tossing deck of the 41. With the deft touch of an expert helmsman, Smitty allowed the boat to slip slowly astern, helping to close the gap. As Dylan took up the slack, the kid had the presence of mind to walk the line to the rear cockpit, where the hull was much lower to the water. Once alongside, Sam made sure the line was secure around Michelle, then he hoisted himself aboard with Dylan's help, and together, they lifted the unconscious girl into the boat.

"Get us in, Smitty!" Mason ordered as he cut the life-vest off the young woman. "Woods Hole. Flank speed!"

Pressing his fingers to the woman's neck, Sam felt for a pulse.

"She's alive!" he shouted in the wind. "Dylan, get on the horn to Woods Hole. Tell them we request emergency medical assistance and transport on the pier. ETA—fifteen minutes!" With that, Sam turned his attention back to Michelle and started CPR.

Seventeen minutes later, the 41 pulled alongside dock A at the Woods Hole Coast Guard station. Michelle had coughed up some seawater in response to Sam's efforts, but she remained unconscious.

"She's still out, but vitals are strong," Sam told the EMTs as they scurried aboard with the gurney. "Probable concussion. She's got a pretty good bump, right side of her head."

"Okay, thanks," one of the technicians said. "We'll take it from here."

They wrapped Michelle in a heated blanket and strapped her to the stretcher. "Looks like she'll make it," the tech said after a quick exam. "Nice job, Chief!" A minute later, Michelle was in the waiting ambulance, speeding toward Falmouth Hospital.

*****

Three days later, Sam had a surprise visitor at the canal docks. Michelle had come accompanied by her mother to thank the man who had risked his own life by plunging into the stormy sea to pull her out. Sam could not believe it was the same girl standing in front of him that he had just seen three days earlier, her body limp and barely alive, her skin pale and soaked to the bone, hair plastered to her face. The young woman standing before him now was one of the most beautiful, vibrant women he had ever seen. Her face glowed with barely a hint of makeup, and her big blue eyes sparkled with life from behind the long golden strands of hair that fell about her smooth, tanned shoulders. She was fit and trim and obviously fully recovered.

Michelle had been completely embarrassed by her foolish ordeal, and it was only at her mother's insistence that she'd agreed to seek out her savior. The pretty young woman had prepared a very brief thank-you speech for the occasion, but as Sam came up from below decks into the bright summer sunlight, Michelle was completely taken aback by the handsome young man, and she found herself barely able to sputter out her gratitude, much to her own annoyance. Never had any man had such an effect on her! Sam could do no better. With his own heart pounding in his throat, he was barely able to croak out an acceptance to the mother's invitation to dinner. Sam kept the dinner date, and the young couple were soon falling deeply in love.

*****

Sam and Michelle were married a year to the day later. They were perfect together. Sam finished his service with the Coast Guard, bought a boat, and started a charter fishing business. Michelle, pregnant with their first child, was finishing her studies at the Oceanographic Institute. Never had two people been happier together. But fate held yet another crushing blow for the young man who'd already come to know death all too well.

It happened on a cold November night. Michelle had been headed home from a late-night class when a bus swerved into her lane, killing both her and the unborn child. Once again, Sam had lost the two people he loved most in the world. This time the loss was more than he could bear, and for all practical purposes, he just dropped off the face of the planet. Deeply depressed and unable to deal with the pain, Sam disappeared for three years without a word to anyone. Mickey Neally finally tracked him down in Canada, working on a logging crew, harvesting giant sequoia in southern Ontario. Sam's friend managed to drag him back to the Cape, where he cleaned him up, sobered him up, and got him to a good therapist.

Once he received the help he'd so desperately needed, Sam's recovery was rapid and complete. He stopped trying to understand the tragedies in his life and came to accept the fact that there was no sense to be made of any of it. There was no blame. No guilt to bear. No "what-ifs" or "if onlys" that held any meaning or truth. It had simply been a matter of fate, and the rest of his life need not be punishment.

After a while, Sam was able to embrace what little time he'd had with Michelle and be thankful for it. In time, he was even able to allow himself to remember her love, and this, more than anything else, helped keep him sane. Her love for him, and his love for her. This became his greatest comfort. This was what Sam chose to believe in. Their love had been true. Finally, and without remorse, he could hold her in his heart and think of her often.

So as Sam made his daily trek along the very stretch of ocean where he had once pulled Michelle from certain death, he once again sent her his love, carried across the waves on the wings of thought. And as always, the love came back tenfold.

Chapter 5

"*Washington Post*. Keri Starr speaking," answered the sexy voice on the other end of the line.

Back in his cottage, Sam had finished his run, showered, fed, and walked Annie, and had just a few arrangements to make for his trip to DC before he could venture out for his own dinner.

"You know," he said, "with that voice and a name like a porn star, you could always get yourself a 900 number should the bottom ever fall out of the gossip column business."

"I don't write gossip! I write behind the scenes news items. And when are you gonna get a real job, huh, Mason?

Keri Starr was like a sister to Sam. She was Mickey's kid sister's best friend. After Michelle's death and Sam's self-induced isolation, these two women were instrumental in helping Sam reestablish emotional contact with the opposite sex.

"Work is overrated," Sam kidded. "Like maturity. Too much is bad for you."

"Maturity?"

"Absolutely. When one becomes too mature, one forgets how to think young. And that leads to cynicism, which as near as I can tell, is the most dangerous element of growing old."

"Well, Sam, no one will ever accuse you of being overly mature!"

"I'll take that as a compliment."

"You would," Keri said, smiling to herself. She'd loved this man like a brother for almost seven years now, dating back to the summer when she had first met Sam.

For the first year or so after bringing Mason back from Canada, Mickey would make frequent trips up to the Cape to check in on him. Back then, Neally had worked for the FBI, stationed in Washington, and his position allowed for a certain amount of freedom to travel. Oftentimes he'd bring along his kid sister Nicole. Of course, everyone called her Nicki. Mickey and Nicki. Mom liked the rhyme scheme she used to say. Nicki would drag her pal Keri along for company, and the two young women spent many a fun weekend in the big cottage by the sea, learning about life from big brother and his mysterious friend.

Though young and irrepressibly mischievous, both women were sensitive, intelligent, and mature beyond their years. Without fussing over him, they provided Sam a female support system that was both comforting and safe, enabling him to take the baby steps needed to make it back into the world of expressive human emotions. Naturally, both girls secretly harbored a crush on this handsome older man, and the fact that he'd experienced so much personal loss in his lifetime touched that inner soft spot that all good women have within themselves, making the ex-SEAL even that much more attractive. Sam's recovery, however, dictated a "hands off" policy, so the relationships became, and remained, purely platonic. That is until the night Nicki slipped into Sam's bedroom to climb naked under the sheets.

The group had been up late, sitting around the kitchen table playing cards and drinking lemon drop shots, Nicki's favorite. Having badly overindulged, she'd worked up the courage to play out her fantasy. But Sam would have none of it. Without hesitation, he wrapped her up in the bedsheet and carried her like a child back to her room. Embarrassed and infuriated but with her arms pinned to her sides, Nicki kicked and squirmed in vain, trying to break Sam's hold. Finally, she leaned over and bit him on the nose, not hard enough to draw blood, but Sam dropped her in the hall, and Nicki stormed into her room, slamming the door behind her.

Sam wrote the incident off to booze and teenage infatuation, but that would be Nicki's last night spent in the big cottage by the sea.

*****

"So," Keri teased in her sexiest voice, "did you call just to harass a hardworking girl, or is there something special I can do for you?"

"Don't make me come down there and spank you, young lady!" Sam scolded in fun. "You're not too old for me to take you over my knee!"

"Oooo, baby!" she purred, and then she could no longer contain her giggle, and the two old friends had a good laugh.

"So how are Nicki and Erin doing?" Sam asked.

"Oh, you know Nicki. Nothing keeps her down, and Erin is just as cute as ever."

Erin was Nicki's four-year-old daughter, Sam's adopted niece. Forty pounds of dynamite.

Nicki had not reacted well at all to the rejection by Sam. Headstrong and impetuous, she ran out and married the first sailor she could find. When the guy turned out to be a major loser, Nicki filed for divorce. And much to her delight, the guy split. Glad to be rid of him, Erin would be the only good to come from the marriage. Though it meant Nicki was left to raise the little girl on her own, she never complained; she just did whatever it took. The success of Sam's books had brought him more money than he would ever need, and he'd offered on several occasions to help out financially. But Nicki would have none of it. Especially from Sam. But even from her brother, she refused all but the most inexpensive gifts at birthdays and Christmastime, bringing back extravagant purchases and returning the money. Sam didn't completely understand Nicki's attitude, and the rift between them hurt him more than he let on. *But she was Mickey's kid sister!* And, therefore, off-limits. Though he worried after her from time to time, he remained respectful of Nicki's wishes, admiring from afar her courage and independence.

"How's Nicki's new job going?" Sam asked.

"Oh, God, she loves it!" Keri said. "One of her favorite professors from the university is doing some kind of research at this place. Don't ask me what, she doesn't say much about it. Some hush-hush thing for the military, I guess. Anyway, this guy's trying to get her assigned to his lab team, and she's really excited about it."

"Good for her. She still cussing like a sailor?"

"Believe it or not, she's almost cured!"

"No way!"

"Yes, way! Get this. She went to a hypnotist! Some doctor who specializes in compulsive disorders. Can you imagine?"

"I can imagine just about anything when it comes to Nicki," Sam said honestly.

"But this is such a trip, Sam! I guess most of this guy's patients have, like, eating disorders, or they want to quit smoking. You know, normal stuff. But Nicki," Keri giggled, "just marches in and says, 'Okay, Doc, put me under so I can stop saying "fuck" every other word'!"

Sam chuckled at the thought. "And it's really working?"

"Well, most of the time. When she gets really tired and stressed out or pissed off, she'll still drop the occasional F-bomb. But yeah, overall, I'd say it's working. She's a riot now to listen to! This guy's got her substituting all these really goofy words for swears. You know, like, instead of calling some guy in a bar a fucking asshole, she'll call him a freaking butthead. And you know how she used to say 'Jesus H. Christ' all the time? Well, now she says 'Jesus H. Christmas Tree Shops'! She's a real scream when she's had a few!"

"Christmas Tree Shops?"

"Yeah, I swear. She's a trip, Sam!"

"I can't wait to put her to the test," Sam said, grinning impishly.

"You be nice, Sam! Nicki's worked really hard on this. Ever since that night, Erin walked out of the kitchen with a finger sandwich in her hand, right into the middle of Nicki's Tupperware party and announced, and I quote, 'This fucking tuna fish tastes like shit'!"

Sam roared. "I hadn't heard about that one!"

"Yeah, well, she was mortified, and she figured she'd better nip it in the bud."

"Ahh, good idea. Erin starts preschool next year, right? I'm pretty sure her teachers would frown on that sort of thing."

"Most definitely," Keri agreed, swiveling in her chair to look out over the city. "So, Mr. Mason, what *can* I do for you?"

"I need a favor. I'm flying down to Washington tomorrow. If you're free tomorrow night, dinner's on me."

"Tomorrow night, huh?" she said, checking her calendar. "Sure, I can make it. I should be out of here by eight or nine at the latest. What's up?"

"I want to pick that clever little brain of yours. I need a little background information on our overpaid, elected public servants' over-spending policies. You know. A little dirt. Big, bad government type of stuff."

"Well, you've come to the right place. Anything specific you're looking for?"

"I'll fill you in at dinner. Pick you up at the paper, say, nine o'clock?"

"Sounds good, Sam. Where're you staying?"

"The Four Seasons."

"Nice. Hey, I hear their new chef makes a shrimp scampi that's to die for. I'll tell you what, get us a table for nine o'clock, and I'll meet you in the dining room."

"You sure?"

"Positive. Just tell the maître d' it's for Keri from the *Post*, and he'll give you a good table."

"Okay, kiddo. I'll see you then."

"Bye, Sam."

Sam made two more quick phone calls. One to arrange room and board for Annie, and the other to his mechanic at the Barnstable airport with instructions to ready his Cessna 172 for flight first thing in the morning. He packed a bag for the trip and, satisfied that all was ready for the morning, headed to Woods Hole and his favorite restaurant, a quaint little place right on the pier called the Landfall. The owner was an old tennis buddy of Sam's, and after dinner, it was customary for the two to sit at the bar and close the place. Jimmy loved Sam's books and was forever trying to pry the "what happens next" out of Sam.

You'll get an earful tonight, old friend, Sam thought to himself as he drove across town, still excited about his story's most recent development.

Chapter 6

Early September 1973, the Province of Guangdong in the Canton military region, China

China's southernmost province, Guangdong is roughly triangular in shape with a long coastline bordering on the South China Sea. It is separated from the Yangtze River plain to the north by the Nanling Mountains, a rugged series of ranges that run east to west. Most of the province is drained by three rivers, the Xi, the Bei, and the Dong, all of which converge in central Guangdong to form the Pearl River, which flows south to the sea where its river delta provides for some of the most productive rice fields in China. Also, under Guangdong's provincial jurisdiction is the large and economically and politically important island of Hainan, Ch'en Li's place of birth and site of Wu Xun's country retreat.

The climate in southern Guangdong and Hainan is tropical—hot, wet, and humid. Though precipitation in China varies greatly, rain is plentiful along the southeast coast, where China's natural elevation draws moist air from the Pacific, creating rainfalls of over eighty inches per year. Eighty percent of this moisture falls during monsoon season, late summer through early fall, and it falls mostly in the Pearl River Valley and the southernmost regions of Guangdong, including the island of Hainan.

Typhoon season hits here with a fury like no other, with the large majority of the storms making landfall most often in the provinces of Fujian, Jiangsu, and Guangdong.

For the better part of two months, the coast of Guangdong and the isle of Hainan are all but shut down, with most inhabitants laying low, battened down against the relentless heavy rains and violently strong winds of these South Pacific monsoon storms. It was under this protective veil of nature, as she vented her seasonal wrath, that eight of the most powerful men in Asia slipped quietly and completely undetected into Wu Xun's seaside retreat. They all came this night after being interviewed and briefed by Wu and Ch'en Li, and though each was motivated by his own cause, they all aspired to the same end result. They all came to become part of an alliance that would change the course of history and place the Asian world, led by themselves, as undisputed ruler of the planet in the coming millennium.

Situated well away from any main roads, Wu's island retreat sat isolated atop a rocky cliff rising straight up from the raging ocean waters a hundred feet below. More of a mansion than a cottage by Chinese standards, the house boasted a large conference room with an east wall of glass overlooking the angry sea. It was in this room that Wu Xun and Ch'en Li would unveil the preliminary details of their long-range plan.

Though no introductions were needed for any of those present, protocol dictated that Wu acknowledge these brilliant and powerful men. Aside from himself, his executive officer Hu Shi, and his military commissar Ch'en Li, Wu had invited three other Chinese, as well as two North Korean officials of great importance to his clandestine congregation. Continuing clockwise around the table, the first was Kao Ting-fa, head of the Chinese National Defense Industries Office, which was responsible for coordinating and integrating military and civilian economies, directly supervising any and all funding for such, in essence, the controller for military finance. Seated on Kao's left was Liu Ying-ch'ao, presently second-in-command of Chinese military intelligence—technically a wing of the PLA, and obligated as such to the general staff, but officially answering directly to the CCP Military Commission. The next man was a cause for wonder. And concern.

Though well known to everyone in the room, the presence of the man seated at the far end of the table, across from Wu Xun, was a great surprise to the rest of Wu's guests. Though no one would question this man's prominence in his chosen profession, they all wondered how he might serve their cause. The leader of the Asian underworld, Lo Fang was the universally acknowledged head of the evil, ancient Chinese society known as the Tong, making him the most powerful and feared criminal in China. His influence and reach extended well beyond the confines of Chinese borders, and though his presence here seemed a mystery to the others, the importance of his role would soon be made quite evident.

Finally, sitting alone to Wu's right were the two North Koreans. Closest to him sat Chung Gi-nam, chairman of the Central People's Committee. Except for President Kim Il Sung, he was the most powerful official in North Korea, and it was well known in certain circles that he had long aspired to replace Kim as the number one man. Beside him sat Chung Kwang-yop, his brother, and head of the Military Foreign Affairs Bureau. Highly placed officials, the two Koreans were obviously extremely influential within their government's political structure, but more importantly to Wu Xun, they represented the leadership of the North Korean contingent presently supervising negotiations with South Korea during the ongoing reunification talks.

Wu needed a liaison to the South Koreans. In years ahead, he would need a go-between to seduce and enlist selected members of certain "free world" Asian economies. Wu would need rich, powerful Asian businessmen with strong Western bonds in order to implement his long-range plans to infiltrate various US and Soviet economic interests and their relevant political arenas. He would need a venue by which he could establish legitimate, privately owned business concerns within the targeted nations, something not possible working from a noncapitalistic society such as China. The North Koreans would have access to such men.

"I trust everyone here was able to make his journey in complete secrecy as was requested?" Wu said after finishing with the formalities. The silent nods from his guests confirmed what he already suspected.

"Excellent. I am sure it is not necessary to stress the importance of security to this operation." Wu paused to scan the faces of his audience.

"Gentlemen," he continued, "we share a common belief. Our current ruling powers are leading the Asian world down a path of doom, and with the absence of a drastic change in that path, our people will inevitably face annihilation at the hands of the monstrous, all-devouring animal that is the ever-developing Western economy!"

Wu stood at the head of the table as he addressed his guests. "Our leaders are blind to this!" he said loudly, hammering his fist on the table in cadence to accentuate his words. "Ever so patient, they cling pathetically to the ancient philosophies of our long-dead ancestors. They continue to build walls around the Chinese people when the time for change is so clearly upon us!"

Wu paused dramatically. It was his moment, and he was going to play it for all he could.

"Each of you," he went on in a quieter voice, "have been abroad, as I have myself. We have visited the great nations. We have seen the enemy where he lives. We have witnessed his awesome might. We are not deluded enough to think that we can match this power just because it is written that it will be so. Just because our leaders, most of whom have never stepped foot outside our own borders, tell us it will be so. I ask you, my comrades, can we afford to be so naive?"

The question was rhetorical. The room remained silent.

"There must be change, my friends, if we as a people are to survive."

The general panned the room as he spoke, taking in each face in turn. "Surely we know this to be true," he said, gesturing with both hands to the group. "But I ask you all, who shall bring about this change?"

Wu's audience was completely captured now, and all eyes remained fixed on the general. "You all know of me," he said softly. "You all know of my reputation. And I see in your eyes, my comrades, that you all know the truth when you hear it."

Wu leaned forward, placing his hands on the table, his face solemn, his voice barely more than a whisper. "So believe me when I tell you that it will be us to make this change." Wu stood straight. "Believe me when I tell you there is a way. And tonight, you shall hear how!"

Wu Xun took his seat at the head of the conference table. "My great friend Ch'en Li," he said, bowing slightly to the commissar, "a senior member of our party's Military Commission, will outline some of the preliminary details."

Ch'en Li stood, returning the shallow bow to the general before turning to address the group. "First," he said, "the matter of security. The privacy of this meeting has been greatly aided by the severity of our monsoon season. No coincidence. The meeting was scheduled at this time for that very reason. However, at future gatherings this will not always be so. Though both General Wu and I wield considerable influence on this island, further safeguards will be put in place to ensure our continued solitude. We will arrange for my nephew, a colonel in the people's army and presently the commander of the Nanjing military region, to be transferred to the Canton region. Here he will serve us well, for aside from governing all military affairs in Guangdong, he will also be responsible for security throughout the Canton region, including the district of Guangxi."

Ch'en Li moved next to a large map hanging on the wall behind Wu Xun.

"As some of you may know," he continued, "a new research and development facility is in the planning stages. Nuclear research and development. Construction is scheduled to begin next spring, after the site is chosen. It is our good fortune that General Wu and I head up the selection committee."

Ch'en drew a circle on the map.

"The site shall be in northern Guangxi," he said, "in the foothills of the Nanling Mountains. General Wu will be named head of research and development, the supreme authority on-site with full control over all laboratory projects. My nephew will be in a position to guarantee our secure passage throughout the region while at the same time supervising security at the new facility."

The commissar allowed himself a thin smile. "Before this night is over, comrades, General Wu Xun will enlighten you all as to what the exact nature of his work will be at 'our' new laboratory."

"How do you intend to maintain secrecy from the party, should an independent investigative body be assigned to the site?" This first question coming, not surprisingly, from Liu Ying-ch'ao, second-in-command at military intelligence.

"I shall defer to Wu Xun in this matter," Ch'en answered as he sat back down, a satisfied look on his face.

Wu remained seated.

"The answer to your question, General Liu, is twofold," he said. "First, as Ch'en Li has indicated, I shall be the ultimate authority at our country's newest and most modern research facility. The entire venture is of my creation. I have been the principal designer and engineer since the project's inception. I alone will determine what technological material is to be released for review. In short, I will tell the commission what I want them to know. As always, regular progress reports will be made to the proper officials, and you can be sure, Ying-ch'ao, that progress will be made. The party will be led to believe we are always on the verge of the next great discovery, and have no doubt, gentlemen, such developments will emerge, for there will be many, many ongoing projects in Guangxi. There will simply be one project that no one outside of this room will ever be aware of."

The general waved a hand in the air as if dismissing the subject. "I will tell the party what they want to hear, and they will be happy."

Wu glanced from face-to-face, encouraged to see confidence reflected in the eyes of such discerning men. His gaze held on Liu Ying-ch'ao as he spoke again.

"Secondly, when you, Ying-ch'ao, are the head of military intelligence, we shall have exclusive access and control over all classified information and confidential communications throughout the entire homeland!"

Nobody's fool, the inference was not lost on Ying-ch'ao.

"When will this take place, my general?"

"General Chang's assassination is planned for the early spring," Wu replied matter-of-factly. "You shall arrange to be out of the country at the time. We will discuss details at a later meeting. Ch'en Li, finance?"

Wu's first lieutenant handed a file folder to Kao Ting-fa.

"Comrade Kao," he said respectfully, "your office will be of the utmost importance to our plans for the obvious reasons. Funds will need to be diverted to our control. The finance of this operation will be your responsibility. How it is done will be left to your discretion. This is an outline of our immediate needs. We will talk in more detail before you leave here tomorrow. At the moment, time is on our side, but we humbly suggest you start formulating financial strategies as soon as possible. You have our complete faith and trust in this matter."

Kao Ting-fa nodded acknowledgment to Ch'en Li, then turned to address Wu. "General Wu," he said humbly, "I do share in your beliefs as to our nation's fragile state. I also am of the opinion that drastic change is needed. And I am completely committed to your service, my general." Then with an emphatic, encompassing sweep of his hand. "I believe we all are, or surely you would not have us here."

"True," Wu said. "And?"

"And I do not propose to speak for the others, Wu Xun, but you have aroused my curiosity beyond all control. Has not the time come for you to enlighten us as to the specifics of what it is we are becoming a party to?"

Kao Ting-fa bowed to the head of the table before going on. "Forgive my bluntness, Wu Xun, but...what exactly is this project in Guangxi?"

Kao looked around the table at the others, then back to Wu Xun.

"What *is* this plan of yours?"

Like a benevolent schoolmaster presiding over a group of his most gifted students, General Wu sat silently smiling for several seconds before answering.

"Yes, my comrade," he said finally, "it is time. You have all been patient long enough."

Wu Xun stood purposefully and walked the few steps to the wall of glass facing the ocean far below. He stood perfectly still for several moments, gazing out over the stormy South China Sea, his back to the room, hands clasped behind him. When at last he spoke, his voice was surprisingly gentle. "Is anyone here familiar with the term 'nuclear winter'?"

The room was quiet, the sound of windblown rain splattering off heavy glass panes the only reply.

After a moment, Wu went on. "Nuclear winter," he said, "is the reason the Cold War persists. It is the reason the Americans and Soviets do not attack each other. They cannot! Nuclear winter, comrades, is the greatest deterrent to war that man has ever encountered!"

The general continued to stare out over the dark water as he spoke. "Science has recently discovered," he went on slowly, "that an all-out nuclear war between the two superpowers would send so much dust and debris spewing into the Earth's atmosphere that it would cause a huge, impenetrable cloud to envelop the Earth, blotting out the sun for dozens of years, creating a nuclear winter. All life on Earth would perish!"

Captivated by Wu's revelation, his guests hung on his every word.

"World War III," he continued, "would mean the end of all humanity. There could be no victor."

The general stepped a foot nearer to the window, so close now his breath fogged the pane. "So I ask you, comrades, when a warrior nation, a superpower, finds that their greatest weapon has been rendered useless, what then do they do?"

The big room was silent except for the howl of the storm raging outside.

"The answer is quite simple, my friends. They build a new one!"

Wu turned now to face his audience. "The enemy builds a new bomb!" he said, his voice rising as he strode back toward the table. "One that will not spew ash into the stratosphere! A bomb that produces extremely high levels of radiation yet causes very little physical damage! A bomb that will kill millions of people yet leave whole buildings intact!"

As Wu Xun reached the head of the table, he again slammed his hand down for effect. "Our enemy builds the neutron bomb!"

Wu's dramatics succeeded in causing a mild murmur of disbelief to circle the table.

"It is true, comrades." It was Liu Ying-ch'ao of Chinese intelligence who spoke above the babble. "I have seen the evidence of such a bomb being tested by the Americans, though they have not yet announced their feat. We do not know of the Soviets, though we suspect they are also pursuing the same line of research."

All eyes turned to Wu Xun, who was leaning into the table, a wide smile upon his face, waiting.

It was Kao Ting-fa who finally dared ask, "What are you saying, Wu Xun?"

The general stood straight, his evil grin still in place.

"I can build this bomb!"

Chapter 7

*J*oo Kwan-jo was running for his life. The fear that gripped him as he scrambled through the back alleys of the Korean slum was paralyzing. It clutched at his guts and radiated through his entire body, causing muscles to tighten and spasm. Driving himself to fight through the terror, Joo stumbled onward, desperately seeking an escape or some dark shadow of a place perhaps, where he might hide until his pursuers passed him by, allowing him to double back to freedom. The thought of capture and the brutal torture that would surely follow were too horrible to imagine, and as the images surfaced in his mind, he immediately stuffed them back down into his subconscious, shaking them off as though they were a physical weight.

With the rest of his gang lying dead or dying, murdered by the henchmen of the devil himself, Joo was left alone. The Korean had only a few rounds left in his Uzi machine pistol, and he could not possibly hope to shoot it out with the dozen or so men that were stalking him. No, stealth was his only chance of escaping alive.

The ambush Joo had planned for his most hated enemy had backfired. Though his scheme had seemed foolproof, someone had betrayed him, and it was his own men he'd seen slaughtered mercilessly by the hatchet-faced man and his troops.

Joo Kwan-jo had always led a dangerous life, he and his people living and dying by the sword. His business dealt in the dark underworld of drug running, prostitution, and gambling. A world where the competition was deadly and one mistake could cost you your life. The Korean gangster had made a power play to regain control of the drug traffic throughout the northern regions by trying to assassinate the current reigning drug lord, Lee Hak-joon—the hatchet-faced man as he was known *on the streets. Named so in part for the distinct sharpness of his facial features as well as for his known preference for the use of an ax as a tool for interrogating his enemies.*

Lee Hak-joon had been the most feared man on the streets of Korea, North or South, for the past five years, and he was barely twenty years old. As a young teen, Lee had earned the reputation as a skilled and fearless warrior capable of obscenely gruesome acts of violence, his ruthless ways leading him, in a very short time, to become the leader of the largest street gang in Seoul. Realizing at an early age the value of fear as a psychological weapon, the young criminal wielded it as no other had before him. Stories of the brutal mutilations of his enemy's bodies shook the courage of all but the bravest of foes, and those daring enough to go up against the madman were easily defeated by Lee's most powerful weapon, his brain.

Lee Hak-joon was a born psychopathic killer for sure, but he had also been blessed with a genius IQ, a combination that proved unimaginably deadly. Lee was a half-breed, the son of a Korean whore and a German arms dealer. A far superior planner and tactician, the young drug lord easily outwitted his adversaries. Rival gangs proved to be no match for his cunning, and the growing tales of his capacity for brutal violence soon discouraged any designs to challenge Lee's supremacy on the streets. By the age of eighteen, the hatchet-faced man had become the sole proprietor of the South Korean drug trade, the mere mention of his name striking fear into the hearts of both criminals and police alike. Free from the dangers of competitors, Lee Hak-joon's only concern was for staying one step ahead of the law, an easy task for the criminal genius as the feeble efforts of the police not on his payroll were constantly undermined by Lee's extensive network of informants.

In time, the drug lord even found the means to expand his trade across North Korean borders, where he'd briefly taken on Joo Kwan-jo as a partner to help with the development of his new territory. Before long, however, Joo found himself relegated to junior status, a mere underling to Lee, with his share of profits dwindling steadily. Faced with the inevitable, the North Korean had made the deadly mistake of trying to overthrow the hatchet-faced man, and now he found himself on the run, hiding in some dark, backstreet alley of Seoul—predator turned prey.

Fearing detection, Joo glanced frantically over his shoulder as he broke from the shadows and sprinted down yet another black alleyway. They were closer now—he could hear them calling to one another through the darkness. He pulled up at another shadowy doorway only to find it unyielding to his frenzied tugs. The night air was hot and excessively humid in the depths of the dank city, and sweat poured down Joo's brow, stinging his eyes. Wired and fully panicked, the Korean gangster pressed on, moving deeper into the bowels of the city, scrambling over the heaps of trash and filth that littered the inner ghettos. Praying he'd slipped his pursuers, Joo stopped again, pressing himself flat against the brick, desperately trying to calm the adrenaline-fed ringing in his head as the blood pounded through his veins. Slowly quieting his breathing, Joo strained to hear any sound of his pursuers, hoping against hope he might have eluded them. But what he heard through the mist behind him robbed the horrified Korean of any remaining courage.

"Lee Hak-joon, he has gone down here!" came the cry from the head of the alleyway. They were closer still! And the hatchet-faced man himself was with them! The fear overwhelmed him, but just then, Joo caught a glimpse of light from a lamp as it flickered briefly in a doorway just a dozen or so yards to his right, someone cautiously investigating the night sounds. His heart leaped and he again broke cover, dashing madly toward the source of the dim light, only to once again have a door slammed in his face. Fully irrational now, Joo pounded on the door as he pleaded for help, forsaking any chance of a silent escape. Visions of victims being tortured, eyes and tongues cut from their heads, flashed through Joo's overwrought mind. Ghostly atrocities he had witnessed firsthand, returning now to haunt him in his final moments of life.

"Over here!" came the call from Lee's men as they moved in for the kill.

Joo Kwan-jo was like a caged animal now. He ceased his battering as he spun catlike in the direction of the voice, harmlessly firing a quick burst at the unseen enemy before breaking cover for the last time, stumbling blindly down one final black alley, finding to his horror, a dead end!

"Take him alive!" Lee commanded from the shadows as Joo pressed his back to the alley wall, seemingly trying to meld into it. His terror

consumed him, and in a final act of defiance, Joo stepped out into the dim light of the half-moon and raised the Uzi to place the barrel in his own mouth. A single shot rang out, hitting Joo in the shoulder, knocking the Korean off his feet and spilling his weapon to the ground. Clutching at his torn shoulder, Joo Kwan-jo scrambled back to the wall behind him, meekly pressing against the cold brick, a steady, high-pitched, indecipherable babble flowing from his lips. Joo was quite mad with fear now, and he lost all physical control. He urinated in his pants, no longer able to suppress the gruesome images that rose from the depths of his subconscious like demons from hell.

From the darkness, two men emerged slowly on either side of the alleyway. They each held a machine gun loosely at their sides, gazing upon Joo with expressionless stares, apparently void of any emotion for what was about to come. Insulated against the din of the city, the damp night air was deathly still, the only sound in the godless alley being the soft, insane whine spilling from the lips of Joo Kwan-jo.

Ever so faint from the darkness beyond, the quiet echo of footsteps came slowly upon the cobblestone street, steadily growing louder as someone approached through the hazy mist, stopping abruptly at the shadow's edge.

"You should not have come back, Joo," Lee said coldly, his face still hidden in the blackness beyond. "Stand him up!" he snapped.

The two gunmen walked over to the wounded man and, taking him under the arms, lifted him to his feet, Joo's only resistance being a slight increase in the volume of his incoherent whine.

The hatchet-faced man stepped into the pale light, his face a mask of evil. "You know the price you must pay for your treachery," he said. "You shall serve me far better in death than you ever did in life, Kwan-jo!"

Lee stepped slowly toward the squirming Korean, removing a small case from inside his breast pocket. He opened it and took out a single long-blade stainless steel scalpel.

"Your heartless body will be found at day-break," Lee said, stepping closer, his piercing black eyes staring without mercy on Joo's look of horror, "a lesson to those who might entertain any future thoughts of crossing my path!"

Lee grabbed the back of Joo's head, clutching him by the hair.

"*Hold him!*" *he commanded, tearing open Joo's shirt, and with his body weight behind him, Lee slowly inserted his long razor-sharp blade into the chest of the wild-eyed Korean. With a sudden jerk of the knife, the hatchet-faced man cut a deep gash over the heart of the screaming man, spraying blood profusely.*

"*Hold him up!*" *Lee shouted at the two gunmen as they looked on in horror. Releasing Joo's head, the madman thrust his hand into the opened chest of the dying Korean, and while staring into his victim's bulging eyes, the blood-crazed killer wrapped his fingers around Joo's still-beating heart and tore it from his body, lifting it over his head to drink in the blood as it drained from the warm flesh.*

As Lee reached for the back of Joo's slumped head, everything suddenly brightened as if the entire alley was awash in floodlights.

"*Let this be a lesson to the rest of the CIA.*" *The hatchet-faced man sneered as he lifted the lifeless head. But it no longer held the face of Joo Kwan-jo. The face on the dead man was now the face of...*

*****

"*Mickey!*"

For the second time in two nights, Sam Mason awoke screaming in his sleep as he surfaced from the depths of a horrid nightmare. This time though, the dream seemed all too real, too personal, and as Sam struggled to pull himself back to reality, he felt his own body racked with fear, a fear not for himself but for his best friend, whom he had just seen butchered in some surrealistic Asian dreamscape.

Beads of sweat trickled down his brow as Sam's own heart pounded in his chest, and without warning, waves of nausea began to sweep over him. Mason raced to his bathroom, where he wretched uncontrollably, unable to shake off the gruesome images that lingered all too real in his mind's eye.

"My God, what a nightmare!" he said to the porcelain bowl as he lifted himself shakily off the floor.

Awakened by the sounds of Sam's violent sickness, Annie had trotted into the large bathroom unnoticed to lay quiet and curious by the door, her jaw resting on her paws, ears flattened back in concern.

"What the hell is goin' on, girl?" Sam asked weakly.

Unsure herself, the little dog nervously inched her way over to Sam on her belly, her big, sad doggie eyes looking up, asking if everything was okay. Sam reached over and scratched her behind the ear, and she immediately responded by licking his hand.

"I'm okay, Annie. I think. But I sure would like to know what the hell these dreams are all about."

Annie offered Sam no opinion, so the ex-SEAL made his way to the sink, where he cleaned up and checked the time.

"Ten past five," he said as he moved to sit on the edge of his bed and stretch. "Almost time to get up anyway."

Out of habit, Mason's mind went to work searching his subconscious for some connection, some clue to help explain the sudden onset of these unusually explicit nocturnal visions. He could sense there was something, but what the hell was it? What was that inner voice trying to tell him?

Something to do with North Korea…and China.

"Mickey and China," he said, thinking out loud. "What about China?"

There was some connection just out of his conscious reach, something hidden deep in the folds of his mind.

What was it, Mickey had said? Something he was working on…

"Damn it!" Sam yelled in frustration. "Think, man, think!"

Then all at once, it came to him. It had been last winter, when Mickey had come up to the Cape just before Christmas. Out for dinner and a night of beer drinking, Sam had asked about Mickey's new position with the CIA. Once he remembered, the whole scene played out in Sam's head as though it were yesterday.

"Sorry, partner," Mickey had joked. "Top-secret stuff. You don't have the security clearance."

"Oh, spare me!" Sam came back. "They've gotta know by now that you can't keep a secret. They've probably got you cleanin' their guns and shinin' their badges!"

"Sam, spies don't carry badges."

"Then you probably work in the mailroom and don't know shit about espionage."

"Shows how much you know. I was voted spook of the month in the last issue of Spy Magazine."

"Seriously, Mick, you like it better than the bureau?"

"To a degree," Mickey had said with reservation. "But I seem to be running into the same dead ends though. Pisses me off."

"What dead ends?"

Neally took a long pull on his Sam Adams before answering. "You remember a few years ago, I was investigating the murder of two of our agents out in San Francisco?"

Sam nodded that he did as he sipped his own beer.

"We'd been sniffing around at what appeared to be some new pipeline for smuggling in Chinese immigrants. We know they come in all over. San Fran and LA on the West Coast. Boston and New York in the east. They pay big bucks to get over here, then they're swallowed up by the cities' Chinatowns where they work like dogs for next to nothing, in restaurants mostly, until they get their debt paid off. Then they save every penny they earn, living like paupers until they have enough money to bring the rest of their families over."

"Isn't that mostly Immigration's problem?" Sam had asked.

"Ordinarily, yes. But in Frisco, there seemed to be some connection to the Tong and their drug-running operations. When two of our guys reported they were on to something, they got snuffed. So some of the rest of us started to take a closer look."

Mickey paused to sip his beer, his eyes discreetly sweeping the room as he did so.

"It seems not all the illegals were going underground in the big city," he went on quietly. "A certain few were herded up through Oregon into Washington State, then up the Columbia River to the Snake and into, of all places, Idaho."

"Idaho!" Sam said. "What the hell would they be doin' in Idaho?"

"You can bet it ain't pickin' potatoes."

"Not likely," the ex-SEAL said, waving to their waitress for another round. "So what'd you find out?"

"Well, that's what's frustrating," Mickey said, leaning toward Sam. "We don't know that the pipeline ends in Idaho, that's just as far as we'd followed it. We'd hit a dead end in Lewiston, and before we could sniff out any new leads, the three of us were transferred. The Oklahoma thing. Just about everyone in the agency was on it, but no one ever picked up the Idaho trail again. And now the file's closed and classified."

"Is that so strange?"

"Not really, but…now I'm in that other three-letter agency, and I still can't get near this thing. It's as though someone is purposely steering me away from it."

"Well, Mick," Sam said with a big grin, "I think it's pretty obvious. It's the Idaho connection. All those potato farms? Just a big cover. Potato Land is actually the espionage capital of the world, and nobody wants you to know!"

"Fuck you!"

And that had been the end of the discussion. Sam and Mickey had spent the rest of the night drinking beer and admiring the festive holiday apparel some of the younger female patrons were sporting.

Still unable to shake the uneasy sensation he felt about his friend, Sam picked up the phone and dialed Mickey's private number in Washington, but got no answer, not even a machine.

Odd, he thought.

Hoping she might have a line on her big brother's whereabouts, Sam tried Nicki's number, only to reach her machine. He left a message saying he was flying into town later that day, and he'd call again as soon as he could.

Mason resigned himself to having to wait until he got into DC to find his friend and turned his attention to gathering up Annie to leave her with friends on his way to the airport. But as he drove to the airfield, something continued to fester in his subconscious mind, like an itch he couldn't scratch. There was something else important Mickey had said that night.

What the hell was it?

Sam knew the puzzle would drive him nuts until he came up with the answer. The preflight check and takeoff had momentarily taken his mind off whatever it was that lurked just beyond its reach, but as the Cessna climbed to cruising altitude, the little buzz started again.

An hour and a half later, flying at four thousand feet, the little plane crossed over the Long Island Turnpike, the site of one of Hollywood's greatest gunfight scenes—Sonny's ambush at the tollbooth in the movie *The Godfather*. And finally, it came to him. *The Mafia!*

Mickey had alluded to the Chinese having some tie to the Mafia.

Chapter 8

September 1973, the island of Hainan, the conference room at Wu Xun's seaside retreat

Though much discussion had ensued following Wu's revelation, no assurances were needed. No one in the group questioned the general's scientific genius, but the practical value of building the neutron bomb was lost on them. It was commonly known throughout the upper echelons of the CCP that weapons-grade fissionable material, specifically uranium-235, was in extremely short supply, but even if Wu could somehow mass produce this weapon, of what use would the bombs be without missiles capable of delivering them to their targets?

"Again, forgive my ignorance in these matters, Wu Xun," said Kao Ting-fa, bowing more deeply to his host. "I do not doubt your preeminence in this field, my general, but assuming you can build a number of these neutron bombs, how do you propose to obtain the undoubtedly large quantities of uranium needed to fuel these weapons?"

"An excellent question, Ting-fa," the general replied with his seemingly ever-present sly grin, "and one that is of particular concern to yourself, whereas you shall be the one to solicit the funding needed for phase two of the Guangxi Project."

"Phase two?"

"Yes, my good friend. In our fifth year of operation we shall propose the construction of a most modern type of nuclear power reactor. It shall be a grand affair. A great technological achievement for the party to lay claim to and a wondrous advancement for the people of China. The new reactor will supply the much-needed electrical power for all of China's south-central provinces. As we bask in the accolades of a grateful people, my team at Guangxi will enjoy an unlimited new source of nuclear fuel. plutonium-239!"

Both Ch'en Li and Major Hu Shi were fully aware of this future segment of Wu's scheme. Hu Shi stood to relate this most necessary element of the master plan.

"As one might expect," the major explained as he walked to an easel standing by the wall behind Wu Xun, "the Americans have been the world leaders in the development of nuclear technology and it's applications. It has become known within the scientific community that they have recently finished experimental work on a new type of reactor, one that is of particular interest to our cause."

The major pointed to the easel as he continued.

"The first experimental model capable of producing commercial quantities of power, designated EBR II, was built in 1964, at the American's National Reactor Testing Station in their northwestern state of Idaho. The facility is called Argonne West, an extension of Argonne East in Chicago, which is the oldest of the National Atomic Laboratories in the United States. Their other sites include Savannah River in Georgia, on their east coast, Hanford laboratories in Washington State on their west coast, their newest facility, and of course, Los Alamos in New Mexico, home of the first atomic bomb and most infamous of the American atomic research facilities."

Major Hu Shi turned to the next page on the easel.

"It is our understanding," he continued, "that a working prototype of the next generation of this new reactor is being built as we speak, at their newest facility in Washington State, the Hanford National Laboratories. Construction is due to be completed next year. It has been designated FFTF, or Fast Flux Test Facility. The Americans call this new type of reactor a breeder reactor. They call it this for the simple reason that through its normal course of operation, this reactor produces more nuclear fuel than it expends. It literally *breeds* fuel!"

The major turned the next page to display a large technical diagram.

"The only naturally occurring isotope capable of fission with thermal neutrons is uranium-235, which constitutes less than 1 percent of all-natural uranium. Other nuclides that can undergo fission with thermal neutrons are plutonium-239 and uranium-233. These do not exist naturally but can be produced by allowing neutrons to interact with uranium-238 and thorium-232 respectively, these isotopes being much more abundant within the Earth's crust. Because of their convertibility into nuclear fuel, these substances are called 'fertile' materials. The neutron capture process with subsequent beta decay is called 'breeding.'"

General Wu's executive officer walked back to the table and stood behind his chair, his hands resting on its back.

"Though the exact details of this reactor's design are unknown to us at this time," he said as if sharing a secret, "we do have a basic understanding of its principal. We know uranium-238 will fission with fast neutrons only. Of most importance to us is that this fast-flux reactor has this capability. An insulated blanket of uranium-238 is wrapped around the reactor core. Normal operation of the reactor creates a discharge of neutrons, some of which escape the core and are 'captured' within the uranium blanket, thereby adding a neutron to the isotope. The subsequent beta decay results in a change of the isotope's atomic properties from 238 to 239. Plutonium-239! Weapons-grade material!"

Major Hu Shi nodded to General Wu then took his seat, peering proudly at his mentor.

"Well done, Major," the general said before continuing the lecture.

"The development and operational placement of this reactor are paramount to our success. We must have this technology! And we must have it soon! But as we have all been taught, a man cannot serve two masters. I cannot afford to split my research between the two projects and realistically hope to attain success at both. We will need to pursue an alternative course of action in order to obtain this much-needed technology."

Wu again leveled his hard gaze on Liu Ying-ch'ao as he spoke.

"One of your first priorities, General Liu, will be to place an agent within the Hanford National Laboratory. He will need to obtain both the details of the design plan and the operational procedures of this reactor. Your man will need to be a scientist. You may take one of my staff to train for the task."

Wu Xun leaned back slightly in his seat—the softening of his hard glare barely evident.

"I am fully aware," he said to the intelligence officer, "of the difficulties you will encounter while trying to place an agent within such a closely guarded, top-secret facility, but my timetable dictates the need for this data by the fall of 1980. You have seven years to complete this assignment."

"Seven years," repeated Liu, acknowledging the challenge. "It shall be done, my general, but," Liu hesitated, not wanting to overstep his bounds, "I should also know now, Wu Xun, if you will also need me to acquire the missile technology I assume we will need to project this new weapon at our enemies?"

As always, Wu beamed whenever a question was put forth. It was part of his great charm. It set his guests at ease, and it gave his audience the appearance that he had all the answers. Which, in fact, he did.

"As promised, comrades," Wu said, gesturing with his hand around the table, "all your questions will be answered before this night is over. As for missile technology…"

Wu's head swiveled ever so slowly to look straight into the eyes of the man seated at the opposite end of the table, his face turning to a mask of stone as he prepared to answer Liu Ying-ch'ao.

"No, my comrade," he said in an icy tone, holding Lo Fang's gaze. "I will not need you to concern yourself with such unnecessary details. When the time comes, we shall be using a far more 'unconventional' delivery system."

Chapter 9

Lo Fang had sat silently throughout the proceedings, taking it all in. Listening intently to each discourse, he heard every question and understood every explanation. He made note of every detail, patiently observing each man's reaction, unobtrusively taking the measure of all those seated around him. Lo Fang missed nothing. He paid close attention to Wu Xun as he spun his yarn, impressed by the ease with which he captivated such venerable men. Though not of as strong a conviction in sharing with the groups' idealistic concepts, the Tong leader was motivated by other considerations. He certainly held the Western world in great contempt, but his hatred was of a more personal nature. Lo Fang knew what he stood to gain from this venture, and as always, he would weigh that against the downside. The Tong leader was known to be of great wisdom, feared and respected by all that knew of him, but he enjoyed his great success and continued reign mainly by being honest. With himself. He never deluded himself into thinking a deal was better than it was. And he trusted no one. Lo Fang was a resolute realist, and he now found himself completely taken with Wu's scheme.

"Perhaps, comrades," Wu asked, "one of you would care to tell me what he thinks is the largest, fastest-growing industry in the world? A business, it is estimated, that currently grosses over one hundred billion American dollars per year!"

Wu Xun was out of his seat now, slowly circling the table as he spoke, his eyes fixed steadily on Lo Fang.

"You will not find the quarterly profit statements or yearly balance sheets of this business in the pages of any of the innumerable capitalist business journals. This industry boasts of no members on the many international stock exchanges around the world. And, comrades, though every government in the world is fully aware of the existence of this global industry, no one in this business pays as much as a single yen in taxes! It is business as usual, seven days a week, three hundred and sixty-five days a year, in every city, in every nation throughout the world! And all completely illegal. Yet it persists."

Wu had stopped just to the right of Lo Fang, hands clasped in front of himself as he addressed the rest of his group, a psychological ploy, aligning himself with the Tong leader.

"I speak, of course, of the illegal drug trade, comrades. A business, which, in spite of the efforts of hundreds of determined nations, continues to flourish and grow at an ever-increasing rate!"

The general turned his head to look at Lo Fang.

"We are fortunate," he said, "to have among us tonight, one of the leaders of this industry, a man of legend, a man whose very existence has been said to be myth. This man needs no one to vouch for him, and I will not insult him by doing so. Yes, my comrades, Lo Fang *is* the reigning head of our ancient, dark society—the Tong!"

With this, Wu Xun bowed deeply to the Tong leader. It was by no means precedent setting for high-ranking Chinese government officials to sit with members of the Tong. For centuries, the ancient organization had maintained a strong behind the scene presence within the political structure of a nation in constant upheaval. Since ancient times, a political leader who made an enemy of the Tong was, more often than not, very short-lived. This, however, had become less of a reality in recent years, no doubt partially accounting for Lo Fang's acceptance of Wu's invitation.

The leader of the Tong remained silent, acknowledging Wu Xun with only a slight nod.

"Tell us please, most honorable Lo Fang," Wu said, "of your 'interests' in this area."

The master criminal continued to stare straight ahead as he answered.

"Drugs are but one of many businesses my organization operates. It is by far, however, the most profitable. Also, the most dependable."

"Opium, heroin, cocaine, marijuana—all in great demand, I suspect?" Wu asked as he walked slowly back toward the head of the table.

"Always."

"May I ask, and please, forgive my ignorance, Lo Fang, but where is your largest market?"

"Depending on the product, either the United States or the Soviet Union."

"Yes, of course. Both countries are very large consumers, are they not?"

"Very."

"Correct me if I am wrong, but I was under the impression that very little of your product is actually produced in these countries. Is that not so?"

"It is so."

"Well then, and again, please forgive my obvious question, but…if your product is not produced in the market countries, and its transport is illegal, how then do you get your product to your consumer?"

"It is smuggled in," Lo fang said without emotion. He'd known all along the point Wu was coming to; he'd simply been obliging him with the appropriate answers.

"Smuggled in!" Wu Xun repeated loudly. "Comrades, as the honorable Lo Fang will attest, every year, billions of dollars' worth of illegal drugs are smuggled into both the United States and Russia despite the considerable efforts by specially tasked law enforcement agencies to deter this trade. May I ask, Lo Fang, what percentage of your contraband is confiscated each year?"

"Less than 10 percent," he said, "and most of that is by arrangement."

For the first time, Lo Fang looked about the table, making eye contact with all in the room, signaling to Wu Xun of his commitment to the operation.

"We have 'agreements' in place with certain officials," the Tong leader explained. "This happens at many levels. The Western world has an expression, 'It takes money to make money.' This is true for sure, and I spend millions on bribery and 'hush' money to protect our investments. But more importantly, I also provide the various inter-national police agencies with a regular number of seizures, 'busts' as they call them, always of our more inferior product of course." Here Lo Fang gave a sly grin. "This helps to placate those we cannot bribe. Politicians are the same the world over. All they truly care about is their image. As long as they appear to be fighting the battle to keep their streets clean, so their public is quiet, they are happy. It is all just lip service. It is their own careers that are of importance to them. They seek power, though they do not truly understand its use. I have encountered very few men of honor. Most can be bought. More eas-ily so, if they can be made to believe that the deal will help them to 'move up.'"

"So what you are telling us," said Wu, "is that over the years, you have established secure routes, through which you move your contraband, by taking whatever steps necessary to ensure its safe pas-sage and arrival at the intended destination. Exactly how secure are these routes?"

"As I have said, very seldom is there a shipment lost that was not done so by design."

"But there is that danger?"

"It is small, but yes, there is always that danger."

"A hypothetical question for you, comrade," Wu said, using the term of implied collaboration for the first time with this man. "If one were so inclined, would it be possible to create smuggling routes that would be *100 percent* secure, with zero chance of discovery or compromise? Is this possible?"

The Tong leader pondered the question for a brief moment before answering.

"It is possible. It would mostly be a matter of money, but to feel totally secure about such an arrangement, I would want my own people 'in place' at both ends of the pipeline. They would need to be in positions of authority. They would need to be privy to any investigation that came near to our secret, so that it may be guided in another direction. One would need a deeply seeded network in place. This would take much time, and as I have said, much money."

"But it could be done!" It was a statement, not a question by Wu.

"Yes."

Wu Xun was positively beaming as he stood before the room, the final piece of the puzzle now revealed.

"And this, comrades, is exactly what we shall do! Over the next two decades, we shall, through the hand of our Tong, develop just such secure routes. We will easily control our own end of the pipeline, and as Lo Fang has suggested, we shall develop an extensive network of spies. Deep undercover agents that will be painstakingly inserted into the target nations. Sleepers, I believe, is the term used. We will spare no time or expense to accomplish this. While we develop the technology needed to manufacture our weapons, we will at the same time be developing our 'delivery' system! Heroin and opium will flow undeterred into our enemies' streets for years to come. And then, when the time is right, weapons of mass destruction will follow! Our weapons! There will be no need for missiles or sophisticated guidance systems. The enemy will have no early radar warnings. No launch detections. Our bombs will already be lying at ground zero awaiting detonation! Hundreds of neutron bombs will explode simultaneously across the US and USSR, destroying both warrior nations in a single millisecond. *Without* creating a nuclear cloud to blot out the sun! Our sun, for we alone shall be left to bask in its warmth. The Asian race, my comrades, will be left to rule the planet! As it should rightfully be. As it is written!"

Led by Ch'en Li and Major Hu Shi, the entire group stood to applaud the general. Even Lo Fang was on his feet, swept up by Wu's hypnotic account of what he knew could truly come to pass. Wu accepted the praise for but a few moments, then motioned for all to be seated.

"There is much work to be done, my comrades. Some most elaborate planning shall be needed. We will want to enlist the services of certain elite Asian businessmen who have the assets we will need to effect the infiltration of the targeted nations."

Wu nodded to his right.

"Our North Korean friends," he said, "will have access to such men through contact with their South Korean brethren. We shall first concentrate our efforts in these matters in the United States, where their more open, permissive society should be easily penetrated."

The general motioned to the left side of the table.

"An item of some urgency, comrades. We shall need to find some special men to be trained for what will perhaps be the most critical part of our plan. The network of sleepers! Ch'en Li, as superintendent of the Board of Military Academies, you will have access to our most promising students. Many, no doubt, will suit our needs perfectly. General Liu, you are to work closely with Ch'en Li on this matter."

Both men nodded their assent.

"And finally, my comrades, and most importantly, we shall need to find one very special man indeed to head up this brotherhood, this most secret and demanding of vocations. A guardian, so to speak, this man shall be an independent force and our only direct contact abroad. This man will need to be highly intelligent. Of a genius IQ, no doubt, and he will need to be physically intimidating so as to command great respect. People should fear this man!" the general said, making a fist and slamming it into his other hand.

Wu Xun lowered his voice as he continued.

"This man will need to be cunning, naturally so, for he may well need to protect his own secret identity from time to time. And our guardian must be ruthless. Brutally so! For should the time ever come when it becomes necessary for him to use deadly force to protect the integrity of our plan, he must not fail!"

Wu Xun opened his arms to infer solidarity. "In the months ahead, comrades, we must all be watchful for such a man, for we need to find him soon. This man has a long path to walk."

The two North Koreans looked at each other at the same time; together they nodded at each other. Chung Gi-nam had already made up his mind. He knew his country had little chance of developing a nuclear program of any global significance on its own, and even if they somehow did find the means, the West would no doubt interfere. No, the only path to true power—to a new world order— lay with Wu Xun. North Korea's number two man turned to General

Wu, and for the first time since the meeting had convened, he bowed to his host and spoke.

"I know this man!"

Chapter 10

The first thing Sam did after checking into the Four Seasons was to try Mickey's private line, again finding the same endless, unanswered ring. With an uneasiness still lingering from the previous night, Sam gave Nicki a call, hoping he might catch her getting home early from work, only to once again hear her answering machine's computerlike voice instructing him to "please leave a message," which he did.

Feeling a bit unnerved, Sam set about unpacking. The flight down from the Cape had been uneventful yet tiring. Though his Cessna 172 is a high-performance single-engine aircraft capable of seating four people comfortably, with a top cruising speed of only 170 miles per hour, the entire trip from preflight and takeoff to landing and tie-down had taken over five hours. With so little sleep the night before and no one to spell him at the controls, Sam was beat. The solo flight had given the ex-SEAL plenty of time to ponder recent events, but he was still at a loss to explain the sudden onset of his vivid nighttime visions. These last two, though more violent in nature, were but two of several dreams he'd had over the past few weeks, all apparently related to the new story he was building. Some were vaguer than others, some he barely remembered. Still, they all seemed to be fueling his imagination with new material for what Sam hoped would be his most thrilling book yet.

Mason decided his obsession with his work was probably the cause of the dreams. He figured the ability he knew he had, that capacity to immerse himself entirely in the project at hand, might just be consuming enough to carry over into his subconscious, and the dreams were possibly just a manifestation of his own overly active imagination. At least that's what he believed for now.

It was close to five in the afternoon, and outside the plush hotel, the nation's capital was bustling with the start of rush hour traffic. Sam was hoping to get a power nap in before his dinner with Keri at nine, and he still needed to phone Irene at her office before she left for the day. He dialed the front desk for a seven thirty wake-up call, then he put his phone call through to New York.

"Leslie-Taylor Publishing, how may I direct your call?" answered a tired, elderly-sounding receptionist.

"Irene, please," Sam asked in a voice nearly as weary.

"May I tell her who's calling?"

"Yes," he said, suddenly full of mischief. "Tell her it's Dr. Peepers, her gynecologist, with the results of her pregnancy tests."

"Umm…I'm sorry," the poor woman said, clearly confused. "What was that name again, Doctor…?"

"Peepers. About her pregnancy tests."

"Yes…Umm…And you wish to speak to Ms. Leslie-Taylor?"

"Yes. It's very urgent."

"Ms. Irene Leslie-Taylor?"

"Correct and tell her I have wonderful news!"

"Oh my! Ah, just a moment, please."

Listening to soft jazz while on hold, Sam felt a slight twinge of guilt at the office rumor that would undoubtedly spread like a virus throughout the firm within hours if not minutes of his call, no doubt creating for Irene some cause for explanation, not to mention embarrassment, but *what the hell!* A moment later the music stopped, and the call rang through.

"You scoundrel!" Irene complained, hiding her amusement. "You shall pay dearly for this one!" Still spunky at sixty-six, she didn't give a damn what her help thought.

"I have good news, and I have bad news," Sam said playfully. "Good news is…you're not pregnant!"

"And the bad news is I'm talking to you again!" she said, cutting in. "What am I to do with you, Mr. Mason?"

"Well, you can start by filling me in on whatever it is you found out for me."

"And what's in this again for me?"

"You get to publish another best seller?"

"Oh, yes. Well, in that case, I did have some success doing *your* research for you."

"For which I am truly grateful. Our next lunch is on me."

"And don't think I won't remember! Hold on a second, Sam," Irene said as she searched briefly for the notes she had taken on her earlier phone conversations.

"Ah, here we are," she said, putting on her glasses. "I made some calls to some people I know down at the Pentagon, but without much luck, I'm afraid. All I got was about an hour of the usual shuffling from one department to the next, no one either knowing or willing to guide me in the right direction. Typical. So then I called Congresswoman Catherine Bradshaw, who is, of course, a dear friend of mine. She's served on the House Ways and Means Committee for the last half dozen years or so and knows as much about what goes on in that town as anyone."

"And she was able to help?"

"Completely. It seems we were right about the military handling all that type of maintenance themselves. For years, only government personnel were allowed to be involved in any way, with anything requiring admission to do work at any of the frontline defense bases as well as at any of our essential government facilities or national laboratories. Basically, any site deemed by the top brass to be vital to national defense was protected against possible communist infiltration, terrorists, or sabotage."

"That's pretty much what we figured. Army Corps of Engineers doing the work?"

"Well, they were. Them and a slew of other military personnel. General staff officers, military management supervisors, the government industries board, project consultants, quality control engineers, you name it. Everyone with their hand in the pie. It was obvious, as with everything else the government does, the systems were overmanaged, overregulated, overstaffed, and of course, overexpensed."

"You said they *were* doing the work—"

"Correct. As you know, following the breakup of the Soviet Union and the apparent demise of her military threat, many on Capitol Hill, specifically the liberals, declared an end to the Cold War and soon started screaming for defense budget cuts. Why the need to spend trillions if we are no longer under nuclear threat from the Russians?"

"Peace at last," Sam said.

"Exactly. But in spite of the great resistance from the right wing and the many arguments made to the contrary, a much more relaxed military posture did evolve. It was a fight, for sure. The hawks trying to save massive programs like the B-2, and the doves trying to get every dollar they could for cancer research and such. Well, as always, trade-offs were made. We'll let this go, but we've got to have that! So with a far less frantic domestic security doctrine in existence, and with everyone in Congress realizing that many corporations in the private sector could perform some of the less vital military tasks as well the government, only for about one-tenth the cost, an effort to trim some of the fat off the budget was incorporated into the national defense policy, and as a result, certain functions that had previously been tagged for military personnel only were then farmed out to private industry."

"Let me guess," Sam said. "Fire control systems were one of the first to go."

"You got it, sunshine."

"You know that fits really well for me."

"I thought you might like it. Catherine was just starting to tell me about the bill that was introduced in the early nineties that enacted the change, but she had an important call and had to go. She said she'd get back to me tomorrow with the rest of the story. So that's all I can tell you for now."

"You are awesome, Irene!" Sam said, pleased with the help.

"Yes, I am. You also wanted the name of the premier manufacturer of firefighting equipment in this country, did you not?"

"Yes, I did."

"Well, I've got that for you as well," she said proudly.

"Irene, I am impressed. You must have spent your whole day working on this thing," Sam said in mock appreciation. "What'd you do, cut back to a two-martini lunch!"

"Now there's gratitude for you."

"You know I love you. Tell me about it."

"Have you a pencil? Do you need to take this down?"

"I'll remember it."

"All right then, listen up," Irene said, consulting her notes again as she began. "There really is only one company, Sam. Far and away the largest designers, manufacturers, and providers of both the installation and maintenance of fire control equipment in the world—I mean, Sam, these people make anything and everything having to do with preventing, containing, and putting out fires. It's really quite astonishing. You name it, they make it. From the smallest, little plastic battery-operated fire alarms you stick on your kitchen ceiling, to the multimillion-dollar sprinkler systems that go into skyscrapers. They make the foam systems for commercial airports, fail-safe mechanisms to prevent oil well fires, they even consulted on the designs for the systems onboard the space shuttles."

"Wow," Sam said, genuinely impressed. "So who are they?"

"Well, it's an international corporation, but their global headquarters are in the US. Some huge facility, from what I understand. Acres and acres of machine shops and laboratories, mostly underground, for safety reasons I would guess. Anyway, the whole complex is built into the side of a mountain, just north of Flagstaff, Arizona. I'm told the company owns the whole mountain as well as most of the land around it."

"You said they're an international corporation," Sam wondered aloud, something gnawing at him. "Did you mean their operations or their ownership?"

"Both. These people do business with 90 percent of the countries in the world, including the Soviet Union. In this industry, they are it. Period. All state-of-the-art, cutting edge technology. Apparently, they pay very well to attract and keep the top people in the field. Upper level management must be very good as well. And all privately owned."

"Irene, who are the owners?"

"That's a bit of a mystery, I'm afraid. Some American interests for sure. On the surface, it appears to be run by US dollars, but there's also a lot of foreign money driving this machine. Multinational Asian investors, which is not all that unusual. Some Japanese players, some Taiwanese, but mostly South Korean money at the top."

Sam felt a tingling sensation, and the hairs on the back of his neck stood up as a little rush of adrenaline surged through him.

"Irene, what did you say the name of this company was?"

"It's called the HAMTIN corporation."

"What did you say!" Sam asked incredulously.

"HAMTIN. It's an acronym for…"

"Hazard Management and Technologies International," Sam said, finishing her sentence.

"Yes. But how did you know that?"

"Irene, the dream I told you about yesterday. The little Asian man in the dream. He was from the HAMTIN corporation! I remember because I thought it sounded pretty good, and I was going to use it in the book. Are you sure about this? Are you sure about the name?"

"Yes, Sam, I am. My sources are impeccable."

"How could that be?"

"Sam, stranger things have happened," Irene offered. "You probably heard or read the name somewhere, sometime ago, and it stuck in your subconscious. Then when you started writing on the subject, it just popped up in your dream."

"I don't know," Sam said unconvinced. "I've had another dream since."

Mason told his publisher in detail about the hatchet-faced man butchering some Korean, and how Mickey's face appeared on the dead man's body.

"That's bizarre, to say the least, Sam," Irene said concerned. "Maybe you've just been working too hard. Maybe you should take a little time off to rest."

"I'm fine, Irene, though I do need a bit of a nap right now. I'm having dinner with your niece at nine, and I could use a little beauty sleep."

"No argument there," she quickly agreed. "Except with your assessment of the quantity needed."

"Ouch," Sam said with a tired smile.

"Where are you staying?" Irene asked.

"The Four Seasons. Room 1812."

"I'll call you when I know more. Give my love to Keri, Sam."

"I will. Good night, Irene."

"Good night, Dr. Peepers."

Chapter 11

The PRC's newest nuclear research and development facility, the Guangxi Project, had been completed on time as General Wu Xun had promised. It had been a massive endeavor, and the general had embraced his work with great enthusiasm and dedication, much to the delight of the chairman and other senior party members, some of whom had cause at one time to question Wu's commitment to the party's chosen doctrine. Forsaking the heated trappings of the political bonfires that continued to flare up throughout party ranks, the general maintained the image of the impassioned scientist whose first loyalty was to his work. While he still offered opinions easily and continued to make his token objections so as not to appear unusually complacent, he did so with much less fervor, always content to return to his new creation, infinitely happy in his work serving the party.

The facility in Guangxi was a masterpiece of design and construction. A massive complex isolated in the foothills of the Nanling Mountains, Wu's brainchild was built to his exact plan and specifications. Many of the research projects here would be of a highly dangerous nature involving risks of exposure to nuclear radiation, and consequently, 90 percent of the facility was placed underground, built into the mountainside as much for safety as for security reasons.

By virtue of his complete control over the construction phase of the project, and coupled with his comrades' abilities to doctor the innumerable progress and cost reports filed with the already overburdened CCP Industrial Development Supervisory Board, General Wu was able to hide an entire underground wing from the party. The very real threat of overexposure to high levels of radiation would help to discourage curious parties touring the facility from entertaining any notion of wandering into one of the many restricted research areas. Wu made sure that his people had posted ample "WARNING! DANGEROUS RADIATION!" signs where they were most needed.

Deep underground, Wu's secret laboratory was accessible only through his private chambers. So much of the classified research done at Guangxi was of such a demanding and time-consuming nature, that on-site living quarters were provided for many of the workers. Wu Xun and his executive officer Major Hu Shi, along with a select group of scientists, hand-picked by Wu himself, virtually lived beneath the Earth in complete isolation and devotion to their work. This condition afforded the general and his people the freedom to move throughout the facility completely unrestricted, and impromptu late-night meetings among certain elite scientists were not uncommon. Tonight's scheduled meeting in Guangxi, however, would include a most unusual visitor.

Present with Wu Xun in the conference room one-half mile beneath the Earth's surface were Major Hu Shi, Ch'en Li, and General Liu Ying-ch'ao, as well as several of the other top scientists Wu had enlisted. General Liu had successfully replaced the previous director of military intelligence, General Lin Chang, six years earlier following Chang's assassination by Lo Fang. Liu had proven to be quite brilliant in his lead role and had distinguished himself honorably. Held now in the highest regard by both military and political party members alike, General Liu was in a strong position to lend aid to the continued success of Wu's secret renegade alliance.

"My comrades," Wu began, seated at the head of the long table, "I have spoken to Kao Ting-fa earlier today, and he has informed me of some very good news. The funding we solicited for the proposed phase two of our Guangxi Project has been approved!"

A modest murmur of congratulations circled the table as this event had clearly been anticipated. No one present held the slightest bit of doubt as to Wu's ability to deliver on his promises, yet with each successful step taken, there developed an even greater sense of camaraderie and solidarity among the group.

"The time has come," Wu said, "to fully initiate the infiltration of our enemy's forces. Ch'en Li, how have our students fared with the final phase of their training?"

"Excellent, my general," Ch'en replied. "Final arrangements for their insertion into the US are being made by General Liu and Lo Fang. My people are well trained, Wu Xun. They will not fail us. Their language skills and relative cultural knowledge are most impressive. Their new identities have been manufactured to the most detailed specifications. When you give the word, Wu Xun, the first one hundred of our brightest young men and women will replace the American born sons and daughters of various chosen families living deep within the Chinese neighborhoods of the selected US cities. Fear of the Tong will keep the neighborhoods in line as our agents assume the identities of US-born citizens. Each tasked with an exact assignment, our people will seek out positions within certain government agencies, many in the field of law enforcement. Ironically, this task will be aided by the American's practice of awarding civil service jobs to minorities. Minorities such as Chinese Americans! Over the next two decades, we shall continue to develop and expand the network. Ultimately, our agents will number in the thousands, and many of our people will no doubt rise to great prominence, gaining for us the leverage we shall need to affect future elements of our plan."

"Excellent, Ch'en Li!" the general said excitedly. There was much work still to be done he knew, but Wu was pleased with the progress to date. "What of our people already in place."

"I believe General Liu is better informed in this matter."

Wu nodded to Ch'en Li, then turned to Liu Ying-ch'ao.

"Of the three agents now operating within the United States," Liu said, "two are scientists. They are both in place and on schedule to be chosen for the necessary work at their target facilities. Both men are patiently awaiting the vacating of positions at their respective sites. As you know, Wu Xun, after a year's training in Peking under my personal tutelage, Chung De'ng, the engineer we chose from your staff several years back, had been enrolled as a graduate student at UCLA in Southern California. Here, as planned, he studied for four more years, obtaining his doctorate in nuclear physics.

A little over a year ago, Chung secured a position as second assistant director of nuclear operations at the US National Laboratory in Idaho. His work ethic and performance in his current arena has been exemplary. He has recently forwarded his letter of intent to the Hanford National Laboratory in Washington State, but Chung De'ng has been unable to secure a position at Hanford as there is simply not one available. Fortunately, the second agent I enlisted last year at your request has successfully attained a position at Los Alamos in New Mexico. Still, he suspects it shall be some time before he will gain a position allowing him to access and extract the information you seek, Wu Xun."

"We shall hear later this evening," Wu said without emotion, "of arrangements being made to 'expedite' the availability of these positions you speak of Ying ch'ao."

General Liu knew well the meaning of Wu's words.

"Can this be done discreetly, my general?"

"Most certainly. Lo Fang himself will join us shortly to reveal the details of this and other developments abroad. Now," Wu Xun said with anticipation, "tell me of our third agent. Our 'guardian.'"

"It was a wise decision you made, Wu Xun, to take on the man the Koreans brought to us. I must admit," Liu said humbly, "that given his history, I had my doubts about the potential that you so clearly saw in him. The success of his training under Ch'en Li at our academy is well-documented. His brilliance and resourcefulness are self-evident, and his brutal deadliness remains unchallenged. However, the questions of his capabilities in the field were unanswered until now. I am most pleased to report that his performance has been stellar. He has adapted to his role with perfect cunning. He is like a shark in a goldfish pond. Less than one year out of their academy, Lee Hak-joon has attained the position of inspector in the United States Federal Bureau of Investigation. The FBI! Lee Hak-joon, the hatchet-faced man as he was known in Korea, is well on his way to the top of the most empowered domestic law enforcement agency in the Western world! A position from which he will no doubt serve us masterfully in future years."

"This is great news to our cause, comrades!" Wu said with pride. He did not bother to disclose that it was only with Lo Fang's endorsement that he had opted to take on the Korean killer for training. Lo Fang had been well aware of the existence of Lee Hak-joon as they had operated in the same dark circles. After the North Koreans had proposed Lee as the man that Wu Xun was seeking, Lo Fang took the general aside and much to Wu's surprise, confessed secretly to him that Lee Hak-joon was the one man in all of Asia that he feared. That was enough for Wu. He instructed the North Koreans to bring this hatchet-faced man to him. Truly of a higher intelligence, and filled with an unmatched hunger for power, Lee immediately saw the promise of Wu Xun's plan and hired on. He had proven to be a most fortuitous find.

"Later tonight," Wu continued, "you shall hear of more good news, for as we speak, Ch'en Li's nephew is personally escorting Lo Fang here from Shanghai where he has just returned from a most productive meeting with his counterpart in the United States."

General Wu looked at his watch. "They are expected in a little over two hours," he said. "I suggest we adjourn now for a long-overdue meal. We shall reconvene at midnight. General Liu, a word in private, please."

After the rest of the meeting had cleared, Wu had a quick conference with the director of Chinese military intelligence. The North Koreans had already secured the services of several of the most powerful businessmen in Asia. Of particular importance was one Kim Ran-hiuk a most successful shipbuilder and owner of the largest and most modern marine facility in the free world. Located in the city of Haeju, on the northwest coast of South Korea, his facility built and delivered high-tech supertankers to oil companies all over the globe. Kim had no desire to continue to toil under the shadow of Western oppression, and he and Wu Xun had spent many long hours in spirited discussion regarding the details and execution of Wu's master plan.

Kim was a strong ally to Wu, and the master shipbuilder had recently made the general aware of a little known yet potentially giant company that was currently emerging as the technological leader in its chosen field. The company specialized in pyro-electronics and was developing products and concepts that were light-years ahead of the competition. With sufficient financial backing and the proper direction and management, the little company could easily grow to corner the world market. Wu agreed with Kim that this particular industry could potentially hold the answer to the distribution and placement questions that lay ahead in the years to come. The company was based in Taiwan, and Liu Ying-ch'ao was dispatched to investigate its ownership.

Chapter 12

Clint Applegate thought he had never been so happy to smell the distant scent of smoke in all his thirty-one years of tracking big game through the Idaho wilderness. It had been a long stretch in the saddle, the last day of a three-week hunting expedition that had traversed some fifty miles of the most rugged and physically challenging terrain in North America. As he led the group of five men, all on horseback, out of the dense tree line a half mile above the south bank of the Salmon River, the welcomed sight of smoke drifting lazily up from the big stone chimney of the Grass Mountain Lodge held the promise of a hot bath, hot food, a strong drink, and a good night's sleep in a warm, soft bed.

For over a half century, the Grass Mountain Lodge had been one of the best-kept secrets in the world of big game hunting and fishing. Located six miles east of Arctic Point and five miles north of Grass Mountain, the old lodge had been built along a completely desolate stretch of the Salmon River, midway between the south and middle forks. The Salmon, known as the River of No Return, flows west through north-central Idaho, where it eventually flows into the Snake River, which originates north at the inland seaport of Lewiston, on the Idaho-Washington State border. Visitors to Lewiston are amazed to find the ocean-faring ships that have traveled the 470 miles from the Pacific up the wide waters of the Columbia and Snake Rivers to the calm, safe dockage at the confluence of the Clearwater and Snake Rivers.

Far removed from any such hint of civilization, the Grass Mountain Lodge sits over twenty-five miles away from its nearest neighbor with no roads leading anywhere near the isolated camp.

The lodge has always been accessible by air or water only, and up until seven years earlier, when Applegate had the existing airstrip built, the only way guests and supplies could be ferried in and out was on small sea-planes capable of landing carefully on the barren expanse of the Salmon River.

One of nature's hidden treasures, the Salmon flows through the north edge of the Payette National Forest, home to the Frank Church River of No Return Wilderness Area, one of the largest designated wilderness areas in the continental United States, boasting over two million acres of near impenetrable mountainous forest. To the north lays the Selway-Bitterroot Wilderness Area with an additional million-plus unspoiled acres. The rugged countryside is unparalleled for its big game hunting and backwater fishing with most of the acreage being accessible only by horseback. For decades, rich sportsmen from all over the country had come to the Grass Mountain Lodge in hopes of bagging a big game trophy. Moose, elk, mountain lions, and grizzly and black bears had roamed the heavily wooded, rocky landscape in great abundance for centuries and rarely did one of Clint Applegate's "clients" go home empty-handed.

A third-generation hunting guide, Applegate was a seasoned, experienced hunter. His grandfather had been a trailblazer in the great northwest in the late 1800s. He'd built the lodge and passed it on to Applegate's father who'd signed a ninety-nine-year lease with the federal government in 1931, signaling the start of a hunting expedition business that would turn into a multimillion-dollar operation. Nothing if not expensive to hunt this great mountain wilderness, by 1980, the price for a three-week trip on horseback for a group of four hunters had risen to fifty thousand dollars, but that did include meals, horses, and an experienced guide. Tips, of course, were expected.

The business grew by word of mouth among the elite, affluent upper-class sports society, luring both the serious and the wannabe hunter alike to the old hunting camp on the river. The Grass Mountain Lodge stood as *the* place to go for big game. The area became known as a hunter's paradise, and Clint Applegate did everything possible to perpetuate that reputation. Since building the airstrip in the early seventies, millionaires had been lured into flying in on their private planes from cities all across the US. Oilmen from Texas, movie stars from LA, senators and congressmen from Washington—any man with enough money and love for the sport flew happily to the isolated, unmarred beauty of this hidden, back-country mecca, all eager to set out on the hunt, each in anxious anticipation of the kill.

Clint Applegate loved his work, loved the beauty of the virgin forest, loved the challenge of leading the hunt for the big animals, but today he was just plain bone tired. For over thirty years, he had been leading hunters deep into the wilderness, making sure his guests got their money's worth. At fifty-eight, he was in better shape than most men twenty years younger, but he could no longer deny that the work was starting to take its toll, and on this last day in the saddle, Applegate was exhausted. This was exactly why he'd promised himself not to take out the three-week expeditions anymore. The long rides were just too much for his old bones, and besides, he really didn't like leaving his wife, Martha, alone for that long of a stretch. These days he left the longer trips to the younger guides. Hell, that's what he paid them the big bucks for. But these clients were special, he reminded himself. They'd been coming up from Vegas for over twenty-five years now, faithfully, at least once a year. They always paid in cash, and they tipped big. They were not the kind of men you said no to.

Anastasia Gambino and his extended crime family were avid hunters, and they always insisted on Applegate himself as their guide. He'd known from the beginning that they were mobsters. He knew what they did for a living.

These guys just like to play with guns, he'd thought to himself at first, and the young tracker figured he'd take Gambino and his hoods a few miles into the woods and they'd shoot up a few trees.

Hell, better than shootin' me, he'd told himself. But the Gambino clan had always treated Applegate and his people with class and respect while conducting themselves as gentlemen, and the young guide found out on the very first trip that the men from Vegas took their hunting quite seriously. Some were better with horses, and some were better with rifles, but they all had the natural cunning and patience, not to mention the nerve, that it took to track and take down a bull moose or elk in grizzly bear territory.

These men were gangsters for sure, tough and hardened criminals who were used to getting their own way in life. Yet for all their hard-nosed ways, when they climbed onto the back of a horse and rode for five days into the heart of bear and mountain lion country, the Vegas hoods soon found themselves completely out of their element and in an environment that was both unforgiving of mistakes, and apathetic of any man's given prowess—physical or otherwise. Still, these men carried with them the same bravado and sense of purpose that sustained them on the dark corners and back alleys of their cities' streets. This was just another proving ground for them. They were born hunters and killers, and they adapted to their surroundings with far more ease than Applegate would have thought possible. As the men from Las Vegas moved through the thick forest, they hunted with solemn respect for the unseen dangers it held, yet they hunted without fear.

Applegate would never forget the fall of '55, when he had taken old man Gambino, much younger back then, up north, high into the Selway-Bitterroot Wilderness Area to the foot of the Bitterroot Mountain Range. Applegate's father had passed the year before, and it had been the young guide's first year of running the place by himself. The crime boss had been up earlier in the season looking to bag his first moose but had gotten shut out. A stranger to failure, he'd come back up by himself to give it another go. At Gambino's insistence and against his better judgment, Applegate led the Vegas hood into the forest alone to find a moose to kill.

Not as familiar with the uncharted northern wilderness as he would have liked to be, the young tracker was often unsure of the safest trails. The rough terrain was no more treacherous than the southern regions of the Payette Forest, but this was also grizzly bear country, and Applegate didn't like the uneasy feeling he had. Determined to get his moose, however, Gambino encouraged his guide to push deeper and deeper into the heavy woods.

As the light started to fade on the third day of their trek, Applegate signaled an end to the day's hunt and indicated a clearing by a mountain creek that appeared to be a good spot to pitch camp. As they led the horses to the stream for water before bedding them down for the night, there was a subtle wind shift that neither man noticed, both being saddle weary from the day's ride. Applegate had taken the tent, and some other supplies off the back of his horse as the animal drank from the cool mountain stream. Weighted down with the heavy load, he headed for the far side of the clearing. He would not make it.

Unbeknownst to either man, the sudden change in wind direction had put them upwind of a mother grizzly and her two cubs as they were taking their nightly drink around the river bend, about a hundred yards upstream. The mother bear had gotten the human scent and had come downstream to investigate the source. Spotting the intruders, she let out a deafening roar from a mere sixty yards away, taking both men completely by surprise. The two hunters froze where they stood, which was exactly the right thing to do.

"Don't run!" Applegate called to Gambino, still standing with the horses in the creek bed. "And don't turn your back on her. Just hold the horses and try to move them back slowly."

As he edged away from the giant grizzly, Applegate realized that he had foolishly left his rifle in the saddle holster on his horse, twenty yards away. If the bear charged, he'd never reach it in time.

Less than two hundred feet away, the mother grizzly continued to voice her displeasure with her angry growls, and though obviously highly agitated, she held her ground, not yet willing to attack.

The two men slowly backed away, Applegate with his hands full of gear and Gambino trying to quietly control the horses. The mother bear was content to stand her ground between the cubs and Applegate, unwilling to invite any further danger to her little ones who, for the moment, were safely out of sight.

"I think it's goin' to be all right," Applegate said softly between the dwindling howls of the big animal. "Just hold the horses, and keep 'em movin' back, slow as you can. Easy, nice and easy... Oh shit!"

From behind the creek-side brush, the two cubs wandered curiously into the open. Applegate saw them just as the mother heard their movement and spun to see what it was. Seeing her cubs, she roared mightily at them in angered admonishment, then she turned toward Applegate, took two steps, and reared up on her hind legs, letting out her loudest cry yet. That was enough to spook the horses and Applegate's bolted, triggering the bear's attack instinct. The young tracker, knowing he could not outrun the huge grizzly, dropped to the ground, covering his neck and head in a desperate attempt to play dead. Maybe she'd chase the horse. Above the roar of the charging bear, he was vaguely aware of several hurried footsteps, followed by six booming rifle shots, and finally a loud thump. Applegate sprang to his feet to find Gambino kneeling between him and the fallen grizzly. The mobster had run to place himself directly in the charging bear's path, calmly emptying his rifle into the target, all six shots finding the mark. Incredibly, the great bear had come to rest less than ten feet from the two men.

The Italian crime boss rose slowly and moved over the fallen beast to appraise his kill. He glanced upstream, but frightened by the gunshots, the cubs were nowhere to be seen. Applegate, his heart still pounding, the adrenaline rush not yet fully subsided, walked to Gambino's side.

"You okay?" he asked in a shaky voice.

Gambino just frowned and raised his eyebrows. "Better than her," he said. Then he turned to Applegate and, with a perfectly straight face, said, "Maybe tomorrow we can shoot my moose. Eh?"

The young tracker marveled at the man's cool. This was not bravado. This was the real thing. He'd been given a glimpse, a small insight as to why Gambino was who he was, and he came to understand, in part at least, the nature of the beast.

"I owe you, Mr. Gambino. Big-time."

Gambino patted Applegate on the cheek. "Hey," he said, flashing his sly smile. "Forget about it."

But Applegate did not forget. And twenty-five years later, as he sat at his bedroom window staring out at the light dancing off the crimson ball of fire sinking slowly behind the distant peaks to the southwest, he knew it would be one of the last times he would watch the darkness fall over his little slice of heaven. The decision was made. Hell, there was never any question. You did not say no to a man like Gambino. Not if you wanted to grow old in good health. The crime boss had made him an offer, and he would have no choice but to accept it. Gambino wanted to buy the Grass Mountain Lodge, the lease Applegate held with Uncle Sam, the horses, the business, and everything else that went with it. The offer was more than fair. It would give Applegate and his wife more money than they could ever spend. He'd hoped to work his beloved ranch for two, maybe three more seasons, but what the hell, Martha would be happy.

*****

There are no windows of light one-half mile below the Earth's crust. No beams of sunshine to illuminate the unseen dust motes that drift lazily through the otherwise sterile subterranean corridors. Day and night lose all meaning in a world without a sun. Time becomes a mere reference point, an abstract concept unrelated to the normal cycles of the Earth. Early morning—late afternoon—evening. Forgotten pieces of time denoted now only by numbers on a clock, a twenty-four-hour military-style clock so as to differentiate between a.m. and p.m. In a world without a sun, every hour is as the next. So much the better to remain focused on the job at hand—no frivolous distractions. At least that's how Wu Xun viewed his underground habitat.

As the group gathered again for the midnight meeting, the room took on a more somber atmosphere. This was due entirely to the presence of Lo Fang. The Tong leader carried about him an aura of such magnitude that by simply walking into a room heads instantly turned in his direction, drawn to his magnetic presence almost against one's will, wanting to look away, but compelled by some unknown force to stare.

Lo Fang frightened people. Being so close to a man of such legendary evil gave cause for most mortal men to squirm in their seats, intimidated to the point of near paranoia. Even men of the strongest will found themselves a bit uncomfortable in this man's presence. This was a phenomenon Lo Fang was quite aware of and one he used to his fullest advantage.

The only man in the room unaffected by Lo Fang's mysterious power, Wu Xun was also well aware of its effect on the others present. From the beginning, Wu had used this menacing entity as a threat of sorts, never actually making mention of it but simply alluding subliminally to the consequence that would befall anyone under the slightest suspicion of betrayal. Though this was understood by all, Lo Fang's physical presence always served as a fearful reminder.

"I trust your trip was both comfortable and rewarding," Wu said as he bowed to the Tong leader.

Lo Fang allowed a rare smile as he settled into his chair opposite Wu Xun.

"It was a most productive and enlightening journey," he said when he was seated. "The arrangements you requested concerning the two nuclear scientists have been confirmed. Our agent needs only to know which man is to be eliminated first. I suggest a minimum three-month interim between 'accidents' so as not to draw undue attention to the events. Which matter do you consider to be the more urgent, Wu Xun?"

"Access to the Hanford plant is far more pressing at the moment. I shall need to submit the final plans for phase two of the Guangxi Project within the year."

"Then it shall be so."

"You expect no problems?"

"I met personally with Lee Hak-joon. He is all that I had suspected he would be. No, there will be no unwanted complications, I assure you."

"Excellent!" Wu said, turning to the rest of his group, who, in turn, bowed their acknowledged approval. "And of the other matter?"

"Better than I had hoped for."

Again, Lo Fang flashed the thin, knowing smile of one who has walked away from the table with perhaps a bit more than anyone else in the game had realized.

"I have a new overseas partner," the Tong leader continued, seemingly amused by his own tale. "The American Mafia was most impressed by the quality of my product, greatly intrigued by my overly generous projections, and completely satisfied by my guarantees of security throughout my responsibility of the pipeline. My counterpart in their society, Mr. Gambino, is head of the various crime families that make up their organization. He revealed to me part of his plan for distributing our 'product.' It is brilliant in its simplicity and a development that will serve us perfectly."

Lo Fang leaned into the table as he shared his new secret.

"Mr. Gambino will buy an isolated hunting lodge deep within the Idaho wilderness. Heavy private air traffic in and out of this location is very common and well established. And all quite legitimate. In fact, that is the only way the lodge is accessible. There are no roads. Planes routinely come and go from this remote airstrip to all points throughout the United States. This will suit us well. Our Korean ships can sail all the way to the inland port of Lewiston, in northern Idaho, where Mr. Gambino's unions control the docks. From there, it is but a short trip to our airstrip in the wilderness, and from this airstrip, we shall have free access to every city in America without arousing the slightest suspicion."

"This is most gratifying to hear," Wu said absently, his mind jumping ahead to another matter.

"Tell me, comrade," he went on, "of our prospects within the Soviet borders."

The Tong leader snorted disdainfully.

"The Russians will present no problems for us, Wu Xun. When the time comes," he said, leaning back in his chair, "all we shall need is money. My contacts tell me it is difficult today to find a man in Russia that *cannot* be bribed, given the degenerate state of their social structure. The Soviet communist republic is a house of cards that is crumbling from below. They cannot even feed their people. Vodka seems to be the only substance in constant good supply. The country has become a society of drunken dissidents and thieving drug addicts. Poverty levels are striking. The peasant masses are unruly, and the anarchy is spreading upward. The structure is breaking down for sure. My sources tell me that within no more than ten years, we shall witness the breakup of the USSR. Communist Russia, comrades, is doomed."

"You are certain of this evaluation, Lo Fang?"

"It is the business of the Tong to know of these things."

"The decline of the Soviet Union," Wu said thoughtfully, "would mean an end to the Cold War and a more relaxed worldwide military posture could be expected."

"That would certainly be one result, yes," Lo Fang agreed.

General Wu remained in silent thought for a long moment, his brilliant mind calculating future probabilities.

"If your estimate is accurate," he said, realizing one possible future, "this development could indeed hold the key to the success of our long-range plans!"

"It is accurate, I assure you," Lo fang said with complete confidence. "By the end of the decade, the great bear to the north will cease to exist!"

Chapter 13

The sign had said "Hanford National Laboratory," and the facility seemed to be located in the southwest corner of Washington State, some fifty miles northwest of the Blue Mountain Range. Part of the US Atomic Energy Commission Reservation, the landscape was a predominantly desolate wasteland, the exception being the areas where the reservation is dissected by the Columbia River. The Hanford Nuclear Facility lay in just such an area on the river's northwestern bank.

As is true with all the US national laboratories, security at the site is of the highest order. A specially trained and heavily armed private security force maintains a twenty-four-hour vigil over the facility, ever alert to the threat of foreign or domestic subversion. One could plainly see the double barbed-wire perimeter fences that formed the first line of defense against any would-be intruders. The major deterrence to any potential assault, however, would no doubt lie hidden in the state-of-the-art technology, which backed up the fence lines and security personnel.

Placed at various intervals throughout the surrounding arid landscape was a network of highly sophisticated sensing equipment. Motion detectors, closed-circuit TV cameras, highly sensitive listening devices, infrared heat sensors, seismic activity receptors, even experimental odor-response monitors were strategically deployed to obtain the earliest possible warning of any potential terrorist attack. One of the technicians who monitored the extensive sensing equipment had once joked that he'd even be able to "smell" the enemy coming, should that event ever occur.

After several test "attacks," when special forces military personnel were sent to try to infiltrate and compromise the security of the site had failed, the Department of Energy (DOE) stated it was satisfied the facility was safe from any outside aggression. The DOE, however, could never have foreseen all their cutting-edge technology being rendered completely useless by the cunning of a single man, for all the security and technology in the world could not stop Dennis Chung! Not when all he had to do was show his DOE photo ID, then slide his encoded pass-card through a magnetic reader in order to open any one of the numerous security doors located throughout the facility, gaining him entry into any building on-site! When you were the assistant director of nuclear operations for the reservation, you enjoyed unrestricted access to the entire facility, including access to the voluminous material stored in the classified computer banks!

The American-born Chinese nuclear physicist had come to Hanford from NRTS, the National Reactor Testing Station, located just west of Idaho Falls. It had taken the sudden, accidental death of the previous assistant director for him to gain the position, but Chung felt no remorse. It was a necessary evil. The Chinese spy needed to access and extract both the plant designs and the operational procedures of the FFTF, and time had been growing short. Chung knew before he arrived at Hanford exactly what his major hurdle would be. Accessing the classified computer system was not the problem; he had Q clearance. The problem was that every user had to log on and off the system, and all work was monitored and reviewed. Certain classified technology was protected and prohibited from copying by a fail-safe system that prevented printouts or disc copying of any kind. No one was even able to look at, never mind extract, classified information without security knowing about it.

Dennis Chung, however, was not your average nuclear scientist. Before leaving mainland China for his assignment, he had been the senior program designer at Wu Xun's central research facility. Chung was a computer genius, yet it had still taken him over three months to design a program that would allow him to discreetly override the security safeguards in the classified system, in turn allowing him to download the necessary technology into the unclassified computer system. The two systems interfaced, but for the obvious reasons, information transfer was only allowed to go one way. Once the computer guru solved that problem, he would be able to retrieve the information from his own PC without any record or documentation. And that was exactly what Dennis Chung was doing at this very moment!

It was after two in the morning, and while Chung's exceptional work ethic was well-documented, he'd also made a point of being seen keeping extremely late hours. Regardless, the Chinese spy had no desire to be accosted at this particular moment. With his program working perfectly, Chung sat at his desk watching anxiously as the download indicator bar moved slowly from 50% to 60%. The amount of information to be copied was massive…60% to 70%…At 78% he would need to insert a second disc he knew…80% now! 85%…Come on, come on…Almost there now! 90%…RRRRRING! What the—RRRRRING! My God, the phone! RRRRRING! Should he answer it! RRRRRING! Why doesn't he answer the phone! RRRRRING! Will someone please answer the phone?!!

*****

"Hello!"

"Hello, Mr. Mason? This is Mikayla from the front desk with your seven thirty wake-up call."

"Huh? Oh, yeah…Umm, thanks. Say, Mikayla, could you have room service send up a pot of coffee, please?"

"Certainly, sir. Anything else?"

"No, that'll be fine."

"The coffee will be right up, Mr. Mason."

"Thank you."

Sam hung up and laid his head back on the bed, stretching his waking muscles, when all at once, the dream came back to him.

"Holy shit!" he said, sitting bolt upright as the images from the strange vision started to replay in his head. He reached for the hotel pen and paper that lay on the night table by the bed. Scribbling furiously, Sam tried to jot down as much of the detail as he could remember before the dream faded to obscurity, as dreams often do.

"Hanford National Lab…Washington State…High tech security…"

Sam listed his thoughts out loud as he wrote. "Department of Energy…Classified computer system…FFTF. Whatever that is…Chinese spy named…Shit!"

He couldn't remember it.

Someone knocked at the door. Sam answered it. The coffee had arrived, maybe that would help. He continued to talk aloud to himself as he poured the coffee.

"Okay, something like…Fung…or Wung…No, Chung! *Dennis Chung!*"

Gratified, Sam quickly wrote it down. But there was something else. Something he wasn't remembering. What the hell was it? No, *who* was it? There was another name he told himself. Someone important. Sam thought hard, but it wouldn't come. *He was Chinese. Someone Chung knew. Someone—*

"He worked for!" Sam said aloud. "The name! What was the name?"

But it was too obscure, buried too deep in his subconscious, and Sam had no more time to spend on it. He needed to get himself ready for dinner. It was already ten minutes of eight, and Sam wanted to give himself a little extra time before meeting Keri at nine. He tried Mickey's number one last time but again had no luck. Still concerned for his friend, he hit the shower and focused his thoughts on the night ahead.

Sam knew that the agreements that were made and signed into law on Capitol Hill didn't always go down in the great assembly halls of the House and Senate. Not really. The deals made between opposing factions were often cut in the back seats of limousines or over a casual breakfast or lunch. Two or three of Washington's heavies would meet discreetly, oftentimes in a bar, and discuss their favorite pet projects. They would agree, off the record, of course, to do each other favors. Withhold objections, for example, or lend support by dropping a word here or there to the right person. To trade votes, so to speak. Favors. An important concept in American politics. Sam knew how the system worked, and he also knew the Four Seasons private elegant cocktail lounge was a likely spot to find just such an informal session. He was hoping to run into a couple of heavies he might recognize, and perhaps pry a little inside information from them. For one thing Sam knew for sure, politicians the world over all loved to hear themselves talk.

A half hour later, shaved and showered and looking fairly nifty he thought in his dark-blue linen suit with his favorite silk tie perfectly knotted, Sam walked into the hotel's stylishly dignified Presidents Lounge, and to his amazement and great relief, found Mickey Neally sitting alone at the far end of the bar.

Chapter 14

Mickey looked like shit. His eyes were tired and dark. He needed a shave and his hair, though always in a bit of disarray, hung down in long unkempt locks about his face. With his left elbow on the bar, Mickey's forehead rested lightly against the thumb of his left hand. A cigarette dangled carelessly between his fingers, the acrid smoke rising languidly to dissolution. With the thumb and middle finger of his right hand, he swished a generous glass of Hennessey on ice, apparently contemplating the contents with deep concern, glancing up occasionally with his eyes to check the room's reflection in the smoky mirror that ran the length of the back wall.

The bar stood in the rear of the lounge beyond an assortment of comfortable chairs and couches arranged around the small low cocktail tables scattered about the darkened room. Sam moved easily past a collection of well dressed, attractive patrons sipping their martinis and manhattans and their chilled glasses of chardonnay as they talked in hushed conversations, impatiently awaiting their dinner tables. The men looked and acted important, whether or not they truly were was unclear, but by virtue of the dazzling display of jewelry and the array of expensive gowns worn by their female companions, they were most certainly quite well-to-do. Sam paid them little or no mind as he made his way to the back of the crowded lounge.

Mickey had seen Sam in the mirror the moment he'd stepped into the room. As he was clearly making his way toward the bar, Sam had undoubtedly seen him as well.

I don't fucking believe it.

Mickey did not want to see Sam. Not tonight. He did not want to be seen with him or anyone else he cared about because he knew it would incriminate them. Anyone Mickey came into contact with over the next twenty-four hours, should he live that long, would come under immediate suspicion and be in real danger for his or her life.

Though Mickey had told Sam some time ago that he worked for the CIA, he'd never really let on exactly what it was that he did for them. He'd preferred that Sam didn't know. Whenever Sam had gotten curious, Mickey would joke around evasively and lead Sam to think that he was administrative help, a paper pusher, or perhaps an analyst or consultant of some kind. Mickey never gave Sam reason to think otherwise, but in truth, he was anything but a paper pusher. He was, in fact, one of the agency's most talented and effective overseas field operatives, and by one of the great, unexplained mysteries of the universe, coincidence, Mickey had just tonight returned from the island of Hainan, in southern China, where he had barely escaped with his own life. He carried with him the end product of his five-year personal investigation into the unlikely and eminently frightening prospect of a Mafia-Tong collaboration.

Frustrated and alarmed by the constant misdirection he had encountered whenever he pursued this evil connection, Mickey had concluded that he could not trust his own government. He had spent the last seven months working "outside the company," supervising a slick and extremely dangerous undercover operation that had backtraced the Asian pipeline all the way to the island retreat of one General Wu Xun!

Mickey had pulled out all the stops on this one. He'd developed an independent network operating exclusively under his direction. He'd used every personal contact at his disposal to infiltrate the renegade organization, including two long-established, deeply seeded Chinese American agents. One of these agents had eventually been able to successfully hack into Wu Xun's personal computer system to obtain the information that Mickey now carried with him. Information that Mickey had previously thought unimaginable.

In the final hour, however, just as he shut it down, the operation had gone very bad, and Mickey's entire network of undercover operatives had been systematically eliminated, murdered by the hand of the Tong. Mickey's closest contact had died in his own arms, but not before the agent was able to warn him of the danger that awaited him back in the US. With his last dying breath, the agent revealed how Wu's renegade alliance had planted their own deeply seeded network of sleepers throughout several American government agencies, confirming Mickey's worst fears. Highly placed agents within virtually every element of US law enforcement sat poised to intercept any hint of suspicion regarding Wu's scheme, effectively leaving Mickey with no one to trust. Sam's friend was a man marked for death, for he alone could prove the existence of Wu's monstrous plot. They'd be coming for him he knew, and they'd be coming soon.

So drink in hand, Mickey sat alone, trying to figure out just what the hell he should do. At the moment, his every option seemed to be blocked. With nowhere to turn, Mickey was truly out in the cold.

Of all the bars in Washington, Sam, you've gotta walk into this one. Shit! I've got to get rid of him.

"Well, well. The things you see when you don't have a gun," Mickey said without looking up as Sam slid onto the stool next to him. "What brings you to town?"

"It's good to see you too, Mick," Sam shot back, feeling a little silly now at having gotten all worked up, apparently over nothing. "I'm having dinner with Keri, actually. Why don't you join us?"

"Ahh, thanks, Sam," Mickey said with a wink, "but I'm happy to say I've got a previous engagement."

"Oh, and how is the lovely Jessica?"

Mickey grinned wolfishly. "Un-fucking-believable."

Jessica was the nickname Sam had given to Mickey's secret lover. Her real name was Dawn DesMoine, and her initials matched her cup-size. One of the sexiest women on the planet and proprietor of Washington's most successful full-service upscale day spa, the woman was both rich and beautiful and blessed with a body that defied description. Sam had once joked that the only near comparison would be the cartoon bombshell girlfriend of Roger Rabbit, one Jessica Rabbit. Sam had tagged the shapely beauty with the nickname, and it had stuck. A befitting codename for the mysterious woman.

"You've been a hard man to find these last couple o' days," Sam said.

Let's hope it stays that way!

"Been out of town awhile," Mickey said, after a taste of his drink.

The barkeep moved in front of Sam, placing a napkin in front of him.

"Sir?"

"Same as him," Sam said. "Make it two."

The barman nodded and hurried off to fetch the brandy.

"So you been out of town on company business?" Sam asked, turning his attention back to Mickey.

"Nah, purely recreational," Mickey lied. "Took a friend down to Key West for a few days."

"Yeah? Didn't get much color down there—"

Christ! Please don't ask a lot of dumb fucking questions tonight, Sam.

Mickey took a long pull on his cigarette, letting the smoke escape slowly through his nostrils, his eyes fixed on the mirror behind the bar.

"Well, Sammy-Boy," he said in his best Irish lilt, "ya don't go to Key West for the beaches. 'Twas mostly 'indoor' recreation, ye see."

The barkeep returned with the drinks.

"Must be nice," Sam said. "I wouldn't know. Some people have to work for a living."

"You writing again, Sammy?" Mickey asked, changing the subject.

Sam tasted the amber liquor, feeling its warmth spreading downward.

"That I am," he said between swallows. "I finally came up with an inspiring new concept. I think you'll like it."

"Yeah? Tell me about it, but be brief. Hate to keep a woman of Jessica's stature waiting."

"Can't say as I blame you," Sam said with a knowing smile as he checked his watch. "I'll give you the short version," he said, taking another quick sip of brandy before starting. Mickey reached for his new drink.

"Well," Sam began, "the name of it is *Made in China*. It's a big plot. Very dramatic stuff. You know, 'the end of the world as we know it' type of thing."

"Your usual story line," Mickey said as he lifted his glass.

"Basically, but this has got a little different twist to it. It's about a mad Chinse scientist who plots to destroy the US and the Soviet Union by smuggling in nuclear weapons with the unknowing help of the Mafia! Wild, huh!"

Mickey's hand stopped midway to his mouth.

What the fuck!

"The cool part is they hide and distribute the weapons in, get this, fire extinguishers!"

I don't fucking believe what I'm hearing!

"Cool, huh?"

Mickey's eyes narrowed, masking his astonishment as he looked from the mirror to Sam. He was having trouble believing his own ears.

The exact fucking story!

"Sam, where the hell did you ever get such a…fantastic idea?"

"Well, that's the strange thing, Mick. Most of the story has come to me in my dreams."

"Your dreams!"

"Yeah, it's been kind of weird. They're so real it's scary. In fact, one of the things I dreamed about is a real goddamn place! It's a real company! The HAMTIN Corporation. Ever hear of it?"

You gotta be fuckin' shittin' me! I do not believe I'm hearin' this!

Mickey stared blankly at Sam for a moment, slowly shaking his head.

"No. No, I haven't," he said, turning his attention back to the mirror just in time to spot two Asian men, conspicuous in their long coats, walk into the lounge and take a seat in the far corner.

Look like Koreans. Didn't take them long to find me. Gotta get away from Sam. Now!

It suddenly struck Mickey. How he felt about Sam. How he admired everything about him. Unlike himself, Sam remained unjaded. Sam still believed in people. Yet though he remained a trusting soul, the ex-SEAL was nobody's fool. He was always engaging, always patient and willing to give the benefit of the doubt, but God help anyone who crossed the line. Mickey knew first hand that Sam's big heart was also the heart of a lion. He loved this man, and thinking about Sam now made him feel sad. It was silly he knew, but it was none the less genuine.

"Sam, you've come up with some real beauties in the past," Mickey said as he stood, dropping some bills on the bar, keeping his back to the Koreans. "But this takes the cake! It sounds just a little too unbelievable, my friend. Do yourself a favor, and don't embarrass yourself. Don't write it. Find yourself another story that's not quite so…outrageous."

"That not like you, Mick, what's the matter with—"

"Drinks are on me, Sammy," Mickey said, cutting Sam off. "Give my love to Keri and do me a favor, will ya? Check in on Nicki and Erin for me from time to time. Okay?"

And with that, Mickey abruptly turned and headed briskly for the door. The two Koreans getting up to follow.

"Yeah, Mick, sure thing," Sam said to his friend's back, more than a little bewildered.

Chapter 15

Sam had finished his drink and was walking through the entrance to the plush Four Seasons dining room where he was mildly surprised to see Keri Starr walking in at exactly the same moment, looking absolutely stunning in a black spaghetti-strap evening dress that seemed to shimmer with gold undertones as she glided across the room.

How does she do that?

Heads turned as Keri moved toward Mason with the grace of a runway model and Sam realized that with her movie-star good looks and tall, slender body, she could have easily chosen a career as such but had opted instead to pursue a life in journalism. A choice Sam was glad of as Keri had developed into a gifted reporter with a wonderful instinct for the truth. She had, in fact, he reminded himself, been the one who had first encouraged Sam to write. He smiled warmly at her as she walked over to take his arm.

"My watch must be slow," Sam teased.

"Oh, you be quiet!" she said as she kissed him on the cheek.

"Well, you are actually on time. Are you feeling okay?"

Keri said nothing.

Standing together, awaiting the maître d', Sam gave her the look a parent might give a naughty child while waiting for the truth to spill. Sam doubted if Keri had ever been on time for anything in her life.

"Oh, all right already!" she said finally. "I got off work an hour and a half early."

"For me? I'm flattered."

"Well, don't be. I was starving. I skipped lunch."

Just then, the maître d' arrived, and greeting Sam and Keri with a flourish, he escorted them to their table.

"Did I just see Mickey leave as I was coming in?" Keri asked as she settled into her seat.

"Yeah, I just had a quick drink with him in the bar."

"He seemed in an awful hurry, blew right by me without even saying hello. What's up?"

"I don't know, he barely said goodbye to me. I had no idea he was even gonna be here. I'd been trying to reach him for a couple of days with no luck. I walked in and there he was, but…he didn't seem to be himself. Seemed like something was bothering him, like he was preoccupied with something."

"Any idea what?"

Sam frowned as he thought about it. As he was about to say he had no clue, their waiter came to the table, introduced himself as Phillipe, and gave them a detailed account of the evening's specials. Keri, as expected, ordered the shrimp scampi, and Sam chose the grilled halibut steak served with a white cream reduction sauce. He picked a nice pinot grigio from Italy to go with their seafood, which Phillipe declared to be a splendid choice.

"Let me ask you something," Sam said as the waiter moved away. "How long have you and Nicki known me now?"

"I don't know. Six, seven years, I guess."

"And aside from you two and Irene, who would you say has been the biggest fan of my writing?"

"Mickey," she said without hesitation, knowing there was a point coming.

"Correct. The man has never been anything but 100 percent supportive. With any of my books, all I've ever heard from Mickey was encouragement."

Sam let his statement dangle for a moment as he sat quietly, peering across the table at Keri. She returned his gaze, noticing the concern in his eyes and the furrow in his brow.

"And tonight," she said perceptively, "he said something that's bothering you. Something out of character."

"Exactly. Mickey is about the warmest guy I've ever known, but tonight he was almost…cold to me. It was like he was in a hurry to get rid of me for some reason. And now that I think about it, he kept lookin' in the mirror as though he were expecting company, yet he told me he was on his way to meet someone."

"Who was he going to meet?"

"A woman. You don't know her," he said, quickly dismissing the subject. "I started to tell him the basic plot of my next story, and he suddenly stood up, told me it was a dumb idea for a book and I shouldn't write it. Then he stormed out of the room."

Sam paused as the wine steward arrived at their table, brandishing the pinot he had ordered. After displaying the label, the steward deftly opened the bottle and poured the customary two ounces into Sam's glass for his approval. Sam admired the color of the pale amber liquid, sniffed the bouquet then tasted the wine, allowing the flavor to rest on his pallet a moment before swallowing it. He announced that it was excellent, and the steward smiled proudly as he filled Nicki and Sam's glasses, then he gracefully departed the table, leaving them alone once again.

"That does not sound like Mickey, Sam."

"No. It's not like him at all. Something's wrong."

"If you don't mind me asking," Keri said after a small sip of her wine. "What *is* your book about?"

Sam gave her the short version of his story, leaving out the gruesome details of the dreams he'd been having.

"Sounds like a cool story to me, Sam," Keri said sincerely. "Clearly well within the bounds of your normal creative scope. I can't imagine why Mickey would want to dump on it the way he did. It's probably got nothing to do with you, and he's just having a bad day at the office. Why don't you just give him a call tomorrow and ask him about it."

"You're probably right, and I will call him, but I've got this nagging feeling that something's not right. I'm worried about him."

"Mickey's a big boy, Sam. He can take care of himself, and you ought to know that better than anyone."

"That's what I keep telling myself, but..." Sam left the thought unfinished, not sure himself of exactly what it was that bothered him.

"Well, you're in town for a couple of days," Keri said helpfully, "so hook up with him tomorrow and see what he's got to say about things. As a matter of fact, why don't I grab Nicki and the four of us can go out for a night on the town. For old times' sake! I could use a little excitement!"

"Sure, why not. And speaking of Nicki, have you talked with her in the last couple of days?"

"No, but that's not unusual. Why?"

"I haven't been able to reach her. And she's not returning my calls."

"Well, I know she's been spending a lot of extra time at her new lab, she really loves the work. But don't worry about Nicki, I can guarantee she'll want to get out."

"I'm not so sure. Every so often, I get the feeling she's pissed at me for no apparent reason, and I can never figure out why."

"I wouldn't say pissed, exactly."

"What then?"

Keri put her wine glass down and leaned toward Sam. "I am continuously amazed," she said quietly, "at how such intelligent men can be so clueless about some things!"

"What?"

"You really don't know, do you?"

"If you're referring to Nicki, no. I must admit she's sometimes a bit of a mystery to me."

"Well, let's think, Sam. How about your house on the Cape?"

"What about it?"

"Well, how about that night we all got drunk playing cards?"

"That! For God's sake, that was years ago."

Keri sat, shaking her head. "Look, Sam," she said, tapping the tabletop with her forefinger, "that night you threw her out of your bed, you did a lot more than bruise her ego."

"I didn't *throw* her out of bed. And what are you talking about?"

"Mickey, of course!" she said, rolling her eyes. "Sam, Nicki idolized her big brother. Christ, he was the one who raised her after their parents died. Mickey was everything to her. She saw the bond you two have, and she wanted to be a part of it. That pass she made at you was not as spontaneous as you might have believed. She wanted more, Sam. A lot more. She was jealous."

"Jealous! Of what?"

"Of you, Sam. Of what you and her big brother had together. That macho male bonding thing you guys do. When she blew her shot at you, she felt like she'd lost a part of her brother too. She was pissed. For a long time. But she was very young back then. She's matured a lot in the past few years if you hadn't noticed. She's over it now."

"What d'ya mean, over it?" Sam asked, a part of him not liking the sound of his own words. "Over what? Me!"

Again, Keri sat, shaking her head sadly. "Don't worry, Sam," she said. "A woman never completely forgets the man who first breaks her heart."

With that, Phillipe came with their dinners, and they ate their meals mostly in silence, making only occasional small talk about the food and the Washington political scene. It wasn't until they settled onto the comfortable high-back leather stools back in the hotel's Presidents Lounge for a quiet after-dinner drink, when Sam asked about the information he needed for his book.

"So, Ms. Starr," he said after ordering two glasses of Sambuca on the rocks with coffee beans and a lemon twist, "what can you tell me about government overspending?"

"Well," she said, putting on her journalist's hat, "I can pretty much sum it up in one word. Flagrant. In spite of all the attention the press gives it and the supposed improved efforts to create better accountability for the dispersion of federal funds, the overspending still persists unchecked. The military is the worst violator, of course, with their huge trillion-dollar budgets. And with all the black-ops projects that are continuously ongoing, it makes it impossible to track the expensing, so…who knows where the money really goes."

"I thought there was a concerted effort being made to trim some of the fat off the military budget."

"Like Einstein said, Sam, everything is relative."

The drinks came, and Keri paused to sample hers. "Ooh, I like it with the lemon twist! It kind of cuts the sweetness a little. Yeah, that's nice. Smoother."

"Stick with me kid, and I'll have you fartin' through silk."

"Classy, Sam."

"Everything's relative."

"I swear I forget sometimes why I like you."

"It is because I am your champion. A doer of good deeds...A slayer of dragons...A friend to animals...And I'm cute."

"You are the oldest adolescent in the world! But you are cute."

"Ah-ha, common ground! A starting place. Who knows where this may lead?"

"Sam," Keri said demurely, "you and I both know you're full of shit, so don't tease me. It's been too long between late mornings, if you catch my drift."

"Hard for me to imagine," Sam said after swallowing a mouthful of the Italian liqueur.

"What, you don't think beautiful women can be lonely?"

"No, I understand that well enough. But you, my lovely, are the complete package. Looks, brains, talent, class. A great career. You've got it all, babe. Hell, if I were ten years younger—"

"Sam, I told you, don't even go there," Keri said in a way that took him aback. Sam leaned away as he gave his pretty friend an appraising look, then he reached over, put his arms around her, and gave her a big hug and kiss on the cheek.

"Let me tell you a little something," he said solemnly, his forehead resting against hers. "Someday, some guy is going to get very lucky with you, and I am going to be very jealous! And that's the truth, sweetheart."

Keri lifted her eyes to meet Sam's. "Yeah?"

"Yeah. The truth is always the truth."

"Well, thanks, Sam," she said humbly, "for the vote of confidence. Now, just what exactly did you want to know?"

"Military spending?"

"Ahh, yes. Christ, Sam, it's ridiculous. Did you ever see that show about the Pentagon? I think it was a made for TV movie. HBO,

I think. What the heck was it? Oh, *The Pentagon Wars*! Did you see that one?"

"I don't think so. I don't watch much TV."

"Well, it was a story about how the military spent like nineteen years developing this troop carrier, the Bradley it's called. Basically, just an armored truck but completely overengineered to the tune of, get this, fourteen *billion* dollars!"

"You're kidding!"

"True story. Stuff like that used to happen all the time."

"Irene was telling me," Sam said, "that there was a movement a little while back on Capitol Hill to cut some of the service-orientated military costs as a trade-off for more vital programs by farming out certain government projects to private industry. As she explained it, the consensus was that several large corporations had become equipped to perform some of the services that were deemed high-security risks just as efficiently as the military but at about one third the cost."

"One-tenth is probably more like it," Keri said. "That was back in the early nineties. The McWilliams-Shahito Bill. It opened up to the private sector a lot of services that had previously only been allowed to be performed by government employees. Saved the American taxpayer a ton of money. And made more than a few people rich. It was one of the first stories I covered. The bill was a step in the right direction, but nothing much along those lines has happened since."

"Miller McWilliams? The secretary of state?"

"The same. He was a congressman at the time. An amazing story he is. A one-time staunch right-wing Republican, he did a complete one-eighty after the death of his wife, Katherine. She lost a long, painful bout with cancer. McWilliams took a year off to basically watch her die, and when he returned to public office, he switched parties and left the legislative branch of government altogether. Ran for Georgia governor practically as a liberal crusader. Won big on the sympathy vote and was a no-brainer for secretary of state a few years later. But before he left Congress, he cowrote this bill with Senator James Shahito, and they pushed it through Congress like you read about. Shahito had to quietly step down from office about a year later though when it became public knowledge that he held a vested interest in the company that won the bid for a vast majority of the contracts. And if I remember correctly, there was also something about him having some connection to organized crime that started to surface as well. It should really have been a much bigger scandal than it was, but somehow it was all kept pretty quiet."

"Shahito, that's Japanese, isn't it?" Sam asked, suddenly very curious.

"Yeah, but he's half Chinese. Japanese father, Chinese mother. He was born in the States, which made him a citizen of course. Very smart, very rich man from what I gathered, but somehow, he just disappeared when the scandal broke. Kind of took the wind out of the sails of those of us who were doing the digging."

"Keri," Sam asked, that little buzz starting again, "what was the name of the company that landed the contracts?"

"The HAMTIN Corporation. They're a big international con-glomerate, but their home base is in—"

"Arizona," Sam said in unison with Keri.

"Yes. How'd you know that?"

Sam explained in much more detail about his earlier conversa-tions with Irene and about his dreams, including how he saw Mickey's face appear on the dead Korean's body. He told Keri about Mickey's suspicions of a possible Mafia-Tong partnership, and he confessed that he was scared for his best friend's life.

"Sam!" Keri said, her face suddenly marred with concern. "When I told you I saw Mickey earlier and he went right by me? Well, I was about to holler after him when these two jerks nearly bowled me over, trying to hustle out the door. I didn't think much of it at the time, other than they were assholes and kind of scary look-ing, not the type you'd expect to find at the Four Seasons. But now I remember that they headed off in a rush"—Keri grabbed Sam by the arm—"in the same direction as Mickey."

Sam waited, afraid to ask.

"Jesus, Sam, the men who took off after Mickey—they were Asian!"

Chapter 16

Mickey didn't need to check the reflection behind him in the angled glass of the storefronts lining Lincoln Avenue. He knew they were behind him. He also knew he needn't worry about taking a bullet in the back. Whoever was running the show over here would have given strict orders to take him alive. The Chinese would expect that Neally held some hard evidence, and they would want it badly. The rogue agent was well aware of the consequences that lay in store for him should he be captured, yet to the casual observer, he simply appeared to be taking a leisurely stroll through the retail district, window shopping perhaps.

Just another block and a half, Mickey told himself, and he'd reach the entrance to the Gavel Club, the most exclusive and prestigious private men's club in Washington, of which he was a member.

Private clubs exist in virtually every city and town across the US, and they vary in size and exclusivity from the small rod and gun clubs found in rural suburbia to the posh and elegant dinner clubs that thrive in the great cities. Though men frequent these clubs for a variety of reasons—sports, liquor, and gambling, to name a few—they all offer one common appeal, quiet refuge from the outside world. Angry bosses or nagging wives are not allowed. Mickey had no such worries; he belonged to the Gavel Club for one reason only—high stakes poker.

The ex-SEAL had acquired a passion for the game during his service time with the Navy. He'd found that his talent for reading people, that same gift that served him so well in the field, could also be put to good use at the card table. In a game of poker, Mickey's powers of observation worked like a finely honed instrument. He caught every nervous habit, every sweaty brow, every facial tic, every hesitant stutter. Nothing escaped his watchful eye. He saw patterns as they developed and knew immediately who was predisposed to either raise or fold. To Mickey, every game had a life of its own with a uniquely distinctive heartbeat, and his fingers were always on the pulse.

It is well known within certain circles that the action is always heavy at the Gavel Club. Big money games go on every night of the week, often lasting until dawn and beyond. The well-stocked bar and gourmet kitchen never close, and as a result of the considerable power wielded by the membership, the players are free to gamble without fear of hassles from the local police. Aside from several judges, including a Supreme Court justice, the club boasts of a number of senators and congressmen as well as two cabinet members among its ranks.

Club rules dictate members only with rare exceptions. Guests and potential new members are allowed only with advance notice and the approval of the club's board of directors. Small fortunes are routinely won and lost here, so great care is taken to ensure that the games are fair and on the level. Applicants for membership are carefully screened, FBI checks are standard, all so members can play without fear of hustlers or card sharks sitting in on their games.

Luck and skill would determine the winners at the Gavel Club. Foolhardy gamblers would go bust early in the night, while those who had trouble controlling their alcohol consumption would follow soon after. Mickey had neither problem and was regarded as one of the club's top players. He sat in on the biggest games with the fattest pots and his skill and somewhat extraordinary luck never failed him, for the crafty Irishman had also been blessed with that most unique of Irish gifts—he was clairvoyant. Neally would almost always play the percentages as good card players do, except on those few rare occasions when he'd get a hunch that was so strong and so clear that he could not consider it a hunch at all. Mickey would never seek out these moments, nor could he explain them; they just happened. He would somehow just *know* when he was about to get lucky, such as drawing to an inside straight and filling it, and though his uncanny success at the tables drove many of the other players into fits of envy, no one ever really complained much beyond the grumbling of a sore loser over a big pot lost to a close hand. The serious players all knew about the law of averages. They all knew about percentages. Mickey was the exception that proved the rule. Someone had to be the consummate winner.

Tonight, however, Mickey would have no time for games. The Gavel Club would serve him only as a means of ditching his Korean shadow. The club was located in the center of a downtown city block on Lincoln Avenue between Congress and Union Streets. The rest of the block at ground level consisted of expensive shops and boutiques, all of which were closed at this late hour, as were the half-dozen entrances to the high-rent apartment buildings and condos that rose above Lincoln Avenue. The stylish apartments all maintained security and offered no chance of entrance to intruders. Mickey knew the Gavel Club's kitchen opened onto a back alley directly across from the rear delivery entrance to the Ritz Hotel. The hotel's front entrance was on Adams Street, on the opposite side of the city block. While Mickey could cut straight through, the only other way to Adams was to circle the entire city block. There was a heavy cloud cover over the city, which would help. Even if his pursuers had the power to obtain a dedicated satellite surveillance task, which he doubted, the thick cloud cover would render him invisible, at least for the moment. If he could just slip the two goons on his tail, he figured he should be in the clear long enough to make his way out of the city.

As he neared the club, Mickey could see that the doorman, one Patrick O'Reilly, a big tough ex-cop, was still on duty as he knew he would be until 2:00 a.m. After hours, any member wishing to gain entrance to the club would need to use his membership card-key. Inside, the member is met by a tuxedo-clad security guard and asked to sign a register. Only then may he enter the inner sanctums of the club, free to wander into the elegant dining room for a specially prepared meal, or to visit the Gavel Club's private bar for a drink or a fine Cuban cigar. Access to any of the private card rooms, however, would need the approval of the steward who, after checking on the games in progress, would steer a player to his usual game, or an appropriate one, this according to the player's relative skill and, of course, his wagering habits.

Everything about the Gavel Club was top-shelf. The house champagne was Dom Perignon served in Tiffany crystal flutes, the ornate oriental rugs were imported from Pakistan, the tiles were from Italy, and the dinnerware, of course, was bone china. The walls of this most dignified of clubs are paneled in rich, dark oak and trimmed with heavy, detailed woodwork. Portraits of distinguished past members adorn the somber hallways, some dating back to the mid-1800s, and new members are always sufficiently impressed to find several former US presidents among them.

All in all, the Gavel Club reeked of upper-class pretension and arrogance and was filled with mostly pompous, condescending bores intent on excluding from their club all but the most sophisticated and prominent gentlemen of the Washington social scene. Though Mickey despised their snobbery, he loved taking their money, and on this particular night, he was counting on their attitude of exclusivity being firmly enforced.

"Well, well, now. A very warm good evening to you, sir," the doorman said with a genuine, broad smile. "Long time, no see, Mr. Neally."

"Good to see you, O'Reilly," Mickey said, slipping the man a bill as he stepped to the opened doorway. "How's it look in there tonight?"

"Not much competition for you, sir," the big man said with a wink. "But that won't stop 'em from tryin' to get a piece of you anyway."

Mickey knew O'Reilly to be a true professional and, as such, always cordial to every member he encountered. But these two Irishmen enjoyed a special bond. Unlike many of the other members with their pompous attitudes, Mickey never acted self-important. He always treated O'Reilly and the rest of the staff more like friends than servants, and they all appreciated him for it.

"There's been more than one or two fish askin' about you over the past couple o' months, sir," O'Reilly said with a wicked grin as he leaned in close to Mickey. "Some of the gentlemen seem to think you've been off spending their money, sir. They'll be happy for a chance to get some of it back!"

"Well, I guess some people never learn," Mickey said with his own wicked grin, taking out a cigarette, which O'Reilly quickly lit with a deft flick of his gold Zippo.

"Thanks," Mickey said.

"You're welcome, sir, and good luck tonight."

"Keep up the good work, Paddy," Mickey said, and then he stepped through the opened door into the Gavel Club. Closing the door behind him, the big Irishman turned to face the street, folding his arms across his chest as two strangers turned into the entrance to the club and started up the walkway.

Once inside, Mickey signed the register then headed straight across the nearly empty lounge into the kitchen where he spoke briefly to the head chef, Jean-Luc. The Frenchman motioned to the back of the kitchen, and Mickey followed him through the service entrance, across a narrow alleyway and up onto a small landing where the chef rang a service bell. Within a few seconds, the door opened, and a man wearing a clean white apron and big floppy hat greeted Jean-Luc excitedly. The two exchanged a few rapid words in French, and the man with the floppy hat motioned for Neally to follow him. The chef led him through the busy kitchen and posh dining room to the front entrance of the Ritz Hotel. Thirty seconds later, Mickey was sitting in the back seat of a cab, heading out of the city.

*****

Sitting alone, smoking a cigar at the bar in the Gavel Club's lounge, Secretary Miller McWilliams awaited a refill of his Kentucky bourbon on the rocks. "Doherty," McWilliams asked of the barman, "wasn't that Mick Neally I just saw walk into the kitchen?" The secretary was one of the fish O'Reilly had referred to.

The white-haired, rosy-cheeked bartender paused, bottle in hand.

"Why, yes, sir," he said, "I believe it was."

"Not like an Irishman to pass by a bar without taking a drink."

"Perhaps he had a special order for Jean-Luc, sir," the barman suggested politely as he poured the whiskey.

"Perhaps."

The secretary of state picked up his drink and headed out of the room.

"Doherty," he called over his shoulder, "have the steward see me in the green room. Right away, please."

Chapter 17

Inspector George Lee answered his phone on the first ring.

"Mary Chu of the National Weather Bureau, inspector, with the update you requested concerning upper-level atmospheric conditions in the DC area."

The female voice on the other end of the line spoke slowly and in clear, perfect English. Lee picked up a pencil and began writing immediately. "Please begin," he said.

The FBI inspector listened intently for the better part of a minute, taking down every word as it was spoken. When the message was through, he asked no questions and ended the connection with a simple "Thank you." Lee then unlocked the bottom drawer of his desk and took out what appeared to be an ordinary desktop calculator. He began rapidly punching keys while referring every few seconds to the message he had just received. Three minutes later, he replaced the instrument in the locked draw and leaned back in his chair. George Lee took several deep breaths to calm himself. His chiseled face was beat red, his dark eyes glowering with anger.

"They've lost him!" he said to the empty room.

*****

The Chesapeake Bay area is home to some of the most beautiful and expensive oceanfront real estate in the world, offering miles and miles of waterfront property to the affluent commuters who labor in and around the nation's capital. The land southeast of the city is formed into a triangular peninsula by the west shore of the bay and the north shore of the Potomac River and is further narrowed by the insurgence of the Patuxent and Wicomico Rivers. Highway 235 runs some forty miles between the two rivers, almost to the end of the peninsula, connecting to Route 5, which continues to Point Lookout at the very tip. On the south side of the peninsula, near the end, lies St. George's Island, connected to the mainland by Route 249. On the tip of this little island, facing south, sitting alone atop a mass of concrete pillars is the thirty-five-hundred-square-foot beach house aptly named the Enchanted Cottage. The beautiful cottage is the summer home of Dawn DesMoine, a.k.a. Jessica, and at a little past midnight, she and Mickey both lay naked, sprawled out upon two large cushioned lounge chairs on the balcony deck off the master bedroom. They had just finished an especially passionate session of lovemaking, and now, drinks in hand, they enjoyed the sweet afterglow in silent reflection, gazing out over the moonlit beach, their hearts slowly quieting.

"You missed me," Jessica said, her dark eyes crinkling brightly from under her long black bangs.

"You think?" Mickey said.

"Yes, I think," she said, turning on her side to face Mickey. "You forget how well I know you, my love." She propped herself up on her elbow, enhancing the soft, slow curve of her hips as the moonlight glimmered off her smooth, tanned skin.

"And just how well is that?" Mickey asked as he rolled onto his side to take in her magnificence.

Jessica let her eyes drift lazily over Mickey's lean, muscular body, a sassy smile etched upon her lips. She enjoyed her brazen sensuality and made no apologies for it. Mickey, she knew, was one of the few men on the planet she was unable to intimidate, a fact that only added to her already-significant attraction to him. Her eyes came to rest on his, and her expression became suddenly sober.

"I know you well enough to know that something's wrong, Mick. Something's bothering you."

Ever so cool, Mickey slowly drained the contents of his glass.

"Now what makes you say that?"

"You have always been a wonderfully passionate and pleasing lover, my darling, but tonight you outdid yourself. It was as though you were making love for the first time." And after a silent moment, she added, "Or the last."

"Now there's a frightful thought," Mickey said, and he abruptly swung his feet to the floor and stood to walk into the bedroom. "You want another drink?" he asked, hoping she'd drop it. But Jessica knew she'd struck a nerve. She stood and followed him to the bed-room slider.

"Tell me about it, Mick," she said.

He turned as he answered her. "Tell you what? There's nothing to…"

As well as Mickey knew every inch of this woman's body, he wasn't prepared for the sight before him. She stood in the doorway stark naked, her head back, hair tousled by the breeze, her feet spread, hands on hips, breasts thrust proudly out at him, her every curve in perfect silhouette against the shimmering moonlit sea. Mickey's senses were momentarily overwhelmed, and he realized instantly that he could never lie to this woman. Their relationship had always been understood. They weren't like most other people. Physically, they were not committed exclusively to each other, but though they'd never talked about it, Mickey knew that emotionally and spiritually they were as one. He loved her, and he knew she loved him. They didn't need to say it. They'd both known it from the beginning. And now she sensed the fear in him, and she needed to know why. He'd have to tell her.

Damn it!

"Sit down, babe," he said tenderly. And he told her. She listened in almost complete silence, asking only occasional questions when something didn't make sense to her. She didn't understand how Sam fit into the story. She wasn't sure of what it was that Sam knew or how he knew it, probably because Mickey was unclear himself.

"I'm confused," she said. "You said Sam's writing a book about this. How can that be if you're the only one, other than the Chinese, to know about it?"

"I don't know," he said. "I have no fucking clue how he knows, but Sam knows. He just doesn't know he knows. If that makes any sense. He thinks it's a story he's made up. He said the story's been coming to him in his dreams. If it had been anyone other than Sam telling me that shit, I would have put a bullet in them right then and there. It's just too fuckin' weird!"

"You think Sam might be with the Chinese?"

"No fucking way!"

"You said they have a huge network in place—"

Mickey took both Jessica's hands in his.

"Look at me," he said. "Look me in the eyes. If Sam is one of those fucks, then everything I've ever believed in is for shit, and the whole world can go to hell!"

Jessica returned Mickey's hard stare for a long moment, searching her own instincts. "No, you're not wrong about him," she said, convinced. "It's something else then. Some psychic connection maybe."

"Well, I sure as hell can't explain it," Mickey said, getting up off the bed and moving to the wet bar for more scotch. "But he even knew about the fire extinguishers. Christ, he even knew the name of their fuckin' company!"

"What company? What fire extinguishers? You've lost me again."

"There was a small company in Taiwan," Mickey explained as he poured the drinks, "that back in the early eighties started to develop state-of-the-art products in the field of pyro-electronics. The founder of the company was Chinese. Fuckin' genius. He was developing concepts way ahead of the rest of the world industry."

Jessica sat listening on the edge of the bed. She took her drink from Mickey as he sat on a bedroom chair across from her, resting his forearms on his knees. Armed with a cigarette in one hand and a scotch in the other, he continued his story.

"This little company probably would have gotten swallowed up by some big Western corporation if this General Wu Xun hadn't found it first. Wu had his Korean friends buy out the company. He's got an extremely powerful Asian syndicate with plenty of money backing him. They dumped a ton of dough into this little venture over the next twenty years or so, and they built the little company into one of the largest international manufacturers in the world!

Hazard Management and Technologies International. HAMTIN for short. Sam had their fucking name."

"So what's with the fire extinguishers?"

"That's what they manufacture. That and everything else having to do with fire control systems." Mickey took a final drag off his cigarette and crushed it out. "Pretty slick move actually. The Chinese knew they could smuggle in their spies and scientists, as well as the components needed to build their bombs. But they also knew they'd need a safe location where they could assemble and store their weapons. And most importantly, they needed a means by which to distribute them, all at once, at just the right time. They saw this industry as a means to do just that. So they took the gamble. They positioned themselves. And then they waited."

"Waited for what?"

"The decline of the Soviet Union, the end of the Cold War. They waited for us to drop our guard. And we did."

"Mick, the Cold War's been over for years."

"Yeah, that's right. And we've gotten so lax about it, we've been giving fucking secrets away. A few years back, we replaced the computers in the Pentagon. Thousands of them. We sold the used systems, and Christ Almighty," Mickey scoffed. "Guess who we sold them to? The fucking Chinese! And apparently, some asshole forgot to make sure all the hard drives were clean."

Mickey sipped his drink, lowering his voice as he went on.

"Jess, do you really think everyone in the intelligence community was surprised by September 11? Hell, anyone privy to a certain stream of Middle Eastern intel knew something big was coming. We just couldn't stop it. And now they're all tripping over each other to close the door after the fucking cow has already left the barn! Our best people are all chasing bin Laden and al-Qaeda! Everyone's looking in the wrong fucking direction, Jess!"

Mickey turned, shaking his head. "They never saw this coming."

"Saw what, Mick?"

"Wu Xun has the neutron bomb, Jess. Thousands of them. Encased in dummy fire extinguishers. Just sitting and waiting. And for the past eight years, guess who's been supplying and servicing the military's firefighting systems?"

The grim reality of Mickey's words fell suddenly and hard upon Jessica as she put it all together, but she was as brave as she was beautiful. Her voice was void of any fear when she asked, "How bad is it?"

Mickey stood and walked to the slider that opened to the balcony deck. With his back to the room, he stood looking out over the beauty of the bay as it reflected the light of the near-full moon. Shore lights were visible in every direction, the sleepy coastal community up late, completely oblivious to the impending catastrophe. He wondered what fate awaited them. Finally, he said, "It's bad enough, but you shouldn't know any more than you already do. I need rest. I haven't had any sleep in nearly three days, and my brain is for shit. Tomorrow I'm gonna try to reach the president. I don't know who else I can trust. And you need to get out of the country."

"Very noble of you to worry after me, darling," Jessica said, slightly miffed. "But if you hadn't noticed, I'm a big girl now. I can handle myself."

"No, you can't!" Mickey said a bit more harshly than he'd intended. "You can't handle the people that are after me and will soon be after you if they find out I've been here. They *will* make you talk, and then they'll kill you!" Mickey turned away. "Fuck!" he yelled, angry with himself. "I'm sorry. I shouldn't have come."

The beautiful Jessica walked over and stood behind her lover. She reached around his waist, pressing her warm flesh against his, slowly caressing his hard, flat body as the first pangs of renewed desire stirred deep within him.

"It's all right, my love," she whispered. "Where else could you have gone?"

Chapter 18

Present day, the island of Hainan

Upon learning of the break-in to his computer system and the extraction of an unknown amount of data relevant to the alliance's master plan, General Wu Xun called an emergency meeting at his island retreat to assess the extent of the theft and to ensure that every means at his disposal was being employed to recover the stolen data.

A security breach of this magnitude had been unimaginable. For so long now, the secrecy of Wu's plan had been absolute. The general and his people had spared no amount of time or expense to conceal every aspect of this massive and intricate operation. To have it all jeopardized at this late date, so close to the plan's final execution, was a most shockingly catastrophic development for Wu and his team. It was both inconceivable and unacceptable. The fact that the theft had taken place right under their very noses merely added insult to injury.

The Chinese had not counted on a rogue agent striking out on his own without authorization, breaking all contact with his government, in effect isolating himself, thereby enabling him to implement a singular, independent investigation. Mickey had used Asian operatives known only to himself. Together they operated completely outside the company, free from communication or contact with his agency through any of the normal channels. *No one* knew what he was working on or even where he was. A concept foreign to them, Wu's intelligence unit could not have anticipated the American spirit of free will and individual resolve coming into play at this most critical of times.

Wu Xun sat at the head of the conference table, struggling to maintain control of his anger. Seated with him were Major Hu Shi, General Liu Ying-ch'ao, and Lo Fang. As commander of military intelligence, General Liu was primarily responsible for the security of the operation. The weight of Wu's silent stare fell upon the general and held there for a long, quiet moment before he finally spoke.

"How did this happen?" Wu asked, visibly disturbed.

"We do not know all the details at this time," Liu answered calmly. "But it appears the system was compromised on the orders of an American agent acting independently. It is, I am afraid, a development we did not foresee."

Liu Ying-ch'ao bowed his apology to Wu Xun before going on.

"Because this agent was operating outside our sphere of influence, we had no indication of his existence or designs. It was only by good fortune that we stumbled upon his network and were able to capture one of his operatives and force a confession. We know who he is and where he is."

"Are you telling me that one man alone has done this?" Wu asked, a look of incredible disbelief on his face. "One man alone threatens the sanctity of our entire operation? With all the safeguards we so carefully developed? All the assurances? How can this be? What manner of man is this?" Wu pounded the table. "Who is this man?" he asked in outrage.

"His name is Neally. He is American CIA," General Liu said, surprisingly at ease with the situation. "A very talented and resourceful man," he continued coolly. "However, this same cunning that had allowed him to remain invisible to us will now work against him."

"Please explain," Wu said, his patience running thin.

"He is but a singular threat, Wu Xun. By virtue of the fact that this man was operating alone, completely isolated from any contact with his government, he is, without a doubt, the only one with any real knowledge of our operation."

The confidence in Liu's voice bordered now on arrogance.

"We know large amounts of data were downloaded," he explained, "so we must assume this man Neally is carrying some type of hard evidence of his discovery, and one of two certainties exist. Without doubt, this American spy will now also know of the extensive network of agents we have in place in his country. The Americans call them moles. Knowing this, he will be unable to trust anyone, unable to come in with his evidence for fear of capture. To be sure of his next move, he will be forced for a time into an idle appraisal of his situation. Time enough for our agents to pick him up and retrieve the evidence."

General Liu bowed his head slightly, tilting it as he did so.

"If, on the other hand," he said, "Neally remains unaware of our forces within his government, then he will simply stumble blindly into our trap. Either way, Wu Xun, this man shall not be a threat for long."

"I want nothing left to chance," Wu said. "We have come much too far to see our life's ambitions imperiled by the work of a single spy."

"The word has already been sent to our agents in the US," Liu said. "This man is under surveillance as we speak. Our guardian has several teams in place, Wu Xun. It shall be but a short time now until we hear confirmation of his capture."

"You are sure of this, Ying-ch'ao?"

"It is a certainty, my general."

Wu turned his attention to Major Hu Shi. "Our communication satellite goes up in ten days," he snapped. "Have the final arrangements been made to reprogram the computer's instructions, Hu Shi?"

"It is all arranged and on schedule, my general."

"Very well then. The operation continues as planned. General Liu, I expect you will keep me informed as to the status of this spy. I trust I shall not have to wait long. We shall reconvene in Guangxi in five days. Lo Fang, a word in private please."

The Tong leader remained seated after the others left the room. Once alone, Wu walked to a cabinet next to the glass wall and, from a crystal decanter, poured a generous portion of Du Kang, an exceptionally potent Chinese liqueur, into two small porcelain cups. He returned to the table, sitting on its edge next to Lo Fang, and handed him a cup.

Wu raised his cup in toast. "To the new world order," he said, his chin held high. The Tong leader merely nodded in silent acknowledgment.

"I need you to go to America, comrade," Wu said after downing the Du Kang. "It is a most critical matter."

"My presence there is not needed, Wu. As I have said before, Lee Hak-joon is a most capable assassin."

"This is not about the hatchet-faced man," Wu said, placing his cup carefully on the table. "There is someone else I need you to make contact with. Someone known only to myself. A last line of defense, if you will. There are new instructions you must bring to him."

*****

Awakening to the smell of coffee brewing, Mickey immediately reached for his watch to check the time. Twenty minutes past noon, he had slept for nearly ten hours. *Damn!* Neally knew he'd needed the sleep, but he'd wanted to be back in the city by now. With her usual uncanny sense of timing, Jessica walked into the room, carrying two steaming cups of coffee just as Mickey sat up in bed.

"Breakfast or lunch?" she asked cheerfully.

"Neither," he said, throwing off the covers. "Why'd you let me sleep so late?"

"You needed it. And you need food as well. Take this to the shower, and I'll fix you something. Go on, and don't argue with me."

He knew she was right.

"Steak and eggs then," he said, taking the coffee from her.

"You got it."

"Thanks, gorgeous," he said, slapping her behind as he headed for the shower.

The two ate their breakfast on the large deck off the kitchen, overlooking the bay. Rested, showered, and fed, Mickey felt like a new man. Able to think clearly once again, his mind was already fast at work planning his strategy for reaching the president, but first, he needed to settle the matter of getting Jessica to a safe hideaway.

"Listen carefully to me," he said. "I want you to fly to Miami today, buy a car, don't rent one. And use cash. Then drive to Marathon Key. Go to the Shark Shanty on the west side of the island and ask for Rudy. Everyone on the island knows the place. Tell Rudy I want him to take you to the 'beach house,' it's a little deserted island with a hut we built—"

"Mick, I'm not running," she interrupted. "Not today. Not ever. You go do whatever it is you need to do. I'll be waiting right here when you get back."

"Jess—"

"No!"

Looking into her eyes, he could see it was pointless to argue with her. She was as strong-willed as any SEAL he'd ever gone to war with. *Fuck it!* He leaned forward to kiss her, and it suddenly hit him. A vision so strong that it swept over him like a wave of undeniable certainty. He shook his head to clear it.

"Are you okay, Mick?"

"Ahh…yeah. Yeah, I'm fine," he said, still dazed. "Wait here a second."

Mickey stood and walked into the bedroom, returning a few seconds later with a long thin jewelry box.

"I almost forgot," he fibbed. "I picked up a little something for you while I was out of town."

Jessica opened the box to find one of the most stunningly beautiful necklaces she had ever seen. No stranger to fine things, she was not a woman easily impressed by material means, but this piece left her nearly speechless. It was a large diamond necklace, over a hundred stones in all. With a total weight of over twenty karats, the center stone alone over three, the necklace was easily the most striking piece of jewelry she had ever held.

"My God, Mick! It's…it's beautiful!" It was an effort for Jessica just to take her eyes from the glittering piece long enough to look up at Mickey. "This must have cost a fortune! Where on earth did you ever find it?"

As at the card tables, the sensation remained so strong and so clear that Mickey could not deny the truth of it. He returned Jessica's loving gaze with his own.

"If anyone ever asks," he said, his eyes locked with hers, "just tell them it was made in China."

Her look turned suddenly curious, and in an instant, the spell was broken. Mickey got up and leaned over to kiss her on the forehead.

"It's late," he said in a hurry. "I've gotta go."

Jessica stood and wrapped herself around her lover and kissed him long and hard on the lips. "I'll be waiting for you, Mick. Be careful, okay?"

"Sure," he said, looking away, knowing he could not lie to her face. "I'll see ya in a couple of days."

Chapter 19

What little sleep Sam had managed the night before had been shallow and restless as once again the dreams had returned. Fragments of dreams really. Fleeting bits and pieces of places and events he could not identify hung suspended in his mind's eye like distant memories slightly out of focus, their meaning unclear. Try as he might, the pieces would not fit together. Perhaps, he thought, they were not memories at all.

Hoping to find a clue to help him make some sense of it all, Sam had spent the morning in the Washington Public Library, where he had gone online to garner information on the HAMTIN corporation's global headquarters in Arizona. After finding all he could, Sam then researched whatever data was available on the Hanford National Laboratories in Washington State. What he found, exact replications of the visions from his earlier dreams, should have surprised him, but did not. Sam was slowly coming to accept that there were forces at work that he did not understand, forces that appeared to be, in part at least, a phenomenon new to his experience. It seemed almost as though he was in a continuous state of déjà vu, and he found himself on new ground, questioning his own sense of reality.

Mason's intellect mandated that he always bear an open mind to such issues, for he believed that the ever-expanding cosmos inherent to all thinking creatures held an infinite number of mysteries, which, as of yet, remain beyond man's understanding. Sam believed that the genius of great thinkers, such as DaVinci, Newton, Einstein, and Chopra, barely scratched the surface of what would be to most, an unimaginable amount of unknown truths.

Lacking any reasonable explanation, Sam decided to simply go with it. For the time being, at least, he would not question his apparent newfound instincts, if that is what they were. He would try instead to use them as a divining rod of sorts, a direction finder for the pieces to his growing puzzle. For that's what his research had now become. Sam could no longer rationalize the stream of recent coincidences. Instinct told him there was more to them.

*****

Back in his hotel room, Sam did not need to rely on his instincts to tell him that his fear for Mickey's life was all the more real, as once again, he came up empty with his attempts to reach him. Since Keri's report the night before of two Asians following after Mickey as he left the Four Seasons, Sam had been at unease with his inability to find his friend. Several times throughout the morning, he had called Mickey's number to no avail. Wondering why neither he nor Nicki was returning his calls, the phone rang just as he reached for it to try Nicki one more time.

"Mason here," he said.

"How the fuck are ya, Sam?"

Apart from the cussing, the female voice on the other end of the line was quite soft, sweet, and almost musical in tone. It belonged to Nicki.

"Well, so much for hypnotic therapy," Sam said.

"I take it you've been talking to Keri."

"Had dinner with her last night. Unlike you, she returns phone calls."

"Shit, I'm really sorry, Sam," Nicki said, sincerely flustered. "I've been so damn busy at work. Erin and I ended up spending the night at Keri's mom's, and I didn't get your messages until just now when I came home for lunch. Honest, Sam, this is the first chance I've had to call you."

"It's okay, Nicki," Sam said in his big brother voice. "How are you and Erin?"

"We're fine, Sam. I guess."

Sam heard the reservation in her voice.

"Well," Nicki added, "Erin is at least, the little shit. She is so full of piss and vinegar she runs me ragged! She's growing so fast, Sam, and…it just seems like I never get to spend any real time with her. I feel like I'm missing seeing her grow up."

Sam was hesitant to comment but, after brief reflection, said, "Nicki, not being a father myself, I can only guess at the choices you must have to make. I know you feel torn about a lot of them, but you are doing an awesome job raising your little girl! You bust your butt all year long, and I happen to know every decision you make is predicated on Erin's well-being. So give yourself a little more credit, you should be proud of the both of you."

"Thanks, Sam, and I'm sorry. I didn't mean to whine at you."

"You're welcome, and you weren't. So tell me," he said. "When's the last time you heard from your brother?"

"Oh Christ, Sam, the last time I actually saw Mickey was about two weeks before Christmas. And then I got a Christmas card from him about a week after New Year's that was mailed from China of all places. Said he was going to be out of town for a while, and he'd call me when he got back. Company business, he said."

"You said Mickey was in China?"

Sam wasn't quite able to keep the anxiety out of his voice.

"Well that's where the letter was postmarked, so yeah…that's what one would assume. Why?"

"No reason," he said quickly, not wanting to get into it with her. "What else did the letter say?"

"Just the usual stuff, you know—'give Erin a hug for me,' 'I'll call you when I get back.' It was a pretty short note."

"Did he say what he was doing in China or how long he'd be gone?"

"No, Sam, he didn't. And what's with all the questions? Is something wrong? What are you two up to now?"

"Nothing, and there's nothing wrong. It's just that I hadn't seen your brother for a while myself. Until I ran into him last night."

"You saw Mickey last night! Where?"

"I had a drink with him in the bar downstairs."

"He's back in town, and he hasn't called me yet," Nicki said, both excited and a little pissed off. "I'll fuckin' kill him!"

"I'm sure you'll hear from him today, Nick. Keri was going to try to get the four of us out tonight. You up for it?"

"Are you kiddin' me? Does a rockin' horse have a wooden pecker?"

"I'll take that as a yes. Keri said you'd probably be psyched."

"Oh, I can't wait to see Mickey! And you too, Sam. Hell, this'll be just like old times! I'm going to call Keri right now."

"Do that. You two plan the night and one of you call me later. You have my room number still?"

"Yeah, it's still on the machine."

"Good. When you hear from your brother, tell him to call me here. Tell him it's important, okay?"

"Sure thing, Sam. But let me go now, okay. I want to call Keri before I have to run back to work. I'll see you tonight. Bye, Sam. Love ya."

Sam said goodbye just as the receiver went click in his ear.

What the hell was Mickey doing in China?

With no answer readily available, he turned his attention back to the phone. He had a couple of long-distance calls he needed to make. One to Irene for an update with her and then a call to an old friend from the Boston North End who had relocated to Las Vegas and still owed Sam a favor or two. This "friend" now managed security for one of the big Vegas hotels, which, unlike most of the casinos in Sin City, had not yet sold out to corporate interests. In spite of continuous pressure from both foreign and domestic sources, this strip icon remained resolutely in the family—so to speak.

Chapter 20

Sam caught Irene just as she was leaving her office for the afternoon. The ensuing conversation merely served to confirm what Sam had already learned from Keri, and though Irene agreed as to the oddity of Sam's new findings so closely paralleling his nighttime visions, she confessed that she could offer no reasonable explanation.

"Perhaps it is all just coincidence," she'd suggested weakly, but on learning of Mickey's incident with the Asians at the Four Seasons and his apparent recent return from China, Irene could no longer hold to that line of rationale.

"There does seem to be more going on here than meets the eye, Sam. Quite troubling actually. I am worried for your friend."

"Yeah, me too," Sam admitted.

"What will you do now?"

"I'm not sure. Hopefully, I'll get to talk to Mickey about all this tonight, and I'll find out what's really goin' on with him."

"And then?"

"And then I think I'll head out west and take a closer look at this HAMTIN facility. There's got to be some good background there for me, at least. And while I'm in that part of the country, I may as well check out the nuclear labs up in Idaho and Washington State. Maybe talk to some people on-site, gather whatever research data I'll need. You know anyone out there who might be of some help?"

"No, but you do."

"Who do I know?"

"Sam, didn't you and Mickey go out there a couple of years ago. Some hunting trip or something? And if I'm not mistaken, wasn't it to be some sort of reunion with an old service buddy?"

"Ron! Damn! How could I not think of him?"

"Well, Sam, it is one of the first things to go."

"What's that?"

"One's memory."

"Touché."

"Ahh, Sam," Irene taunted, "I trust you're not suffering from any other age-related condition, or should I say lack of condition?"

"Umm, no, everything is working just fine, Irene, but thank you very much for asking," Sam said, caught off guard. "And I have several more important calls to make, so—"

"You know they have pills for that sort of thing now," Irene interrupted, thoroughly enjoying the upper hand.

"Goodbye, Irene."

"I know of a good doctor, would you like his number?"

"No! Say goodbye, Irene!"

"Goodbye, Irene," she said, laughing.

"Okay, you win this time. Thanks for Ron. I'll call you in a couple of days."

"Goodbye, Sam," Irene said, still smiling. Then in a more serious tone, she said, "Be careful out there, Sam. I'm suddenly getting a very bad feeling about all of this."

"I'll be careful," he said and he hung up.

"The old girl's getting awfully feisty in her old age," Sam noted, smiling to himself as he picked the receiver back up to dial the operator.

*****

Mickey was on a payphone dialing the White House. He didn't dare use his cell. He'd had a cab drop him off at the Smithsonian. The hotels and restaurants would all be closely watched, as would the airports and bus and train terminals, but there would be no reason for anyone to look for him at the famous museum.

Neally needed more time, and the large crowds of visitors touring the museum would help him remain invisible long enough to arrange a way in. He used the payphone to call Miller McWilliams's office line as his cell would also be too risky.

"Secretary of State McWilliams's office, how may I direct your call?" The female voice was bright, cheerful, and completely devoid of any accent.

"Lemme speak with Secretary McWilliams, please," Mickey said, coloring his speech with a Southern drawl.

"I'm sorry, sir, the secretary is unavailable at the moment."

"I see. The secretary's a little busy right now, is that it?"

"Yes, sir, he is."

"Well, darlin', why don't you just be a dear an' go ahead an' interrupt him for me?"

"I'm sorry, sir, who did you say was calling?"

"I didn't."

"Well, sir," the voice said with a hint of indignation, "the secretary is in an important meeting at the moment, but if you would care to leave me your name and number, I would be happy to…"

"I'm sorry darlin'," Mickey cut in. "I did not catch your name. To whom am I speakin'?"

"This is Ms. Allison."

Like most women in the business world, she used the neutral prefix "Ms." There would be no way to know if Allison might be her married name. Without a hint of accent, Mickey had no reason to suspect she was Chinese American.

"Well, *Ms.* Allison, I am a very dear, old friend of the secretary, and this call is of a most personal nature. Now, I can guarantee that your boss will want to talk to me. I can also promise you that ol' Hoof will be sorer than a blind man in a room full of cactus plants if he misses my call. And you, Ms. Allison, will be in deep shit, if you catch my drift! So, darlin', why don't you just slide into that meeting nice'n quiet like, an' slip ol' Hoof a note sayin' he's got an important phone call?"

"I will need your name, sir," Ms. Allison said after a moment's consideration.

Mickey was hoping to charm his way through to McWilliams without divulging his identity. *Fuck!* He'd have to chance it.

"Tell the secretary that Mick Neally is on the phone."

Ms. Allison did not miss a beat.

"Very well, Mr. Neally," she said. "Please hold."

A full minute later, having left his meeting, McWilliams stood next to Ms. Allison's desk to take the call.

"Mick, you ol' son of a gun, where the hell have you been, boy?"

A lifelong politician from the glorious state of Georgia, the secretary was the embodiment of all that typified the Southern expression "good ol' boy." Nicknamed Hoof because he was as stubborn as a mule with a kick just as hard, McWilliams was no Southern gentleman. He had schmoozed and bullied his way to the Capitol by making it his business to know everyone else's business, professional, personal, or otherwise. He could play hardball with the best of them and had his hand in more pockets than he could count. He was both affable and charming, or loud and obnoxious, depending on one's inclination or political persuasion. Though Mickey didn't care much about the man's politics, he enjoyed the spirited ribbing and fierce competitive nature that McWilliams always brought to the poker table. The two quite often found themselves playing head to head, long into the early morning hours, the last two survivors of a brutally weary night of cards. They were rivals for sure, but they had also become friends, and Mickey trusted him.

"I've been out of town a while, Hoof," Neally confessed.

"Well, I guess so! Seems like you've had yourself a nice long vacation at my expense. I do hope you're plannin' on givin' me a chance to recoup sometime soon?"

"Sure thing, Hoof. You know I love taking your money, but…"

Mickey paused, and his voice turned as grave as he could ever remember.

"That'll have to wait, I'm afraid. I need your help, Mr. Secretary. I need you to get me in to see the president. Today, sir, as soon as possible. It is a matter of national security of the highest priority!"

"You're serious, Mick."

"Yes, sir."

"What's this all about?"

"I can't say over the phone, sir, but…you know who I work for."

"I do."

"Well, sir, let's just say that my actual job description doesn't exist. If you know what I mean."

"You a spook, Boy?"

Mickey didn't need to answer.

"Well, I'll be damned…"

"This can't wait, Hoof. If you want to sit in on it, that's fine. Just get me in to see him. ASAP!"

"Hold on a sec, Mick. Linda, what time am I scheduled with the president this afternoon?"

"Three ten, Mr. Secretary."

"Can you make it here by three, Mick?"

"No problem, sir."

"Okay. Come to the north gate. I'll leave your name. Someone will meet you inside an' bring you up to the Oval Office."

"Thanks, Hoof."

"Do you need help, Mick?"

"No, sir, and I suggest that you tell no one of this."

"I'll talk to you then, son."

McWilliams turned to his secretary. "Linda, arrange for Mr. Neally to enter the north gate and have someone meet him and bring him upstairs. Then call the Oval Office and let them know that I've added a guest to the agenda. Advise the Secret Service. Make all the necessary calls. Understand?"

"Perfectly, sir."

As McWilliams went back to his meeting, Ms. Allison quickly made the calls, and when she finished, she placed one more, a personal call to her friend Mary over at the National Weather Bureau.

Chapter 21

R on Knight was Sam's friend in Idaho of whom Irene had spoken. He was, in fact, the third surviving SEAL from that long-ago, ill-fated covert operation down in South America. Ron had recovered from his wounds to return home to Idaho, where he'd entered a career in law enforcement. Knight had done well and was currently the sheriff of Bonneville County, which, as Sam was about to find out, held partial jurisdiction over the land surrounding the Idaho National Engineering and Environmental Laboratory (INEEL).

On Sam's first call to the Bonneville County offices, the dispatcher informed him that the sheriff was out on a road call but was due back within the hour. Sam left his number, and a message to please have the sheriff call him back when he got in.

Having had no luck reaching Ron, Sam took out his wallet and, sifting through it, came up with an old worn business card with a phone number scratched on the back. He dialed it and got an answer on the first ring.

A recorded voice said, "You have reached Caesar's Palace security. Please dial your extension now or hold for a security agent." Sam held.

Half a minute later, a dull, gruff voice came on the line. "Security, Costa."

"Jack Stavros, please."

"Who wants him?"

"Tell him it's Sam Mason."

"Sorry, don't know ya."

"Your loss I'm sure."

"Huh?"

"Just get your boss on the phone, meat."

"Sorry, pal, Stavros is on the floor."

"Listen, Costa, your boss will be wearin' a headset. You wanna keep your job till tomorrow, press a button and patch me through to him!"

"Is that so?"

"Yeah, it is."

"What are you, some kind of fuckin' tough guy?"

"Yeah, I am."

The line was silent for a few seconds while Costa considered the sincerity in Sam's voice.

"What was that name again?"

"Mason, Sam Mason."

"Hold on."

Sam held for no more than ten seconds this time for Costa to come back on the line. "I'm putting you through now, Mr. Mason. Sorry about bustin' 'em."

"Hardly noticed."

"Sammy, you hot shit! Where the fuck are ya?" The voice on the line now was much higher pitched and practically screaming.

"Hey, Jackie, I'm in DC. How's Vegas treatin' ya?"

"Are you fuckin' shittin' me? There's more action out here than even I can handle. So, when are you comin' out to see me, huh, Sammy? For Christ's sake, I'll put you up in the best room we got. On me. Just get your ass out here!"

"I might just take you up on that in a few days, Jack, but right now, I need to talk."

"Sure thing, pally. What's up?"

"Is this a secure line?"

"No."

"Call me back on one."

"Gimme half an hour."

Sam left his number and hung up the phone. It rang immediately. The front desk was calling to say a Sheriff Knight had called and had left the number for his direct line. Sam dialed it.

"Sheriff Knight."

The booming voice was even deeper than Sam had remembered it.

"I thought I'd called the wrong county before when they told me the sheriff was busy working."

"Sammy!"

And for the second time within a minute, Sam heard the loud, warm greeting of an old friend. They spent a couple of minutes catching up on lost time, and then Ron asked, "So to what do I owe the honor of this call?"

"I'm headed out your way in a few days to do some research on the new book I'm workin' on. Thought I'd stop by to say hello, and maybe you could point me in the right direction."

"Anything I can do to help Sammy. You know that."

"Thanks, Ronnie. Right now, you could help me out with a little intel about that nuclear lab you've got out there."

"INEEL?" Ron asked with mild curiosity.

"What'd you call it?"

"INEEL. I-N-E-E-L. Stands for the Idaho National Engineering and Environmental Laboratory."

"I thought it was the National Reactor Testing Station?"

"It was till the mideighties. Then they changed it to INEL. Idaho National Engineering Lab. They added the extra *E* a few years back to help pacify the environmentalists."

"Make a lot of noise out there, too, do they?"

"You bet they do. Heck, you've been out here, Sammy. You know how beautiful the countryside is. People here take to protectin' it mighty seriously."

"Can't say as I blame 'em. Okay, so it's called INEEL." Sam made notes as he talked. "So what can you tell me about the place?"

"Not much to tell anymore. Most of the site is inactive. About all they do out there now is the downgrading of spent fuel and related research to find better, more efficient ways to affect the process. That's the environmental part, I guess, making the stuff less radioactive. They call it pacification. State-of-the-art procedures from what I understand. Once they get the stuff to a safe enough level, they transport it down to Arizona, where they bury it a couple of miles underground in the salt mines. That's where I come in."

"Security?"

"Exactly. Half the site lies in Bonneville County, and half lies in Butte County. Whenever they transport that shit, it always goes through Bonneville, and I'm responsible for security along the route throughout my county. Protesters, accidents, breakdowns, terrorists. I have to cover it all. The feds are always in on it, and they're a pain in the ass, of course. Other than that, I don't have much to say about what goes on out there."

"Why not? Ain't you da Sheriff?"

"Yeah, but the DOE has its own private security force on-site. Pretty good one too. I help out from time to time with some of the training, you know, weapons and tactics. Antiterrorist stuff mostly. And now the state has given those boys jurisdiction over the roadways that run through the reservation, so watch your ass if you go out there, Sam. They can be a might overzealous. Love to write speedin' tickets."

"So there's still heavy security on-site."

"Well, it's still pretty good, Sam, but not like it used to be. Like I said, not much goin' on out there anymore."

"They ever do any weapons research out there?"

Sam's friend didn't answer right away.

"None that I could speak of."

"Does that mean there wasn't any, or that there was, and you just can't talk about it?"

"I dunno Sam, what do you think it means?"

"Okay, Ron, one last question. Ever know of any Chinese working on-site?"

"Chinese?"

"Yeah, Chinese."

"Well, sure. Heck, we got our share of foreigners movin' in just like everywhere else. There's been a big migration to this area the past ten years or so. Some from back east or down Mexico way, but mostly we get folks movin' east from California. Big trend lately. I don't like it to tell you the truth. It starts gettin' too crowded and all of a sudden people don't get along so good. Makes my job tougher."

"Ron, you're spoiled. Idaho's bigger than all of New England, and what have you got? Maybe a million people?"

"A million, two-five."

"Gee, a regular meltin' pot."

"More than enough for me. So why the interest in the Chinese?"

"Actually, I'm only interested in one particular scientist. As county sheriff, Ron, could you gain access to past employment records out at the site?"

"I dunno, Sam, do you think I could?"

"Okay. If, for the sake of argument, you could, why don't you see if the name Dennis Chung comes up anywhere?"

"If I could, and if this Dennis Chung were to show up, I would call you back in about half an hour. But that's only if I could, of course."

"Of course."

"So, Sammy, when do you think you might be comin' out this way?"

"I dunno, Ron, when do you think I might be comin' out?"

"Heh, heh. Okay, wise guy, I'll see what I can do."

"Thanks, Ron."

"No sweat, amigo. Later."

Sam hung up to wait for Jack's call. He couldn't help but smile as he remembered his little pal from the North End.

*****

Jack Stavros was in the mob, and he wasn't even Italian, he was half-Greek, but the wise guys loved him anyway. True, he could never become a "made man" because his blood wasn't pure Sicilian, which meant he would always remain on the outside of that inner "family" circle, but Jack didn't care. He knew he would always be taken care of. The Italians loved Jack not so much because he had big balls and was cute and funny. It was more for the fact that he'd twice done time for one of the main men. On two different occasions, Jack had taken the fall for one of the Salemi brothers when one of their deals went bust. He did the time, and he kept his mouth shut, and because of it, Jack was forever in their good graces.

Sam had come to know Jack quite by luck. Lucky for Jack, that is. The little guy had more balls than brains sometimes, and when he stiffed one of South Boston's Irish mobsters by the name of Jimmy Greene for about twenty big ones, Greene came looking for him.

Just outside the Boston North End, in the Quincy Market district, was a nightclub Jack was known to hang out in. The club was called Il Peninos, and it was run by the mob. The Irish knew they couldn't touch Jack inside the North End neighborhood, but here he was fair game. The place was pretty upscale for the area with five levels of bars and dance floors to choose from, each with its own music and unique atmosphere. At the back of the club was an open stairwell running between the five floors that the patrons used to move up and down from bar to bar. On hot summer nights, the fire doors would be left open to let smoke out and fresh air in.

When a fight they'd staged broke out, distracting the bouncers, two of Greene's men grabbed Jack as he stood alone by the fire escape. They dragged him deep into the back alley, out behind a dumpster, where Greene planned to extract his pound of flesh. To Jack's good fortune, Sam happened to be leaving the smoky club when, spying the unattended opening, he quickly slipped through the door, down the metal stairway, out into the alley, and turning the wrong way, he stumbled right into the middle of the imminent murder scene. Mason heard the ruckus before the Irish saw him, and he quickly assessed the situation. He tried to talk himself into leaving it alone.

It's none of your business, Sam.

But Mason knew by the time the cops could get there, the little guy being held at knifepoint would be long dead. So putting on his best drunk act, Sam staggered straight into the middle of it. Pretending to be in great need of relieving himself, he ignored Greene's angry warnings until he was within a few feet of the group.

"Sean, break this motherfucker's neck," the boss man said to the big freckled face goon pointing a shotgun at Sam.

"Love to," the big man said with a sneer, and shifting the shotgun to his left hand, he moved to get behind the swaying drunk. Sam staggered a couple of feet closer to Greene, who was holding a stiletto in his right hand. A man wearing a scally cap stood behind Jack, his left hand at Jack's throat, his right holding a gun to the little guy's head. *Won't get to him in time.*

Freckle-Face let the shotgun lower to his side as he made a clumsy move to grab Sam around the neck with his right arm. The ex-SEAL hit him hard with an elbow in the solar plexus as he kicked the knife out of Greene's hand. With the same foot, he kicked the Irish mobster in the head, knocking him out. Mason spun around before Freckle-Face could straighten up, hitting him with a massive uppercut. Knocked unconscious, the big man collapsed to the ground, his jaw broken.

Taken by surprise, the man in the scally hesitated for no more than a second before taking the gun from Jack's head to aim it at Sam. But he'd made the amateur's mistake. He should have shot Jack first. As soon as the gun came away from his head, Jack grabbed Scally Cap's gun arm with both of his own and shoved up for all he was worth. Two shots whistled harmlessly over Sam's head, and he quickly stepped in to clip the gunman on the temple, putting him to sleep.

The little guy, who a moment earlier was facing a sure and unpleasant death, became suddenly animated, bouncing around and screaming a string of obscenities at the fallen hoods. Sam stood watching, mildly amused, until Jack grabbed up the shotgun and pointed it at Greene's head.

"No!" Sam yelled, taking the gun away.

"Look, pal," Jack said, pleading his case, "you saved my ass. Thank you. But if I don't finish this prick now, he's just gonna come after me again. So gimme the fuckin' shotgun!"

"No."

"What are you, some kind of fuckin' Boy Scout? This piece of shit over here was about to put a bullet in your fuckin' noggin.' What the hell do you care if I ace 'em?"

"Not gonna happen, so forget it," Sam said as he picked up the other weapons, wiped them, and threw them in the dumpster.

"That's just fuckin' great. I won' be able to show my face south of Hanover Street now without lookin' over my shoulder."

"So, relocate," Sam said without sympathy.

"Hey, you're all fuckin' heart."

The faint sound of distant sirens drifting down the alleyway suddenly caught Jack's attention.

"Let's get the fuck outta here," he said, realizing a crowd was starting to gather up by the street. "Stick with me if you don't want to get pinched."

Jack led Sam through the crowd and across the street where they slipped into a parking garage just as a cruiser came around the corner. When they came out the other side, he whistled down a cab.

"North End and hit it!" he yelled at the cabbie as they slid in back.

Jack took Sam to "his" restaurant, which of course he didn't really own, but that didn't seem to matter to Jack. Once he'd told everyone the story of how his new friend had saved his ass, Sam was treated just like one of the "family." They ate the best Italian food Sam had ever tasted and drank red wine and Ouzo long into the night. In spite of his better judgment, the little guy was beginning to grow on Sam, and by the morning, the two men had become pals.

*****

Jack had ended up taking Sam's advice about relocating. One of the wise guys set him up out in Vegas, and whenever Sam came into town, everything was on the house. Sam was just realizing that he was truly looking forward to seeing the little guy again when the phone rang.

"Mason."

"It's Jackie, Sam. What's up?"

"You ever hear of the Tong, Jack?"

"The fuckin' Chinks? Sure."

"Any of the people you work for ever do any business with them?"

There wasn't much of a pause, but it was there.

"Fuck, no, Sam! They're our fuckin' competition now for Christ's sake!"

"You sure, Jack?"

"Fuck, yeah, Sammy. Hell, you can't trust the slant-eye motherfuckers!"

"How would you know that?"

"Well, shit, Sam. I've seen some of the boys doin' a little action on the side with some of 'em. I mean, I don't know for sure if they were even Tong guys. It was just nickel 'n dime stuff, Sammy. Some dope, a few whores. You know, nothin' big. But I can tell you for sure, pally, official family policy is to keep them the fuck out of our business."

Sam knew Jack's personality all too well. Jack was talking just a little too fast.

"You bein' straight with me, Jack?"

"Yeah, Sammy. I'm tellin' ya, I don't know nothin' about their business. Honest. Hell, I'd do anything to help you, pally, you know that. There's just nothin' to tell."

"Okay, Jackie, thanks anyway," Sam said. "Do me a favor, will ya, an' keep your ears open? If you hear anything, let me know, I should be out your way in a few days."

"No fuckin' problem, Sam. Hey, I love ya, pal."

"Oh, and Jackie, I picked up a present for you. I'll send it out."

"Yeah? Hey, I fuckin' love presents. What is it?"

"A vocabulary book!"

"Hey," the little guy said as though genuinely hurt, "what the fuck's wrong with my vocabulary?"

"Later, Jack," Sam said, shaking his head at Jack's racist comments. The little guy wasn't always so funny.

Sam hung up the phone, and again it rang almost immediately.

"It's Ron, Sam. Got a line on that scientist you inquired about."

The cop in him had taken over now, and the sheriff was all business.

"We had a Dennis Chung out at what was then the National Reactor Testing Station from November 1978 to June 1980. He worked for the DOE. He was the second assistant director for nuclear operations at the station. He left to take a position up at the Hanford National Laboratory in Washington State. Sorry, Sammy, but I can't help you up there. Out of my jurisdiction."

Sam was quiet, stunned by the new information.

"If you want, Sam, I can try an' make a few calls up to Hanford. See if I can find out what this guy does up there."

"That's okay, Ron," Sam said in a faraway voice, "I think I already know."

"Who is this guy anyway?"

"Huh? Oh, ahh…just a character in the book is all."

"Yeah? What's this book about, Sam?"

"I'll fill you in when I get out there, Ron. Thanks for all the help. I'll see ya in a couple of days."

Sam hung up still in a daze, hoping in his heart the phone would ring one more time, and it would be Mickey calling to say, "Let's go get a beer, bro!"

But the phone did not ring.

Chapter 22

Mickey was less than five minutes from an audience with the president when they came to take him. As planned, one of McWilliams's staff had met the rogue agent after he had passed through the security check, and the two were accompanied by a member of the Secret Service directly up to the reception area just outside the Oval Office. Here Neally was left to wait for the secretary of state. He sat in silent contemplation under a portrait of John F. Kennedy, a Marine honor guard in full dress standing watch over President Dean's doorway a mere ten feet away.

With the seconds dragging by like hours, Mickey checked his watch one last time. It was three ten.

Damn it, Hoof, where the hell are you?

Just then, he heard the sound of soft footsteps at the far end of the carpeted hallway. Looking up, he saw four men approaching him, all in suits, all wearing earplugs, and all looking far too serious for his liking. With practiced casual efficiency, the four men carefully encircled the ex-SEAL. The bulges made by the weapons worn under their specially tailored jackets were barely noticeable.

The man closest to Mickey stepped forward to speak, "Mr. Neally, I am Agent Daniels, Secret Service, would you please come with us, sir." It was not a request. *Fuck, so close! Okay, be cool. See what this is about.*

"I was told to wait here for Secretary McWilliams," Mickey protested. "We have an appointment to see the president."

"Please just come with us now, sir."

As tough and as skilled as he was, Mickey knew these men were every bit as good. Any resistance would be futile.

"Why don't I follow you then?" he said, standing up carefully.

Flanked by the four Secret Service agents, Mickey was led to a room near the north gate entrance. Inside, three more men in suits stood waiting. Mickey's gaze fell immediately on the man in the middle. His face appeared to be chiseled from stone, his eyes mere dark slits. When he spoke, his voice belied his obvious Asian heritage.

"Michael Neally?" he said without emotion.

"That would be me."

"Inspector George Lee, FBI." The hatchet-faced man took a step closer. "You are under arrest," he said, "for conspiring to assassinate the president of the United States."

Mickey said nothing. A deep cold flooded through his veins, and he stepped back in stunned disbelief, causing one of the Secret Service agents to move to block any intended escape. Every nerve in Mickey's body was supercharged now, and the agent's movement triggered his survival instinct. Mickey whirled around, knocking away the outstretched arm of the agent with his left forearm while lashing out at another with his right foot. The fracas ended quickly when one of the agents produced an electric stun gun, apparently out of thin air, and hit Mickey in the chest with three hundred thousand volts, knocking him unconscious to the floor.

Inspector Lee turned to Agent Daniels.

"I have orders to take this man to FBI headquarters," he said, handing over the paperwork. "My employers would like a few words with Mr. Neally in private."

"He's all yours, Inspector," Daniels said.

Lee looked at the two young FBI agents.

"Take him to Quantico for interrogation and put a gag on it!" he ordered forcefully. "This incident never happened. Do you understand?"

"Yes, sir," the two said as one.

"You know the route. I will tie up the loose ends here. Now move!"

*****

When Mickey finally regained full consciousness, he found himself lying in the back of an FBI car with the same two agents he'd seen at the White House now riding up front. His hands were cuffed behind his back, and his ankles were in chains, but Mickey managed to push himself up to a sitting position. The two agents in front took note of the movement but said nothing. The one riding shotgun turned to confirm that their prisoner was still fully restrained. Satisfied, he turned to his partner driving.

"Our boy's awake," he said with little concern.

The driver, glancing at Mickey in the rearview mirror, grinned and said, "Have that tingling sensation, do you?"

The comment surprised Mickey. The FBI were usually more professional. Then he noticed how young both agents appeared to be.

"Where are you boys taking me, to your scoutmaster?"

"I am Agent Wilkins, and this is Agent Perry," said the man in the driver's seat, working hard on his cool. "Just sit quietly, Mr. Neally. The doors and windows are locked, so please do not entertain any thoughts of escape."

Mickey looked around at the landscape they were speeding past. They were well outside the city now on some rural stretch of back road. Mickey didn't recognize it.

"You kids lost?"

"Mr. Neally, we will gag you if necessary," Agent Perry said with more force than was needed.

"I used to work for the bureau a few years back," Neally said, hoping to strike a conversation with his captors. He named off a half dozen of his old buddies from his time spent with the agency, none of whom solicited a response from either of the youthful agents.

That's why so young…

"Your boss is a double agent, Wilkins," Neally said with nothing to lose. "He's part of a plot by a terrorist faction of the Chinese militia to destroy both the United States and Russia. I have the proof on a…"

"Shut the fuck up, you fucking traitor!"

Agent Wilkins was screaming into the rearview mirror.

"We're the ones with the proof, asshole. We know you were hired by Libyan terrorists to assassinate President Dean. So just keep your mouth shut or—"

"Take it easy, John," Perry said to his driver.

"Fuck him, Vern!"

"Libyans?" Mickey said, his eyes wide. "Are you serious?"

Clearly the one in charge, Agent Perry turned to warn Mickey one last time that if he would not remain silent, then he would be rendered so, and he held up the electric stun gun to further make his point.

Turned in his seat and distracted by Neally, Wilkins did not notice the Ford panel van that was pulled up to the light at the intersection ahead. An exotically pretty, dark-haired woman was leaning out the passenger window holding out an opened road map. She smiled sheepishly at the young FBI driver as he pulled alongside her. Holding the map in both hands, she made the universal shrug of her shoulders to indicate she was lost. Agent Wilkins either did not notice the woman was of Middle Eastern heritage or he just didn't make the connection. Either way, the young agent made the fatal mistake and rolled down his bulletproof window. It was Mickey who first recognized the bloodline in the woman's face. He immediately put it together and yelled a warning at the young agent.

"No, don't!"

But it was too late. The woman shot Wilkins between the eyes with a silenced Glock semiautomatic pistol. With precision timing, a man came around from behind the van and dropped a gas grenade into the open window. In the passenger seat, Agent Perry had reacted far too slowly, firing shots harmlessly out the open window as he tried to slide behind the wheel of the car. But he could not move Wilkin's lifeless body out of the way in time, and the car rolled out of control through the intersection where it was slammed by another car in the left rear quarter, spinning it around violently.

Within seconds the gas from the grenade took effect, and both Mickey and Perry fell unconscious. Squealing its tires, the van pulled alongside the FBI car in the now crowded intersection, and two swarthy-looking dark men got out and hustled Mickey out of the back seat. To the shock and dismay of a dozen witnesses, the men loaded their prize into the van and sped off. No one thought to get the plate number.

The next time Neally awoke, he found himself sitting in a dark room, his hands and feet still bound. The room seemed to be some type of large warehouse, though he could not tell for sure, the effects of the gas still fogging his mind. He thought he could hear the soft murmur of voices in the distance. Shaking his head to clear it, Mickey strained to make out whatever it was the strange voices were saying. In the pale light that shone through a darkened skylight high above, he could barely distinguish the outline of several forms moving toward him through the hazy darkness. The voices and echoed footsteps grew slowly louder as the shapes came nearer, stopping just beyond the light.

"And what of our Libyan friends?" a voice asked.

"They wait next door for their money," another voice said. "Should I pay them?"

"No. You should kill them."

The footsteps came closer to where Mickey sat helplessly bound.

"Mr. Neally," said a voice from the shadows, "I regret that we do not have the time to do a thorough interrogation. Your body must be found within the hour before the press becomes aware of your assassination attempt. That way, the whole affair can be easily covered up. Something your government is most adept at. You and any knowledge you might have will simply cease to exist."

"Don't bet on it!"

"Stand him up!" the voice commanded loudly, moving closer. "Hold him!"

Two men appeared out of the shadows and lifted Mickey from his chair.

"Turn on the floodlights!" the hatchet-faced man ordered, reaching into his breast pocket as he walked slowly toward his defenseless prey.

Chapter 23

The cover-up was the quintessential bureaucratic work of art. When a postal worker found Mickey's body lying in the trunk of an abandoned car in one of the most run-down, crime-ridden sections of DC, the feds were on the scene within minutes. They quickly took command of the investigation, holding the press and local authorities at bay. The same thing happened at the site of Mickey's kidnapping, where, according to eye witness accounts at the scene, the three men and one woman involved in the attack appeared to be Middle Eastern terrorists. Later that evening, an FBI spokesman made the official statement to the press.

The government agency claimed that an ex-IRA arms supplier currently suspected of international gunrunning had been detained for interrogation. The man was believed to maintain many aliases but was most recently known to operate under the name of Michael Kelly. It was believed that Kelly was collaborating with fellow compatriots in a conspiracy to supply a splinter group of Libyan terrorists with military-style arms. While he was being transported for questioning, what was presumed to be a sect of this group attacked the two FBI agents guarding Kelly and successfully abducted him. The whereabouts of Kelly and his abductors were still unknown. The FBI reported that tragically, agent John Wilkins had been killed during the attack. A second agent, Vernon Perry, had survived the attack with only minor injuries. It had also been reported that Agent Perry was later able to identify the woman involved at the scene as a known associate of the suspected Libyan terrorist group. A massive manhunt had been initiated.

*****

In a separate announcement receiving far less attention, former FBI Agent Michael Neally was said to have been found stabbed to death in a west-side section of Washington, DC. The area was riddled with crime of late. Neally's was the third murder in the past two weeks in the predominantly black section of the capital city. There were no suspects or motives known at the time. The two incidents were not believed to be related in any way.

Not only was there no mention of Neally's alleged assassination attempt, there was no report made of any disturbance of any kind at 1600 Pennsylvania Avenue.

*****

Earlier in the evening, in a briefing at the White House, the FBI's chief investigator, Inspector George Lee, advised a small, select group of top government officials as to what really happened. Due to his apparent unwitting involvement, the secretary of state, Miller McWilliams, was present along with national security adviser, Bob Clancy; the deputy director of the CIA, Tom Parker; and the US attorney general, Jim Anderson.

Inspector Lee explained that Neally had turned and become a double agent. A fact seemingly supported by Parker's report that Neally had been missing in action, so to speak, for the better part of six months. There had been no contact at all by the rogue agent with anyone in the agency. Unable to find any trace of him, the CIA assumed he was either dead or gone underground for some unknown reason. Parker expressed that Neally had become a "concern."

Lee went on to explain that Neally had used McWilliams to gain access to the president, but because Neally had been abducted before he could be interrogated and fully searched, the FBI had no clue as to the means by which he planned to kill President Dean. Some type of miniature biological weapon had been one possible suggestion. Lee expressed hope that the autopsy report could perhaps shed some light on this question. The FBI, the chief inspector confessed, had only very recently and, quite by accident, become aware of Neally's intentions through their investigative surveillance of the Libyan cell's operations within US borders. It was assumed the terrorists had killed Neally after his failed attempt simply to prevent him from talking.

"We were very fortunate to intercept him," the inspector said, looking at McWilliams.

"God, what a fool!" the secretary said, clearly embarrassed. "Hell, I've known Mick Neally for years. Played cards with the man. Never would have believed this."

"Don't beat yourself up too badly, Mr. Secretary," Clancy said kindly. "Neally was a professional. From what Deputy Director Parker tells me, he was one of the best."

"He was," Parker said, "and I'm as surprised as anyone. I liked the man."

"Christ, Tom," McWilliams sighed, "he was once, well hell, he was once my friend. Is there anything we can do?"

The national security adviser, Clancy, looked from Secretary McWilliams to Deputy Director Parker. The two men read each other's eyes and Parker shrugged his shoulders. Clancy got a barely perceptible nod of the head from the attorney general before he turned to the FBI's chief investigator.

"No sense alarming the American public," he said, "with stories of assassination attempts and double agents. And, Inspector, given that the man is already dead, I see no need to expose Mr. Neally's crime. Can we count on your full cooperation in this matter, sir? If need be, Attorney General Anderson here can call Director Harrison."

"That won't be necessary, sir," Lee said respectfully. "I will, of course, do what is in the best interest of the American people."

"Thank you, Inspector Lee. We'll keep this quiet then. My people will draft a press release for your agency within the hour. Neally and this whole affair should just…go away."

"I couldn't agree more, sir."

"Thanks, Bob," McWilliams said graciously, having just been spared a great public embarrassment.

"Did Neally have any family that you know of, Mr. Secretary?" Parker asked.

"Just a sister, I believe," the secretary said with a sigh. "I suppose I should be the one to tell her."

As the meeting was clearly over, Deputy Director Parker stood to leave.

"Better make it damn soon, Mr. Secretary," he said, "unless you want her to hear about it on CNN."

The secretary of state wasted no time getting to Mickey's sister. Wisely, he brought a doctor along to administer a sedative should one be needed. This proved to be quite prudent as Nicki did not take the news well at all. Mercifully, Keri happened to be over in anticipation of their night out. She had, in fact, just picked up the phone to call Sam to see if he'd heard anything from Mickey yet, when the doorbell rang.

Nicki was crushed by the news and immediately became hysterical. Keri had all she could do to help calm her friend down long enough for the doctor to administer the sedative. In shock herself, the young reporter somehow managed to hold it together. She needed to be strong, she told herself, for Nicki and Erin's sake. Later, however, she would find that she could remember almost nothing about her conversations with McWilliams and the good doctor. The two stayed until Nicki was resting quietly, and Keri had been able to reach her mom. With Erin sleeping soundly in her bed, Keri thanked the doctor and assured the secretary of state that everything would be okay. She would stay to keep an eye on things until help arrived.

As soon as the two men were gone, Keri called Sam. What remaining bit of self-control she'd once had vanished when she heard Sam's voice. She was barely able to choke out the words between her heaving sobs as the flood of emotion welling inside her spilled over.

"Oh…God…Sam…They really did it. They…killed…him. They…killed him, Sam!"

"Keri, calm down, honey, calm down. It's okay," Sam said, knowing it was not, knowing his worst fear had come to pass. "Who, Keri? Who did they kill?"

"Mickey, Sam! They've…killed…Mickey!"

Chapter 24

The funeral took place three days later on a cloudy, drizzly June morning, one of two being held that day in the Arlington National Cemetery. Sam was surprised and mildly curious at the light turnout. For some reason, only a couple of Mickey's closest friends from the bureau had shown. Most of the mourners seemed to be friends of either Nicki or Sam. McWilliams was there, but he kept a low profile, as did the other government people in attendance.

The graveside liturgy was short and sweet with no celebration of Mickey's military or government service, no eulogy for the public servant, no official ceremony for the fallen soldier, just a short passage read from the Bible by an Irish Catholic priest from Nicki's neighborhood parish. Mason wondered, why the downplay? Why so low-key? Since learning of Mickey's murder, Sam had spent most of his time helping with the arrangements and tending to Nicki and Erin. When he did find time to ask questions, his every attempt to uncover any information at all to help explain his friend's death had ended in fruitless frustration. No one seemed to know anything, or if they did, they weren't talking. Sam's grief was quickly turning to anger.

Standing beside Nicki throughout the service, Sam held her close, keeping an arm around her waist and taking her weight from time to time as she drifted near the edge of consciousness. The depth of Nicki's grief and sense of helplessness, piled onto to his own, further fueled Sam's anger, and right then and there, he vowed to find whoever was responsible and make them pay. One way or another, the ex-SEAL would get his answers.

At the end of the ceremony, as the mourners filed past the grieving sister to pay their final respects, Sam noticed Secretary McWilliams apparently staring off into space as he moved toward Nicki. Sam followed the secretary's line of sight to see what had caught his eye. There alone, up by the road overlooking the cemetery, stood the shapely figure of a woman clad in black, her head bowed, her face hidden behind a dark veil of lace. Sam's heart grew heavier still at the sight of her.

Then it hit him.

Mickey was going to see Jessica!

With an effort, Sam returned his focus to Nicki as it was time to take her and Erin back to the house where an even smaller group showed to help. Keri kept an eye on Erin while Sam and Irene helped put some food out for the dozen or so guests that had come from the funeral. Sam was pleased to see the secretary of state among those that had come back, impressed that a man of his importance had taken so much time from his busy schedule to pay tribute to his friend. Setting down a basket of rolls on the makeshift buffet table, Sam noticed McWilliams sitting alone next to the grieving sister, holding Nicki's hand and talking softly to her. A fatherly figure doing his part to help make things right. As Sam started toward them, two of Mickey's friends from the bureau approached him.

Barry Bassett and Brian Gillis were two of the sharpest and most honest men Mason had ever known. He'd met them both several times during Mickey's time with the FBI. Sam liked and respected them both. It was Gillis who spoke first.

"How are you holding up, Sam?"

"About as good as can be expected, I guess. Nicki's the one I'm worried about."

"Gotta be pretty tough on her," Bassett said with genuine concern. "I know they were pretty close."

"Yeah, they were tight. Nicki idolized her big brother. Hell, so did I."

"We loved him too, Sam," Gillis said, and then he leaned close to Mason. "Ahh, Sam, think Barry and I could have a quick word with you in private?"

Sam was watching Nicki with McWilliams, and only half heard the question.

"Sure. Yeah, sure," he said, his eyes still on Nicki. "Why don't we grab some fresh air."

Outside, the two agents seemed uneasy. Discreetly scanning their surroundings, the FBI men moved just a little too stiffly as they led Mason across the lawn away from the house. Sam noticed.

"What's up with you two?"

"We know how tight you were with Mickey, Sam," Gillis said. "He told us about you being in the SEALs with him and all the shit you two went through together."

"Yeah," Sam said, waiting.

"Well, there's something not right, and we thought you should know about it."

"There's plenty not right at the moment, Brian. My best friend was just murdered, and nobody seems to be doing anything about it. Heck, I can't even get anyone to talk to me about it."

"That's just it, Sam, nobody can. Not even us. But that's not the worst part."

Sam waited.

"There's rumors spreading through the bureau about Mickey, Sam."

"What rumors?"

"It's crazy stuff, Sam. Some people are trying to say. I mean, the word going around is…well, it's not good."

Gillis was having trouble getting it out.

Bassett laid it on the line.

"Sam," he said, "they're saying Mickey tried to assassinate the president."

"That's crazy!"

"We know that, Sam," Bassett said. "But that's what's being said. And now all of a sudden, it seems no one wants anything to do with either one of us."

"Somebody's covering something up, Sam," Gillis added, looking around. "And this is some heavyweight shit. So watch your back if you decide to go around asking a lot of questions."

"Oh, I'll be askin' questions all right," Sam said. "And I may as well start with you two. Either of you have any idea what Mickey might have been doin' in China?"

"Sam," Bassett said, "neither of us has heard from Mickey in over six months. Whatever he was working on, we were out of the loop."

"I saw him the night before he was killed," Sam said. "There was something wrong with…"

Sam stopped in midsentence as Secretary McWilliams came through the back door looking to say his goodbyes.

"Ahh, there you are, Mr. Mason."

"We'll talk later, Sam," Gillis said, slipping Sam a card before turning to walk past McWilliams into the house.

"I wanted to say again, Mr. Mason," McWilliams said, offering his deepest sympathy, "how very sorry I am about your friend. He was a good man."

"There's no truth to it, sir," Sam said solemnly.

"Excuse me?"

"Mickey tryin' to kill the president. There's no way, sir."

"I see," the secretary said, lowering his voice. "What do you know of this, Mr. Mason?"

"I know it's not true, sir. Probably part of some high-level cover-up."

McWilliams put his arm around Sam to lead him further away from the house.

"I'm not buying it either, son," he confessed in a hushed voice. "How much do you know about what Mick had been working on before he was killed?"

"Not enough, Mr. Secretary," Sam said, deciding at that moment to trust no one. "But I can promise you, I will find the truth."

McWilliams reached into his vest pocket and pulled out a card. He handed it to Sam.

"You be careful, son," he warned. "I'm going to pull at this thing from another end. You may need a friend…you start poking around in this. You hear of anything you think is important, anything at all, you give me a call, you hear?"

"Yes, sir."

"We'll get to the bottom of this, Mr. Mason, I promise you."

"Thank you, sir."

With that, the secretary turned and walked back into the house, leaving Sam alone with his thoughts.

*****

Much later, as the evening grew late, the rest of the guests gradually made their way out the door, leaving Keri and Sam alone with Nicki. Sam closed the door behind Keri's mom, the last to leave, then went to sit with the two women.

"You want more coffee, Sam?" Keri asked.

"I'm all coffeed out, Kerr. A brandy would do me more good right now, I think."

"Make it two," Keri said tiredly.

"Three," Nicki added.

The meds the doctor had prescribed for her had kept Nicki in a near-catatonic state. The pills were Librium, and they were strong. For the past two days, Nicki had been not much more than a walking zombie, and Mason didn't like it. Though he knew it would help her get through the worst of it, Sam wanted to wean her off the powerful sedative as soon as possible. She'd taken just the one pill before the funeral that morning, and Sam thought he could notice the effects of the drug starting to wear off.

"You think it's okay to be drinking while you're on those pills?" Keri asked.

"Fuck the pills!"

Yup, the meds are wearing off.

"Glad to see you're feelin' a little better, Nicki," Sam said.

"I feel like shit, Sam," she said as the tears started down her cheeks.

With less Librium in her system, the demands of the day past, and with everyone finally gone, Nicki's emotions were finally able to release. She sat and cried softly, clutching a pillow to her breast as her shoulders shook with her sobs.

"Let her cry," Sam said, heading for the kitchen. "She needs to get it out. I'll make the drinks."

He came back a couple of minutes later and handed Keri her drink. He set Nicki's on the coffee table in front of her. Sam sunk into the seat next to Keri, and the two sat quietly, sipping their Remy Martin on the rocks as they watched their friend say goodbye to her brother.

A good bit later, when the heavy sobs had finally subsided, Nicki reached for her glass. The ice had melted. She didn't care.

"Brandy," she said. "Feels good going down."

"You gonna be okay tonight, kid?" Sam asked.

"I don't know," she said, holding out her empty glass. "How much of this we got left?"

"I think she'll be fine, Sam," Keri said, standing to fetch more brandy. "I'll stay with her overnight. My mom will be here in the morning to stay with her while I go to work."

"Okay, it's late," Sam said, "and I've got some things to do early tomorrow, so I'm gonna shove off for now. You two need anything, call me."

"We'll be okay, Sam," Keri said.

Sam leaned over to hug Nicki goodbye. She returned the hug, holding on tightly, and with her lips next to his ear, she whispered, "I'm gonna need some answers, Sam."

"Yeah, I know," he whispered back. "Me too. I love you."

"I love you too, Sam. Thanks."

Sam stood and walked to the door. He opened it to leave, and there stood Dawn DesMoine, dressed in designer black from head to toe, her face still hidden behind her dark veil.

"Jessica!" he blurted out. "I mean...I'm sorry...Ms. DesMoine, please...come in."

"It's all right, Sam," she said kindly as she glided through the door. "Mickey had adopted your nickname for me. He was forever calling me Jessica or Jess. To tell the truth, I rather liked it. He was so cute about it, and it is somewhat...flattering."

Sam felt like a jerk anyway. Still blushing, he said, "Ms. DesMoine, I, ahh, I don't believe you've met Mickey's sister, Nicole, and this is her friend, Keri Starr."

The magnitude of the woman's presence was eerie. As she stood before Nicki and Keri, still seated on the couch together, Sam felt himself a bit out of touch with the moment. He knew Nicki was starting to feel the effects of the brandy, and he was a little afraid of what might come out of her mouth. She did not disappoint him.

"Jesus H. Christ, Sam! Who the hell is this?"

"Nicki, this is Dawn DesMoine. She is...I mean she was... ahh..."

"I was your brother's lover, my dear."

Both girls' jaws had already dropped, yet somehow their expressions grew even more incredulous. They stared blankly at each other, mouths open.

"I wanted to tell you how very sorry I am for your loss," Jessica said. "I loved your brother very much."

Nicki was dumbfounded. She looked at Sam, then to Jessica, then back to Sam again. Sam nodded that it was so.

"Jesus..." was all Nicki could manage until she realized there were tears falling from behind the woman's veil. "Oh my God! I'm so sorry, please...sit down. Sam, would you please get Ms. DesMoine a drink?"

"Thank you. Scotch, please, neat," she said to Sam. Then she turned to Nicki, and through her veil, she said, "Your brother was murdered! You are all in great danger!"

*****

Alone in his office, Inspector George Lee was speaking on an electronically scrambled line. Only the person with the right equipment and the proper decoding frequency could decipher his words. The inspector had no idea, nor did he care, who belonged to the voice on the other end. The mechanical sound was so perfectly devoid of human quality that one could not even discern if the speaker was either male or female. Always the one to be contacted, Lee, even if he so desired, had no means by which to reverse the procedure. As always, the hatchet-faced man either listened without interruption to instructions or answered questions. He never asked them.

"No, he did not have it with him," he said to the voice, pausing then to listen.

"Yes, the autopsy would have found it," he said, pausing again.

"Yes, I can do that."

A longer silence this time.

"We are watching them all, of course."

Another long pause.

"Yes, I saw her. We don't know."

After a final short silence, the inspector answered the mystery voice one last time.

"I understand."

Chapter 25

Sam had quickly splashed a few ounces of Glenlivet into a glass before handing it to Jessica.

"Mickey went to see you the night before he was killed," he stated gently.

"Yes," she said, taking the drink in both hands, her eyes staring down at the scotch. "He came to my summer home on the bay."

"I saw him the night before he was killed," Sam said. "He wasn't himself."

"Yes, I noticed it as well," she admitted. "Something I had never seen in him before." Jessica lifted her head to look at Sam, her face only partly visible through her black veil. "He was scared."

"Scared of what? Of who?" Nicki asked.

Jessica held her gaze on Sam. "He said you already knew, Sam. He said you were writing about it."

"What are you talking about?"

"Your book, Sam. It's not a fantasy! It's real! Everything you told him that night, Mickey knew to be real. The Chinese, the bombs, the fire extinguishers. It's all true!"

"Jesus, Sam," Keri said, concern on her face.

"No. It's not possible," Sam said, not willing to believe it. "You're confused, Jess. Mickey was just telling you the story that I told him in the bar at the Four Seasons."

"Would someone please tell me," Nicki asked, "what the fuck you people are talking about!" She had her full wits about her now, and Nicki did not like being out of the know.

"Remember I told you I saw your brother at the Four Seasons the night Keri and I had dinner," Sam explained. "Well, I told him about the new book."

"What about it?"

"Mickey must have told Ms. DesMoine the plot as I told it to him that night, and she thought he meant it for real."

Sam turned back to the mysterious woman in black.

"It's not real," he said. "It is just a fantasy. The whole story. It couldn't possibly be true."

"But, Sam," Keri cut in, "what about the dreams? You said yourself there are so many coincidences."

"No. Not possible. It's got to be something else."

"Well, what about the two Asians I saw?" Keri persisted.

"What Asians!" Nicki asked, shaking her fists in frustration.

"Keri thought she saw two Asian men follow Mickey out of the hotel the night I saw him in the bar," Sam said blankly.

"She did," Jessica said, turning to Nicki. "Your brother told me he was being followed, but he lost them in the city. He was scared for me. For all of us. He wanted me to leave, to go to some safe house in the Caribbean."

"And what was my brother going to do?"

"He said he had proof. He wanted to get to the president. He said there was no one else he could trust. Except you, Sam."

"Then why didn't he confide in me that night?"

"Because he didn't want to get you killed. When he couldn't explain how it was that you knew everything, I suggested maybe you were with the Chinese. Mickey wouldn't hear of it. He believed in you, Sam. Right till the very end."

"You said he had proof," Keri said.

"Yes," Jessica said. "But he wouldn't tell me what or where." She paused to sip her scotch. "He said I knew too much already. He was afraid they'd find me and make me talk. He said they'd kill me."

"How did he say he planned to get to the president?" Sam asked.

"He didn't," Jessica said, turning to Nicki. "He just kissed me goodbye and left."

"We've got to do something, Sam," Keri urged. "We've got to tell someone!"

"Who? Who would believe it?" Sam asked. "Hell, I don't even believe it myself."

"Well, we just need to find the proof then," Nicki said as if it were that simple.

"If it even exists," Sam said, sitting down, his head hurting, his mind overloaded with the strain of his brain scramming to make some sense of it all.

It can't be true.

"Believe what you want, Mr. Mason," Jessica said. "But as absurd as it sounds, Mickey was killed by the Chinese to prevent him from exposing the very plot that you have somehow conjured up. I cannot explain it, yet I know it to be true."

With that the black-veiled beauty stood to leave. "It is very late," she said to Nicki. "I should leave you now."

Nicki rose with her. "I'll see you to the door."

Sam remained seated, lost in his thoughts.

As Nicki opened the door, Jessica lifted her veil to kiss Nicki goodbye on the cheek. The two women embraced for several seconds, sharing the pain of their loss. As they separated, Nicki was struck by the beauty of the most stunningly brilliant diamond necklace she had ever seen. Hidden before by Jessica's veil, it had gone unnoticed throughout her visit.

"My God, what a beautiful necklace!" Nicki exclaimed. "Did my brother give that to you?"

"Yes, just before he left me that last day. Strange," the woman in black said, remembering. "But he told me that if anyone ever asked about it, I was to tell them that it was…made in China."

"Well, it is positively stunning on you. I'm glad you came, Ms. DesMoine. Thank you."

"Goodbye," Jessica said, and then she turned and started out the door.

"What did you say!" Sam asked, coming out of his fog.

"What did who say?" Nicki asked.

"Ms. DesMoine," Sam said, bolting from his chair to the opened door, "what did you just say?"

"About…"

"The necklace, yes!"

"Mickey told me that if anyone ever asked, I was to say it was made in China."

No, it couldn't be that simple!

Her own curiosity aroused, Jessica asked, "Why? Does this hold some special meaning for you?"

"It's the name of my book," Sam answered in disbelief.

"Made in China?" Jessica asked.

"So what's your point, Sam?" Nicki wondered, not getting it.

"I told Mickey the name of the book that night!"

"So…" Keri said, joining the group by the door.

"Come on, you two! *Made in China.* The book! The necklace!"

"Holy shit!" the two girls said as one, eyes wide, mouths open. "You don't think…"

Together the three turned their gaze on the string of diamonds that lay glittering around Jessica's exquisitely beautiful neck.

"Ms. DesMoine, may I see your necklace for a moment, please?" Sam asked, his eyes still fixed on the brilliant stones.

Jessica stood there a moment, her turn to be dumbfounded, the three in front of her all glaring anxiously at her throat.

"Of course," she said, unsure still of the significance.

The beautiful woman in black stepped back inside the house, reached behind her neck to undo the clasp, then carefully handed the necklace to Sam. With Nicki and Keri close behind, he walked deliberately over to a table lamp to hold the sparkling work of art over the light for inspection. Jessica looked on in dismay as the three crowded around each other, straining to see the stones up close as Sam turned the necklace several ways to the light.

"I can assure you the jewels are quite real," Jessica said.

"No doubt, but I need to get this to a jeweler, ASAP!" Sam said absently, still examining the stones. "Anybody know a good one? One we can see tonight?"

Instantly realizing the answer to his own question Sam turned together with Nicki and Keri to again stare at the beautiful woman in black.

"What?" she asked, still in the dark. "What would you need with a jeweler at this late hour of the night, and what has any of this got to do with my...Oh my God!" she whispered as it finally came to her.

"It's a possibility," Sam said, seeing the realization on Jessica's face. "We need someone to examine it. Do you know anyone?"

"Of course," she said, walking over to Sam, holding out her hand. "May I?"

Sam handed her the necklace. She held it up in front of herself, nodding as though suddenly, it all made sense to her.

"I'll take you," she said to Sam. Then to Nicki, "May I use your phone?"

*****

Herb Ludington was a man with fine tastes. He enjoyed fine food, fine wines, fine women, and most of all, fine jewelry. A very gifted artist and craftsman, jewels had been his passion for almost fifty years. Ludington owned Chesapeake Jewelers, one of the most prestigious chains of jewelry stores on the East Coast, making him a very rich man. For more reasons than one, Dawn DesMoine was perhaps his most valued customer. So when his home phone rang at ten minutes before midnight on a Sunday evening, it was, of course, no intrusion what so ever. He would be more than happy to meet Ms. DesMoine at his store by the bay in thirty minutes.

Ludington made it to his shop a few minutes before Sam and Jessica arrived. The jeweler had just turned the alarms off and the lights on as the two climbed out of Jessica's silver Jaguar to tap on the glass front window. The little man came scurrying out from the back, keys in hand, to open the door for his favorite customer. Obviously disheartened to see Sam with Ms. DesMoine, Ludington did his best to hide it, putting forth his best professional behavior.

"Herbie, you're a doll," Jessica purred as the jeweler stepped aside. "Give me a big hug."

At five feet, four inches, the little English jeweler barely came up to Jessica's shoulders, and as she wrapped her arms around him, pulling him to her, his face all but disappeared in the depths of her voluptuous bosom. Sam wasn't sure if he should feel sorry for the little guy or not. Jessica released him just before he ran out of air. Backing up, the poor little man straightened his glasses and cleared his throat, hoping some sound would come out when he opened his mouth to speak.

"So, ahh, Ms. DesMoine," he said, his voice weak and throaty, "you said you needed my help. How may I be of service to you this evening? Something for a late-night soiree, perhaps?"

"No, Herb. Sadly, I'm not here to purchase anything tonight. Herbie, this is Sam Mason, a very dear friend of mine. Mr. Mason has come into possession of a very special piece at, well, shall we just say a bargain price. We'd like you to take a look at it for us. An appraisal, if you would be so kind."

Again, the little man hid his disappointment well.

"But of course, Ms. DesMoine, anything at all for you. May I see the piece?"

Sam took the necklace out of a velvet bag that he'd pulled from his pocket and handed it to the jeweler.

"My, my, my," the shopkeeper said, genuinely impressed by the shimmering necklace. "This is a special piece indeed," he said, looking Sam up and down, reappraising him. "Yes, yes indeed," Ludington said, motioning to his back room. "Come, let's take a closer look, shall we?"

The little jeweler shuffled quickly out back to his workroom, where he put on his magnifying glasses, adjusted them slightly, then spread the necklace out on a felt-covered worktable. He sat examining the piece for a full minute, making only occasional grunting sounds as he worked his way through the stones.

Finally, he looked up at Sam, and lifting the glasses to his forehead, he said, "Would you be interested in selling this piece, Mr. Mason?"

"Ohh…I'm afraid not. I'm mostly concerned with its worth. I wanted to make sure there were no flaws in the necklace or anything unusual about it that might diminish its value."

"My dear man, I can already tell you that this *is* a most unusual piece, but that does not detract from its value. Oh no, no. On the contrary, its uniqueness only adds to its desirability."

"What's so different about it?" Sam asked, apparently only casually interested.

"Well, it was not made in this country, or Europe for that matter, that much I can assure you. I've rarely seen workmanship of this quality before. Extraordinary!"

"Can you tell us where it was made," Jessica asked.

This time the little man merely peered up over the tops of his glasses to look at Ms. DesMoine. "Of course, my Dear," he said. Then looking back down to his work, he said quite plainly, "this magnificent piece was made in Southeast Asia."

Sam and Jessica exchanged looks.

"The quality is okay then?" Sam asked. "Nothing strange about it in any way?"

The jeweler continued with his examination. "Well, Mr. Mason, I've barely looked at half the stones, but I can assure you there will be no flaws in a piece of work of this…"

The little man stopped dead quiet.

"Dear me," he muttered, a sudden concern in his voice. "What have we got here?"

The jeweler adjusted his glasses and wiped the lenses.

"I don't believe it," he said, taking off the headset and picking up an eyepiece. He held the necklace right up to the lens for a moment, tuning it in his hand. "Now that is odd!"

Finally, he put the eyepiece down and held the necklace up to his naked eye.

"Well, I've never seen anything like it!" he said to Sam and Jessica, looking somewhat astonished. "I'm sorry to be the one to tell you this, Mr. Mason, but there is a major flaw in the center stone of your necklace. Here, you see…"

The jeweler held the piece under the light, turning it for Sam to see. "If you know what to look for, you can even see it with the naked eye. It's almost as if something were embedded in the stone," he said, thinking aloud to himself. "Impossible, of course. Just an illusion of light, but quite a detriment, I'm afraid."

"Oh my," Jessica said, laying her hand gently on Sam's arm.

"Of course, it is still a very expensive piece, but the center stone really should be replaced to fulfill its potential value. I cannot believe anyone would actually have used it. The rest of the necklace is perfect. What a shame!"

"Just my luck, I'm afraid," Sam said, taking the necklace from the jeweler, in a hurry now to get back to Nicki's.

"I'd still be willing to take it off your hands, Mr. Mason, for a reasonable price."

"Thanks anyway, Herb, but I...ahh..."

"The piece has been in Mr. Mason's family for years, Herbie," Jessica said, coming to Sam's aid. "I'm afraid it holds far too much sentimental value for him to ever let it go."

"Ah, well..."

Outside in the car, Jessica asked, "Sam, what does this mean?"

Pulling the sleek sedan away from the curb, Sam checked his rearview mirror before looking tiredly at the mysterious beauty beside him.

"What it means is...we are going to need a computer scientist."

Chapter 26

The Massachusetts Institute of Technology (MIT) is widely regarded to house the greatest collection of scientific minds on the planet. Aside from the exceptional level of studies offered by the school in the fields of mathematics and physical sciences, there is always a large number of ongoing university studies and federally funded experimental research programs in progress to sufficiently challenge the great minds of this most prolific East Coast think tank. Experimental programs such as the research and development being done in the field of atomic supercomputers for example—machines that will be filled with liquid rather than circuit boards and will process information at the atomic level using positive and negatively charged neutrons instead of microchips. Scientists working on the project predict this new breed of computers will work a million times faster than conventional computers with a potentially infinite permanent memory storage capable of transcending time and space. The concepts under study in this program are so deep that it is difficult for the great minds at MIT to articulate them.

One such mind belonged to Dr. Frederick Graff, the assistant director of computer sciences at the institute, who at twenty-nine was one of the youngest of the brilliant scientists leading this research. As fate would have it, Dr. Graff had been renting a summer home in Falmouth for the past two years that just happened to be next-door to Sam's. An avid sportfishermen, the young doctor and Sam had quickly become summertime fishing buddies despite the fact that the two exhibited few similarities beyond enjoying the thrill of hooking into a big fish and a love of imported beers, these joys apparently offering more than enough common ground to form a warm friendship.

So upon his return from the jewelers, Sam didn't think twice about calling his young summertime neighbor the moment he got in, regardless of the fact that it was almost one in the morning. He lucked out. Dr. Fred was in Falmouth, starting a week's vacation from his research at the institute. Telling him as little as necessary over the phone, Sam was able to convince his brainy buddy to hop on a plane the next day and fly down to Washington. Sam and Nicki picked the MIT scientist up at Dulles International Airport at seven that next evening.

After the introductions, Dr. Graff offered his deepest sympathy to Nicki for the loss of her brother, and as Sam drove the three out of the airport concourse, Nicki turned in her seat to address the bespectacled young scientist.

"Sam and I held off eating dinner, Dr. Graff. We figured you might be hungry after the flight, airline food being as it is."

"That was very thoughtful of you both, thank you, I am starved," he said, "But, please, Ms. Neally, my friends call me Freddy or Doc."

"Sure thing, Doc," she said, "and please call me Nicki."

"What do you feel like eating, Freddy?" Sam asked.

"I haven't had Chinese in a while—"

"*No!*" Sam and Nicki said together, exchanging sideward glances.

"Ahh…Freddy, how does pizza and beer sound instead," Sam said, looking in the rearview. "We're not big on Chinese restaurants at the moment. I'll explain later."

They ordered the pizza to go and ate it sitting around Nicki's kitchen table, washing it down with bottles of Corona. As they ate, Sam brought Freddy up to speed on everything he either knew or suspected to be true regarding his book's research and the apparent connection to Mickey's death.

Fascinated by the intrigue and hanging anxiously on Sam's every word, young Dr. Graff was living up to Sam's description of him as the ultimate computer geek. By the time Sam reached the part about the necklace and the possibility of a computer chip being hidden in one of the stones, the MIT scientist was bubbling over with excited anticipation.

"Wow!" Freddy blurted, hopping to his feet. "A microchip, embedded in a diamond, possibly full of secrets that could"—he paused as the reality fully hit him—"save the world."

"So it is possible?" Sam asked. "You can make chips that small?"

"Oh, absolutely," the young genius said, starting to pace the kitchen floor now, his mind shifting gears. "The size of a pinhead," he continued. "Eventually, we'll have microchips even smaller that will be capable of digitally storing the total volume of information contained in the Library of Congress."

Freddy slipped into his lecture mode as he continued to educate his small audience.

"One of our long-running projects at the institute is the development of microscopic chips that could be surgically implanted into a human brain to repair, well, brain damage. Restore motor skills lost from head injuries, that sort of thing. We're close. Very close. We have not as yet been able to develop the organic coupling device that will allow the connection between hardware and human flesh, thereby creating the link through which electronic impulses carrying information or instructions for the brain could pass. Once we solve this 'bridging problem,' there are no limits to the possibilities. Imagine a chip containing the total knowledge contained in the Library of Congress being implanted into a man's memory circuitry! It boggles the mind! The recipient could instantly access all the information known to mankind! He could walk into a hospital in the morning to perform brain surgery and that night be the featured violinist with the New York Philharmonic! His skills would be limitless!"

"Or," Nicki asserted, "the sudden massive influx of information into this otherwise normal human brain would fry the man's thought processing circuitry, reducing the poor bastard to nothing more than a blubbering idiot, barely capable of drooling on himself or peeing in his pants."

"Ahh, yes, well," the young scientist frowned as he admitted, "there is that possibility, I'm afraid. As I said, our research is ongoing."

"But your point is well made, Freddy," Sam said, bringing him back on track. "It *is* possible that a chip could have been hidden in one of the stones."

"No question. May I see the necklace?"

Sam pulled the felt bag out of his pocket and laid the necklace on the table, "The center stone," he said. "You can see a shadow in it if you hold it to the light. It's more evident if you look at it from the back."

"Yes, I see it," the scientist said, turning the piece to the light. "Surely seems to be something there."

"So how do we get it out, Doc?" Nicki asked.

"We cut it out," he said, handing the necklace back to Sam. "I'll need a lab, do you two want to come with me? We can fly back up to Boston tomorrow and take this to the institute. I have everything I'll need right there."

"No," Nicki said quickly. "We can go to my work, Sam. We can do it tonight, right here!"

"Nicki," Freddy said, trying not to sound condescending. "I'm going to need some very specialized equipment. Instruments usually only found in a scientific laboratory. What exactly is this place you work at?"

"The Dahlgren Marine Laboratory. We're part of the new annex to the US Naval Weapons Lab at Dahlgren."

"Oh, well, I had no idea. Are you a scientist?"

"Not yet, I have one more year to get my doctorate."

"Fantastic!" Freddy said, pleasantly surprised. "Beauty and brains. What field of study?"

"Marine geology. I'm sure we'll have everything you'll need, Doc. The annex is just off base, we can be there in half an hour."

"Nicki," Sam said, thinking he must not have heard her correctly. "Did you say Dahlgren Marine Laboratory?"

"Yeah, Sam, I thought Keri told you. I started on a research team there about three weeks ago. Why?"

"Your lab was in one of my dreams."

"Is that so?" she said, reflecting Sam's pensive look. "Well, maybe you should see it for real."

"Yes. Maybe I should."

Forty-five minutes later, after dropping Erin off at Keri's Mom's for the night, the three pulled into the secured employee parking lot across the street from the main entrance to the facility. Nicki's lab was located on the basement floor in the rear of the main building, one of several structures that comprised the new complex at Dahlgren. As they crossed the street and walked up the short flight of steep stone steps to the main entrance, Sam stopped midway up to read the inscription on the front of the building. Noticing at the top of the steps that Sam was not beside her, Nicki turned to look back.

"Something wrong, Sam?" she asked.

"This place," he said, still looking up, his head panning from left to right. "It's exactly as I saw it in my dream."

"You ever been here before, Sam?" Freddy asked.

"No."

"Maybe drove by once?"

"Never," Sam said as he walked to the top of the steps. He stood looking back and forth from Nicki to Freddy, waiting for one of them to offer some plausible explanation. Neither did. Nicki just nodded quietly to herself.

The hairs on the back of Sam's neck were standing up, a cold chill suddenly seeping through his body.

"I've got a bad feeling about this place, guys," he said, looking at Freddy.

The man from MIT was all business. "Sam," he said, anxious to do his part, "we need to cut that stone open."

"I know," said Sam, still staring at the young scientist.

"Well, what the fuck, Sam," Nicki said, pressing forward. Her brother was dead, and she wanted some answers. "Are we goin' in or not?"

Sam wanted answers too. "Yeah," he said, walking past her to hold open the door. "Let's do it."

Inside Nicki signed for her two guests. She'd called ahead to arrange for their visits, which posed no problem as both men carried a military security clearance. It was almost midnight, and the building was virtually empty, with nearly all the labs shut down that late at night.

Sam left Freddy and Nicki to the task of retrieving and accessing the hidden microchip, taking the opportunity to explore the corridors and entrances of the building. He was quite sure the Navy provided an adequate security force for the facility, and though he told himself he needn't be concerned with the possibility of unwanted visitors, he still couldn't shake the uneasy feeling he had. So the ex-SEAL toured the entire building, opening every unlocked door he could find, spying out windows and watching the entrances, all in an effort to spot any other late-night visitor who might happen to wander into the naval laboratory. There were none. So with an effort, Mason quieted that little voice in the back of his head and returned to the lab to see how his friends were progressing. As Sam reached for the lab door, something caught his eye. He turned slowly. Outside the lab entrance, mounted on the opposite wall, hung what appeared to be an ordinary-looking fire extinguisher. Sam stared at it for several seconds before walking over to examine the silver nameplate attached to the side of the unit. It read,

PROPERTY OF THE HAMTIN CORPORATION
ASSEMBLED IN THE UNITED STATES
ALL COMPONENTS: MADE IN CHINA

What else did you expect, Sam?

*****

Dr. Graff and Nicki were now working in a different area of the lab from where Sam had left them. Both sat at an island workstation that ran parallel to a countertop along the outside wall. The top two feet of the room were above ground level, affording for a high, long, narrow set of wire-mesh windows to run the length of the room. Completely engrossed in their work, neither of the two scientists heard the ex-Navy SEAL as he came quietly up behind them.

"How's it goin' guys?" he asked.

"Jesus H. Christ, Sam!" Nicki yelled, nearly jumping out of her seat. "You scared the shit out of me!"

"Hey, easy, girl…take it easy," Sam said, smiling broadly, amused by her overreaction. "I'm sorry, I didn't mean to startle you."

"It's not fucking funny, Sam!"

"Okay, okay. I'm sorry. So what's got you so uptight?"

"She keeps hearing things, Sam," Freddy said, looking up from his work. "Thinks there's somebody moving around outside."

"You hear anything, Freddy?" Sam asked, now serious.

The myopic young scientist looked apologetically at Nicki, then to Sam. "No," he said, shaking his head. "I think you spooked her, Sam."

"Christ, Sam," Nicki argued. "You could set a bomb off next to this guy while he's working, and he wouldn't hear it!"

"All right, Nicki, calm down," Sam said, reassuring her. "Look, I just spent the last half hour checkin' this place out. We're the only ones here other than the posted Marine sentries. Maybe that's what you heard. One of them patrolling the grounds."

"Are you sure, Sam?"

"It's just us and the Marines, kiddo."

Nicki let out a deep breath.

"Okay," she said. "You're probably right. I guess I'm just a little edgy. All this talk about your dreams coming true is weirding me out."

"It's all right, Nicki," said Sam, resting a hand on her shoulder as he stepped closer to the work station. "I don't know what to make of it all either. So what'd you two find, anything?"

"It's a microchip all right, Sam," Nicki said. "Tiny little fucker. Doc's got it under the scope now, trying to set it to the reader."

"How's it look, Freddy?"

"All…most…done. Just…one…more…There!"

The screen on the computer monitor to their right suddenly came to life, and the three quickly turned to it, only to find a single window staring back at them requesting a seven-letter password.

Freddy rolled his chair in front of the screen, and with his hands posed over the keyboard, he looked up over his wire-rimmed glasses at Sam and Nicki.

"Any ideas?"

Chapter 27

Present day, the research facility at Guangxi

Wu Xun and Lo Fang sat alone in Wu's private chambers—Lo Fang having just returned from his trip to America. The two sat in momentary silence as one of Wu's staff poured tea for the two men. When the servant had left the room, the Tong leader bowed modestly to General Wu.

"I have personally delivered the instructions to your 'agent' as you had requested, Wu Xun. I must confess," he said sincerely, "I did not expect someone of such standing. I am most impressed. How did you manage this?"

Wu Xun acknowledged his great respect for Lo Fang by returning the shallow bow. "As you yourself said, there are very few people of honor. Most can be bought. I merely offered money and power. But that proved to be enough, particularly considering the alternative offer. Now, what news do you bring me?"

"The CIA agent, Neally, is dead, as you know. There was no chip or evidence of any kind found on him. Your agent has been in contact with Lee Hak-joon. I'm afraid the autopsy also produced nothing."

"He must have passed it to someone before he was captured," Wu said, worry in his voice.

"We believe he did, and we are acting on that assumption. Your agent is confident. The hatchet-faced man has been watching those close to Neally. We have learned of a necklace that Neally brought back from his visit to Asia. A diamond necklace, one with a large flaw in its center stone."

"A microchip?"

"We believe so. There are teams in place at this very moment to retrieve it. It will not take long."

"See that there are no mistakes," Wu said adamantly. "Get the chip and kill those who have it and anyone else who may have come into contact with them!"

"The order has already been given, my general."

*****

Back in the lab at Dahlgren, Sam and Nicki had racked their brains for twenty minutes trying to piece together every relevant sequence of seven letters or digits they could think of that Mickey might have used as a password. Nicki tried combinations of names and birthdays for herself, Mickey, Sam, Erin—anyone she thought was of some significance to her brother, all with no luck. Sam tried to find something from Mickey's military background, codenames, dog tags, serial numbers, black-ops locations, all with the same result. As fast as Freddy could type the sequences into the computer, the screen would simply respond every time by flashing,

The password you have entered is invalid.

"There's got to be something you guys are missing," Freddy said, still hopeful. "Something that was important to Mickey, yet obscure at the same time..."

"Christ, it could be anything," Nicki said, completely frustrated. "We may as well be searching for a needle in a haystack. I'm sorry, Sam," she said at a loss. "Whatever it is, it's not coming to me."

"Maybe it wasn't meant to," the man from MIT said.

"What do you mean?"

"Sam," Freddy said, apparently on to something, "if Mickey somehow meant for the necklace to find its way to you, then it follows that the password would be something known exclusively to the two of you, right? How did you say you came by it again?"

"Well, we were at Nicki's house after the funeral when—"

"Jesus, Sam!" Nicki exclaimed. "The night of the funeral, when Ms. DesMoine first stopped by, you opened the door for her and called her by some other name. Yeah, I remember now. She said it was a nickname that only you and my brother called her. I think it was—"

"Jessica!" Sam yelled. "Seven letters! That's it! Put it in, Freddy!"

This time the screen went suddenly blank for a few long seconds until the black screen was abruptly replaced by something far darker—an alphabetical list of US cities, military sites, and government facilities that ran the full length of the page. Each listing was followed by the number 26, 27, or 28, and then by another number followed by the letters *mgtn*. The three looked on in stunned silence as Freddy started to scroll down the pages. When after several clicks, he had only reached the Cs, the young scientist hit Control and End, which brought him to the thirty-seventh page, over seven hundred sites, all on US or allied soil.

The undeniable reality of what the three were seeing before them was a true epiphany, and it hit Sam like a car wreck. When he finally spoke, his voice was barely more than a throaty whisper.

"My God," he said. "It is true. They've done it! They've actually gone and done it!"

Freddy opened the next file to show a similar listing of what were obviously strategic Soviet sites. Another six-hundred-plus targets.

"Holy Christ, Sam!" Nicki said, grabbing his arm. "What does it all mean? What are those numbers? What's *mgtn*?"

"Stands for *megaton*," Freddy said calmly. "The destructive capability of the bomb to be used is listed for each specific target."

"What do you think those numbers mean?" Sam asked. "Twenty-six, twenty-seven, and twenty-eight?"

"I don't know," Freddy said, scanning through the screens. "But there must be some significance. Every entry has one of those same three numbers beside it."

"Maybe they're days of the month," Sam offered. "Maybe they're dates. Maybe they're…" He paused as an earlier vision flashed in his mind's eye. "Maybe they're delivery dates!"

"Delivery dates for what?" Freddy asked.

"The delivery date of the weapon for the site indicated."

"No indication of month or year if they are dates," Nicki pointed out.

"Let's look at some more files," Freddy said.

The next file provided the final piece to their most horrific puzzle. It detailed the procedures and timetable of an upcoming world event. A rocket launching. A joint multinational effort led by the Chinese, the rocket was to deploy the final link needed to complete a network of orbiting satellites, thereby creating for the Asian world countries their own global communication system.

The file detailed a secret payload change. Once the network linkup was complete, the bogus satellite would be capable of sending the detonation signal simultaneously around the globe. All the bombs, an assortment of small, conventional tactical nuclear weapons, coupled with thousands of extremely powerful neutron bombs, would all go off at once.

"This is incredible!" Freddy said, unable to believe his own eyes.

Nicki was starting to cry now as a sudden realization came to her. "My God, Sam!" she said, her face once again streaked with tears. "I just saw this story on CNN last week. Sam, that rocket launch is scheduled for the twenty-ninth!"

"Are you sure? That's only six days from now."

"She's right, Sam," Freddy confirmed. "I read about it a couple of days ago. Big media event. It's set to go up this Sunday!"

"All right," Sam said with a sense of urgency. "Let's get the hell out of here. Freddy, pull the plug on that thing and give it to me. Leave it in the reader."

Overly excited, the young scientist tried to move a little too fast, and his nervous hands dropped the chip and its reader assembly onto the floor between Sam and Nicki. They both bent down to the floor at the same time to pick it up, bumping heads as they did so. Crouched low, the two paused only a moment to smile at one another over one of those silly, awkward moments. That one smile saved their lives.

Chapter 28

S am would remember thinking at the time of how odd it is, those seemingly insignificant thoughts that can run through one's mind at a time of great crisis. Lingering near the edge of consciousness following the explosion, the first thing that popped into Sam's head was that they'd used far more C-4 than they'd needed, and they were lucky not to have toppled the entire building. Someone had lined the entire length of the basement laboratory windows with the potent plastic explosive, and the resulting blast had decimated the lab and nearly everything in it. Shards of glass with chunks of wire mesh and torn metal were blown across the workspace at the speed of sound, killing Freddy instantly, his head nearly decapitated.

As the shattered, faint remains of the laboratory came gradually back into focus. Sam realized that both he and Nicki would surely have suffered the same demise had they not been protected by the stainless-steel island workstation. Because the built-in cabinets beneath the countertops were designed to store hazardous and often-times radioactive materials, their walls were lead-lined and steel-reinforced. The structural integrity of the island had remained completely uncompromised by the explosion, sheltering Sam and Nicki from the deadly flying debris. Though protected from the brunt of the blast, the concussion caused by the sudden compression of air at detonation had knocked them both flat, leaving them badly stunned and temporarily deaf, their ears ringing painfully.

Rising up out of the black hole he knew would become everlasting sleep should he surrender to its call, Sam fought to regain full consciousness. He pushed himself to his knees and, with his hands on the countertop, pulled himself up to peer over the work-station at the origin of the blast. All the lights in the room had been blown out by the explosion, the only illumination now being the dim beams of light from the night sky that filtered down through the haze of dust and smoky debris. Sam could see no movement, nor could he hear any sound. Water poured down from the damaged sprinkler system, and Sam figured the fire alarm he knew must be sounding, probably accounted for at least some of the ringing in his ears. He became aware of Nicki beside him, hands holding her head, knees wobbling weakly as she tried to stand. Sam quickly put a hand on her shoulder and, turning her away from Freddy's dead body, gently pulled her down to a crouching position. He shook his head to her, then pointed toward the end of the island countertop, motioning with his hand to stay low. Sam took Nicki's hand, and after a short bit of resistance from her, the two crab-walked their way through the debris and heavy air toward the exit.

Keeping the island between themselves and the window, Sam and Nicki soon reached the end of their cover. With no other choice, they crossed to the row of cabinets along the corridor wall, exposing themselves to view from the blown-in windows. No sooner had Sam started to edge his way around the last cabinet toward the exit door, then someone shone a light into the cloudy room. Sam and Nicki both froze. Whoever it was holding the light was sweeping the room slowly from the far end.

Time to move!

With one hand holding on to Nicki, Sam reached around the end of the counter with his free hand, trying to feel his way to the door. His hand hit upon something metallic and cylindrical mounted on the cabinet's end about three inches in diameter by a foot and a half tall.

A fire extinguisher.

Potentially his only weapon, Mason lifted it off its cradle, and just as he pulled the safety pin, the corridor door burst open, and two men wearing ninja suits and night-vision goggles tumbled into the room, rolling to a crouch a mere five feet from Sam and Nicki. Kneeling back to back, each man pointed a suppressed automatic weapon at opposite ends of the lab. With the night goggles limiting their peripheral vision, neither man had yet to see Sam. He wasted no time. Mason hit the closest assassin hard on the base of the skull with the little fire extinguisher, then sprayed foam in the face of the second ninja as he turned to the sound. Sliding under the man's weapon, Sam kicked him square in the goggles, tearing the weapon out of his hands. Sam shot both men with short bursts, then pulled Nicki to her feet, the two pressing flat against the wall beside the open exit. Sam mouthed the words "Stay here" to Nicki, and with the weapon tucked, he tumbled into the empty hallway. Knowing there'd be more than the two, Sam grabbed Nicki and hurried her toward the rear fire door.

Reaching the back exit, it seemed to Sam as though the ringing in his ears was finally and thankfully starting to subside. He put his mouth close to Nicki's ear.

"Wait here while I check it out," he said not too loudly.

The basement exit opened onto a brick stairwell leading up to a brightly lit courtyard spanning a wide area between three buildings. Sam figured correctly that their backdoor escape route would be closely covered, but he also realized his advantage. The enemy couldn't afford to wait him out. With police and fire racing to the scene, they'd have to come for him soon.

Slipping silently through the door, Sam took up cover beneath the top of the stairwell and waited. It wasn't a long wait. Creeping out of the shadows from behind the building across the courtyard, two pairs of men leapfrogged each other with perfect military precision, taking turns dropping to the ground, then running in the open, steadily closing the distance to Sam's position. The ex-Navy SEAL waited until the group was within easy range, then, as two of the enemy sprang to their feet in turn, he shot them both dead center, spraying a long burst at the two still lying prone as they returned fire at Sam's muzzle flash.

Unconcerned about the remaining two assassins, Sam retreated back down the stairwell and through the fire door to where Nicki waited. Pulling her behind him, Sam and Nicki hustled up one flight of stairs to the main floor, then ran full tilt down the center corridor, past the two Marine guards lying dead on the reception area floor and straight out the front door.

Weaving their way through the gathering crowd, Sam decided not to risk going anywhere near Nicki's car, so they avoided the parking lot. With the sirens approaching, the two strolled casually along to the next block where Sam flagged down a cab.

Once in the back seat, Nicki opened her mouth to speak as she started to brush the dust and smudge from her clothes. Sam grabbed her arm gently and, with a finger to his lips, shook his head no. They rode in silence for several minutes until Sam saw the meter hit eight fifty, then he motioned for their cabbie to pull over. He paid the fare with a ten so as not to over tip and draw unwanted attention. As soon as the first cab drove off, Sam flagged down a second, and again they rode in silence for another dozen city blocks.

*****

The scene back at Dahlgren was one of controlled chaos. Police cars and fire engines lined the street as military and city police cordoned off an area out front in an attempt to hold back the growing mob of television and newspaper reporters. From the front entrance, three men emerged and stopped to confer at the top of the steps. Inspector George Lee was one of them. After a brief exchange, the other two men went back inside, and the inspector came quickly down the steps to head purposefully for his car. As he walked, he pulled his cell phone from his vest pocket and placed it to his ear. He held his other hand over his ear as though blocking out the crowd noise. The inspector made sure the media people were within easy earshot as he stopped to speak loudly into the phone, as if to be heard above the clamor.

"Yes, the bombing was undoubtedly the work of terrorists," he told the empty line. "Yes, probably the same Libyan group we are already chasing."

*****

Now a couple of miles from Dahlgren, Sam and Nicki cleaned up as best they could while waiting for their third cab. Though unhurt physically, Nicki was badly shaken by the ordeal. She leaned into Sam's chest to hide her tear-streaked face.

"Poor Freddy," she said after her sobbing had slowed.

"I know," Sam said, tenderly. "The poor kid never knew what hit him."

"Sam," she said, lifting her head from his chest to look up, "why are we running? Why don't we just go to the police?"

"For one, I don't trust them, or anyone else for that matter. And two, no one would believe us without proof."

Sam looked sorrowfully at Nicki. "I dropped the chip in the explosion."

Nicki's sad eyes brightened, and a weak smile pursed her lips. She let go of Sam as she pulled away from him. Holding his eyes with her own, she reached inside her blouse to her bra and pulled out the reader card with the microchip still intact.

"Damn good thing you brought me along," she said, wagging the card with her fingers.

"Oh, good girl!" Sam said, letting out a sigh of relief. He took the chip from her just as another cab finally pulled to the curb.

"So can we go to the police now?" she asked, climbing in the back.

"No."

"No? Sam, why the hell not?"

Sam didn't get to answer her right away as their cabbie turned in his seat. "Name's Sal, folks," Obviously Italian, the driver asked, "Where to?"

They'd finally gotten an English-speaking cabdriver, the type who will make perpetual conversation, hoping for bigger tips.

With a wink, Sam told the cabbie they needed a quiet, obscure motel anywhere on the outskirts of town.

"Sure thing, pal, no problem. Hey, you hear 'bout the bombing?"

"A bombing?" Sam asked, looking sideways at Nicki. "No. Where? When?"

"Just happened," Sal said, excited to share the news. "Some terrorists tried to blow up the naval lab over at Dahlgren! You believe that shit?"

"Terrorists!" Nicki exclaimed. "But—"

"Where'd you hear that, Sal?" Sam asked, cutting Nicki off and pinching her arm.

"Ow, you shit!" Nicki cried, slapping Sam on the arm.

Sal looked up in the rearview but missed it.

"It's all over the radio," he said. "They say a man and a woman were seen leaving the scene that fit the description of two of those Libyans that capped that FBI guy the other day. They think it may be related. Duh!"

Nicki was quiet now.

"Anyone killed?" Sam asked.

"Three they know of so far. A couple of Marines and one of the lab people they haven't been able to identify yet. Guy's probably pretty messed up. From the bomb, I mean."

"Jesus, Sam," Nicki said with a shudder.

"Oh, ahh, sorry, ma'am," Sal said. "Didn't mean to upset you."

"Pretty scary stuff," Sam said.

"You said it, pal!" the cabbie said. "This terrorist shit is gettin' way the hell outta control. First the towers, now this!"

Sam had nothing to add.

"Hey, here's your place," Sal said, turning off the road.

Sam paid and tipped the cabbie then he and Nicki checked into the sleazy motel. As he had hoped, the out of the way place did a large part of its business with hookers and cheating spouses sneaking away for a one-night stand. The old woman behind the desk had no aversion at all to taking cash for the room. No credit cards needed here.

Once inside the room, Nicki went ballistic. "Christ Almighty, Sam! Do they mean us? Are they saying we're the fucking terrorists!"

"Seems that way. Now you know why I don't want to go to the cops just yet."

"Sam, what are we going to do?"

"First things first. We need to get Erin to a safe place. Keri and Irene too. Anyone close to us that we've been in contact with since Mickey was killed will be in danger."

"Why, you don't think—"

"Nicki," Sam said, knowing he was about to scare her even more than she already was. "These people will stop at nothing to get this chip. If they get a hold of Erin, they'll use her to get to us."

"Oh my God!" Nicki immediately ran for the phone.

"Nicki, no!" Sam yelled, stopping her. "We can't call anyone we know. Their lines may be tapped, and they'll be able to trace the call here."

"What then?"

"Didn't Keri's mom say she was taking Erin to a friend's house for the night? So she could play with her friend's granddaughter?"

"Yes, Mrs. Sullivan. Why?"

"They should be all right there for a while. Do you know the friend? Do you have the address?"

"Yes. Why? What are you going to do?"

"Jessica, Ms. DesMoine, gave me the number for her beach house. She can hide them."

"Sam, are you sure? How do you know you can trust her to do this?"

"I just know."

"But how?"

"Because Micky trusted her."

"Then what about us? What about the chip? Who can we trust, Sam?"

The ex-SEAL walked over to the phone and picked it up.

"In the morning, I'm calling your brother's friends at the FBI."

Chapter 29

There is a man in a dark suit and tie browsing. He looks so familiar. He seems to be looking at everything I have just looked at, but I can't see his face. Is he following me? I think he is, but why? What does he want? Wait, he's found something. He's taking it to the register. No, he's turning. He's bringing it to me. I know this man! He's the Korean, the hatchet-faced man! But what is he doing here in the jewelry store? What is he holding? My God, it's the necklace! He has the necklace! How did he get the necklace?

"Did you think you could hide this from me forever? No, Mr. Mason, now that I have it, I shall kill you and the woman, just as I did your friend. You are a fool living in a fantasy world, Mr. Mason. Wake up, man, wake up! Wake up, man, wake up!"

*****

"Wake up, Sam, wake up. Come on Sam, it's six o'clock."

Nicki was gently shaking Sam's shoulder. They had spent the night in the cheap motel taking turns watching the parking lot. Sam had let Nicki rest first, getting her up at 4:00 a.m. and instructing her to let him sleep until six. She was having trouble waking him, but finally, his eyes opened, and he sat up with a start.

"Another dream, Sam?" Nicki asked.

"Yeah," he said, rubbing his eyes. "Sort of a repeat."

"Same dream?"

"No," Sam said, his mind's eye remembering. "Just the same face."

"You want to tell me about it?"

"I wouldn't know what to say about it, Nick," he said, standing up. "Why don't you take the first shower. I'll get us some breakfast."

By six fifteen, with the sky just starting to brighten, Sam had ventured across the street to a twenty-four-hour market where he bought some coffee, fresh bagels, and a few other items. By six thirty, with Nicki headed for the shower, Sam was back sitting on the edge of the bed with his coffee, fishing out the business card Brian Gillis had given him in Nicki's backyard the night of her brother's funeral.

"Do you need the bathroom, Sam?" Nicki asked, pausing in the doorway. "I'll probably be in here awhile."

"All set," he said, reaching into the bag he'd brought back from the market. He tossed her a small box. "Here, take this with you."

"Hair coloring? *Blond* hair coloring! No fucking way, Sam!"

"Nicki," Sam reasoned, "the cops are looking for a dark-haired man with a dark-haired woman. They won't look twice at a man with a blond."

"Jesus, Sam! Blond?"

"These people are playing for keeps, Nicki. We need every advantage we can think of."

"But fucking blond!"

"Nicki, you'll look great," Sam promised. "Come on, you need to do this. Think of Erin."

"I am, Sam, and I'm worried to death about her," the young mother confessed. "How do you know this Jessica person won't fuck things up?"

"Your brother didn't hang out with idiots, Nicki. Go take your shower."

Sam had called Jessica from a payphone the night before, reaching her at her home on the bay. Glad at first to hear Sam's voice, she quickly picked up on his tone. She listened in silence to his brief instructions.

"Do you know a place?" Sam asked at the end.

"Yes. Mickey told me of one. And he told me what to do."

"Okay, go there and stay there. I don't want to know where right now. You have the number. You can call me when it's safe, and I'll come get you."

"How long, Sam?"

He told her the truth. "You'll know one way or the other by Monday."

Jessica nodded to herself. "Six days," she said thoughtfully. "They say, Sam, that God created the world in six days. If you believe in that sort of thing."

"If you believe."

"It seems you now have but six days left to save it."

Sam said nothing.

"Tread carefully, Sam," Jessica said. "The tall grass is full of snakes."

"Come again?"

"I'll talk to you Monday," she said, and five minutes later, the exotic beauty was out the door.

Sipping his coffee on the edge of the bed, Sam dialed the number on the back of the card, assuming it was Gillis's home phone. He was right. A tired voice answered on the third ring.

"Yeah, Gillis here."

"It's Sam, Brian."

"Sam!" the sleepy voice said, suddenly coming awake. "Man, am I glad to hear from you. Where are you and is—"

"Yes, and never mind all that now." Sam had cut him off before he could say Nicki's name.

"Listen, Brian," Sam said, nonchalantly, "I'm calling you early just to let you know that I've found that Asian import you were looking for."

"Import?" Gillis said, still a bit sleepy and a little slow on the uptake.

"Yeah," Sam went on. "That little oriental piece you've been looking for to finish off your study. You know, for your computer room."

"Something from Asia for my computer room?"

"From China, actually."

"Oh! Oh, yeah, right," the FBI man said, finally catching on, "You found something that will fit in there, huh?"

"Yes, and it's something you really need to see soon. There's a pretty heavy demand for this particular piece. It being one of a kind."

"Where is this piece now?"

"In a little shop at one of the malls. I can't remember the name of it, but if you want to meet me tonight, I can show it to you."

"Sure. Where? What time?"

"I'll check my schedule and call you back tonight."

"Should I bring an appraiser along?"

"Why don't you bring Barry. He knows a lot about these things. I wouldn't mention it to anyone else. Wouldn't want to see it get stolen out from under you."

"I understand. I'll talk to you tonight."

An hour later, Nicki finally emerged from the bathroom. The transformation was both complete and amazing. Her clothes were the same, but Sam felt as though he were seeing a completely different woman. Her hair, now a golden honey-blond, was still somewhat wet, so Nicki had brushed it out and pulled it back to one side, holding it in place with a near-invisible hairpiece, creating a sleeker, more sensual look for the pretty young mother. Her makeup appeared to be different too, Sam thought. Her cheekbones seemed higher and more prominent, and her lips seemed fuller somehow. She looked beautiful and Sam found himself staring.

"Wow! Nicki, you look…different."

"Does it look okay?"

"It looks great!"

"You really think so?" she asked, secretly pleased with the results.

"Yes, I do."

Sam was staring again.

"I guess it's not so bad," Nicki said, turning her head in front of the dresser mirror. "So, Sam," she said, hands on hips, tuning to face him, "Now that you've got your blond, where do we go from here?"

"Well," he said, refocusing, "first we find a new home for the day, and then we're going to the mall."

"The mall?" she said, turning back to the mirror with a smirk on her face, "Good. You can buy me some new clothes!"

*****

Inspector Lee was in his car, listening to the electronic voice again. The device was supposed to remove any hint of emotion from the human tongue, but Lee swore he could sense anger in the garbled words. The conversation this time was not one way.

"I'm not sure," Lee said. "I was not there, but the men we used were all well trained."

"Four," Lee said after listening a moment. "But my people were able to extract all the bodies."

"No, that will not be a problem. I will follow up with a press statement. At this point, I can say whatever I choose. There will not be enough time for anyone to validate the facts one way or the other."

"Yes, it does appear as though we underestimated this man."

"Yes. He has made contact as we thought he would."

"Tonight. I will have the exact time and location later."

"I will see to it myself."

*****

Sam had a cab pick them up in front of the market across the street and take them to an even shabbier motel. Nicki was less than thrilled. Lunch from McDonald's didn't do much to improve her mood. At two in the afternoon, though, they took another cab to the Bayside Mall so Sam could scout out a meeting place while Nicki picked them up some new clothes. Sam thought she almost smiled in the cab.

The mall was huge, and Sam was pleased with the layout. He wanted a big public place for the rendezvous, one with plenty of open space. And in the event something went wrong, one with lots of ways out. He also wanted people around, but not so many that he couldn't spot trouble coming. The mall was open until midnight, and Sam figured an hour before closing would work best. The meeting with the two FBI men had to come off okay. Sam was counting on Gillis and Basset to bring Nicki and himself in. If it didn't happen, he knew they'd be out on their own.

After another fast-food takeout dinner in their new room, Sam and Nicki watched reports of the bombing on the news, glad at least not to hear their names or see their faces on TV. They spent the rest of the evening getting their new outfits ready and taking turns catching up on their sleep. At ten forty, with a cab waiting outside, Sam called Gillis.

"The phone next to Starbuck's in the Bayside Mall, center of the lower level. Twenty minutes," was all he said.

"We'll be there," Gillis said.

Sam had already hung up.

*****

The two-story Bayside Mall was L-shaped, with the entire center of the top floor being open to the main level below. Railings along the inside of the walkways fronting the second story shops allowed patrons to lean over and look down upon the storefronts and vendor carts that lined the center portion of the lower mall. On the outside corner of the L, on the lower level, was the food court, complete with restrooms, a newsstand and a short bank of payphones. Starbuck's was next to the food court, on the short leg of the L, heading toward the east mall exit. The upper-level balconies were rounded off at the corner of the L, with benches lining the railings on both sides of the opening affording a resting place for weary shoppers. On one of the inside corner benches, dressed as mall rats in baggy clothes, with backpacks and shopping bags at their feet, Sam and Nicki sat with a group of five kids, all apparently just hanging out.

From this vantage point, Mason could easily peer down into the open food court, taking in the adjacent storefronts as well as the bank of payphones next to Starbuck's. He watched as Brian Gillis walked past the food court to stand by the phones. Using a cell phone he'd pickpocketed just ten minutes earlier, Sam dialed the number to the first payphone. The FBI agent casually picked up the ringing phone.

"This is Gillis," he said.

"It's Sam, Brian. Where's Bassett?"

"In the food court watching my six. Where's Nicki?"

"She's with me. Is Barry wired?"

"Yes."

"Just you two?" Sam asked, scanning the food court, spotting Bassett sitting at a middle table with a newspaper spread out in front of him.

"Just us, Sam."

"Okay, let's talk. What's the word on the inside?"

"They're on you like white on rice, Sam. Someone spotted you two coming out of the lab at Dahlgren right after the explosion, and the chief investigator has tagged you and Nicki for the bombing. You've been officially labeled subversives, Sam. He's even got you tied in with the Libyans somehow, and now they're changing the official story about Mickey, saying the three of you were all in this thing together. The whole bureau's buzzin' like a bee's nest."

"There's somebody dirty behind all this, Brian. What do you and Barry think?"

The FBI man didn't hesitate. "We don't buy it, Sam. We'd like to hear what you've got to say, hear what Dahlgren was all about."

"We'll get to that," Sam said, thinking hard. "Who'd you say was pushing me and Nicki for this thing?"

"Guy named George Lee. One of the top men in the bureau, Sam. He's the man running the show."

"Last name spelled L-E-E?"

"Yeah."

"Is he Asian?"

"Yeah, why?"

Snakes in the tall grass!

"He's it!" Sam said, sure of himself. "He's bent, Brian! He's a double agent."

"That's impossible, Sam. The man's being groomed to be the next assistant director for Christ's sake!"

"Brian, you have no idea how big this thing is. Trust me, it's possible, and I've got the proof."

"What exactly do you have, Sam?"

"I told you Mickey had been in China. The night I saw him, he had just gotten back. That's why he wouldn't talk to me. He didn't want to involve me. He'd uncovered a nuclear threat to both the US and Russia. He'd documented the intelligence and stored it on a microchip that he was carrying with him. That's why they killed him. I have the chip."

"Do you know what's on it?"

"Yeah. That's what Nicki and I were doin' at Dahlgren with Freddy."

"That the guy we found dead?"

"Yeah. A kid I knew from MIT."

"Sorry about your friend, Sam," Gillis said sincerely. "But… what happened there? What's on this chip?"

"Later, Brian. We can't stay on the phone much longer."

"Okay, Sam. Let's get the two of you in safe and take a look at what you've got. You can fill in the blanks on the ride in."

"Not to the bureau!" Sam said emphatically. "We've got to secure this evidence. It's the only way anyone will believe any of this."

"Barry and I already talked about that, and we agree, Sam. He's got an uncle with the Maryland State Police. A captain. They'll be a lot tougher to push around than the locals. He should be able to buy us the time we need. His barracks are in Leonardtown, in St. Mary's County. We can be there in half an hour."

Sam considered the proposal. He'd have to trust someone sooner or later.

"All right," he decided, "let's do it."

"Where are you and Nicki now?"

"Close. Where's the car?"

"Outside the East exit."

"Okay. Pull it up to the door. Tell Barry to wait at the exit. When we show, he can take us out."

"Done."

Sam kept pace on the upper level a little behind Gillis, watching him as he walked briskly past the storefronts toward the exit. Sam knew he would be relaying instructions to Bassett. He took a quick glance to his left in time to see the FBI man stand and head out of the near-empty food court. When Sam looked back after Gillis, a familiar shape caught his eye. Gillis was passing by a jewelry store, and there standing alone in front of a glass display window was a dark-haired man in a dark suit, a newspaper tucked under his left arm, his back to the mall. Sam couldn't see the man's face, but as he strained for a closer look, he spotted the earplug in the man's right ear. The man in the dark suit seemed to be talking to himself. When Gillis was about ten feet past, the man suddenly whirled about and set off behind the FBI agent. Sam got a good look at the man's face and stopped dead in his tracks, putting an arm out to stop Nicki as well.

"What is it? What's wrong, Sam?"

"It's him!"

"Who?"

"The face in my dreams! It's a trap!"

Sam glanced quickly back at Bassett just as the FBI agent passed by two Asian kids dressed much like Sam and Nicki sitting at one of the food court tables. One of the kids held a newspaper, and spreading both arms wide as though stretching, he shot Bassett point blank with a silenced pistol concealed in the newspaper. Appearing to have tripped, the FBI man stumbled forward, falling on his face in the center of the mall concourse to lay dead still.

Sam turned to run after Gillis. He saw the man in the dark suit remove the newspaper from under his arm as he closed in behind the remaining FBI agent.

"Brian, behind you!" Sam yelled down too late.

Gillis spun around and, with a surprised look on his face, said something to the approaching man in the dark suit. Sam read his friend's lips as the hatchet-faced man raised the newspaper.

"Inspector Lee..." was all Gillis got out before he was knocked backward by the force of three rapid-fire shots in the chest from a silenced nine-millimeter at a range of six feet. Lee continued walking by the fallen man as though nothing had happened. Ten feet past, with the newspaper tucked back under his arm, he stopped to turn in the direction of Sam's voice. An empty balcony was all he saw, but he knew he had flushed his quarry. He spoke rapidly into the microphone hidden in his lapel.

Sam and Nicki had ducked down the corridor that led to the upper-level restrooms. Hurrying past the bathrooms, they went straight through a door marked "Mall Personnel Only." They ran down a metal stairwell, out a service entrance, and into one of the three waiting cabs Sam had prearranged.

"Where to?" the black cabbie asked.

"How long to the airport!" Sam shouted.

"'Bout twenty minutes," the cabbie said, looking over his shoulder.

"A C-note if you get us there in ten!" Sam said, holding up the bill.

The black driver whirled forward in his seat, stomping on the gas as he focused his skills on the task at hand. He issued one simple warning.

"You folks might wanna put on yo' seat belts!"

Chapter 30

America West flight 2118 is the red-eye from Washington, DC, to Phoenix, Arizona. It was on schedule to depart DC at 12:10 a.m., Wednesday morning. Sam and Nicki were on it.

"Sam, the damn plane is practically empty. Do we really need to sit all the way in the back of this fucking monster?" Nicki was exhausted, and it showed in her voice as they made their way down the long narrow aisle.

"You take the window seat," Sam said as they reached the last row of the massive 747. Nicki did as she was told, though not too happy about it. Sam stowed their backpacks with an extra change of clothes in the overhead bay. The outfits they wore now they'd been carrying in the mall shopping bags. They'd made a quick change in one of the airport restrooms, ditching the bags and their old clothes in the trash.

"Look, Nicki," Sam said gently. "I know you're tired, but please, try not to get us thrown off the plane for foul language."

"Christ, Sam, who the hell's going to hear us all the way back here? We practically have the whole damn plane to ourselves."

"Just humor me. Okay?"

"Sure thing, Sam," she whispered, settling into her seat. "No fucking problem." With that, Nicki let her seat back, tucked a pillow under her head, and closed her eyes, letting out a long, tired sigh. "So why are we sitting in the back of the bus?"

"We lucked out getting on this flight before the feds got to the airport," Sam said, looking at his watch. "But within the hour they'll know were on it. They'll know exactly where we're going and what time we're going to get there."

Nicki sat up. She was one tough little woman, but the events of the past few days had shaken her badly. She was both scared and tired, and it showed in her eyes.

"Jesus, Sam, what are we going to do?"

"Well, that's why we're in the back of the plane," he explained. "First, so I can see any trouble coming and second…"

"Shit!" Nicki cut in, grabbing Sam by the arm. "You think they might be on the plane?"

"No, not enough time. We barely made it ourselves, and we knew where we were going."

"That's true, huh?" she said, her voice still shaky.

"Yes, it is. And I covered our tracks somewhat. Not enough to throw them off for very long, but it should get us out of DC at least."

"How? What'd you do? What'd I miss?"

"Remember when you came out of the women's room, and I was on the payphone?"

"Yeah, we almost missed the last boarding call."

"Well, I booked us on three other flights on three different airlines, all leaving within the next half hour. An expensive little misdirection but one bill I'll be happy to pay. They'll figure it right eventually, but it should buy us some time."

Sam was confident, but Nicki wasn't buying it. She glanced anxiously about the cabin.

"I don't like it, Sam," she said. "Why don't we just go to the cops and get some police protection?" Nicki looked as though she might start to cry. "There must be someone we can trust!"

She was panicky, and Mason knew it. He also knew her only chance of staying alive was with him, but he needed her calm and rational. He reached over and laid his hand gently over hers.

"Take it easy, Nicki," he said tenderly. "There's no way in hell I'm going to let anything happen to you. That's a promise."

Nicki looked up, and their eyes met and held for a long moment. There was something about this man she couldn't argue with. Somehow, she knew she could trust him. Even with her life. She let her head lay back on the cushion, and the tension drained from her body. She gave Sam's hand a weak squeeze and, smiling shyly, said, "Okay, Sam, thanks."

Sam returned the smile with a little more warmth than he had intended. He suddenly realized his pulse was racing, and his face was starting to flush. The moment was quickly spoiled though by the sound of overhead cabinets slamming shut. A tall and curvy black flight attendant was working her way toward the back of the plane, doing her final preflight check. When she finally reached the back row, she flashed a huge bright smile that could only be genuine.

"And how're y'all doin' a way back here by yo' lone selves? Lookin' for a bit of privacy, are ya?" The pretty attendant made no attempt to hide her Southern drawl. She drew out the word "privacy" so as to insinuate an intimacy between the attractive young couple. A natural presumption, but when she winked at Sam, he felt his face flush even deeper. He recovered quickly, though, and decided to use her misinterpretation to his advantage. Her nametag read "Darnell" in bold letters, and above her name were the words "Senior Flight Attendant."

"Uh, Darnell," Sam said as if sharing a secret, "we we're hoping to, ahh, spend a little quality time together, if you know what I mean." And he reached over to take Nicki's hand, returning Darnell's wink.

Though it didn't seem possible, her smile broadened.

"Well, shoot, y'all got the whole back half of the plane to yo'selves. And you folks lucked out. We don't usually fly the 747 on this leg. This one just happens to be comin' out of some unscheduled maintenance, back into the regular rotation. We're takin' her out to the coast where she'll fly the LA to Hawaii run."

"That is fortunate," Sam agreed.

"So," Darnell said, flashing her big smile again, "I just need y'all to pull your seats forward an' buckle up for me, then I can leave you two alone for a bit."

"Do I have time to visit the head before we take off?" Sam asked.

"Go ahead, but be quick," she warned, glancing at her watch. "We'll be liftin' off in less than five minutes."

Sam leaned over as if whispering some sweet nothing in Nicki's ear.

"I'm gonna do a quick sweep of the plane," he said softly. "Make sure there's no unwanted company aboard."

Nicki played along with the charade. "Don't be long, honey," she purred as Sam slid out of his seat and headed forward.

Darnell looked after him a bit, then turned to Nicki. "Damn, girl, that is one fine lookin' man you got yo'self there. Can't say I blame you for wantin' to be alone with him." Seeing no ring on Nicki's finger, she asked, "He yo'r husband?"

Nicki couldn't resist. "No," she said, leaning back in her seat, closing her eyes. "Just the man I'm sleeping with."

"Well, honey," Darnell said, amused but not fooled. "Everybody's on the plane now an' we're all buttoned up, so you won't be get-tin' any more company back here." With her big smile in place, she turned and headed back up front.

Sam returned a minute later. "We're okay for now," he said. "No unfriendlies onboard."

"How do you know for sure?" Nicki asked.

Sam shot her a look that said, *"Because I just know…"*

She shot him a look back that said, *"Don't fuck with me!"*

"Sam," she said, the edge still in her voice, "you said they'll be waiting for us when we get to Phoenix. What do we do then?"

"Well," he explained, "that's the other reason we're sitting in the back of the plane. Right behind us is the elevator the attendants use to bring up the food carts from cold storage below. It also accesses the rear baggage compartment, one deck below that. I'm afraid that'll be our only way off the plane."

"How do you know all this?"

"The military. When I was in the SEALs with your brother, we were part of a special unit that trained to do hostage rescue missions on Air Force One, in the event some terrorist group managed their way onboard and held the president and the plane hostage. We had to learn the entire layout, inside and out. Air Force One is a 747, same as this. Well, same basic construction anyway. Air Force One is just a whole lot more luxurious, with a heck of a lot more technology on her. The plane carries the newest radar systems, state-of-the-art defense mechanisms, even stealth technology. It also flies with everything the president would need to command a war. Specifically, the most sophisticated communication equipment in the world, complete with satellite uplink capabilities and all the up-to-date fail-safes and codes. Now, of course, there are several underground bunkers in secret secure locations that would be the government's first option given a pending catastrophe, one is right under the White House, the PEOC, the Presidential Emergency Operations Center. And there is also a group of four even more advanced 747s called the Doomsday Fleet that the president and his staff could board if necessary, should a crisis arise while the president was away from Washington. But if a disaster threatens while the president is in flight, on Air Force One, with no time to reach a secure bunker location, the thinking is that thirty-seven thousand feet above ground could then be the safest place for the president.

"Great plan. His ass is safe and to hell with the rest of us!"

"Now, Nicki, that's our beloved president you're talking about—"

"Fuck him," she said, turning away. "I didn't vote for him."

Sam just shook his head, only half-amused with her rebounding spirit.

"Anyway," he went on. "The feds will be waiting for us at the gate. They'll probably want to pick us up just outside the terminal. Less chance of drawing attention that way."

"Why should they care about that?"

"This Inspector Lee has the best of both worlds, and he's playing it to the max. When it behooves him to use the FBI people, he does, but those weren't FBI people at Dahlgren, and the ones who killed Gillis and Bassett in the mall last night certainly weren't either. When Lee thinks he can get away with using his hit teams, he'll use them, but the airport will be too public with too much security. He'll sick the feds on us for sure. But whoever's really calling the shots in this operation, someone above Lee, well…he'll want to make us disappear, and the less people who know about it, the better."

"So how do we get away from them, Sam?"

Mason had it all planned.

"The feds will have to watch and wait for the last of the passengers to deplane," he said. "Then when they don't see us get off, they'll identify themselves, go onboard and search the plane. That should buy us enough time. If we don't get too much hassle from the baggage handlers, we should be okay."

"And then we go to the cops?"

"Nicki, we can't go to the cops because the first thing they'll do is call the feds. Gillis told me we've been labeled subversives. The locals will have no choice but to turn us over to the FBI. If that happens, we're dead and the world as we know it ends."

The look on Sam's face was almost apologetic. "I hate to use the old cliché, kiddo, but I'm afraid we're out in the cold."

*****

The 747 taxied to the head of the runway and paused only a moment as the pilot got word from the tower. Seconds later, with all four engines at full throttle, the giant machine lifted effortlessly into the starlit night sky. As the plane climbed, banking steeply to its westerly heading, Sam wondered what fate awaited them in Arizona.

Standing alone in front of Delta Airline's main ticket counter in terminal C of Dulles International Airport's north concourse, Agent Richard Larsen recognized the chief inspector immediately. Larsen was only nine months out of the academy, but he already knew well of this man's reputation. Rumored to be the next in line when the AD stepped down, Inspector George Lee was a legend within the bureau, acknowledged by many to be the smartest and toughest man in law enforcement. Surely his Korean heritage had something to do with his remarkable talents, the young agent thought to himself, believing the myth claiming Asians to be exceedingly clever. He only wished he were meeting this man under different circumstances, for he was about to become the bearer of bad news.

As Inspector Lee and his entourage approached, Larsen straightened to receive his superior and give his report. "Agent Larsen," he said, holding out his hand. "It's an honor, sir."

Lee acknowledged the agent with but a slight nod of the head.

"Please tell me," the inspector suggested with an icy coolness, his words slow and precise, "that you have some useful information for me, Agent Larsen."

The young agent was not prepared for the magnitude of this man's presence. The sheer weight of Lee's stare was hypnotic, his facial features so sharp as to lend an almost physical intensity to his hard, steady gaze.

"Umm, I'm afraid that we've…uh, missed them, sir."

"How so, Agent Larsen?"

"Well, sir, it seems, ahh, it appears that is." The young agent was fumbling badly for his reply. "It seems," he said weakly, "that the fugitives were…I mean they are…confirmed at least…on four different flights. On four different airlines…to four different cities. This apparently to confuse us, sir…"

"And successfully so it would appear." Inspector Lee held his glare fixed on the wilting agent. "You have a list of these flights, Agent Larsen?"

"Yes, sir," Larsen said, handing over his notepad. The hatchet-faced man quickly scanned the open page, stopping at the fourth entry.

"Flight 2118 to Phoenix," he said to no one in particular. Then looking away, Lee handed back the notepad with a curt, "Thank you, Agent Larsen."

The inspector turned sharply on his heel and strode toward the exit.

Chapter 31

Route 77 runs northeast from Globe, Arizona, a small city about an hour east of Phoenix, far up into the Navajo Indian Reservation to intersect Route 15. This high, back-country road heads west toward Flagstaff, through the Painted Desert, skirting the southwestern ridges of the Rocky Mountains. Sam and Nicki were driving the road in a rented hunter-green Ford Bronco, making their way steadily up through the narrow mountain passes, flanked on either side by sheer walls of rock that climbed skyward, towering over them. Though she had often heard of the red rock of the Arizona landscape, Nicki was surprised at the depth of the color. As they drove on, she was continuously awed by the magnificence and grandeur of the seemingly infinite views they would come upon as they skirted the steep roadside cliffs.

Mason had decided to avoid the main highways whenever possible, so he had forsaken Route 17 north, heading east instead out of Phoenix on Route 88, the Apache Trail, up past Theodore Roosevelt Lake to Globe, where he picked up 77. The diversion would turn their two-hour drive into four, but it couldn't be helped, and besides, they had some time to spare. It was only a little after noon now, and Sam would not attempt to break into the HAMTIN facility until well after midnight. The detour would provide the ex-SEAL some quiet space in which to assess their situation, while still allowing ample time to recon the site.

*****

Their escape from the airport had been without incident, almost too easy, in fact. There had been, but a few feeble objections from the baggage handlers as Sam and Nicki made their way across the airport tarmac to the ground level of the terminal. Here an idle maintenance worker shouted at them to "hold it right there" as Sam bulled past him with Nicki in tow. The mechanic threatened to call airport security, which he did as the two fled through a fire door and up an adjoining stairwell, but Sam and Nicki were into the main terminal lobby, through the exit, and into a waiting cab, before security dispatch could even pick up. They had seen no sign of the welcoming committee Sam had expected. What he could not have known was that there was none. The hatchet-faced man would lay his snare further down trail.

Leaving the airport as quickly possible, Sam had the cab take them to the west side of the city where he rented the Bronco from an all-night dealership. He had no choice but to use his credit card. Lee would be able to trace him to the rental, he knew, but it was unavoidable, he'd just have to ditch the truck at the first opportunity.

While waiting for the papers to process, Sam consulted a phone book and, to Nicki's great dismay, announced that he needed to see a dentist.

"But you've never had a cavity in your life," Nicki protested. "Your teeth are perfect!"

"Not anymore," was all Sam would say on the matter.

With the two hours they had gained by flying west, it was still only a few minutes past five in the morning. So they drove to the address Sam had picked out of the phone book, parked behind the small brick and glass building, put their seats back, and grabbed a couple of hours of much-needed sleep. At 7:30 a.m., a shiny black Lincoln Navigator pulled into the lot and a tall athletic-looking man dressed in shirt and tie got out carrying a briefcase. As Sam had hoped, the dentist himself was the first in to open his practice. While Nicki waited in the car, Sam followed the doctor to the door where they spoke briefly. Over his shoulder, Sam mouthed the words "wait here" to Nicki as he entered the office.

"Wait here, he says," Nicki said to herself, sitting alone in the bright morning sunlight. "Where're am I gonna go? You've got the damn keys there, Sammy-Boy."

She looked around at the flat, barren landscape stretching off in all directions. "And where the hell would I possibly want to go?" she wondered aloud as she lay back down to rest.

Thirty minutes later, Sam climbed back into the rented truck, apparently no worse for wear, and with Nicki asleep beside him, set off across the open desert floor.

*****

"If you don't find me a damn bathroom soon Sam, so help me God, you're gonna see a side of me you will not want to remember!"

Nicki had become a little "fussy" again. They had not seen any sign of civilization in almost two hours now, not since the little strip mall they'd pulled into as they were leaving Globe. They'd bought some coffee and doughnuts to go, and Sam had picked up a few items he'd needed at a local Army-Navy surplus store, but there were no public bathrooms to be found there or anywhere since. Nicki was now in dire need.

As if in answer to her plea, as they crested the rise ahead to start down the long gentle slope onto the next desert plateau, Sam spotted what appeared to be a roadside diner and gas station. Dreamlike, the place just seemed to materialize out of the dusty, blurred air that rose off the super-heated Arizona hardtop. Sam slowed and pulled into the mostly empty gravel lot, parking just to the left of a battered old pale-blue Chevy pickup. A shabby wooden hitching post stood between them and a short flight of tread-worn steps leading up to the open veranda that ran the length of the front of the building. Past the steps was the main entrance, complete with a pair of swinging saloon doors.

The log structure was ancient, over a hundred years old Sam guessed. Sun-bleached and weather-beaten, the cafe was a vision straight out of an old Wild West movie, but it was the faded wood-burned sign hanging over the doorway that held Sam and Nicki's attention. They both sat quietly for a time, staring up at it. The sign read,

O'Brien's Irish Saloon est. 1859
Food and Spirits

Nicki burst into laughter. "You've got to be shitting me!" she cried. "An Irish pub! In the desert? In the middle of nowhere? Now I've seen it all!"

Sam continued to stare.

Apparently, as they would soon learn, the young son of an Irish tavern owner by the name of Patrick O'Brien, had immigrated to America in the mid-1800s. Finding New York City a little too crowded for his liking, he followed the horde west when the great gold rush struck. Like most, he found no gold, but he did find a wife, a beautiful young Indian girl who'd been enslaved to a gang of claim-jumping, murderous horse thieves. O'Brien fell madly in love with the girl at first sight and could not bear to see her abused as she was. When his offer to buy the squaw was refused, he stole away with her in the middle of the night as the outlaws lay in a drunken sleep. She led him to her village, where they were married by way of Indian ceremony. Together they built the trading post and went on to raise a band of half-Irish, half-Navajo children who grew to terrorize the countryside, their adventuresome exploits remaining legendary to this day. The outpost flourished over the years and the watering hole as it came to be known, was passed from father to son, evolving into the wonder that now stood before Sam and Nicki. A combination of restaurant, gas station, general store, and ginmill, O'Brien's had become all things to the local folk who managed a life in these parts, a life for most as barren and desolate as the landscape itself. Desert living is hard, and hard men and women are what one finds here, mostly of Indian or Mexican bloodlines, families that have worked the hot land for generations with never a thought of prosperity. Survival is the only ambition in the desert. They stay for the beauty of the landscape and the harmony they find here with nature. O'Brien's is their oasis.

To this day there are still mining crews in the hills tirelessly working the arid land alongside a scattering of farmers and cattlemen. All tough, hard men in their own right, and all known to frequent O'Brien's bar to quench their desert thirst. The saloon is also a favorite stop for the packs of bikers that roam freely across the back roads of the western plains, and though most bikers today are decent, law-abiding, spirited folk, some of the more notorious types, Hells Angels or Mongols, would occasionally find their way through O'Brien's swinging doors as well. This is when the place would get really exciting. The combination of hard whiskey and hard men with attitudes would inevitably lead to drunken brawling, and though usually harmless, someone would eventually get hurt bad—a knife slash or broken bottle over the skull—once in a while a gunshot wound. Then the county sheriff would have to come by with a couple of his tougher deputies to lean on certain folks for a bit, and the place would quiet down again with everyone getting along just fine—for a bit.

On its good days, O'Brien's was not for the timid—no place to bring the wife and kids. But the old watering hole had been nice and peaceful like for quite some time now.

"Are you coming or not?" Nicki asked as she reached for the car door handle. Sam didn't answer. He continued to gaze up at the sign, clearly entranced, his mind somewhere far away.

"Sam. Hello, Sam? Hey!" she said loudly to break the spell. "You okay?"

"It's happening again," he said softly.

"What is?"

"I'm not sure," he said, still staring up at the sign. "It's like déjà vu, I guess. That's the only way I can describe it." He turned to face Nicki, "I've seen this place before."

Nicki glanced up at the building, then back at Sam.

"An Irish pub? In the middle of the desert? Sam, you've never even been to Arizona before, you bonehead!"

"I know! I can't explain it, but I'm telling you I've seen this exact place before. I think in one of my dreams maybe. I don't know."

"Aquarius, right?"

212

"Huh?"

"You were born in early February, weren't you?"

"Yeah. Why?"

"That explains it. You're a whack-job, Sam. All Aquarians are whack-jobs. I'm in the desert with a fucking whack-job!"

"I'm serious, Nick."

"Yeah, me too, Sam," she said. "Maybe you did see this in a dream. They say you only remember your last dream, you know, the one you have just before waking up. Maybe that's why you can't remember it. Maybe you saw this wondrous establishment sometime in the middle of the night! Probably in a nightmare! Who knows? But right now, I couldn't possibly care less. I have to pee!"

"I'm telling you, Nicki, I've got a very bad feeling about this place."

"Sam, you're not hearing me! I have to pee like a friggin' race-horse! I'm goin' in."

Nicki started to swing her legs out of the truck, when two very large, rugged-looking men with long, straight reddish-brown hair held in place by headbands came through the swinging doors. Dressed in plain white-cotton long-sleeve shirts with dusty vests and faded jeans, they padded lightly down the wooden steps, passed in front of the Bronco, and climbed into the old Chevy pickup. As the driver turned to look out his window, he stole a long glance at Nicki. His face held no expression, just a deadpan stare. Their eyes locked, and as the Indian held her gaze, she felt as though he was looking right through her. Appraising her. Searching her soul. A chill started up Nicki's spine, when suddenly the man's deep green eyes crinkled with light and the crow's feet at his temples deepened. A moment later, his whole face broke into an amused smile. He stomped on the accelerator, and the old truck slued backward, spraying gravel in its wake. In an instant, they were gone. Then it dawned on her.

"That Indian had green eyes!"

"And freckles," Sam added.

"That's it," Nicki declared, climbing out of the truck. "I need a drink. Sam, you comin' or not?"

"Yeah, but let's make it a quick one," he said, following her up the steps.

Nicki paused at the saloon doors. "Tell me, Sam," she said, "in your dream, was there a clean bathroom anywhere in this joint?"

Sam cracked a wry smile. "Does the word 'straddle' mean anything to you?"

"Nice, Sam. You really know how to show a lady a good time."

He decided to leave the "lady" comment alone, and as they passed through the swinging doors, he whispered, "Let's just please try to keep a low profile in here, okay, Nick?"

"Sure thing, Sam," she whispered back. "No fucking problem."

Chapter 32

O'Brien's Irish Saloon, Sam and Nicki realized very quickly, was Irish in name only. Once through the swinging doors and out of the bright desert sun, the interior, by contrast, seemed exceedingly dark. It took them both a few seconds for their eyes to adjust to the dim lighting before they could see the layout of the place clearly. The design was simple, and Sam instinctively took note of it as they looked around.

Built with hand-cut logs, heavy wooden beams, and wide pine planking, O'Brien's was rustic, to say the least. Contrary to its name, the whole interior was lavishly adorned with native Southwestern decor—not a four-leaf clover to be found. The place was surprisingly clean, though, and an extensive array of ceiling fans did an efficient enough job at cooling the interior air.

As Sam and Nicki moved inside, they could see the bar and dining area to their right. A half dozen booths were sided along the outside front wall, and across from the booths, a heavy wooden bar ran the length of the room. Cut into the wall behind the bar was an open doorway to a rather large kitchen. To their immediate left as they walked in was a small general store with an old mechanical cash register sitting on an even older wooden barrel top. Next to the register was a sign which read, "Pay for gas here."

Behind the store, across from the kitchen area, was a big room with tables and chairs in the front half and two pool tables in the rear. The loud sound of pool balls breaking moved Sam to guide Nicki into the empty bar. A sturdy-looking, rosy-faced man sporting a full red beard and wearing a white apron and chefs-hat was busying himself just inside the kitchen door. When he noticed Sam and Nicki standing by the bar, he came right out and around to greet them.

"Well, you folks are sure off the beaten path," he said, flashing a big smile. "Welcome to O'Brien's. Danny O'Brien at your service an' this here's my place. Not much to look at, but the beer's cold an' the food's hot. So what can I get you two nice people?"

"A clean toilet seat would be nice," Nicki muttered under her breath.

"Say again, miss?"

"Ahh, your restrooms, please," Sam said, covering quickly. "I'm afraid it's been a long drive, Mr. O'Brien, and she needs to, umm, freshen up."

"Oh, sure thing," O'Brien said. "Straight through that doorway, miss, then right past the pool tables to the back wall. 'Fraid there's just the one toilet though, but you're sure welcome to it."

Sam held his gaze on Nicki as a warning.

"Get me a beer, will ya, Sam," was all she said before making a beeline for the bathroom.

Much to her surprise and delight, the small room was quite clean and bright. Someone had installed a skylight in the high wood ceiling, flooding the room with sunshine. A basket of freshly cut desert blossoms hung from the window's lower sill, adding color and fragrance to the little room.

Refreshed and greatly relieved, and with her mood boosted considerably, Nicki returned to find Sam seated at the bar, sipping a Dos Equis beer, and listening intently to Danny O'Brien as he finished the tale of O'Brien's pub. Sam's initial apprehensions about the desert oasis had started to fade, so he agreed to ordering sandwiches, and the weary couple took their beers to a far corner booth where they could talk in private.

So as to see the entire room, the ex-SEAL sat in the bench seat on the outside wall as Nicki slipped easily into her side of the booth. Sam couldn't help but notice the gentle curve of her slender hips as she scooched across the bench to lean her back against the front wall. As she pulled her long, shapely legs to her chest, she reached up and loosened the band that held her golden hair back, allowing it to fall softly about her delicate neck and shoulders. She closed her eyes and leaned her head back.

It was all instinct. Natural feminine instinct. To the casual observer, Nicki would seem completely oblivious to her own striking sensuality, and consciously she truly was. Still, on some level never to be understood by men, she knew exactly what she was doing, yet to Sam's eye, her innocent unawareness only served to heighten her feminine appeal.

"So, Sam," Nicki asked between sips of her beer, "what'd you have in mind for sleeping arrangements tonight?"

Sam was still off with his thoughts.

"Sam. Hello, Sam!"

"Ahh, sorry," he said, coming back to his senses. "My mind drifted."

"Yeah, where to?"

"Never mind. What'd you say about sleep?"

"Well, I doubt we're going to come across a Holiday Inn any time soon, so I was wondering what your plan was for tonight."

Sam took a long pull on his beer before answering. He didn't want to upset her again, but he needed to be straight with her.

"No motels, I'm afraid. Too dangerous. We'll be camping out tonight. I've got us a couple of sleeping bags and a small tent in the back of the truck. We'll make our way as close as we dare to the HAMTIN plant, find a safe spot off the road a bit, build a fire, and catch up on some sleep. About 3:00 a.m., I'll go over the fence and find a way inside."

He saw the concern creeping back in her face. "It'll be fine, Nicki. I've done this sort of thing before, many times. And I'm good at it, so don't worry, okay?"

"No! It's not okay," she said on the verge of tears once more. "And I am worried, Sam. In fact, I'm scared! I'm scared to death for Erin, for myself, for you, for the whole damn planet! Sam, I don't know where my daughter is or even if she's safe. The poor thing's probably scared half to death! Christ, I haven't talked to her in a day and a half, and I wouldn't know how to even begin to find her. Shit, Sam, if anything happens to you, I'll never see her again! And if we don't get through to someone we can trust within the next"—she looked at the date on her watch, her arm trembling—"three and a half days."

And suddenly it was all too much for her. Her eyes welled up, and the tears started to stream down her cheeks. "And Mickey's dead."

Nicki didn't sob or wail. She barely made a sound. She sat there looking at Sam with her big, beautiful, sad eyes wide open, full of pain, asking for help. It had been a long time since a woman had touched Sam this way. He'd never let anyone get close enough. Not since Michelle had been killed. This had snuck-up on him. Hell, he'd known this girl since she was a teen. This was Micky's kid sister for God's sake! But clearly, she was no longer a kid, and Sam could not deny what he was feeling.

So for the second time in twelve hours, Sam held Nicki's hand and promised her everything would be all right. Somehow, he told himself, he would find a way. As if on cue, Danny O'Brien bustled over to their booth with their food. Sam seized the chance to give Nicki a few minutes to herself.

"My turn to use the facilities," he said, sliding out of his seat, "Try to eat some if you can. We'll take the rest to go. We might not see real food again for a while."

Mason headed to the 'john,' and as he passed the front entrance, he heard the unmistakable roar of several big bikes passing the front of the building and circling around back to stop by the open rear door. Passing by the pool tables, the ex-SEAL caught a quick glimpse of four, maybe five men climbing off their Harleys. As the bathroom door closed behind him, Sam heard the gang clamor through the back doorway. Regulars of a sort apparently, the crew was loud and abrasive, shouting obscene greetings to anyone they spied as they made their way straight to the bar. Sam heard Danny O'Brien's insincere welcome, and that little bell started ringing in the back of his head. His early warning system.

Mason could always sense trouble coming. He just noticed things in ways that others didn't. His senses were sharper than average, and his brain had been trained to process information differently and more efficiently than most. Through some subliminal process, he did not himself fully understand, his mind would calculate and signal the probability of imminent violence before others would notice—and the bells would go off. It was an instinct that had kept him alive many times in the past, and he'd learned to trust it.

Walking back into the bar, Sam's instinct proved immediately correct. The ex-SEAL was not surprised to see one of the men— he could now see there were five—stand back abruptly from where Nicki still sat with her back against the wall. The man was huge, a full six inches taller than Sam. He was very dark, probably of Latino blood, and his jet-black hair was cut short and slicked straight back. He wore a bright-red shirt, open to the waist with the sleeves rolled up tightly over his thick forearms. A wide black belt with a big silver buckle pulled snug over faded black jeans. He was baked hard as leather by the desert sun, and his sinewy muscles glistened with sweat. He towered over Nicki, glaring down at her. He flashed an evil grin and said something over his shoulder to her as he turned back to join his friends at the bar.

This was a tough, mean-looking bunch, Sam thought. He paused a moment at the first booth, using the old "tie the shoelace" routine to garner a closer look. These were not recreational riders for sure. These men were thugs. Social outcasts, misfits big enough or bad enough to make their own rules in life. Having either acquired or been born with a strong aversion to authority, these men would avoid the law at all costs, but when confronted, they wouldn't hesitate to use violence to get their way. The scars and prison tattoos that adorned their exposed skin were testimony to their lifestyles. Mason was careful not to make eye contact with any of them. He knew men like this always viewed that as a challenge or an excuse to flaunt their machismo. Using only his peripheral vision as he'd been trained, Sam appraised the enemy, for he had already come to think of them as such.

Red-Shirt was the tallest but not the biggest, the two seated at the end of the bar nearest to Sam had a good forty pounds on him. Big, dull-looking white men, they appeared to be twins, brothers at least. They both shaved their heads bald, and they each wore a multitude of earrings in both left and right ears. They'd dressed alike in black T-shirts and black jeans with heavy silver chains draped from belts to rear pockets. Built alike, they were broad, barrel-chested men, no-neck types with thick arms and legs and the great natural strength that is born to their kind. The only discernible way of telling them apart was their facial hair. The man on the end wore a big, droopy mustache while his twin sported a bushy goatee. Over a quarter ton of ugly trouble.

The biker next to Red-Shirt was nearly as tall as the Latino, though not as heavily built. He wore faded blue jeans, a brown cotton shirt, and brown leather vest. He was the rangy type, with wiry long arms and legs that belied his strength. His big hands were all knuckly and gnarly, and Sam suspected they had split open more than a few unsuspecting skulls in their time. The man's long blond hair was tied in a ponytail and fell midway down his back. He was listening to Red-Shirt while looking over his shoulder at Nicki. He turned back to face the bar, threw back the contents of his shot glass, then said something out of the side of his mouth to Red-Shirt, and they both laughed. Ponytail yelled for more tequila. A dangerous pair, Sam thought.

It was the man in the middle, however, who worried Sam the most. The smallest, he was also probably the deadliest. Also dressed in black jeans but with a white T-shirt, he seemed to be the leader of the group, confident and arrogant. With dark hair and dark skin, he also seemed to be of Latino blood, and when he talked, he used his hands to make his point. His movements were quick and precise. *Very* quick hands, Sam noted. His eyes looked hard and mean as they glanced about, constantly assessing his surroundings. He was the kind who survived on speed and cunning. Mason knew this man would rely on surprise to take out an opponent. He would always strike first and would not hesitate to stab you in the back. The fact that he commanded the respect of such an ungodly group spoke in earnest of his toughness. Like the rest of his friends, he carried a large knife on his belt.

A very dangerous creature indeed, Sam thought to himself as he walked behind the group to the booth where Nicki still sat with her legs tucked up under her arms.

"Everything okay?" he asked, sliding into his seat.

"Fucking asshole!" she said a little too loudly.

Sam cringed. He knew she'd had words with the big man in the red shirt. He'd hoped she would let it go, and he could get her out of there without incident. That prospect seemed dim at the moment.

"Problem?" he asked.

"Not anymore," she said defiantly, but her eyes said differently.

"Good," Sam said. "Let's go then."

"I want to finish my beer."

"I'll buy you another one at the next fun spot."

Sam stood and threw a twenty on the table to cover their bill. "Come on," he said, "let's get out of here."

She didn't move.

"Nicki, we need to leave."

"That big piece of shit doesn't scare me," she lied.

"So this is you keeping a low profile?"

Nicki said nothing.

"Nick, did you get a good look at these guys?" Sam asked softly, leaning into the booth.

"Fuck them!" she said. "That big prick just waltzes right over to me and says, 'Hey, little Mama,'" Nicki lowered her voice in mock imitation, "'how's 'bout you 'n me have us some kicks together?' So, I say, 'Thanks, but no thanks.' But he ain't takin' no for an answer, and he says to me, 'Hey, baby, you one lucky muchacha, you know that? You 'bout to have the ride of your sweet life.'" Nicki shuddered in disgust at the thought. "So I told him to go tell it to his mama. And he left. Said something to me in Spanish, but I didn't catch it."

The damage was done, and Sam knew it, but he couldn't help admiring the young woman's courage.

"Well," he said, "at least you didn't swear at him."

That brought a wry smile to her lips. Twenty feet away, Red-Shirt called for more tequila.

"Look, Nicki," Sam pleaded. "Ordinarily I'd relish the chance to defend your honor, but we've got bigger fish to fry. And we don't exactly want to be drawing any undue attention to ourselves. So how 'bout you and me make like horseshit and hit the trail?"

She stayed quiet for several seconds, then let out a long, deep breath, "You owe me a beer."

"You got it," Sam said, standing straight. He took Nicki's hand. "Stay behind me," he said, and he started to lead her out.

There was only about eight feet separating the booths from the stools facing the bar. Sam tried to give the bikers a wide berth, hoping he and Nicki might be lucky enough to slip by unnoticed.

Midway past the group, the big bald man with the mustache slid off his stool to block their way. At the same moment, Ponytail stepped out behind them. Mustache's brother swiveled slowly on his barstool to face them, grinning the way a coyote must just as it's about to pounce on the helpless baby rabbit. Red-Shirt and the little man with the quick hands continued to stand facing the bar.

The big man in the red shirt lifted his shot glass and drained it, then without turning said, "Your woman, she's got a pretty fresh mouth on her, amigo. You shouldn't let her talk that way to strangers. Someone might take offense and close it for her. Permanently!"

"Look, friend," Sam reasoned, "we don't want any trouble. So how about I buy you boys a drink and we'll be on our way."

"Friend!" Quick-Hands snarled. "We're not your fuckin' friends, gringo! And we don't need you to buy us no fucking drinks!"

Knowing it would place Nicki in mortal danger, Sam wanted to avoid a fight at all costs.

"Okay, fine," he said. "Hey, we're sorry if we've offended you. You don't want to drink with us, no problem. We'll just get out of your face."

As Mason spoke, his head panned from one end of the bar to the other, but his eyes never left the little man in the middle.

Red-Shirt stepped away from the bar and took a step toward Sam and Nicki. He'd had half a dozen tequilas by now, and the effects of the alcohol were starting to show. His movements were stiff, and his speech slow and careful.

"I think," he said with a wicked, half-drunken grin, "that maybe your woman needs to learn some respect, amigo. No?"

Just then, Danny O'Brien stepped through the kitchen door with a tray of food and, no stranger to a fight himself, quickly assessed the situation.

"All right, boys," he said carefully. "Let's not have any trouble. We don't need the sheriff nosin' around here again. So what say we all relax n' have a drink. On the house—"

"Shut the fuck up, Irish!" Quick-Hands shouted.

Sam knew the tone. Things weren't about to improve anytime soon. He risked a glance up and down the bar. The two bald brothers were a few feet to his left, with Goatee still sitting. Red-Shirt with Ponytail right behind him stood ten feet to Sam's right. The little man in the middle was standing directly across from Mason, still facing the bar. Sam could feel Nicki pressed up behind him; to her credit, she was still breathing.

The ex-SEAL kept his focus on Quick-Hands. Mason knew the others would look to follow his lead. The slick little Latino remained facing the bar, his head down, apparently contemplating his empty shot glass. From behind him, Sam stared over the man's shoulder at his reflection in the mirror behind the bar, holding his gaze on the biker's eyes. Quick-Hands looked up and caught Sam's reflection. They locked eyes in the mirror, and for a moment, the two men stood as if alone, frozen together in that reflective parallel universe. Neither man flinched or even blinked for several long seconds, but the Latino saw something in the mirror he didn't like. Sam's eyes were projecting one single thought.

You may get us, but you will be the first to die!

Quick-Hands looked away from the glass to O'Brien, who stood tense behind the bar, his knees flexed, his hand poised to grab for the shotgun the biker knew he kept under the cash register.

"Irish," the Latino said, his face suddenly breaking into a wide grin, "the gringo here wants to buy us a drink. Make it your best tequila, eh?"

Red-Shirt started to mouth an angry protest, but Quick-Hands barked something at him in rapid Spanish, and the big man turned slowly back to the bar with the others.

O'Brien stood straight and let out a slow breath. He knew it was over, as did Sam. He walked up to the bar next to the little biker with the quick hands and, without looking at him, dropped a hundred on the bar.

"The rest is for you," he said to O'Brien. Then he turned and led Nicki out to the Bronco.

"I'll drive," Nicki said, her spirit renewed once again. Sam didn't argue. She got behind the wheel, and spraying gravel and dust behind her, she pointed the big rented truck north again, further up into the mountains.

As O'Brien's slowly disappeared in her rearview, Nicki couldn't help but think, *Out of the frying pan, into the fire.*

Chapter 33

The last sliver of fiery red ball that was the setting sun slipped unhurried below the tree line to the west just as Sam and Nicki pulled off the main road. Since leaving O'Brien's, most of the ride had been made in silence. Consulting one of the maps he'd picked up in Phoenix, Sam's only conversation came as he directed Nicki to Mount Flinte, the site of the HAMTIN facility. An old service road wound its way up the mountainside, emerging above the tree line to end at a fire observation tower on top of the mountain. The trail skirted the boundaries of the plant's grounds, at times coming within a few hundred yards of the outer perimeter fences. Sam had timed their arrival at the old dirt road for dusk, leaving himself barely enough light to find his way up the narrow trail without using the headlights, hoping to allow for no chance of their ascent being observed through the thick cover of trees.

Mason took the wheel and pushed the Bronco steadily up the rugged path, finally settling on a level stretch of trail about three miles off the main road. He pulled the truck into a small clearing that crested away from the HAMTIN plant, and he and Nicki pitched camp on the far side. While exploring their surroundings by moonlight, Nicki found a narrow path that led down the slope about fifty yards to a mountain stream. Someone had blocked the water with a makeshift stone dam, creating a small waterfall on one side and a rocky pool on the other. The empty beer cans and cigarette packs littering the ground gave evidence to the spot being a favorite of local teens. Desperate now for a bath of any kind, Nicki immediately informed Sam that the first dip in the pool was hers. So while Nicki shed her clothes and slipped gingerly into the cool mountain water, the ex-SEAL busied himself and his thoughts with gathering wood to build a fire, trying hard not to think about Nicki skinny-dipping. When it was Sam's turn to clean up, Nicki opened some of the canned food they'd bought back in Globe and heated it over the fire. The hot food and cold water greatly reenergized them both, but Nicki's repeated attempts at conversation were met with either silence or single-word answers as Sam remained quiet, suddenly uncomfortable with being this alone now with Nicki. The clear moonlit sky and roaring campfire weren't helping.

"Well, Sam," Nicki said finally after ten minutes of listening only to the crackle of the fire and the night sounds drifting from the deep woods, "it seems like I've managed to tough it out this far."

Sam just nodded.

"Christ, Sam, those men would have raped and killed me. And not necessarily in that order!"

Nicki's spunky attempt at humor brought a smile back to Sam.

"You know, Nicki," he said thoughtfully, "I think you're a lot tougher than you give yourself credit for."

"What do you mean?" she objected. "I think I'm plenty tough!"

"No, you don't, and that's why you're always putting up the big act. You won't let yourself appear to be soft because you have no idea how tough you truly are."

Nicki did not wish to pursue that line of reasoning any further. "Well, Sam," she said, dismissing the subject, "I guess we'll find out soon enough."

"It was one of the things I loved about your brother, you know," Sam said, not letting it go.

"What was?"

"His big heart. As tough as he was, he never had the need to act it. He was always so kind with people, so open and up front. Within minutes of meeting you, no matter who you were, Mickey could draw you out of your shell and set you right at ease, make you feel right at home, like you'd known him all your life. You're the same way with people, Nicki. You just do your best to hide it is all."

"Oh, really?"

"Yeah. You try to cover it up by projecting that tomboy image of yours, but you've never really fooled me. You're just like Mickey, if you like someone, you're an open book."

"An open book, huh?" Nicki found herself somewhat flattered by Sam's obvious interest. "How so?"

Sam picked up a twig from beside the fire and drew a stick figure in the dirt.

"Everyone draws their line in the sand," he said, making a line about a foot away from his little man drawn in the dirt. "Most draw it way out here, you see, keeping things at a nice safe distance. Gives them more time and lots of room that way. No one gets too close. No surprises that way. Makes them feel as though they're in control."

"In control of what?"

"Their lives. But you believe that control doesn't really exist in this world. To you, it's just an illusion that people latch onto so they can sleep at night and continue to get out of bed in the morning with some sense of direction to their life. You believe in fate. You believe that what's meant to be will be. So you draw your line here." Sam drew a mark right next to the little stickman. "Like an open book you're an invitation to anyone who's interested, to step right up and flip through a couple of pages. 'Here I am you say, come an' see if there's anything in here that you like.'"

Sam paused to throw the twig in the fire.

"And you are this way by choice," he went on, "even though you know it's a lot tougher to go through life this way because, in relationships, it makes you…"

"Vulnerable?"

"Easier to get burnt," Sam agreed. "But your brother was so cool, so strong. He could walk that fine line and never worry about getting burnt. He just trusted in the truth, and in his own beliefs. You have that same strength in you, Nicki, you just don't quite believe it."

"I'm going to miss him so much," Nicki said sadly.

"Yeah, me too," Sam said as he stood.

At sixty-five hundred feet above sea level, the night air was cooling rapidly. Sam got another log and threw it on the fire, sitting back down a little closer to Nicki.

"What's going to happen to us, Sam?" she asked, sliding closer still.

"We are going to expose this thing, that's what."

"But how?"

"Tomorrow's the twenty-sixth, first day of deliveries. I've got a hunch that all the weapons that we saw listed on the microchip are sitting right down there, on the other side of this hill. In a couple of hours, I'm goin' in to find out for sure. If I can confirm that the bombs are all here, I'll find someone to move on it."

"Who, though?"

"I've got an idea or two."

"Tell me."

"No. You're better off the less you know."

"Always looking out for poor little Nicki," she said under her breath.

"Say again?"

"Do you think I'm vulnerable, Sam?" Nicki asked, leaning into him.

If able to measure its strength at that exact moment, the physical attraction between the two would have been off the charts. The chemistry had always been there for sure, for the both of them, they'd simply suppressed it over the years due to Mickey's impact on their relationship.

They were sitting very close now, as if to fend off the night chill. Sam could almost feel her breath on him as the fire warmed them, its orange glow dancing across their faces. Nicki leaned closer.

"Well, do you, Sam?" she persisted.

"Yeah, I do," he said, lost in the depth of her eyes. "It's one of the things I've always loved…ahh…I mean…liked about you."

Sam's pulse was racing, and he was sure Nicki could hear his heart pounding in his chest. *Mickey's kid sister,* he reminded himself one last time.

"Sam, remember that night at your cottage," Nicki asked, looking down at her finger tracing circles on Sam's thigh, "when you carried me back to my room?"

"I didn't mean to hurt you," Sam said quickly. "It…it wasn't an easy thing for me to do."

"Then why did you?"

"You were Mickey's little sister—"

"Sam, Mickey loved the both of us. Do you really think he would disapprove?"

"When you were eighteen, and I was twenty-seven? Yes."

"Well, I'm not eighteen anymore."

Sam opened his mouth to speak, but nothing came out. Nicki knew she'd have to help this poor man if things were to progress properly. She leaned over to kiss him, but Sam stopped her.

"You're not going to bite me on the nose again, are you?"

"Not on the nose," she said, smiling, and she kissed him gently on the lips. No longer of a mind to fight it, Sam kissed her back, softly at first, and then more deeply as their passion consumed them. Space and time seemed to cease as everything around them faded to obscurity. The two were lost in each other, swept away by the years of repressed desire that now flooded over them like a tidal wave of emotion. On and on they tumbled, cascading further and deeper into the depths of their lust, exploding as one in a final brilliant release, their bodies merely bearing witness to a love born of a much higher plane, as it always is, when soul mates come to find each other.

Afterward, they slept in each other's arms until it was time for Sam to get himself ready for his assault on the HAMTIN plant. Dressed in black with his face darkened, Sam kissed Nicki long and hard on the lips.

"Wait here until I come back for you," he said, knowing full well how things would never be the same. "I'll try to be back before dawn, but if I'm late, do not come looking for me. Understand?"

"Sam, I'm scared," Nicki said, holding tightly to Sam's hand. "What if you don't come back?"

"I will, Nicki, I promise. I could do this in my sleep."

"That's what I'm afraid of. Sam…"

"All right, remember this name. Ron Knight. He's the sheriff of Bonneville County up in Idaho. If I'm not back by dusk, make your way out of here as soon as it gets dark and head north. It's about a ten-hour drive from here. Find Ron and tell him everything you know, he'll help you."

Nicki threw her arms around Sam and squeezed for all she was worth. "You just come back to me, Sam Mason!"

"I will, Nicki. I always will."

He pulled away and kissed her on the forehead. Then armed with only a hunting knife, pencil flashlight, and a small spade, he disappeared into the dark woods.

*****

Mason found what he was looking for within ten minutes of hitting the fence line. From out of a pouch in his pants, he pulled a cluster of maple leaves he'd brought along for the occasion. He took the gum that he'd been chewing out of his mouth and stuck one of the larger leaves over the lens of a video camera mounted on top of the fence. The camera had been set to continuously pan this particular remote section of the grounds. Sam had dug under the fence about a hundred feet away and had already prepared a hiding place for himself. He knew the blackened video picture the security people were undoubtedly now seeing would probably be interpreted as a malfunction, calling for the night-shift supervisor to send someone immediately to investigate. Sam took up his hiding spot and waited.

Less than ten minutes later, he heard what sounded like a jeep approaching along the fence line. It stopped just under the camera.

"Just a fuckin' leaf," said a voice from the open vehicle.

"Pull up close to the fence, Dicky," a second voice ordered, "and I can get it from the hood. You call it in."

"Rover three to base," the first voice said. "Come in base."

"Go ahead, Rover three."

"We're at camera twenty-two. No malfunction, just a leaf caught on the lens. We'll clear it and finish the sweep before headin' in. Should be back in about forty-five minutes. Put a fresh pot on for us if you would."

"Roger that, Rover three."

Sam heard the jeep move forward a few feet, then a strained grunt as one of the security men climbed up onto the hood. The ex-SEAL rose silently out of his shallow grave no more than ten feet behind the jeep and its two unsuspecting passengers.

"Can you reach it?" the man behind the wheel said.

"Yeah, I got it. Hey, what the fuck!"

Having already sapped the driver with the heavy butt end of his knife, Sam swung his feet up over the hood and cut the feet out from under the man reaching up to clear the camera. The guard came down hard, hitting the back of his head on the side of the hood, crumbling to the ground in a heap. Mason quickly secured both men with a roll of duct tape he pulled from his pouch. He took both men's wallets, then stripped the uniform jacket and cap off the guard closest to his size and laid him up against the fence directly under the camera, out of its range of view. The other man he propped up in the passenger seat of the jeep. He looped a string around the wad of gum, and as he headed the jeep back down the fence line, he yanked the camera lens clear.

Driving back toward the facility, Sam went through the guards' jacket pockets and wallets. His luck was holding. In a front outside pocket, Sam found the security man's pass-card that would open the magnetic locks on the plant doors. The wallet told Sam the guard's name was Richard Marino, and he worked for HAMTIN security. The ex-SEAL had also taken both men's weapons—two Heckler & Koch USP .45-caliber automatics with ten-round magazines. The feel of the hard metal tucked into his waistband was some measure of comfort at least as he pulled up to the rear of the facility by the delivery bays.

Figuring he had less than an hour before the two guards would be missed, Mason tucked his unconscious passenger under the jeep, jumped up onto the loading platform, swiped the pass-card, and at three forty-five, Thursday morning, slipped into the rear of the HAMTIN plant completely undetected.

Chapter 34

Mason knew the basic layout of the facility from his visit to the plant's website. With nine floors in all, two above and seven below ground extending well into the base of the mountain, the facility was massive. The two floors above ground were administrative offices only and occupied the front two-thirds of the structure. The back third of the building was the shipping and receiving area. Two stories high, the extensive loading platforms and storage areas were now mostly empty.

Though Sam had taken a virtual tour of the plant and had committed what he'd learned to memory, he was confident that what he now searched for would not have been disclosed on the web or anywhere else for that matter. No, the secret lab that he expected to find would be well hidden in some remote corner of the facility, probably deep within the mountainside.

Alone in the huge loading area, Sam crouched low by the overhead bay doors. Opposite the doors, across the empty storage area, was a bank of five service elevators. The number five car had a bold sign posted above its doors that read AUTHORIZED PERSONNEL ONLY. The ex-SEAL crossed to the elevators, investigating each one in turn. The selection panel read the same in each of them. The top button was marked G, for ground level, the rest were marked in descending order, SL1 through SL7—sublevels one through seven.

Mason pulled one of the .45s from his waistband and pushed SL7 in service elevator number five. The big over and under doors closed with a thump, and the car started its descent into the Earth. As the elevator passed level six, the ex-SEAL dropped to one knee against the side of the big car and leveled his weapon at the center of the doors. The precaution proved to be unnecessary as the doors opened onto an empty, dimly lit hallway not much larger than the width of the service elevator. Directly in front of Sam was a locked steel security door. To his right, the corridor was interrupted by a firewall and a second security door. Sam tried the door across from the elevator first, swiping the pass-card through the reader. The door opened on hydraulics into a darkened room. With gun in hand, he entered the room crouched low, listening for a few moments before sweeping the empty room with his pencil flash. Satisfied he was alone, he hit the close button for the door, waiting for it to shut completely before flipping on the lights. Obviously, a machine shop, the large room was filled with tools and workbenches. The only item of interest to Sam was a single empty red metal canister measuring about eight by thirty inches.

A fire extinguisher? Perhaps not.

Mason left the room to try the corridor. He swiped the pass-card, and again the heavy steel door swung slowly open, this time onto an empty hallway that stretched as far as he could see, fading from sight in the dim lighting. Sam would have thought an operation of this size would have been on a 24-7 production schedule. He realized now that some downtime would be necessary to afford secrecy when needed, so this floor at least was deserted.

Sensing he was close, but with time running short, Sam started to doubt whether he had enough left to fully explore the entire level. He would need to get lucky.

Resigning himself to having to systematically search every room, Mason started through the doorway when suddenly the doors on elevator five started to close. The ex-SEAL whirled about at the first sound, pressing himself flat against the wall, his weapon drawn and aimed. Realizing what it was, he quickly moved next to the elevator, pressing against the service doors, listening. When the doors were fully shut, the car started to move. Downward!

One more level!

Sam knew this must be it. He took out his knife and pried open the outer service doors, and as the elevator stopped one floor below, he stepped onto the top of the empty car roof. Kneeling down, Sam lifted the access hatch just enough to peer into the empty car. He was in time to see two Chinese men dressed in lab coats carrying books and clipboards enter the elevator from a hallway below. One of the men produced a key and opened a small compartment next to the selection panel. He reached inside, apparently to push a button because the doors closed and the car started to move upward. The man closed and locked the little door, and he and his companion rode up to the ground floor, speaking to each other in rapid Chinese.

At ground level, the two scientists exited the service elevator, the doors remaining open. Sam waited, listening a few moments before dropping through the hatch and pressing SL7. As the car dropped, he used his knife to jimmy the lock on the little cubicle door to pry it open. Inside he found two unmarked buttons, one over the other. As soon as the car stopped at sublevel seven, Sam pressed the lower button, and the car dropped one last floor. He checked his watch. He'd been inside the plant for over a half hour now.

As the big service elevator stopped with a thud, Sam again dropped and aimed one of the .45s out the front of the car, again finding an empty hallway. This time, however, there was but a single door twenty feet directly across from him. Sam did not hesitate. With weapon in hand, he crossed to the door and swiped the card. As soon as the door opened wide enough, he somersaulted into the dark room, rolling to his knees just as all the lights in the room came on.

There, standing in plain view, flanked by two ninja guards holding automatic weapons, was Inspector Lee. Sam lowered his weapon but not because of the two men pointing machine guns at him. The hatchet-faced man held Nicki tightly beside him with a knife to her throat.

"We've been expecting you, Mr. Mason," Lee said coldly. He gestured to his left. "Looking for these?"

Stretching to the back of the large room, all neatly lined in row after row, stood hundreds of shiny new fire extinguishers, all tagged with the proper paperwork for delivery.

Pressing his blade tightly to Nicki's throat, there was no mistaking the tone of Lee's voice.

"Please place your weapon on the floor, Mr. Mason, stand up and turn around."

Sam did as he was told, and two technicians flanked by two armed guards moved next to him.

"Take them and search them," Lee commanded. "Though I doubt you will find anything. Mr. Mason has proven to be quite resourceful. Drug them and hold them separate until my plane is ready."

"Shall we do a full-body cavity search?" one of the scientists asked.

"No. I will do the interrogation and a more thorough search at the lodge. I am expected there by noon, Mr. Wong, so please instruct the mechanics to hurry my plane. Mr. Mason has me several hours behind schedule already."

*****

The next thing Sam would remember was the sensation of cold air flowing over his body. Gradually regaining consciousness, he thought he must surely be awakening from a dream once again—a dream of New England in winter, with its blowing snow and harsh, bitter winds.

Too cold, much too cold. Got to get up off this ice.

Slowly, Sam's eyes came to focus, and he saw that the silvery white beneath his face was not ice at all, but the metal flooring twelve inches from the opened side door of a jet plane in flight. The plane was flying at an altitude of ten thousand feet, as high as it could safely fly with an open fuselage.

"Ahh, Mr. Mason," Lee said loudly, "so good of you to join us."

Sitting on the far side of the plane, away from the frigid wind, the bogus FBI inspector smiled his evil grin, for this was the part the madman truly loved—watching the fear grow in his victim's eyes.

"I'm afraid the shivering you are experiencing is not completely due to the cold air," Lee said, motioning with his head to Nicki, who was beginning to stir just a few feet away from Sam. "It was necessary to give you both an injection of adrenaline to bring you out of your sleep. I did not want either of you to miss the view."

The hatchet-faced man was merely amusing himself by toying with his captives, softening them up for the real torture to come later.

Thanks to the effects of the stimulant, Sam's mind was very quickly coming clear. He could not determine exactly what type of plane they were in, but their situation, he quickly realized, was not good. Both he and Nicki lay head to head, facing out the opened hatch. Their hands and feet were bound behind them, and at least four men with automatic weapons watched over them. It soon got worse. Nicki came to full consciousness a moment later and realizing her predicament started to scream. In trying to roll away from the opened door, she ended up rolling back even closer and might have fallen right out had Lee not reacted quickly to grab her.

"Careful, Ms. Neally," he chided sarcastically, speaking at the top of his voice to be heard over the constant roar of the howling wind. "We do not want to lose you just yet."

"Sam!" Nicki called in distress, unable to see him behind her. "Oh God, Sam, where are you!"

"I'm here, Nicki!" Sam yelled. "I'm right here behind you."

"Yes, we are all here now," Lee said in a mock consoling tone. "Untie them!" he ordered harshly. "If he moves, kill her!"

Two of the guards slit the tape that held their feet and hands. One of the guards lifted Nicki off the floor. Sam got up on his own. They each had a machine gun pushed painfully into their ribs.

Suffering from vertigo, Nicki was in a near panic. Dizzy and disoriented, she swayed dangerously close to the cockpit door. Pleased by this, Lee decided it was Sam who now needed debilitating. He was curious to see how long it might take to unnerve this man who had cost him so much time and trouble. The hatchet-faced man was enjoying his plane ride immensely.

"Bring her to me," he ordered above the howling wind, and once again, Lee placed his blade against Nicki's throat. Glaring hatefully at Sam, he began his morning's entertainment.

"It won't work, Lee," Sam said defiantly.

"And what is that, Mr. Mason?"

"The bombs. Even if you manage to destroy our mainland, our forces abroad would retaliate."

"Retaliate at whom, Mr. Mason? There will be no evidence of an attack. Who will they blame?"

"They'll figure it right eventually, and when they do, our subs alone have enough firepower to annihilate half of Asia."

The hatchet-faced man threw his head back in amused laughter.

"Mr. Mason, did you think that there are no fire extinguishers aboard your submarines!" Lee tightened his hold on Nicki as the anger spread across Sam's face. "No, Mr. Mason," Lee explained. "There will be no retaliation. General Wu has a carefully planned coup in place, and once he is in power, his military forces will quickly mobilize to invade what is left of your decadent society! Now please," the madman said, his face darkening, "step a little closer to the door, Mr. Mason."

Sam held Lee's gaze and did as instructed. Unlike Nicki, however, the ex-Navy SEAL did not suffer from vertigo, quite the contrary. A veteran of over two hundred free-fall jumps in every conceivable condition, Sam was completely unaffected by the dizzying height. Battered by the force of the wind, he stood unwavering.

"Closer, please, Mr. Mason," Lee ordered, reminding Sam of the knife held at Nicki's throat.

Sam turned head-on into the wind blowing through the opened hatch, putting both hands out to brace himself against the plane's bulkhead. He knew Lee's game and was forced to play along, but as the ex-SEAL went through the motions, his brain was fast at work.

Mason knew Lee could not kill either Nicki or himself until the chip was found, but that was an eventual certainty. Dr. Wong had x-rayed Nicki's teeth, but not Sam's as the oral examination had revealed his teeth to be perfect, no cavities in which to hide the minuscule chip. The dentist Sam had visited in Phoenix had done a perfect job of bonding over the tiny drill hole, exactly matching Sam's natural tooth coloring, fooling the Chinese spy. The hatchet-faced man would not be so easily duped. Sam was well aware of the fate that awaited both he and Nicki once this madman got them to his hideaway. The ex-SEAL needed to come up with something fast, but at the moment, there seemed to be no way out—short of jumping out of the plane without a parachute.

"Now, Mr. Mason," Lee said wickedly, "take a last look at your countryside. You will not be seeing it again, I'm afraid."

Lee was determined to extract the desired effect from this man—this most troublesome adversary. He motioned for the guard nearest to Sam to prod him closer to the doorway.

With a machine gun pressed hard into his back, Sam was forced halfway out of the plane, his feet teetering on the doorway's edge, both hands holding tight to the fuselage above him. Sam fought back the rage building within him.

Stay cool, man. Be patient.

But for his SEAL training, Sam would not have been able to keep his focus, waiting things out for a possible escape opportunity. Forced to look down, he watched the land below as it crept slowly by, and something on the ground caught his eye.

Could that be the Snake?

Sam let a show of fear creep across his face as he continued to stare downward. The madman Lee said something in Chinese to his men, and they roared with laughter. Straining to make out the terrain below him, Sam paid them no mind, and seconds later, in the distance to the north and directly below their flight path, Sam's miracle came into view.

Yes! It is the Snake River, and those are the Lower Mesa Falls!

Sam knew it was the only way. Whether he made it or not, Lee could not kill Nicki without the chip. If he didn't make it, Sam knew that when his body was found, the autopsy that was certain to be performed had a chance at least of producing the microchip. If he stayed on the plane, there was no chance.

Lee's men continued to taunt Sam now, but he ignored them, keeping his eyes glued to the ground below, still giving the appearance of being overtaken by fear.

Mason knew well the ground beneath him, having studied it on maps before his hunting trips with Ron. He knew the lower falls were no good for what he planned—too shallow and rocky. But the

Upper Mesa Falls were much higher and steeper, falling into much deeper water.

Back in the SEALs, Sam and his buddies had once speculated that the only way a man could survive a free-fall with a failed chute would be to fall into broken water—such as is found at the base of a water fall. Mason had no option now but to test the theory.

Apparently having had enough entertainment, Lee stood and shouted an order at one of the guards.

No, not yet.

Mason needed several more seconds for the plane to fly closer to the upper falls. He'd have to stall. Lee motioned for one of the guards to pull the prisoner in. Sam resisted, pretending to be frozen with fear.

There they are! Just another few seconds now.

Lee repeated the order more forcefully. It was now or never.

Sam looked over his shoulder at Nicki standing horrified beside Lee.

"You stay alive no matter what!" he yelled to her, and then the ex-Navy SEAL stepped out of the plane and in a split second was gone before even Lee could react.

Chapter 35

Two hundred feet per second. Twelve thousand feet per minute. From ten thousand feet, Sam would plummet to Earth at well over one hundred miles per hour, landing in the river in a little more than forty-five seconds. From almost two miles up, he would need to hit an area no larger than fifty by twenty feet. Sam would need to call upon every ounce of skill and courage he'd ever known to pull this off.

Having left the plane a few seconds before he wanted, the ex-SEAL was south of the Upper Mesa Falls. Roughly three hundred feet from his target, the falls were still well within Sam's lateral range of movement. For every twenty feet a skydiver drops vertically, he was able to slip one foot horizontally in whatever direction he chooses, simply by shaping his body and changing his aerodynamics. Sam's first priority would be to fly himself directly over his target to allow enough time to check the alignment of his descent and make any last second adjustments. This would take the first thirty seconds of the fall.

If he were to survive, Sam knew he had to nail the splash-down. Just a few feet upstream and he'd land in less than six feet of raging water pouring over a solid rock cliff. He would break every bone in his body. Should he miss downstream in the lower riverbed by so much as an arm's length, he would hit flat water with much the same result. No, the ex-SEAL needed to fly directly into the heart of the overflow, entering the pool below together with the downflow of fifty thousand gallons of falling water.

The theory was that from a height of over one hundred feet, the weight of the falling water, continuously breaking the surface at the base of the falls, would penetrate deep into the pool, thereby minimizing the impact from Sam's fall, allowing for a much softer entry into the water—in effect, cushioning his landing. Enough he hoped to at least slow his hundred-twenty-mile-per-hour high-dive to a point he could survive.

Sam had two elements working in his favor. The lack of a cross-wind and a large abundance of water. It was a perfectly calm late-spring day with very little air movement in the lower levels of the atmosphere, allowing for a smoother and straighter descent. Also, the rivers were always swollen at this time of year by the waters feeding down from the melting snow-fields high in the mountains. The annual runoff this spring was exceptionally heavy, and the water flow over the falls would be at peak rates, creating the largest possible target and the greatest disruption of surface water.

These advantages, though helpful, seemed of little comfort to the ex-SEAL as he fell to Earth. He knew the jump had been his only option at the time; still, Sam did not want to die. Not now. There was too much to live for, and Nicki needed him, but he could not afford to think of her now, nor of the consequences should the landing go bad. Blocking out the fear and ignoring the cold, Sam focused his every molecule of brainpower on the falls below. He wished he had goggles. Without them, his eyes were stinging and tearing badly, forcing him to blink them tightly shut every few seconds. He briefly tried redirecting the airflow with his hands, but it inhibited his control over the descent, which he could not afford. He would just have to endure it.

Thirty seconds into the jump and more than halfway down, Sam was just coming over his target. The ground below looked to be rising at a snail's pace, and the falls still appeared to be nothing more than a growing white blotch in the middle of the river. Sam knew from experience that would soon change. He'd made many a jump that had required late pulls, under five hundred feet, and the ex-SEAL knew that in the last thousand feet of a fall, the Earth would race up at you like a runaway freight train. It was all a matter of relative distance.

Less than fifteen seconds from impact now and the ground below was starting it's run at Sam. His descent looked good and as best as he could tell he was directly over the center of the falling water. He'd better be, he thought, for he knew there was no margin for error. The ex-SEAL lay flat out in the standard pose of a skydiver in free fall. The best he could hope for would be to maintain his present line of flight until just over the falls. At the last second, Sam would try to jack-knife his body into a feetfirst dive. The timing would be critical. Too soon and he could waver offline. Too late and he would belly-flop into the pool below—probably fatally.

The water was charging up at him now. Ten seconds to splash down.

Remember to keep the knees flexed. Seven seconds. *Still online.* Five. *Wait.* Three. *Now!*

Like a cliff diver, Sam snapped his legs out beneath him, and crossing his arms over his chest with his fists tucked under his chin, he prayed the pool would be deep enough. The last memory Sam would have of the dive was flying past the top of the falls a split second before disappearing into the roar of fifty thousand gallons of gushing white water.

*****

Most of the kids in the tour group from Camp Wianno were getting restless. They wanted to see some animals, some bears and some moose, not some stupid waterfalls in the middle of nowhere. The tour was headed up north to Yellowstone National Park from Pocatello, Idaho. About a four-hour drive altogether, the Lower and Upper Mesa Falls were always an interesting diversion in the middle of the trip, nicely breaking the drive about in half. At least that's what Cory Lang thought.

Lang was Camp Wianno's senior counselor, activities director, field trip supervisor, and bus driver, all rolled into one, at least for this day. He was supposed to have help on these tours, but the female camp instructor had not showed, and the camp director insisted the tour leave on time. The parents had paid big bucks to send their kids to this camp, the director pointed out, and this tour was one of the advertised highlights. So with twenty-two preteens, ten to twelve years old to watch over by himself, the young instructor had been saddled with more than he cared to handle.

Next summer, I'm takin' that white-water rafting job, he said to himself as he started to round up the campers and head them back up to the bus.

The group had viewed the lower falls from a distance, stopping at a scenic overlook. The Upper Mesa Falls, however, offered a much more intimate viewing area. An extensive network of wooden catwalks had been built to that purpose, winding all the way down to the edge of the river and falls. All the walkways have railings on them, allowing tourists to stand and lean directly over the east edge of the falls to look straight down on the huge volumes of water flowing over the cliff—fifteen hundred cubic feet per second—967 million gallons per day. Less than one meter beneath the visitors' feet, the raging river suddenly shoots some twenty feet out beyond the cliff before dropping straight down, disappearing into a misty spray to crash down with a thunderous roar into the river pool 114 feet below.

In spite of the lone instructor's efforts to keep the group tight, the kids from camp Wianno had spread out all over the place. Exhibiting great patience, Cory managed to herd all but two of the group back up to the parking lot. As usual, Jimmy was missing, with his sister probably off looking for him. Leaving the rest of the group alone with orders to stay put in the bus, the young instructor headed back down to the river to look for the two stragglers.

Two minutes later, he came upon a cute, freckled-faced twelve-year-old girl walking up from the falls.

"Ashley, where's your brother?" Cory asked, clearly aggravated.

"I told him it was time to leave, Mr. Lang, but he wouldn't come. I hope the little creep falls in the river!"

"No, you don't," Cory corrected. "Come on, help me find him."

"Why me?" she complained. "I can't help it the little jerk is my brother!"

"He's not a jerk, Ashley. He's just a little boy, and little boys like to irritate little girls. Especially sisters. It's just a fact of life."

"Yeah, well, he's always screwin' up an' gettin' me in trouble!"

The two were at a point where the trail down to the falls split in two directions.

"It's okay, Ashley," Cory assured her. "You're not in trouble, just tell me where's the last place you saw him?"

"Leanin' over the falls."

"Oh, that's just great. All right, you go downriver, and I'll go up. The trails come out at the edge of the falls. We'll meet in the middle. If you find your brother, keep him with you. Okay?"

"Yeah, okay."

Most of the kids on the tour had shied away from the catwalk directly over the falls. The roar of the raging water was deafening, and that, coupled with the close proximity to the cliff, was enough to make even most adults step back in caution. But not Jimmy—he loved it. He was, in fact, standing on the lower railing and leaning out over the edge of the cliff, completely thrilled by the spectacle of it all. Alone at the brink of the falls, Jimmy was the only one who saw the man fall out of the sky, dead into the center of the waterfall a mere thirty feet away from him.

"Holy shit!" the young boy exclaimed, his eyes almost popping out of his head. He looked down into the spray but could see nothing through the mist. He looked quickly up, wondering where the man might have come from, but saw only blue sky.

"I know I saw him!" Jimmy cried out, and he jumped down from the railing and started to run along the catwalk, winding his way downriver. As fast as he could, the boy ran down from one level to the next, stopping every few seconds to stare into the white water a hundred feet below. The third time he stopped, he saw what looked like a body floating along the near side of the river, heading downstream toward the next set of falls. Jimmy ran down three more flights and, out of breath, stopped to search the river again from much closer this time.

"There he is!" he cried. "It is a man, I knew it!"

The young boy looked around, but there was no one in sight. Frantic, he started screaming for help.

Climbing her way up the walkway from downstream, Ashley heard the shouting. Knowing her brother's voice well, she knew right away the cries were genuine. Thinking he was in trouble, she started running up the catwalk as fast as she could, screaming back at him.

"Jimmy, I'm coming, Jimmy!"

Hearing the screams from below and downriver, the camp instructor also broke into a run toward the cries for help.

Ashley got to her brother first. The two had come together on one of the lower sections of walkway, about thirty feet above the river. "Jimmy, are you all right?" She cried, out of breath but relieved. "What's the matter?"

Never taking his eyes off the river, Jimmy ran right past his sister to the end of the catwalk. "There's a man in the river, Ash!" he yelled. "He fell into the waterfall! We have to save him!"

"What! Jimmy, if this is another one of your—"

"I'm not foolin', Ashley!" the young boy shouted, turning to run down the next flight of steps.

"Jimmy! Get back here, Jimmy!" Ashley took off after her brother, catching up with him as he climbed onto the last railing closest to the river, screaming and pointing.

"There he is! See him? He's right there, Ash!"

Reluctant to play along, something in her brother's voice convinced the young girl to look, and sure enough, there he was.

"Oh my God, Jimmy!"

"We've got to save him, Ash, before he goes over the other falls! Come on!"

"Jimmy, no!"

But she was too late. Her impetuous younger brother had climbed over the rail and dropped the remaining ten feet to the rocky riverbank below.

Running alongside the rushing water, Jimmy yelled back at his sister. "Go get Mr. Lang, Ash, hurry!"

The young girl stood undecided for a moment, then turned to run for help.

*****

Unconscious, Sam's body had popped to the surface near the east side of the river and had immediately been swept downstream. The force of the impact had collapsed his bent knees up into his chest, forcing most of the air from his lungs. The back of Sam's head had hit the water pretty hard during entry as well, knocking him out. His body had plunged over twenty feet to the bottom of the pool, but dragged up by the strong current, Sam had resurfaced, miraculously alive and floating face up.

Less than a hundred yards from the lower falls, Jimmy had managed to get far enough ahead of the man to stop and try to reach him as he came floating by. The man was only about twenty feet offshore now, and though the current was very fast, the water looked shallow enough along the river's edge. Jimmy waded in gingerly, holding on when he could to any protruding rocks. When he was in up to his thighs, he stopped, afraid to go out any further. Reaching as far as he could, the young boy just caught hold of a pant-leg as the body rushed by, but the current was too strong, and the weight of the body pulled Jimmy into the river. Letting go, the boy was barely able to grab hold of a rock and pull himself out of the water before he too was swept away.

Scared but with no thought of quit in him, Jimmy leaned over to catch his breath. Looking back downriver, he saw the man come to rest about fifty yards downstream, hung up on one of the fallen trees that occasionally jut out into the river. In a flash, the boy was on the run again. Wading out about twenty feet on the upstream side of the heavy fallen log, Jimmy reached the man in waist-deep water. With one hand holding tight to a tree branch and the other around the man's belt, the young boy held on for dear life, fighting to keep them both from being swept out into the river and over the lower falls a mere sixty yards downstream.

Less than a minute later, Ashley and Cory came running along the bank.

"Hold on, Jimmy!" Ashley yelled over the roar of the river as it sped over the lower falls. "We're coming!"

Without hesitation, the young camp instructor plunged into the river, splashing straight out to the boy.

Cory's immediate concern was to get the boy safely ashore, but as he pulled him from the water, he found that Jimmy would not release his grip on the unconscious stranger, and the man who fell from the sky was pulled safely to shore as well.

"Is he alive?" Jimmy asked, winded from his efforts.

Cory was kneeling over the man, his fingers on the man's neck, feeling for a pulse.

"Yes!" he said, starting CPR. "Thanks to you, kid!"

"Way to go, Jimmy-pie!" Ashley shouted, hugging her kid brother.

Half an hour later and still unconscious, Sam was loaded into the back of an ambulance and sped off to Rexford County Hospital.

Chapter 36

*T*he bear was closing fast. Sam could turn the corners of the cabin much tighter than the lumbering beast, lengthening his lead, but the big animal was much swifter on the straightaway, and the gap narrowed after each turn he made. If he could just get to the front door before the grizzly pounced on him, he could dive in and save Nicki. He could see her as he ran past the open windows, sitting alone in the middle of the big room, tied to a chair. He had to get to her before the bear got him, but after each turn he made around the big log cabin, there always seemed to be one more waiting ahead.

Sam could sense the bear coming up behind him again as he reached yet another corner. This would have to be the last, or the beast would catch him for sure! He swung himself around to the front of the building just as the grizzly went roaring past, his claws sliding in the dirt, digging for traction as he tried to turn. There was the door! But Sam felt like he was running in mud now, barely able to lift one foot in front of the other. Where did the mud come from? He was so close he could see Nicki through the opening, but he was moving so slow, and the bear was still coming! He could feel the beast was almost on top of him now, its hot breath scorching the back of his neck! Move, man, move! Not going to make it! He's rearing up to pounce!

"NICKI...!!"

*****

Betsy Olsen was the RN working the second shift at Rexford County Hospital. Sitting alone at the computer in the second-floor nursing station, she had just started to enter the data from her ten o'clock rounds when one of the monitor alarms started beeping, signaling with little red flashing lights that the patient in room 211 had come out of his coma.

The duty nurse lifted a phone and pressed a button. Downstairs in emergency, the attending physician picked up.

"Dr. McCampbell."

"Our swimmer's awake."

"He's conscious?"

"Don't know. Heart rate and BP just spiked. I'm going in to check him now."

"I'm on my way. Sheriff Knight still in with him?"

"Just went down for coffee."

"Get him up there now. I want a familiar face in the room if this guy's about to come around."

Dr. Bonnie McCampbell hung up the phone and turned to one of the interns. "Guy in 211 just woke up."

"You're shittin' me!"

"Fucking miracle he's even alive," she said, rushing out the door.

*****

Everything was fuzzy to Sam. He could hear voices talking, but he couldn't make out what they were saying. It hurt too much whenever he tried to open his eyes. Maybe he could try again in a few minutes.

Who is that, anyway? And why does he keep calling my name? What's so important that I need to get up right now?

"Nicki," Sam whispered.

"That's the same name he said when I first came in the room."

Nurse Olsen was standing next to Dr. McCampbell and Sheriff Knight. The three leaned anxiously over Sam's bed.

"Keep talking to him, Ron," the doctor said. "He's almost with us, and I don't want him to slip back again. Try to get him to open his eyes."

"Sam, it's Ron, Sam. What about Nicki, Sam? Open your eyes and tell me about Nicki. Come on, bro, talk to me."

With all the strength he could muster, Sam forced his eyes open. He could see shapes leaning over him, but they were too blurry to recognize. The lights were so bright they hurt his eyes.

"Sam, it's Ron, Sam. Tell me about Nicki."

Nicki! My God, Nicki's in trouble!

The amount of effort it took for Sam to turn his head was exhausting, but he managed to look at the image closest to him and bring it into focus.

"Ron," Sam said in a voice little more than a whisper. "Nicki's in trouble. I need your help, Ron. They killed Mickey."

"I'll take it from here," Dr. McCampbell interrupted, "nice job, Sheriff." She leaned over Sam, shining a light in one eye, then the next, checking for pupil dilation. "Welcome back to the living, Mr. Mason," she said as she worked. "How are you feeling?"

"Head hurts."

"I'm not surprised," the pretty doctor said, smiling. "You're lucky to be alive. That was quite a swim you went for, do you remember any of it?"

Sam's head was pounding worse than any tequila hangover he'd ever had, but his wits were steadily returning.

"Some. How long have I been out?" he asked, looking at Ron.

The sheriff looked at the doctor, who nodded.

"About ten hours," he said. "A couple of kids fished you out of the Snake River about noon. Ambulance brought you in here a little after one. Rooster...remember Rooster, Sam? One of my deputies? Flew us up to Coeur d' Alene to fish, last time you were out?"

Sam nodded once that he remembered.

"Rooster happened to be in emergency writing a report on a DUI when they brought you in. He recognized you right off and called me. Been here ever since. Feel like tellin' me about it?"

Sam looked at the doctor and nurse standing over him, then back at Ron.

"Ahh, Doc, honey," the sheriff said. "Do you think you could trust Mr. Mason to my care for a few minutes?"

"Five minutes, Ron," the doctor said firmly. "He's stabilizing nicely, and I don't want that to change. If what I've heard about his fall is true, it's a miracle he's come through with nothing more than a mild concussion and a couple of bruised ribs. He needs rest. Just to be safe, I'm going to keep him for twenty-four hours to run a few more tests. Then barring complications, he's all yours."

"Thanks, Bonnie."

The two hospital workers left the room leaving the two ex-SEALs alone.

"Doc, honey?" Sam said with a raised eyebrow.

"For someone who's supposed to be half-dead," Ron said, "you don't miss a trick. Yeah, ol' Bonnie and me got a little 'thing' together."

"She's got a nice smile."

"Yeah, and nipples you could hang a hat on. Now, you care to tell me what's up. One of the kids that pulled you out of the river swears you fell out of the sky into the upper Mesa falls. Anyone other than you, Sam, I'd have figured the kid was lying. Was he?"

"No. I jumped out of a plane."

"Your chute fail?"

"No chute."

Sheriff Knight leaned back in his chair.

"When you were comin' to," he said somberly, "you said they killed Mickey. Who's they, and what the hell's goin' on, Sam?"

"I'll tell you everything, Ron, but it's gonna take more than five minutes."

"Just let me worry about the doc. What happened to Mickey?"

Sam filled Knight in on the whole story. Twice Dr. McCampbell came in to shoo him out of the room, and twice the sheriff sent her away, the second time with a look that she knew meant she should not come in a third time.

"You still have your sniper rifle?" Sam asked when he'd finished the briefing.

"You bet," his old SEAL teammate said. "But don't you think we ought to call in reinforcements."

"We can't chance it, Ron. This Lee character has the clout to put a muzzle on the both of us. We've got barely over forty-eight hours till the satellite launch. We need to find Nicki first and get her someplace safe. So long as I've got the chip here in."

Sam stopped, his heart in his throat. Feeling his tooth where he'd had the microchip implanted, he found an empty pinhole.

"It's gone!"

"What is?"

"The microchip," Sam said. "It must have gotten knocked loose when I hit the water."

"Well, Sammy," Knight said as he stood, "looks like it's just you and me now for sure. It's your call, amigo."

"Okay, we go!" Sam said, lifting himself slowly to a sitting position. "You got a map of the Panhandle?"

"Sure, got one in the car. I'll get it. Anything else?"

"Just some food for now."

The sheriff returned five minutes later with a detailed map of the Idaho Panhandle.

"Bonnie says it's a good sign that you've got your appetite already. She's sendin' something up."

They spread the map out on Sam's bed and traced a line up from the HAMTIN plant, over the Snake River Falls, and on up into the Panhandle.

"They must have been headin' up to Lewiston," Ron guessed. "Or maybe Coeur d' Alene. Hell, Sam, they could have flown all the way up into Canada."

"No," Sam asserted. "They're in Idaho somewhere, and Lee's holding Nicki…"

The ex-SEAL paused as just then an image of Nicki tied to a chair in some big log cabin flashed in his head.

"In a hunting lodge!" Sam said with certainty. "We're looking for a camp where people hunt for grizzly bear, Ron. One with an airstrip. You got one of those up here?"

The sheriff stared at Sam in disbelief for a second, then put his finger on the map, directly on the line they'd just traced.

"The Grass Mountain Lodge!"

Chapter 37

S am and Ron had finalized their plan of attack by midnight, and less than six hours later, the two ex-Navy SEALs had worked their way through the forest above the Grass Mountain Lodge to a high ground overlooking the camp and airfield. Though both had agreed there was little time to waste, Ron had been insistent that Sam get a few more hours' rest. He'd be of little help, the sheriff pointed out, if he wasn't strong enough to make the jump and then the short hike through the heavy woods. Ron promised his ex-team leader he would gather all the equipment and weapons they would need and then come back for him at 4:00 a.m., along with Rooster to fly them up to Grass Mountain. Sam reluctantly agreed.

Sheriff Knight was true to his word, and by 0500 hours, the two had made their predawn jump. Now, thirty minutes later, a half mile from the lodge, Ron was busy sighting his sniper scope while Sam, fed, rested, and feeling stronger with each passing minute, made ready to infiltrate the enemy camp.

The plan was simple. Ron would cover Sam from a thousand yards away with his Barrett M82A1 .50-caliber sniper rifle. The rifle had been adopted by the military specifically for sniper work and, depending on the skill of the shooter, was deadly accurate to a range of up to two thousand yards. Other than the legendary Vietnam sniper codenamed White-Feather, Ron was the best Sam had ever seen or heard of. While most shooters needed to use a wind gauge and complicated formulas to determine the necessary adjustment for wind and drift, Ron could exactly calculate the correction needed in his head, sometimes by simply watching the trees or by gauging the amount of mirage refraction he saw through his four-power scope.

When looking through long distances of air through a high-powered scope, a mirage effect will appear, like blurred air rising off a hot roadway. Wind will influence the mirage, bending and shaping it to different degrees. Ron had a unique knack for interpreting both wind strength and direction from this distortion.

The Barrett M82, though exceptionally accurate from long distances, was not a silent weapon, so Ron would not take any shots until it was absolutely necessary. Sam, on the other hand, would be carrying a Heckler & Koch MP5, equipped with a laser sighting scope and fifty-round clip. Accurate to about seventy-five yards, the fully suppressed German-made gun was capable of single, semi-, or full-automatic fire and was designed specifically for close-in combat.

Sam would enter the lodge under cover of early morning darkness while hopefully, most inside were still sleeping. He would find Nicki and take her out, with Ron giving cover from afar. Sam and Nicki would then make their way to the airfield where Sam would steal a plane and fly Nicki and himself away. Ron would take out the tires of the other planes, then backtrack through the forest to the Salmon River, making his way downstream on the inflatable Zodiac raft they'd brought with them. Rooster would be waiting several miles downriver. Just a walk in the park for these two men.

Able to stay in communication with his teammate via radio headsets, Sam slipped silently through the trees to the edge of the woods above the lodge. Using his Bushnell night-vision glasses, Sam surveyed the area immediately surrounding the lodge.

"Four posted sentries," he said softly, relaying the information to Ron, over a half mile away. "Two strolling up and down the airstrip, watching over the planes, and two on the deck in front."

"I got 'em, amigo."

The end of the runway came within fifty yards of the big log cabin, and there were four planes parked on it, two Lear jets, a twin-engine Cessna, and a small Piper. Sam watched the guards for several minutes, trying to determine if they were in radio contact with each other. When one of the guards roaming the airstrip waved to his comrade on the lodge deck, Sam assumed not. That would be helpful. Though Lee had some pretty tight security in place for such a remote camp, it was by no means a military operation up here. Nor did it need to be. There would be no reason to expect any unwanted visit this far removed from civilization and surely not one from a man who had just fallen out of an airplane to his certain death.

Sam made his way through the woods to the rear of the building and found two more guards casually smoking cigarettes by a back entrance. He did a quick sweep of the forest around him. Satisfied these two were the only sentries out back, he decided to take them out. Two less to have to deal with later.

"I've got two targets at the back door," Sam said softly into his headset. "I'm thinking I should take them out now."

"Affirmative, Sammy. The less the better."

"Roger that. I will go in, and hopefully out, through the front door. You let me know when the two goons on the airstrip are about halfway to the end and headed away from me, and I'll snuff the two on the front deck."

"You got that Sammy but be quick in there. If I have to take a shot, the whole forest is gonna know we're here."

Sam waited until the men finished smoking their cigarettes and separated. Then, unable to determine whether they were wearing body armor or not, he shot them both in the head, the only sound made being that of the bodies hitting the ground. The ex-SEAL then edged along the far side of the lodge, away from the airstrip, up to the front of the big log cabin, and waited for the okay from Ron. The second he got it, he shot both sentries out front the same way, then slid unseen through the front door.

Inside, Sam found a two-story cathedral parlor in the center of which was a huge stone fireplace surrounded by a scattering of sofas and reclining chairs. On the front wall across from the big fireplace was a massive two-story window overlooking the airfield and the river beyond. To the left of the great hearth was a wide stairway up to a second-story balcony. In the center of the balcony was a hallway that Sam suspected would lead to the guest bedrooms. Nicki should be in one of them.

Wasting no time, Sam crossed the big empty room and moved silently up the stairs to the head of the hallway. The first early morning light was starting to brighten the sky to the east, and Sam knew there was not much time left before the whole place would be waking.

Peering carefully around the corner of the hall, Sam spied a solitary guard sitting at the end of the corridor, facing down the length of the hallway, watching over the last door on the right of the hallway. The door was padlocked. The man was reading. From a prone position, the ex-SEAL put the little red dot from his laser sight between the base of the man's nose and his upper lip and pulled the trigger. The guard slumped quietly dead in his chair. Sam slipped down the hallway, and taking a small pair of hydraulic cutters from his belt, he cut the padlock off the door, slipped inside, and placed his hand over the mouth of a sleeping Nicki. The young girl's eyes popped open with a fright, her expression turning slowly from fear to disbelief, then to pure joy as she came to realize that it truly was Sam kneeling beside her and not some ghostly apparition from a wishful dream.

Sam shook his head before taking his hand from Nicki's mouth.

"Oh, Sam!" she whispered, throwing her arms around his neck. "I thought you were dead. How? How are you here? How did you find me?"

"Later," he whispered back. "Are you all right?"

"Yes, I think. They drugged me, that much I know. Then I woke up here. Sam, I have no idea what I might have told them while I was under."

"It doesn't matter now, babe."

"Sam," Nicki said, squeezing him tight. "I was so scared!"

Sam let her hold on as long as he could. "Come on," he said, helping her up. "Time to check out."

With Nicki close behind him, Sam led them quickly down the hallway, stopping at the top of the stairs to carefully scan the big room below. It looked empty.

"You still with me, Ronny?" Sam whispered into his headset.

"Me and the .50-cal, bro," the sheriff said softly. "But our two friends on the runway are headed back your way. What's your situation, Sammy?"

"I've got Nicki. I'm takin' her out the front in about ten seconds. We'll be coming fast, Ron. As soon as you see us come through the door, take out the two by the planes. And we'd appreciate it, Ronny, if you'd discourage any of their pals from following after us."

"No problem, amigo. I could use the target practice."

"Roger that. We're on our way."

Sam took Nicki by the hand, and the two ran down the stairs and started across the big room where two ninjas jumped them from under the stairway. One of them grabbed Nicki and, with an Uzi machine pistol jammed into her throat, dragged her across the room away from Sam, holding her by the big window. The other had jumped Sam from behind, looping a strangle wire around his throat. Sam threw the smaller man over his shoulder, dropping on him hard with a knee to the man's solar plexus. He put the barrel of his MP5 under the ninja's chin in a standoff with the man holding Nicki.

"Trouble, Ron!"

"I see it, bro."

"Have you got him!"

"I got him, but he's too close to Nicki, Sam. Can't risk the deflection through the glass."

"Mr. Mason! Like a cat, you seem to have many lives."

Wearing only a pair of baby-blue boxer briefs, the hatchet-faced man walked boldly down the stairs, his half-naked body ripped with sinewy muscle. Seemingly unimpressed by Sam's apparent return from the dead, Lee carried a pistol loosely by his side.

"I will enjoy taking all of them," he said, stopping midway down the staircase.

"Inspector Lee," Sam said, pressing the MP5 more tightly to the throat of his prisoner, "what pretty shorts."

With that, Lee could no longer contain his hatred, and he suddenly lifted his weapon to shoot, but Sam was quicker, diving and rolling behind one of the couches, shooting out the big window as he rolled, yelling at Nicki to duck.

The man holding Nicki instinctively turned away from the shattering glass, exposing his silhouette to Ron. From a thousand yards away, the sniper sighted what is referred to as the no-flinch zone. Ron put his crosshairs just above the man's left ear and took the shot. The .50-caliber BMG bullet flew clean through the shattered window blowing off the top off the man's spinal column, allowing for no reflex pulling of the trigger.

Mason popped up from behind the couch, spraying gunfire across the room and yelling at Nicki to run. He shot the ninja he'd left lying on the floor, but Lee had ducked out of sight. Backing out of the room, the ex-SEAL continued to spray fire as he grabbed Nicki and shoved her out the door.

Immediately after Ron saw his shot hit the mark, he turned his sights on the two guards on the airstrip who had started running toward the gunfire coming from the lodge. He took them down with two quick shots, then turned his scope back to the front door of the lodge in time to see, to his great relief, Sam and Nicki come through it and head for the runway. Two men came through the doorway seconds after them, one dropping to his knees to take aim. Ron shot him, then quickly lifted the Barrett to sight the second man when, through his scope, he saw the face of the man staring straight up at him, a face of evil unlike any he'd ever seen. He hesitated a split second before squeezing off the shot, allowing the man to duck back into the doorway, the bullet crashing harmlessly into the face of the building.

Ron heard the sound of engines starting on the airstrip a few seconds later, and as Sam headed the twin-engine Cessna down the runway, the sniper took out the tires on the remaining planes one at a time. Some small-arms fire started up at him from the lodge below, but he was well out of their range.

"Time to go," he said to the empty forest around him.

As the Cessna lifted off at the far end of the runway, Ron stood and hefted his weapon, watching the plane turn to fly over him, wagging its wings as it passed overhead.

"Good luck, amigo," he said, waving back. Then he turned and headed for the river.

In the Cessna, Mason climbed to five hundred feet. He knew Lee could still bring forces to bear, forcing Sam to fly low in order to stay under any radar that might try to track him. He headed the plane southwest and checked his fuel. The Cessna's tanks were full, but at this altitude, she would burn fuel much faster than normal.

Sam checked the flight manual. The plane's optimum range was twelve hundred miles. It was going to be close.

Nicki's nerves were shot. Too tired to be afraid anymore, she asked, "Where to now, Sam?"

"Right now, there's more good guys chasing us than bad guys."

"Yeah, so?"

"So when you want to hide out from the good guys, you need to find some bad guys of your own."

"Sam, what the fuck are you talking about!"

"The mob, Nicki!" Sam said with determination. "We're headed to Las Vegas!"

Chapter 38

Special Agent Richard Larsen was excited to make the call. He'd been embarrassed at Dulles in his last encounter with the FBI's chief investigator, and this was a second chance for him to make points with the bureau's top man.

Inspector Lee had called the Washington office two hours earlier, requesting information concerning the suspected terrorist bomber. Lee wanted the phone records from anywhere the bureau was able to place Mason during his stay in DC. Larsen was one of the investigators to draw the assignment, and the young agent intended to make the best of it. Larsen was able to trace Sam's credit card to the Four Seasons Hotel and acquire a list of six numbers called from his room.

"Special Agent Larsen," Lee said, his voice totally devoid of emotion. "This is Chief Investigator George Lee. You have the information I requested?"

"Yes, sir. And may I say that it's an honor to be working with you again, Inspector. We met at the terminal in Dulles International, the night..."

"The information, Agent Larsen. Now please."

"Ahh...yes, of course, sir. Mason made calls to six numbers, some more than once."

"I am only interested in the destinations of the calls."

"Three local numbers and three out of state, sir."

Inspector Lee was on his cell phone, standing at the far end of the runway outside the Grass Mountain Lodge. A state police chopper was inbound from Lewiston to pick him up, but by the time the FBI man would get to faster transportation, Mason would have at least a three-hour lead on him, and as yet Lee had no knowledge of where his prey might be headed. He was anxious and running out of patience.

"Just the out of state numbers, please," Lee said, controlling his anger.

"Mason called his publisher in New York," Larsen said, reading from his notes. "A Ms. Irene Leslie-Taylor. We tried contacting her, but the people in her office say she is presently traveling abroad with her niece, a Miss Keri Starr."

"Not what I am looking for. What else do you have, Agent Larsen?"

"Mason also called the sheriff's office in Bonneville County, Idaho, sir." The young agent had done some follow up with the out-of-state police department, and he wanted to be sure the inspector knew about it.

"I contacted the sheriff's office myself, sir, and talked to the deputy sheriff. Sheriff Knight was unavailable, and when no one seemed to know of his whereabouts, I ran a check on him. It seems Sheriff Ronald Knight and Mason served in the Navy together, Inspector. Navy SEALs. For three years, they were assigned to the same special operations unit. Mason was a squadron leader, and Knight was…"

"A sniper."

"Ahh…yes, sir. How did you know?"

Lee ignored the question. "Call our Boise office," he said. "I want Sheriff Knight, and anyone found with him picked up immediately and held in isolation for questioning. Do you think you can handle that, Agent Larsen?"

"Absolutely, sir!"

Inspector Lee whirled about suddenly as the rhythmic, beating sound of a helicopter's rotor blades came floating across the tarmac from some distance downriver. Lee turned away from the approaching clamor so as to be better heard.

"Agent Larsen," he shouted into the phone, "to where was the last call placed?"

"Caesar's Palace Casino Hotel, sir. In Las Vegas."

*****

The stress of flying at very low altitude for an extended period of time is similar to driving in heavy traffic, in a fog, at a hundred and sixty miles an hour. Things can come at you seemingly out of nowhere, allowing no time to relax. For over five hours now, Sam had kept his eyes glued to the onrushing landscape, following the contour of the land as he headed the Cessna south to Las Vegas.

After their escape from the lodge, Nicki had given Sam an account of her ordeal as best as she could remember it. She had been drugged for a good part of the time, and her memory was sketchy and unclear. She was unsure if some of the events her mind was try-ing to recall were real or imagined.

"I remember thinking," she said pensively, "that there were a lot of people coming and going…a lot of bustling around."

Nicki thought hard for a moment, trying to place herself back in her captive state. "It seemed to me there was some kind of meeting being held."

"What makes you think that?" Sam asked.

"Well, there were a lot of voices coming from the big room below, you know, like the babble of a large crowd, and then the noise suddenly went quiet and—"

Again, Nicki paused to search the fog that clouded her memory.

"That voice!" she said, remembering. "I know that voice! Or I thought I did at the time—"

"Whose voice? Inspector Lee?"

"No. Well, yes, he was there too. But there was another man's voice. A voice I know, or I've heard on TV or something. Shit! I'm sorry, Sam, I can't remember it."

"But you thought, at the time, you knew it?"

"I think so. I was drifting in and out of consciousness. I'm sorry, Sam, it just won't come to me."

"Well, how many times did you hear this voice?" Sam was try-ing to jog Nicki's memory. "Once? Twice? Was it male or female? Did you hear it in conversation? What did the voice say?"

"It was male, and I couldn't really make out the words," Nicki said, remembering something, "but I recall thinking…this man was important…because everyone was listening to him! That's right, he spoke to the whole group. I remember now! It was like a lecture. Or a rally. Everyone cheered at the end!"

"A victory speech," Sam said. "A pep talk for the troops and last-minute instructions for the aftermath."

"I think your right, Sam, because afterward I heard the voice talking alone in the hallway with that Lee character. Yes, I think he was giving Lee orders. Sam, I think he was Lee's boss!"

"Can you remember the voice, Nicki? Try to recognize that voice!"

"I can't, Sam. I don't think I ever actually recognized it. I just know I thought at the time that it sounded familiar, like I'd heard it before. I'm sorry."

"It's okay, babe, maybe it will come to you later. Why don't you try to get some rest while you can."

"I'd like to, Sam, but first tell me why it is you think you can trust this mob friend of yours in Vegas. What's his name again?"

"Jack Stavros."

"Yeah, Jack...Stavros? Christ, Sam, he's not even Italian!"

"Trust me, he's connected. All the way to the top. And I can't tell you how I know I can trust him, I just know.

"Sam, how can you 'just know'?"

"How is it that you know you can trust me?"

"That's different!"

"How so?"

"I know you."

"I know, Jack."

"But not like I know you," Nicki teased.

"True. But I know him well enough. And you are just going to have to trust me on that one."

"Christ, Sam. The fucking mob!"

"They played an important part in this thing, Nicki. Your brother knew it, and that's what led him to China. The Tong and the Mafia were working together, to some capacity at least, but I'm betting the wise guys are in the dark about the bombs."

"What makes you think they don't know?"

Sam hesitated. "Because that's how I would have written it."

"Your story...."

Nicki turned sideways to look at Sam, squinting her eyes.

"How much of this had you imagined, Sam?"

"Too much. Too much for it all to be coincidence."

"How else can you explain it then?"

"I can't. And I honestly don't know what to think about that."

Nicki took Sam by the hand. "You really see this mob guy helping us?"

"Yeah. Jack and his friends will be able to keep us hidden for a while, and we certainly won't have to worry about them turning us over to the police. I'll be able to find out from Jack just how much the wise guys know about what their Chinese friends have been up to. Anyway, who else can we trust?"

"I don't know, Sam, but...talk about a leap of faith."

Six hours into the flight, Sam realized they weren't going to make it. At least not to an airfield, not unless one miraculously appeared in the middle of the Nevada desert. The combination of flying through heavier air while having to wind their way around the mountains by following the river valleys had burned through fuel far too fast. As best as Sam could figure it, they would come up about a hundred and fifty miles short of Glitter City. The ex-SEAL would keep the twin-engine plane low for as long as he dared, then he'd have to risk climbing to a few thousand feet. He would need the altitude for glide time and distance once the tanks ran dry. Running out of gas at five hundred feet left no options other than straight down. From three or four thousand feet, Sam would have time to glide the plane to a suitable emergency landing site.

Nicki was not going to be happy.

When the warning light on the reserve fuel tank started to flash, Sam started the plane on a gradual climb. He reached over to gently shake Nicki awake.

"Have a nice rest?" he asked as she opened her eyes.

"Yeah, thanks," she said, sitting up and peering out her window at the barren landscape below. "Where the hell are we, Sam?"

"Over the Nevada desert, about a hundred and fifty miles north of the city."

"Hey, are we...yes, we're climbing! Sam, why are you climbing? I thought we needed to stay under..."

Nicki fell quiet when she noticed the flashing red light on the fuel indicator panel.

"Pull your seat belt as tight as you can," Sam said, seemingly without worry, "and start looking around for a nice level place to land. An old dirt road would be nice."

"An old dirt road would be nice!" Nicki glared at Sam in shocked disbelief. "No, Sam, a fucking runway would be nice!"

"Sorry, I was hoping to make it to the outskirts of the city where I could have put us down on some private strip, but..."

Sam nodded at the flashing light.

"So why are you taking us higher? You want to make a bigger hole in the ground!"

Sam suppressed a smile. "Just look for someplace that suits you, and I'll put us there. Make it quick, though, and make it close, we've only got a few minutes fuel left."

"Jesus H. Christ, Sam!" Nicki exclaimed as she pulled her seat belt snug. "What next?"

"You don't want to know."

Sam got the Cessna up to thirty-eight hundred feet where, one after the other, both engines suddenly sputtered and quit. The sudden quiet was eerie, underscoring the gravity of their situation. The silence took Nicki by surprise, and she realized, in a moment of serene contemplation, the possibility of her imminent death.

"Oh, fuck!"

"We're okay, Nick," Sam reassured. "I can see pavement about ten miles ahead. We won't be able to reach it, but there's some kind of an access road running off it to the northwest. I think I can get us down there."

"You think?"

"Yeah. Piece of cake."

The landing would not be near as simple as Sam had alluded. Though the dirt road was plenty long enough, it led into the foot-hills and mountains now passing under their right wing. There the road quickly turned to the right and then up, winding through a rocky pass. Sam could not risk dropping down over the mountains where he might suddenly run out of altitude. He would have to try to glide far enough past the hills, then bank almost 180 degrees back to set the Cessna down on the narrow stretch of dirt, hopefully having given himself enough runway. His main concern was that if he tried to stretch his glide too far from the hills, he wouldn't have enough altitude left to make the turn back to the road, leaving himself no choice other than to put down on the desert floor, which, though it looked flat from high above, was a maze of ruts and gorges. Should they hit one of the rock outcroppings that littered the landscape, the plane's fuselage, as well as he and Nicki, would be torn to shreds. The ex-SEAL would get only one chance to do it right.

Gliding a plane not meant to fly without power is a delicate balancing act. One needs to maintain enough airspeed to create lift, and without power from an engine, the only way to do that is by pointing the plane down. Too steep and she'll go into an irrecoverable dive. Too shallow and she'll lose lift, and again, straight down she goes.

The twin-engine plane they were in was much heavier than Sam's own single-engine Cessna and the glide path was a bit steeper, but that didn't worry Sam. The ex-SEAL knew most emergency landings went bad because the pilot overshot the landing area. This common mistake made by the inexperienced flyer is caused by a natural fear of sacrificing altitude, knowing there is no power available to regain it. Consequently, the plane comes in too high, ending up more often than not in the trees or rocks beyond the clearing. Sam would not make that mistake. His challenge would simply be to create enough runway for himself and then to get to it.

With his flaps three-quarters in, Sam had the Cessna into a comfortable, fast glide path, trying to make some distance. At a thousand feet, he put in full flaps, and easing her back slightly to slow their descent, he started a shallow bank toward the road a half mile to the west. Nicki's knuckles were white from squeezing the bottom of her seat as ever so slowly the heavy plane turned silently toward the long stretch of dirt. Somewhat mesmerized by the quiet stillness, it almost seemed to Nicki as though the plane, with her and Sam in it, was holding fast while the road and the world below turned to meet them.

"Sam," she said, coming out of her funk, "don't you think you ought to put the landing gear down now?"

"Can't use the landing gear."

"No? Why not!"

"The increased drag will slow us down, cause us to lose altitude too fast. And the road's too rough. Could cause a wheel to collapse and send us spinning into the rocks."

"Fucking wonderful."

"Besides," Sam said without thinking. "She'll stop much quicker on her belly."

"Stop much quicker? Why? Why do we need to stop much quicker!"

Realizing he'd said too much already, Sam turned his attention back to his flying as they passed five hundred feet with an eighth of a mile still to go before coming over their makeshift runway. He knew he'd cut it very close.

"Almost there," he said as though he were driving the family car home from a long trip. "Make sure your straps are as tight as you can get them, it's going to get bumpy and very loud in a few seconds."

"Loud don't bother me," Nicki said stiffly. "How bumpy?"

She found out a moment later as the Cessna finally came level over the road and, after aligning her to the end of their runway, Sam pulled back lightly on the stick, dropping the plane the last ten feet to the ground. He hadn't lied. The scraping noise of the fuselage grinding over the dirt and stone road reverberated throughout the thin metal cabin like a tin drum. The sound of the metal underbelly tearing was much worse than the actual damage being done, though Nicki didn't know that. The plane bounced once for a brief second, then continued its violent slide down the narrow path, shaking and shuttering all the way, and though Sam had slowed the Cessna as much as he dared before putting her down, their airspeed at touch-down was still over seventy miles per hour. The rocks ahead were coming up fast.

"Hold on!" Sam yelled above the screech of metal against rock as they both braced themselves for impact.

With feet pressing on imaginary brakes, Nicki was desperately trying to will the plane to a stop as the rocks ahead raced at them.

"Stop, damn it! Stop, stop, stop!" she screamed, ordering the plane to obey her. Miraculously it did as all at once the plane lost momentum and their slide ground to a sudden halt.

The two sat momentarily frozen, together once again in a sudden quiet, coming to terms with their apparent, if only temporary, safety. As they slowly relaxed from their braced positions and the tension flowed from their bodies, Nicki turned to Sam. She tilted her head, squinted her eyes, and smiled a fake smile.

"I don't *ever* want to do that again!"

Chapter 39

"Like I said before, Sam, you really know how to show a girl a good time."

Sam and Nicki were trudging through the desert on foot, heading for the paved road Sam had seen just before they ditched.

"At least it's never boring."

"No, that's true, Sam. Never boring. Weird, terrifying, and life-threatening but never boring."

Sam figured they had about five or six miles to cover on the dirt road before they'd hit the highway, if that's what it was. About a two and a half hour walk in the desert heat. He'd left the MP5 in the plane, knowing the automatic weapon would be far too conspicuous to carry in public. He did, however, take along the SIG 220 .45-caliber pistol Ron had provided along with two extra seven-round clips.

"It could be worse," he said.

"How in God's name could it possibly be worse, Sam?"

"Well, at least we have some water from the emergency kit, and the worst heat of the day is almost past. It should start cooling down over the next couple of hours."

"Sam, it's like a hundred and fucking thirty out here! What's it going to cool down to? A hundred and fucking ten!"

"And," Sam said, ignoring her mood, "there's no snakes."

Nicki stopped dead in her tracks.

"What d'ya mean!" she said. "What snakes!"

Sam stopped a few feet past her.

"This is rattlesnake country," he said, turning back to her. "You probably want to stay on the road and watch your step."

Glancing nervously at the ground around her feet, Nicki quickly moved to the center of the road.

"Damn it, Sam, you could have warned me!"

"Didn't want to alarm you unnecessarily," he said honestly, walking a couple of steps back to where she stood. "I take it you don't like snakes?"

"And I suppose you do?" she said, still looking at the ground.

"Not particularly, but they don't really bother me either."

Sam put his fingertips on Nicki's cheeks and gently pulled her head up to look at him.

"It'll be okay, babe," the ex-SEAL said, his eyes smiling down at her. "Just stay right behind me, and we'll be on the highway before you know it."

Nicki looked up into Sam's eyes, then threw her arms around his neck and kissed him long and hard on the lips.

"Anything else I should know about?" she asked after the kiss.

Sam took her by the hand and started walking, pulling her lightly behind him. "Yeah," he said over his shoulder. "We have to steal a car."

Nicki looked to the heavens.

"Lord, let the good times keep a-rollin'!"

Four hours later, as the sun was starting its long drop down to the western horizon, Sam and Nicki were a little more than an hour north of Las Vegas, cruising down Route 93 in the front of a brand-new El Dorado they had stolen from a mall parking lot.

The pavement Sam had seen from the air had turned out to be a secondary road running from the Humboldt National Forest to the town of Ash Springs, Nevada. They had made it to the lightly traveled road without encountering a single rattler, much to Nicki's relief, and within twenty minutes, had managed to flag down the first pickup that came by. Some ranger's kid running errands had stopped, happy for some company on his ride into Ash Springs. The teenager was only mildly curious about the military camouflage Sam still wore, the getup apparently not all that uncommon in those parts.

Sam had the boy take them to the closest mall, dropping them at the back entrance where the first thing they did was to buy clean new outfits. They changed and cleaned up as best they could in one of the mall's public bathrooms, then they walked to a grocery store where they waited by the entrance. When a silver-haired little old lady parked her shiny new Cadillac in one of the handicap spots right in front, they knew they had their mark. They followed the elderly woman into the store, and at the right moment, Nicki distracted the unknowing victim while Sam lifted her purse from the cart. He took only her car keys and replaced the purse. The poor woman would not miss them until she finished her shopping almost an hour later.

*****

Inspector George Lee decided not to return the phone call to his boss, FBI Director Leroy Harrison. This man Mason's relentless interference had indeed threatened the sanctity of the operation Lee had been entrusted to protect, but worse still, it had frustrated and embarrassed the Korean madman, triggering his bloodthirst. Sam's resilience and allusiveness stung, unlike anything Lee had ever encountered, driving the killer to an irrational state of mind. The hatchet-faced man was consumed with anger and hatred for the ex-SEAL, and those long suppressed, deeply hidden workings of the psychopathic killer mind had surfaced once again. It was personal now, and Lee would not rest until he tasted Sam's blood.

On impulse, the madman made a critical mistake, choosing to forsake the FBI and all the forces the bureau could have placed at his disposal, opting instead to use his Asian hit squads to find and eliminate the American thorn in his side. Putting all his eggs in one basket, the hatchet-faced man gambled on Caesar's Palace as Sam's destination and ordered his teams of killers to take up positions in and around the casino with himself directing the hunt.

*****

Making great time in their new ride, Sam and Nicki were headed straight into Lee's trap. It was barely a half hour after sunset as they started their slow drive up the glittering, pulsating spectacle that is the Las Vegas strip. Ignoring the distraction of a million brilliant lights, Sam sighted the Palace and immediately pulled off the busy street to ditch the car in the parking garage of the Bali, one of the massive neighboring casino-hotels. Here he used a payphone by the garage elevators to give Jack a heads-up call. Sam's mob friend was again working the casino floor, so saying as little as possible over the phone, Sam arranged for Jack to meet Nicki and himself just outside Caesar's front entrance in ten minutes.

The garage elevators opened onto a lobby that was both an entrance to Bali's and the entrance to the pedestrian bridge crossing over the strip. Fully enclosed in a plexiglass tunnel, the bridge spanned about 150 yards of sidewalks and courtyards as well as six-plus lanes of constant heavy traffic, allowing tourists to pass comfortably over the busy street, making for easy access to casinos and hotels on either side.

As Sam and Nicki made their way through the long glass tube, Sam slowed his pace as he approached the midway point, a distant ringing starting in his head.

"What is it, Sam?" Nicki asked, sensing his uneasiness. "Why are you stopping?"

"Something's wrong. This doesn't feel right."

"What doesn't feel right?"

"This," Sam said, stopping completely and pulling Nicki to the side of the tunnel, out of the flow of traffic. "It's all been too easy."

"Too easy! You call the past five days easy!"

Sam didn't hear her. He stood dead still, blankly staring through the glass into the distance.

"This is not how I'd envisioned it," he said finally. "There should be trouble."

"Trouble? What kind of trouble?" Nicki asked, afraid to hear the answer. "What exactly *did* you see, Sam?"

"Sunglasses."

"Say again, Sam. Did you say sunglasses?"

"Yes. Men wearing sunglasses and long coats to hide their weapons."

Nicki's mouth opened as if to speak and then froze. She nodded over Sam's shoulder in the direction they had been heading.

"You mean like them!"

Mason spun to see two Asian men sporting Wayfarers and trench coats entering the far end of the tunnel and heading purposefully in their direction. Sam immediately started Nicki moving back up the tunnel only to find their retreat blocked by an identical set of killers. Sam glanced back and forth from one end of the long tube to the other, realizing there was no escape in either direction.

Steadily closing in, the men in the dark glasses were reaching under their long coats as Sam looked frantically out both sides of the glass tunnel, scanning the ground below. All at once, he grabbed Nicki and dragged her back across the twenty-foot width of the bridge. He pulled the .45 out of his waistband and yelled for the people around him to get down. The plexiglass tube was rainproof and windproof, but there was no reason for it to be bulletproof. The ex-SEAL put seven rapid shots through the thin plastic, then dragging Nicki by the hand, sprinted across the tunnel as both pairs of killers pulled their weapons from under their coats. Sam lowered his shoulder, busting clean though the shattered glass, he and Nicki falling a mere four feet onto the top of a slow passing eighteen-wheeler. As Sam and Nicki scampered forward to the truck's cab, all four of their stalkers ran to the jagged opening in an effort to get off a burst of fire from their Uzi machine pistols. Sam fed a new clip into the .45 and emptied it at them, all four diving to the floor for cover. When Sam jumped onto the truck's cab, the driver immediately pulled to a stop to see what the hell was going on. Nicki followed suit, and the two climbed down off the big rig. Dodging traffic, they ran straight across the strip to the front doors of Caesar's Palace.

Slowing to a brisk walk, Sam slid his last clip into the .45, then tucked it back into his waistband just before passing through the entrance. He glanced back at the overpass in time to see all four hit men reach the end of the tube and start hurriedly down the stairs leading to the Palace. Wasting no time, he led Nicki across the lobby to join the large noisy stream of gamblers headed into the massive first-floor casino, hoping to get lost in the crowd. At almost that exact instant, Jack Stavros came down a balcony staircase and passed through the revolving front doors of the Palace, out onto Caesar's front courtyard to wait for his friend, his trained eye taking note of the four men in long coats and dark glasses turning into the casino. Jack spoke briefly into his lapel microphone, then moved off to investigate the commotion down the street, scanning the crowd for his friend as he went.

Inside, Sam and Nicki moved further into the big room, hoping Jack would find them before the Koreans did, but it was not to be. Moving past the endless rows of one-arm bandits to mingle with the big crowds standing around the crap tables, Sam felt Nicki tug on his arm. Closing on them from the far-right side of the room was another pair of Asian assassins. Sam turned to lead Nicki in the opposite direction only to spy two more killers to their left, lurking behind the blackjack tables. Both pairs had obviously spotted them and were now angling to intercept.

"Christ, Sam, they're everywhere!" Nicki cried. "What are we going to do!"

With trouble to the left, right, and behind, Sam searched out their only remaining option, an elevator lobby straight ahead. Once again, he led Nicki by the arm to what he hoped would be an escape route to safety.

"This way," he said. "Stay close and follow my lead."

Ignoring their pursuers, Sam and Nicki moved away from the dice games and out into the open, slowly edging toward the elevators.

"Now, run!" Sam yelled when they were close enough, and the two made a mad dash for the hallway, no longer concerned about drawing attention to themselves.

Short of breaking into a full sprint, the Koreans moved as quickly as possible to follow, but Sam and Nicki beat them to the elevators by a full ten seconds. Pressing all the buttons as they ran past, they quickly ducked under a velvet rope that cordoned off an adjoining stairway to disappear unseen.

The long stairwell down led to one of the casino's lower levels, made up mostly of theaters and function rooms, all of which were now unused due to renovations. Finding themselves alone in a wide-open, empty corridor, Sam and Nicki ducked into the first unlocked room they found. Sam bolted the door behind them and hit the lights. They found themselves in what appeared to be the backstage area for one of the big theaters. A huge curtain hung from high above, running the length of the stage. No sooner had the two started across the backstage than they heard voices speaking in rapid Korean coming from outside the door they had just come through. Sam and Nicki moved quietly over to the backstage curtain, and as they slipped through a separation in the heavy drapes, someone shot the lock off the rear stage door. The gunshots startled Nicki, and she let out a little scream, which Sam quickly muffled by putting a hand over her mouth.

"Shhhh!" he said, whispering in her ear. "This way, stay low."

They were in between the front and rear stage curtains. Both of the heavy sets of drapes were tightly closed, allowing for very little light to reach them. Crouched down on their ankles, Sam led them across the forty feet of open stage to the front curtain. Feeling for an opening, they heard a murmur of voices coming from the theater. Sam took out the .45 and snuck a peek through the curtain. Two gunmen were working their way down the aisles, checking the rows of folded seats. Two more stood poised at the back of the theater, weapons in hand.

"No good this way," Sam whispered, trying to sound as though there was another perfectly safe escape route at hand, but even in the dim light, Nicki could read the look on his face.

"We're fucked, right?"

Sam couldn't lie to her.

"It doesn't look good."

They could hear someone poking around behind the rear curtain, searching through the piles of props and racks of costumes that cluttered the backstage. It would only be a matter of moments until the gunmen came through the drapes.

"What do we do, Sam?"

The ex-SEAL weighed his options and realized there were none.

"I don't know."

"What do mean you don't know?" Nicki whispered harshly. "You always know what to do!"

"I'm sorry, Nicki. There's just too many of them."

"That's bullshit, Sam! Think of something!"

"This isn't a novel, Nicki! I can't just write our way out of…"

And a light suddenly went on in Nicki's head. "That's it! That's it, Sam!"

"What is?"

"Your book! What did you do in the book?"

"Are you serious!"

"Yes! Sam, what happens in the book!"

"Nicki, this isn't my book."

"No, it isn't, but think about it. Everything else you'd imagined in it has come true, right? So for the love of God, Sam, what the hell happens next! What did you write?"

Mason turned away, lowering his eyes.

"Sam."

"Nicki," Sam whispered wearily, "I didn't get this far! I'm sorry."

"Oh, he didn't get this far!" she said sarcastically, straining to keep her voice as low as she could. "Well, what did you *imagine*, Sam? You must have imagined this at some point. Think man! You've seen everything else that's happened so far. You know you have, Sam!"

Mason stared at Nicki for a long moment as that reality sunk in.

"A door," he said finally, seeing it again in his mind. "There's a door somewhere."

"Where, Sam? There're no walls we can get to! Only drapes!"

"In the floor!" he whispered urgently. "There should be a trap-door in the stage-floor for…"

"Magic acts!" Nicki finished. "Quick, find it!"

On hands and knees, the two scurried back toward the middle of the stage, feeling the floor for seams.

"Here!"

It was Nicki who found the recessed foot pedal that operated the mechanism. With the voices from the back nearing the curtain, Sam and Nicki positioned themselves in the center of the trapdoor and stepped on the switch just as someone jumped up onto the front stage. With much more velocity than either had anticipated, the three-foot square piece of stage dropped silently to the floor of the room below as a second door slid from beneath the stage-floor into its place.

The room below was pitch black. Hand in hand, the two felt their way to the sidewall and found the lights. The room was long and narrow with a stairway leading back up to the rear stage, and a single door at the near side that Sam figured must open into what should be the orchestra pit. They had no other choice. They could hear from the footsteps above them that both gunmen from the front of the theater were now on the stage with the two from the rear. It would only be a matter of time before one of them came down the stairway. Sam would have to risk taking Nicki up the side aisle along the wall of the theater. If they stayed low, they might make it. Maybe the two gunmen Sam had seen at the back of the theater would be gone. If not, he'd have to shoot it out with them. At least the odds would be better.

Nicki shut the lights off as Sam opened the door a crack. Thankfully, the theater was still mostly dark, the only light coming from the opened rear doors and some balcony lighting above. Sam could see no one anywhere in the theater.

"Okay," he said. "Let's do it."

One after the other, Sam and then Nicki slithered out and across the far end of the orchestra pit to the side aisle, where, hugging the ends of the seats, they crawled their way toward the back. Halfway up the aisle things went bad. One of the gunmen in the back of the theater had remained, hiding out of sight. When he spotted Nicki's blond hair bob above the seats, he ran to the top of the aisle, yelling to his friends as he opened fire on Sam and Nicki. His hurried aim was off, and the bullets slammed harmlessly into the heavily padded seats along the aisle.

"Get down and stay down!" Sam yelled at Nicki as he shoved her into the row of seats beside them. The ex-SEAL rolled to the sidewall as the second burst of fire chewed up the carpeted aisle. Sam took aim and put two .45 shells into the center of the gunman, then dove on top of Nicki just before the four others ran out onto the stage.

One of the killers shouted orders, and the group spread out along the front of the stage and began systematically spraying gunfire throughout the rows of seats. Chunks of cloth and pieces of wood flew through the air as the seats splintered apart, ripped to shreds by machine gun fire. The second gunman from the rear of the theater was back, standing now in the center aisle, spraying the rows of seats from behind, creating a crossfire. The Korean killers didn't know which row Sam and Nicki were hiding in, nor did they seem to care, content apparently in using their deadly process of elimination. All Sam could do was cover Nicki with his body.

The four gunmen on stage were reloading fresh clips as fast as they could, intent on maintaining a constant stream of fire. The killers were so obsessed with mass murdering the theater seats, that none of them noticed the little man in the gray silk suit walk casually up behind the lone gunman in the middle aisle. He put a sawed-off shotgun to the back of the Korean's head and pulled the trigger. A split second later, the theater lights came on, and eight men opened fire from the two balconies above, killing all four gunmen on stage.

The little man in the gray suit walked down the aisle, turning into the row of seats behind Sam and Nicki. Coming aware of the sudden silence, Sam, still lying on top of Nicki, uncovered his head to look up. Jack Stavros was standing over them, smiling like the cat that ate the canary.

"Hey, pally," he said, the shotgun resting on his shoulder. "How'd you like the show?"

Chapter 40

"You're sure none of them is this Lee character?"

Jack and several of his security force had escorted Sam and Nicki upstairs to one of the hotel's penthouse apartments. With two professional hoods standing watch over the corridor outside their room and two more sitting in the foyer, Jack stood relaxed in the kitchen pouring drinks. Sam stood at the glass slider to the balcony high above the Vegas strip, gazing down on the dazzling sprawl of lights below while he considered the implications of Jack's question. Nicki stood in the shower.

"I'm positive," Sam said, turning his gaze on Jack. "It's not a face you'd forget."

"Fuckers all look the same to me," the little man said, handing Sam a glass of scotch neat. "An' you went with Tony an' checked those other two we capped down by the stairs?"

"Yeah," Sam said, looking back out the window. "They're all just hired guns, Jack. Lee's still out there."

"Then fuck him, Sammy!" Jack said, cocky as ever. "I already whacked eight of his boys, right? Hey, guineas eight, gooks nothin'! Heh, heh."

"He'll be comin' again, Jackie. You can bet on it."

"Let him. I got plenty of muscle watchin' our backs. Lou an' Tony are two of my best with a gun. You're safe up here, pally. Stay as long as you want."

"Thanks, Jack, but I can't. I'm takin' Nicki to New York first thing in the morning."

Sam downed the whiskey then turned to his friend.

"And you're coming with me," he said.

"New York!" Jack objected. "I thought you needed to see the president. Who the fuck's in New York?"

"The only man I can trust to get me safely to the president."

"Yeah, an' who the fuck is that?"

"The head of the New York crime families," Mason said, walking over to lay his hands on his friend's shoulders. "Anastasia Gambino. And you're gonna take me to see him!"

Sam explained in detail to his mob friend the Mafia-Tong connection, as he understood it to be. He explained what the Chinese had really been up to and the timetable he and Nicki had been racing against. Jack had trouble imagining the scope of such a vast operation and the consequences it held, but he knew Sam wouldn't be lying about something so important, and he agreed to help in any way he could.

"I never trusted those chink motherfuckers!" the little man said disdainfully.

"It's not like that, Jack," Sam corrected. "This is not an act of the Chinese people or their government. These people are renegades! A power-crazed terrorist group intent on ruling the world. At any cost! It's not a race thing, Jackie."

"Fuck 'em anyway!" Jack said, dismissing the subject. "What do you need me to do?"

"Set up a meeting with Gambino," Sam said. "For tomorrow, as early as possible. We're running out of time, Jack. That launch is scheduled for two o'clock, Sunday afternoon. Peking time. They're twelve hours ahead of us, which means it'll be two in the morning on the East Coast."

"Cuttin' it a little close there, ain't ya, Sammy?"

"Not by choice, my friend. But…" Sam looked at his watch. "we now have just over twenty-six hours to get me an audience with the president of the United States, or the world as we know it ends!"

Jack got to work. His priorities being as they are, he first ordered food from room service, then called the airlines to book three first-class seats to La Guardia, arranging afterward for security on their ride to the airport. Finally, he made the call to New York.

While Jack was making his calls, Sam went into the bedroom to check on Nicki. He found her fast asleep on top of the bed, too exhausted to even crawl under the covers. He threw an extra blanket over her, kissed her on the forehead, and rejoined Jack and the two bodyguards in the sitting room.

"All set, Sammy," Jack said as one of the hoods let room service in with their dinner. "Plane leaves at seven ten, gets into New York at one forty. We'll be on Long Island by three in the afternoon."

"And Gambino?"

"He'll be expecting us."

"Good."

"Yeah," Jack said with a hint of apprehension. "Hope he's a fan."

Room service came with the food, and the four men ate making small talk mostly about gambling and women. When they were finished, Jack said, "Get yourself a few hours' sleep, Sammy. Lou and Tony will stay with ya till we leave in the morning. I got a couple more of the boys watchin' the outside too. If your buddy comes lookin' for ya, we'll have a nice, warm Vegas welcome waitin' for him. Heh, heh."

Sam nodded, unconvinced.

"Thanks, Jack," he said, "See you in a few."

The ex-SEAL said good night to the two thugs standing watch, then went into the bedroom, closing and locking the door behind him. He stood for a moment watching Nicki as she slept on the bed, a worried furrow lining his brow as if he were struggling with something. Making up his mind, Sam abruptly took the pillows from the bed along with the extras from the closet and, with whatever blankets he could gather, put together a makeshift bed on the bathroom floor. He picked Nicki up as if she were a child and gently placed her on it. She barely stirred. Sam closed the bathroom door, locked from within, then pulled a chair up next to the bed. He chambered a round in the .45, and facing the door to the sitting room, the ex-SEAL shut off the lights to wait.

*****

The Japanese throwing star, or shuriken, one is invariably surprised to find, is a much heavier object than imagined. At six and a half ounces, the iron weapon can, in the right hands, be propelled at speeds approaching ninety miles per hour, approximately the velocity of an average major league fastball. At such a speed, any one of the eight razor-sharp, steel-hardened points of the shuriken is capable of slicing clean through the metal panel of a car door. What one of these ancient missiles can do to human flesh is unspeakable.

Though not of Japanese heritage, Lee Hak-joon had become expertly proficient with the deadly weapon as a young teen surviving the ghettos of Seoul. He had further mastered the art of throwing the shuriken during his ninja training arranged by Wu Xun. It was a skill he was most fond of, and one he'd never lost.

*****

"Hah. Gin!"

"You fuckin' prick, Lou! That's three in a row!"

The two hoods had been hard at their game of gin rummy for over two hours. Sitting face-to-face at the dining table, a hanging tiffany lamp providing the only light in the darkened room, Lucky Lou, as he was known to his pals, was giving poor Tony the Trigger a beating.

"Hey," Lou said, trying to sound innocent. "Can I help it you keep throwin' me every fuckin' card I need!"

"Fuck you an' deal the cards you lucky prick."

Lucky Lou took a long sip off his glass of whiskey, then shuffled and dealt the next hand while Tony sat in silent anger with his hands folded across his chest.

Neither man noticed the slight ruffling of the curtain in front of the balcony slider as Lee Hak-joon slipped silently through the glass door. The Korean madman, dressed now in his ninja uniform, had rappelled silently down from the hotel roof to the balcony outside the sitting room, the lone guard Jack had posted on the rooftop left to quietly bleed to death. The outdated alarm system on the slider had posed even less of a problem. Lee had looped a wire to bypass the circuit contacts, then, using a glass cutter, he opened the locked door and stepped into the room.

Twenty feet across the room, the two shooters sat arranging their cards. Tony sat with his back to the balcony considering his hand and the up card on the table.

"Hey, Tone, you want the fuckin' card or what?"

"Bite me," the big Italian said, bending from the waist to reach for the card. As he sat back straight, a shuriken buried itself deep into the base of the gunman's skull, completely severing his spinal column and killing him instantly. The card still in hand, the dead man slipped slowly back toward the table as if putting the card back.

"Hey, Tone! You can't—"

Lucky Lou never saw the second star come hurtling over Tony's slumping head. It struck him in the forehead, just above the bridge of the nose, also killing instantly.

Lee moved silently to check his handiwork. Both men lay face down on the table, dead still, blood spilling from their wounds across the tabletop to the floor. Satisfied, the Korean killer turned instinctively to Sam and Nicki's bedroom.

Inside the bedroom, Sam lifted the .45 off his lap and reached a hand to the light switch. He had been sitting listening to the constant murmur of the two hoods as they went at each other throughout the night. The only prolonged silence had come when one or the other announced he had to use the bathroom, and those moments aside, there had been a continuous stream of obscenities and wisecracks flowing from the lips of both men as the two joined in verbal combat over their card game. The sudden quiet signaled trouble.

Easily picking the bedroom lock, Lee slipped into the black room. When he closed the door noiselessly behind him, Sam hit the lights.

"Freeze!" he yelled, pointing the .45 at the Korean, but Lee was faster than Sam could have imagined. In almost the same instant the lights came on, the killer flicked his wrist, flinging a shuriken across the room to strike the gun from Sam's hand before the ex-SEAL could get off a shot. The force of the blow knocked Sam's arm across his body as the deadly star caromed off the .45 to slice into the wall next to the headboard, burying itself deep in one of the wall studs about two feet off the floor.

Unleashing his full fury, the hatchet-faced man appeared to fly across the room as he launched a karate kick that would surely have broken Sam's neck had he not dove to the floor beside the bed. The kick missed Sam's head by a hair, smashing the bed's corner post and punching a hole clean through the sheet-rock wall.

On his back on the floor, Sam found himself wedged between the chair and the sidewall of the room. He scrambled to get up, but again, the Korean killer was too quick, pouncing on the ex-SEAL like a big cat. Lee had his blade in hand, and he stabbed down at Sam while pinning him with the weight of his body. Flat on his back and unable to move from side to side, all Sam could do was block Lee's thrust, grabbing hold of the madman's knife arm with both hands. Using all his strength, Sam fought to hold back the killer's blade, but he was fighting a losing battle. Lee had the advantage of adding his body weight to his considerable strength, and the scalpel started its slow descent toward Sam's chest. Sam tried to rock the Korean off him by rolling from side to side, but the wall and chair held Lee fast atop of the ex-SEAL.

Centimeter by centimeter, the blade moved downward, neither man making a sound as every ounce of energy was channeled into the silent death match. Sam's arms burned from the strain, yet still the knife dropped lower and lower. So close to the kill, Lee Hak-joon was crazed now by his thirst for blood. His eyes burned with hatred as his face hovered inches over Sam's. The pure evil glowering in Lee's eyes was so repulsive it gave the ex-SEAL a momentary burst of renewed strength. In a last desperate attempt to throw the Korean off him, Mason bucked his lower body off the floor with all the strength he had left, violently arching his back again and again as he tried to throw Lee forward over his head. But Lee merely bounced headfirst, off the wall beside the bed, each time coming back on balance over Sam to regenerate his efforts with the knife.

Sam's arms felt dead. The blade was touching his chest, and the ex-SEAL could feel the pressure of the tip through his shirt. His muscles were tiring badly, maxed out by the strain. With death staring him in the eyes and nothing he could do about it, Sam's mind drifted briefly to thoughts of Nicki. He feared for what Lee might do to her.

The pinch of the blade as it pierced his skin brought Sam back to the here and now. He *must* not give in!

Vowing to fight until there was no life left in his body, Sam felt a warm liquid drip into his eyes, trickling from Lee's brow, blurring the ex-SEAL's vision.

So much sweat, not normal.

Sam's muscles screamed with agony as the ex-SEAL willed his every last bit of strength into holding back the blade that was starting to enter his chest. With his eyes squeezed tightly shut, wincing from the pain, Sam thought he felt the pressure on the knife lessen by a fraction.

Is he weakening? Could he be tiring too?

Sam shoved up against the knife with what little strength he had left, and the blade lifted out of his flesh!

So much sweat. So warm.

Sam shoved up again, and again the blade rose, perhaps an inch this time.

Not sweat—blood! He's bleeding!

Inch by inch, Sam lifted the knife away from his heart as the weight behind it lightened steadily. Agonizingly, his tired arms moved Lee higher and higher, every inch a major victory won. When he had lifted Lee's body to an almost-sitting position, the scalpel suddenly fell from the Korean's hands. With one final shove, Sam pushed the killer to the sidewall, where Lee's limp body slumped slowly back to the floor. Sam had been holding up a dead man.

After a minute's rest, the ex-SEAL lifted himself off his back to examine the body. The top of Lee's head was scarred with a cluster of deep puncture wounds. Large slices of scalp and chunks of skull had been cut open, exposing the madman's damaged brain. Sam looked at the wall next to the head of the bed. The bloodstained shuriken remained firmly embedded in the stud, little pieces of Lee's head still clinging to the sharp metal. The hatchet-faced man had died by his own hand.

Chapter 41

The flight to New York was routine and without incident. There was no sign of ambush by Asian killers lurking on the roadways, nor were there any feds waiting for them at the airport. The mess back at the hotel room had been all taken care of by dawn. Nicki had slept through the entire ordeal, but Jack had not as Sam had called his friend immediately after his battle with Lee. The little mobster was outraged to hear that the Korean assassin had managed to get past five of his best men, killing three of them in the process, and Sam's friend from back east had not yet stopped apologizing to him. To be sure there would be no more such intrusions, Jack whisked Sam and Nicki to a room on another floor, needlessly doubling the security, for there would be no more trouble that night.

Their plane arrived at La Guardia on schedule, where the three were met by two large men in dark suits who escorted them to a waiting limousine for the slow ride out of the city to Long Island. The Sunrise highway took them east out to the Hamptons where the limo turned north to the coast, eventually turning into one of the seaside estates. After passing through a heavily guarded security gate, the big Lincoln glided down a half mile of tree-lined driveway to stop in front of one of the largest mansions on the bay. Before the car had even rolled to a stop, four more large men in suits appeared from inside to greet the guests. Two of the bodyguards opened the limo's doors while the other two stood back a safe distance, closely watching every move the visitors made.

In spite of the fact that all the gunmen seemed to know Jack and treated him with obvious great respect, Nicki was extremely uncomfortable with the whole idea of waltzing into "fucking hood heaven," as she put it, to look for help. She wanted to go to the cops. With Inspector Lee dead, she thought it should be safe now to tell their story to the authorities. Sam reminded her that Lee's boss was still in the picture and they had no clue as to his identity.

"If this guy you heard back on Grass Mountain is indeed Lee's superior," Sam reasoned as he stepped out of the limo, "then he may even hold a higher position of authority. Meaning we aren't out of the woods yet, babe."

"And you think this mob guy is the answer?" Nicki questioned doubtfully.

"He'd better be," Sam said, "because there's no time for anyone else. The Chinese launch their rocket in a little over ten hours. Ten hours! Hell, it may already be too late to stop it..."

"Don't say that, Sam!" Nicki pleaded.

"Yeah," Jack agreed. "Don't fuckin' quit on us now, Sammy-boy!"

The little man stopped to straighten his jacket and tie.

"Gambino will help us," he said, quite sure of himself. "Don't you fuckin' worry."

"What makes you so sure?" Nicki asked.

"The guy loves me, that's what!"

With a wink Jack headed up the front steps of the mansion. Nicki cast a dubious look at Sam.

"You gotta admit," the ex-SEAL said, "he is lovable."

"Yeah, he is," Nicki admitted, following after Jack, "and so are raccoons, but try and pet one and see what happens."

Reaching the top step, one of the hoods held the massive front door open for them. Jack stopped and turned to Sam and Nicki.

"The man also happens to be my uncle," he said with his best wise-guy smile.

*****

Inside the mansion the three were led to a large sitting room overlooking the Long Island Sound. Here they were left alone to wait for the crime boss. It was a short wait. From the outside, one of Gambino's bodyguards opened the French doors to the adjoining patio while a second bodyguard pushing a wheelchair rolled the mob king in from the afternoon sunlight, positioning his boss in the center of the room facing the three visitors. The two hoods took up silent stances on either side of the old man, hands clasped in front of them.

At eighty-three, the old mobster looked his age. Ravaged by a life of crime, his once-handsome face was now deeply lined. His noted thick head of jet-black hair had thinned and turned to gray, and the Italian's once-strong, proud body had been reduced now to a frail frame of skin and bones, yet Gambino's mind remained as sharp and tough as ever. Even from a wheelchair, this man wielded more power and commanded more respect than any criminal in the free world, his word still feared by both ally and enemy alike. To underestimate him would be a fatal mistake.

The old man sat quietly inspecting his guests in turn. His hard gaze moved back and forth from Sam to Nicki, then back to Sam again, finally coming to rest on Jack. Nobody spoke. Finally, the crime boss lifted a tired hand and motioned for Jack to approach. The little man did so, and when he was close enough, the mobster reached up and tenderly patted Jack on the cheek.

"How come you don't get back to see me so much anymore, eh, Jackie?" the old man asked, his voice, though raspy, still strong and decisive.

"You're right, Uncle G," Jack said, humbly. "I should come more often, and I will, I promise."

Sounding almost reverent, Sam was sure he'd never heard his friend speak with such respect.

Jack had always been the old man's favorite, and Gambino's eyes beamed with love as he peered up at his nephew.

"Okay, Jackie," he said, nodding slowly. "Now tell me, who are these people you bring to see me, eh?"

Jack took a step back, turning slightly and beckoning to Sam and Nicki to step forward.

"Uncle G," he said, facing the old man, "these are my very good friends, Ms. Nicole Neally and Mr. Sam Mason. They have ahhh… discovered a problem that they need your help with."

"Is this the same Mr. Mason who writes the books?" Gambino asked with new interest. "The one who helped you up in Boston?"

"Yes, sir," Jack said.

Gambino looked Sam up and down a second time.

"Come forward, Mr. Mason," he said. "Please."

Sam stepped closer to the legendary criminal.

"Yes, you have the look," the crime boss said, nodding to himself. "I enjoy your stories, Mr. Mason," he said, changing his tone. "A bit far-fetched, but fun to read. That is mostly all I do now," the old man said, gesturing to his wheelchair.

Sam simply nodded his understanding.

"So, Mr. Mason, my nephew has told me much about you. I thank you for saving his ass from that Irish pig. My Jackie has a nose for finding trouble, oftentimes more than he can handle. But he is my sister's only son, God rest her soul, so…"

The old man waved his hand through the air as if to say the little mobster was his cross to bear.

"My nephew," he continued, "tells me you have a problem that concerns me, Mr. Mason. Tell me about it."

Old man Gambino's presence was threatening, to say the least, but Sam had come through far too much to mince words now. When he spoke, his voice was clear, strong, and without a trace of fear. Pulling no punches, the ex-SEAL got right to the point.

"Mr. Gambino, for the past twenty years or so, you and your organization have been involved in a partnership with the Chinese, the Tong, to be specific. The sole function of this alliance, as far as you knew, was to smuggle and distribute illegal drugs for profit. I am sorry to be the one to tell you, sir, but you have been played for a fool!"

Sam paused to let his words take their effect. Though not exactly genial with being tagged for a fool, the old man remained unruffled, waiting to hear more. Sam was boldly spilling the truth, unconcerned for the personal consequences for himself should he anger the crime boss, and this intrigued Gambino.

"For two decades," Sam continued, "you and your Asian counterparts have flooded the streets of both the United Stated and Russia with high-grade opiates and cocaine, inflicting addiction on millions. At great expense, you and the Chinese have created pipelines into both countries. Safe, impenetrable routes by which you could smuggle in your deadly product, and for years now, you have witnessed the success of your joint venture." Mason waved a hand around the magnificent room. "You have enjoyed the fruits of your enterprise, sir, but you were blinded by your greed. You did not see that your partners had a hidden agenda…" Sam lowered his voice. "You have been used, sir. Like a common street corner whore!"

Jack was squirming as though he might pee his pants. No one talked to Anastasia Gambino that way! Not and lived to tell about it, anyway.

Sam had struck a nerve for sure, but the old man seemed to be taking it all in stride. The mob king held Sam in deep contemplation for several seconds.

"Go on," he said finally.

"Drugs are not the only evil substance the Chinese have been smuggling across international borders. With your unwitting assistance, Mr. Gambino, over thirteen hundred atomic devices have been distributed across both the United States and Russia by your Chinese friends. Thirteen hundred nuclear bombs! All placed in strategic locations! All awaiting a single detonation signal! A signal that will be sent in just under ten hours unless you help us!"

Gambino had been totally focused on Sam, listening patiently to his story. Now he shifted his attention briefly to Jack, inquiring of the little man simply by raising his eyebrows.

"I'm afraid it's true, Uncle G," Jack said. "Several hit teams, gooks, came into Caesar's chasing Sam and Ms. Neally. I had to ahh…intervene on my friends' behalf."

Gambino turned back to Sam.

"This sounds like one of your novels, Mr. Mason. A little too fantastic to be real."

"Does the name George Lee mean anything to you?" Sam asked.

Gambino shook his head silently from side to side.

"*Inspector* George Lee?" Sam elaborated. "Of the FBI? The number two man at the Bureau?"

The crime boss remained silent.

"This Lee person," Jack interjected, "killed three of my men trying to get to Sam, Uncle G."

"He was a double agent working for the Chinese," Sam added. "He wanted me dead because of what I know. Because of what I have just told you."

"So why don't you simply go to the police now?" Gambino offered.

"He is not the only double agent," Sam answered. "There are hundreds more, perhaps thousands. And at least one more highly placed. Mr. Gambino, I need to talk directly to the president. The bombs are to be detonated from space by a satellite. The president is the only one who can authorize its destruction, and you are the only man I can trust powerful enough to get me in to see him."

"You can prove all of this, Mr. Mason?" Gambino asked.

Sam hesitated, his mind suddenly drifting as something began to rise up from his subconscious. "No," he said absently. "The proof is lost…"

"Lost?" Gambino snorted. "How could you possibly lose something of such importance, Mr. Mason?"

Sam barely heard the question, his mind searching deep within itself for whatever it was trying to surface.

"I fell…" he said.

"You what?" Nicki spouted. Completely flabbergasted, she could no longer hold her tongue. "He didn't fall, Mr. Gambino… sir," she said, venting her frustration at the mob king. "He jumped! Out of an airplane from ten thousand feet. *Without* a parachute! And do you know why?"

Gambino had kept his gaze fixed on Sam, as if Nicki was so unimportant as to not exist. The feisty young woman waited, hands on hips, and without moving his head, Gambino finally shifted his eyes to Nicki.

"Because it was the *only* way!" she said, scolding the old man. "It was the only chance he had to save me and to keep himself alive so he could try to save the rest of the free world! Including your sorry ass!"

The big room suddenly became incredibly still. Jack thought he could hear his guts rumbling. Gambino was steaming, unsure himself if it was the insolence of this woman that more angered him or the fact that it could all be true. The great and all-powerful Gambino… played for a patsy!

"Look, Mr. Gambino," Nicki went on in a kinder voice, "I don't know what you've done with your life, what crimes or evil you've committed. I don't know and I don't care. But I can see that you love your nephew here. And there must be others, Mr. Gambino. People that you care about. People that you don't want to see die just yet…"

Nicki's plea seemed to be falling on deaf ears. She lifted her head, throwing her hands to the sky as if begging divine intervention.

"Don't you get it?" she contended. "All this will be gone if you don't help us! Everyone you hold dear! Everything you have worked for! Your legacy. Gone! Your country. Gone! And all because *you* were played for a fool by—"

"Enough!"

The old man's voice resonated loudly in the big room. He looked up at Sam as he spoke.

"How can I be sure I am not giving myself up to a trap?"

The ex-SEAL stood quietly, pondering the question a moment before answering. "You can't," he said. "I can offer you no proof. Some of what we know is from a microchip that is now lost. And some, I just know. I can't explain how I know. I just know some things to be true. Like the Grass Mountain lodge, for instance."

"What about it?"

"I know you bought it as a base of operations. And I know that's where you first made your deal with the Chinese."

The old man sat silently nodding to himself again.

"Yes," he conceded. "I met in private with one man. A ghost of a man. And we struck a bargain. That is true. But in over twenty years, I have never revealed his identity. Not to anyone. Not even…"

"His name is Lo Fang," Sam said.

Gambino didn't flinch, or even blink an eye, but as the gradual realization of his betrayal and the significance it held penetrated deep within his tired bones, the aging crime boss seemed to sink down into himself. When he spoke again, his voice sounded very old.

"Frankie," he said to one of his bodyguards. "Would you be so kind as to get Jim Anderson on the phone for me?"

"Jim Anderson?" Nicki whispered, "Isn't he—"

"Yes," Sam interrupted somberly. "The US attorney general."

Chapter 42

Returning from London, President Dean had been in the air over the Atlantic aboard Air force One on approach to Washington, DC, when the classified call came. Once advised of a potential national emergency requiring his immediate attention, the president promptly entered the Emergency Operations Center of the plane and ordered an immediate emergency landing at Andrews Air Force Base. Now sequestered in one of the conference rooms aboard Air Force One along with Jack and Gambino, Sam and Nicki awaited a meeting with the president. A Secret Service agent standing by the locked door watched over the group. There was little to watch over. The crime boss sat sullen in his wheelchair, alone with his thoughts, while Sam and Jack sat across from each other at the large conference table in the middle of the room. Nicki paced the floor nervously.

The four had been on the plane for only a few minutes. Using his personal Lear jet, Gambino had flown the group down to DC, where Sam had told his story to Attorney General Jim Anderson. Just before midnight, the nation's top lawman brought in the national security adviser, Bob Clancy, to be briefed, and together on the strength of Gambino's confession and corroboration of Sam's story, they contacted the FBI director, Leroy Harrison. Director Harrison verified the apparent disappearance of Chief Inspector George Lee, as well as the murder of several of the bureau's agents connected with Lee and his investigation. Harrison confessed his concern for Lee's recent lack of communication with the bureau, expressing his own suspicions while citing ongoing revelations regarding the chief inspector's activities. Something about George Lee appeared to be very wrong indeed, and everything the director said seemed to support Sam's story.

As fantastic and outrageously improbable as the threat seemed, Clancy was compelled to alert the president, placing a call first to General Joseph E. Blythe, chairman of the joint chiefs of staff. Always one to err on the side of safety, Blythe immediately called for a step-up of the country's defense condition to DEFCON 3 and suggested to Clancy that given the issue of time, and whereas the president was currently inbound to DC, that Air Force One be used as the Crisis Operations Center. The national security adviser concurred, agreeing to meet the general at Andrews AFB. Sam was then able to convince Clancy to have Director Harrison dispatch FBI agents to investigate the HAMTIN plant, hoping they would find further evidence to back his story. The president's chief adviser stopped short, however, of initiating an all-out search of any frontline government facilities. He would leave that call to the president.

At twenty-seven minutes past midnight, Sunday, the morning of the twenty-ninth, the national security adviser made his call to Air Force One. President Dean would not land until almost an hour later, at 1:15 a.m., a mere forty-five minutes before the Chinese would launch their rocket. The president was quickly hustled into an in-depth briefing with Clancy, Anderson, and General Blythe, as well as several of his other top advisers, including the secretary of state, Miller McWilliams, who just happened to be with the general when the call had come nearly two hours earlier.

Though it was unclear as to what the president would choose to do about it, everyone, including the president, considered the situation to be serious and potentially catastrophic, at least until it could be proven otherwise. General Blythe, in particular, was alarmed, having fought long and hard against any compromise of the military's domestic security policies, all along warning of just such a possible breakdown.

*****

"Christ, what time is it?" Nicki asked of no one in particular.

"About five minutes later than the last time you asked," Jack said.

Nicki turned her silent glare on Sam's friend, and the little man shrugged and checked his watch once again.

"One thirty," he said.

"Thirty minutes!" Nicki exclaimed. "Sam, that rocket goes up in thirty fucking minutes! Where the hell is the president?"

Nicki's anxiety was mounting with every passing minute. The young mother missed her baby girl terribly, and the very real fear of never seeing her again was starting to overwhelm her.

"It's okay, babe," Sam reassured. "He'll be here. They wouldn't have brought us aboard otherwise."

"And that's another thing," she said, looking at Gambino. "Can you tell me how the fuck is it that one of the world's most notorious criminals was able to get us aboard Air Force One!"

Sam sat silent, not knowing how to answer.

"Secrets," Jack said softly after a moment of quiet.

Sam and Nicki both turned to look at the little mobster.

"Cops and robbers," he explained. "We all know each other. All up and down the food chain."

"What do you mean?" Nicki asked.

"Hey, you think a cop walkin' a beat, don't know who the neighborhood assholes are? Don't you think the State cops have a pretty good idea of who the local wise guys are and what they're up to? Remember Leo Finny? The fuckin' mayor of Boston? I remember when he used to drink in the same bars in Southie as Whitey Bulger for Christ's sake! And what? You think they didn't know each other? You think there was no communication goin' on? Well, let me tell ya. Ain't many cops out there that're all that snowy white. Most of 'em gotta get a little dirty just to do their jobs. Hey, people don't talk to each other, they don't learn nothin'. Don't make the cops bad. It's just the way it is."

"Well," Nicki rationalized, "naturally the US attorney general would know of the head of the Mafia and vice versa, but are you suggesting they know each other personally?"

"Hey," Jack said, "top cop and number one bad guy. You figure it out."

"Jim Anderson, and Anastasia Gambino?" she questioned doubtfully. "Talk to each other?"

"Talk?" Jack scoffed. "They probably keep each other's number on speed dial!"

"So," Sam followed, "Gambino calls Anderson, Anderson calls the president's national security adviser, he calls the president, and here we are."

"Jack, what time is it now?" Nicki asked.

This time the little man didn't bother to object. He checked his watch and looked up at Nicki almost apologetically.

"Quarter of two."

"Oh, God, Sam!" Nicki cried. "There's not enough time left to explain! It's too late!"

"No, not yet," he said, standing to move beside her. "They can't deploy the satellite until the rocket reaches its orbit. That'll take about twenty minutes. There's still time."

No sooner had those words left Sam's lips than the Secret Service agent standing by the door reached up to touch his earplug. He spoke into his lapel microphone before stepping to the door to open it.

Though Air Force One was climbing to an altitude of nearly forty thousand feet at a speed of just under six hundred miles per hour, there was virtually no sensation of movement aboard the giant plane. For all practical purposes, Sam and Nicki could have been standing in a penthouse boardroom on Wall Street, awaiting the arrival of a corporate CEO, rather than the leader of the free world. That distinction became eminently apparent, however, when President Dean strode through the opened door into the big conference room as he always did, tall, proud, and full of purpose. The president carried with him an air of unmatched confidence, and without hesitation, he walked directly to Sam, personally taking charge of the situation.

"Mr. Mason," he said, introducing himself, "Mathew Dean. I am a great fan of your work, sir."

"Thank you, Mr. President," Sam said humbly as he took the president's hand. "I am honored to meet you, sir."

The president turned his head to acknowledge Nicki's presence.

"Mr. President," Sam said, "may I introduce Ms. Nicole Neally."

President Dean took Nicki's hand.

"My pleasure, Ms. Neally."

"The honor is mine, Mr. President."

"I have been informed," the president said to Nicki, "that you are the sister of Michael Neally. I am very sorry for your loss, Ms. Neally. I'm told now that the circumstances regarding your brother's death may not be as we were earlier led to believe."

"I can assure you they are not at all, Mr. President."

The president nodded silently a moment before looking curiously across the table at Jack and Gambino.

Sam did the honors.

"Mr. President," he said, "Mr. Jack Stavros and Mr. Anastasia Gambino."

The president nodded curtly in their direction.

"I thank you all for coming," he said, turning back to Sam. "But I'm afraid it is necessary to dispense with any further pleasantries. Mr. Mason, I have just been informed that Air Force One is currently flying under the codename Looking Glass. Are you aware of the significance of this, sir?"

"Yes, Mr. President, I am."

Mildly surprised, President Dean raised an eyebrow in the direction of General Blythe.

"Mr. Mason is ex-Navy, sir," the general explained. "SEALs, Special Operations. He was once part of Air Force One's antiterrorist unit."

The president turned back to Sam.

"I see," he said. "So you know then, Mr. Mason, that Air Force One only flies as Looking Glass when the United States is under immediate threat of nuclear attack."

"Yes, sir. I do."

"Then you probably also know the significance of DEFCON 2."

"Defense condition two," Sam answered. "Our military's final level of readiness before…well, before war, sir."

President Dean took two paces to his right, folding his arms across his chest as he turned back to Sam.

"That is exactly correct, Mr. Mason. And I can assure you that any sudden step-up of our military's level of readiness never goes undetected. Pretty much every major power in the world becomes aware of the escalation. A very serious matter, Mr. Mason. And possibly one with very grave global repercussions."

The president locked eyes with Sam, taking the measure of his words on the man. The ex-SEAL stood tall under the president's stare.

"Five minutes ago," Dean continued profoundly, "it was necessary for me to bring our military forces to DEFCON 2 in order to bring certain defense systems online. Whether or not these systems are deployed will depend on what I learn in the next few minutes."

The president took a step closer to Sam.

"Mr. Mason," he said, hands on hips, "would you please tell me why it is that some of my advisers think I should risk starting a war with the Chinese by blowing one of their satellites out of the sky!"

"Mr. President, if you don't do exactly that, you won't have to worry about a war, sir. You'll have nothing left to fight one with!"

Sam stood straight as he made his case.

"Sir, a renegade faction of the Chinese militia, call them terrorists if you like, have at this very moment over thirteen hundred nuclear warheads spread across the US and Russia. When that satellite reaches orbit, Mr. President, it will complete an existing network of satellites, thereby giving their system complete global coverage. The terrorists plan to detonate the weapons from space, sir. They'll send the detonation signal as soon as the linkup is complete."

"So I've been told, Mr. Mason. And I also understand you have no real proof of any of this. No witnesses. Other than Ms. Neally, that is, and the word of a couple of career criminals."

"Sir, Mr. Gambino has confirmed the involvement of his organization with the Chinese Tong. This is how the Chinese managed to smuggle the weapons into place. Why would he lie about that, Mr. President? What would he stand to gain by such a confession?"

Dean considered that fact, looking to his national security adviser for input.

Clancy motioned to Attorney General Anderson, saying, "Jim believes him, Mr. President."

"Mr. President," Sam continued, "Ms. Neally's brother, Mickey, my best friend, was with the CIA. He traced the Mafia-Tong partnership to China where he somehow gathered proof of all of this and hid it on a microchip. He managed to get the chip to me just before he was murdered. I'm sorry, sir, but the chip is lost, and I'm afraid we only got to scan it for a few brief seconds before..."

"The explosion at Dahlgren. Yes, Mr. Mason, I've been fully briefed. The fact that you've lost the only hard evidence of your claim does not help your case."

Sam turned to the national security adviser, then back to the president.

"Sir, what about the HAMTIN plant?" he asked. "Your security adviser sent the FBI to investigate, they must have found something."

"The plant is deserted," Clancy said, answering for the president. "Which, though curious, neither confirms nor denies that part of your story, Mr. Mason."

"Well, what about George Lee?" Sam said to the security adviser.

"What about him?"

"He was a double agent!"

"That has not been absolutely confirmed yet."

"Oh, for God's sake, man!"

"I'm sorry, Mr. Mason," Clancy said firmly, "but so far, all the evidence is circumstantial. No one knows for sure that Inspector Lee was working for the Chinese..."

"That's not true."

It was the first sound from Gambino since he'd boarded the plane.

"I know," he said. "I have known of his existence from the beginning."

The old man sat staring straight ahead, his words harsh and bitterly self-deprecating.

"For twenty years, I watched his rise through the bureau. This man Lee, you see, was to be the most important part of the deal I made with the Tong. He was to be their guarantee for a safe pipeline. They called him their 'guardian.'" The old man lifted his weary head to look up at President Dean. "I never knew of his true purpose."

Dean acknowledged Gambino's confession with a silent nod.

"Even if this is true," he said, turning back to Sam, "it only proves that Lee was a double agent running interference for an international drug ring. It says nothing of nuclear weapons."

"Then you're just gonna have to find one of the bombs!" Nicki said, stepping forward. "And please tell me, Mr. President, that would be proof enough!"

"Ms. Neally," Dean said sincerely, "I can assure you, should our people on the ground find a single weapon anywhere on US soil that even remotely resembles a fire extinguisher, I will blow that Chinese rocket out of the sky faster than you could order a Pu-Pu platter!"

"Then you are looking," Sam said to the president.

"Yes," he said. "I issued the order to initiate the immediate full inspection of all fire control systems at every base and frontline government facility throughout…"

"But how long ago, sir!" Mason interrupted, already knowing the answer.

Dean hesitated, knowing what the ex-SEAL would be thinking. "Five minutes."

"With all due respect, Mr. President, that rocket will reach orbit in." Sam looked at General Blythe.

"Nine minutes," the general said.

"Nine minutes!" Sam repeated. "In just nine minutes, sir, that rocket will launch their satellite! Mr. President, you just gave the search order five minutes ago! It's two o'clock in the morning! In nine minutes, your teams on the ground will have barely started their inspections! What are the chances they'll get lucky within the first minute, sir! It's not enough time, Mr. President! You can't afford to wait."

"Mr. Mason!" Dean said loudly, cutting Sam off, "you are asking me to commit an act of war!" The president turned away in frustration. "For God's sake, man, you're asking me to shoot down a multinational launch for peace! The Chinese will go nuts! Christ, we're just getting over that damn spy-plane business. This would set relations back years!" The president looked directly at General

Blythe. "I'm sorry, Joe, but I can't give the order to destroy that rocket without solid proof."

"Mr. President," the general replied, "there is a good possibility the Chinese won't know what happened to their bird. The laser burst is undetectable from Earth. They might just interpret the explosion as being caused by an internal malfunction."

"That's highly unlikely, Mr. President." It was the national security adviser speaking up. "Once they analyze their data, they'll know what happened all right. It'll take a few days, no doubt, but they'll eventually figure out that an extreme heat source, both external and foreign in nature, was brought to bear on their craft, causing the massive temperature spike and complete disintegration of their satellite. They *will* know what it was, and they *will* know it could only have been us. No, Mr. President, I'm afraid I'm inclined to agree with you. We need to see proof, sir."

With a shift of his eyes, Dean inquired of McWilliams, who had been uncharacteristically quiet throughout the entire discourse. The secretary of state remained silent, giving his answer with a discreet shake of his head.

General Blythe saw it and stepped forward.

"Mr. President," he said with some urgency, "may I then suggest we move to operations at this time. In the event you may yet find it necessary to give the order to destroy the satellite, I would like permission now to retask the appropriate K-SATS with the necessary firing solutions. We need to be ready should you get the word, sir. All we'll need do then is input the fail-safe code."

"Yes, of course, Joe. Let's move to operations, gentleman. Mr. Mason, you're welcome to join us, sir." With that, the president turned sharply and left the room with the others quick on his heels.

As Sam started to follow, Nicki grabbed his arm. "Sam, what the hell are they talking about? What laser and what the fuck are K-SATS?"

"Killer satellites," he said. "An orbiting global laser-defense system. *Star Wars*, Nicki."

"*Star Wars*? I thought they scrapped that project?"

"That's just what they wanted you to think," the ex-SEAL said. "It's up there all right. And it's obviously fully operational. The general wants to target the rocket and wait."

"Wait for what?"

"Word from the ground. If they find one of the bombs in time, the president will issue the fail-safe code. It's a big if."

Nicki grabbed Sam by both arms.

"Sam, that's it!"

"What is?" he said, but Nicki was already running after the president.

"The fail-safe, of course!" she yelled over her shoulder as she ran out of the room. "You can give them the code!"

Chapter 43

The Crisis Operations Center (COC) aboard Air force One fills most of the front lower level of the massive, specially built 747. This high-tech portion of the president's plane gives first-time visitors more the impression of standing in the command center of one of the US Navy's frontline aircraft carriers than of flying aboard the otherwise luxurious craft. The state-of-the-art equipment and technology in the COC is manned by some of the sharpest, best-trained people in the world, making the plane one of the most sophisticated aircraft in the world. More than safe and comfortable transportation, Air Force One doubles as the president's airborne emergency war room.

Nicki searched out the president immediately on entering the COC. Completely focused on her mission, she was oblivious to the sheer electric energy the room generated with its row upon row of computer consoles, and it's two dozen airmen, all busy at their work stations, their commanders hurrying about their duties as they hastened to deal with the crisis at hand. Nicki spotted General Blythe speaking to another officer, standing by what appeared to be a three-dimensional radar display. The president, she could see, stood ten feet beyond him, listening to Adviser Bob Clancy report the context of his communications with search teams on the ground. Nicki made a beeline for the general just as Sam entered the war room.

"General Blythe, sir," she said slightly out of breath from her sprint. "How much time before the rocket reaches orbit?"

The general looked to the officer he'd been speaking with, Air Force Captain Alosa, who in turn addressed the airman sitting at the console behind him.

"Sergeant Haggett," he said, "you have that data on screen?"

"Yes, sir. Present speed and trajectory indicate target will attain orbit in five minutes, thirty seconds, sir."

Blythe looked at Nicki, waiting.

"We can give you the proof you need, General!" Nicki blurted. "We can prove Sam is telling the truth!"

Already fearing the worst, Blythe was willing to listen. "And how might you do that, Ms. Neally?"

"The fail-safe code," she said. "You need the code to activate the lasers, right?"

"Correct, the system won't fire without it." The general tilted his head curiously. "Why?"

"What if Sam could give you that code, sir."

Blythe considered that possibility for a long, hard moment, looking from Nicki to Sam as the ex-SEAL approached the group. "That probability is highly unlikely," the general said finally.

"Exactly!" Nicki said.

The general's eyes narrowed. "I see your point, Ms. Neally. However," he said, motioning to the president. "I'm not the one you need to convince."

Nicki looked to the president, then back to the general. "Will you help us, sir?"

Blythe looked over to the president, who was still in conversation with his national security adviser. He turned to Captain Alosa and asked, "Do you have target acquisition, Captain?"

Alosa addressed the airman manning the next console. "Sergeant Salvadore?"

"Yes, sir. Firing solutions are computed and entered, sir."

Blythe was a man of action, and the young woman's proposal was an option other than just waiting.

"Give me one-minute updates, Sergeant," the general said to Sergeant Haggett before turning to Nicki. "Come with me, Ms. Neally."

They walked the few feet to where President Dean stood in discussion with Clancy and Anderson. McWilliams stood away from the group, leaning against one of the bulkhead consoles with his arms folded casually across his chest. Clancy had a phone to his ear, listening.

"Still nothing, sir," he said to the president as the general approached with Nicki.

"Mr. President," Blythe said, interrupting, "there's less than five minutes until the Chinese rocket reaches orbit."

Dean looked away from his advisers. He could tell by his friend's tone that the general had something more to add.

"What's on your mind, Joe?"

"Sir, Ms. Neally has a proposition," the general said, lowering his voice. "I think you should listen to her, Mathew."

General Blythe was one of the president's oldest and most trusted friends, yet this was the first time since his inauguration that Dean could ever recall the general using his first name. Even in private, it had always been 'Mr. President." It spoke for the weight of the situation. Dean turned his attention to the young woman standing before him, and Nicki gathered herself to make her plea.

"Ms. Neally?"

"Mr. President," she started, "I can't explain it, sir. I couldn't even begin to tell you how any of it could be possible. But somehow, sir, Sam has known almost everything about this whole affair before any of it even happened!"

Behind them, Sergeant Haggett counted down the time.

"General Blythe, sir, target will reach orbit in four minutes, sir."

Nicki turned to the voice, then looked back to the president.

"You've got to believe me, sir!" she pleaded. "Everything that's happened, Sam has seen it beforehand, either in his dreams or just before it's happened. I know it sounds crazy, sir, but it's true. I've seen it and lived it for the past six days!"

"Ms. Neally," the president said patiently, "what you are saying does sound less than rational. What exactly are you suggesting?"

"The fail-safe code, Mr. President! If Sam could give you the code needed to fire the laser weapons, wouldn't that convince you that everything else we've told you is true? I mean…how else could he possibly know it, sir?"

"He couldn't," the president said with absolute certainty. "Ms. Neally, the fail-safe is a random computer-generated eleven-character code. It is updated every four hours and encased by machine in a sealed packet. Anyone holding the code with the ability to transmit it could theoretically activate and even deploy a portion of our nuclear arsenal. Consequently, only three men on the planet have access to it. Two of them are on this plane, Ms. Neally, and I can promise you, Mr. Mason isn't one of them!"

"So it would be impossible for him to know it."

"Completely."

"Unless, of course, what I'm telling you is true."

The president had nothing to say to that.

"Sir, you said it yourself. It should be impossible." Nicki grabbed a pen and pad of paper off a nearby console. "So," she said, holding them up, "if Sam can write down that exact code, Mr. President. You've got destroy that rocket!"

Dean looked at General Blythe.

"I know where you stand, Joe," he said before turning to his national security adviser. "Bob?"

"Nothing to lose, sir."

The room was eerily quiet for what seemed to Nicki an eternity as President Dean stood in silent contemplation. Finally, he said, "All right, Ms. Neally. Give that pen and paper to Mr. Mason."

Nicki didn't hesitate. She whirled about and headed straight for Sam.

"Well, ain't that a hoot! I thought I'd pretty much seen 'n heard just 'bout everything in this ol' world. Till now, that is!"

Nicki stopped dead in her tracks as her head snapped back to the sound of the voice. *It was McWilliams!* The young woman stood frozen, staring at the secretary of state.

Sergeant Haggett broke the trance. "Three minutes till orbit is reached, General."

Nicki faced ahead, still unmoving, unsure of what to do. Slowly she started forward again. Taking him by the arm as she handed him the pen and paper, Nicki led Sam to an empty table in the middle of the room and motioned for him to sit. The ex-SEAL caught the look in her eye and followed her lead, sitting down next to her.

"You can do this, Sam," she said loudly for the room's benefit. Then she leaned in close to the ex-SEAL. "It's him!" she whispered.

"Who?" Sam whispered back.

"The voice from the lodge on Grass Mountain! Lee's boss! It's McWilliams!"

"Are you sure!"

"Yes! That's why I couldn't remember it. I was sedated both times I heard it!"

"The funeral," Sam said.

"Exactly!"

"Are you sure, Nicki?"

"On Erin's life, I'm positive!"

The ex-SEAL looked over at the secretary, who was shaking his head in disgust. "That's good enough for me," he said. "Don't say anything yet."

Sam studied McWilliams for several seconds, realizing just then that all eyes in the room not glued to a computer screen were staring at him and Nicki—and that's when it came to him. The ex-SEAL closed his eyes tightly, rubbing them with his fingertips.

"Sam, are you all right?"

"Yeah…yeah, I'm fine," he said, looking back up at McWilliams. "I know what he's up to, Nick."

"What, Sam?"

But the ex-SEAL didn't answer. He was busy scribbling out a series of numbers and letters on the pad of paper.

"Here," he said, abruptly tearing off the page when he'd finished. "Take this to the president."

Nicki grabbed the piece of paper from Sam's hand, knowing full well it held the proof that would save her world. Holding it out in front of her, she ran straight to the president, ignoring McWilliams as she did so.

President Dean took the piece of paper from Nicki with one hand and with the other he reached into his left inside breast pocket. The president removed a three by five-inch plastic packet, and holding it with both hands, he snapped it in two, breaking the seal. The COC fell quiet as a cold winter's night, the faint electric hum from the computer consoles the only sound in the room. Every pair of eyes in the operations center were trained on the president as he took the code card from the packet and held it up to Sam's note to compare the two.

"Two minutes, sir." Sergeant Haggett called.

Nicki stood not more than three feet in front of the president, her heart pounding in her chest. She knew the codes would match. Dean looked carefully back and forth from the fail-safe card to Sam's scribble, his face unreadable. Then without fanfare, he handed Sam's note back to Nicki.

"I'm sorry, Ms. Neally," he said. "It's not even close."

"What! But that can't be!" Nicki couldn't believe her ears. "Sam!" she yelled, turning to where he'd been sitting. But Mason's chair was empty. While all eyes were watching the president, Sam had moved unnoticed to stand beside McWilliams, who'd been casually inching his way nearer to the console housing the K-SAT's firing controls. The ex-SEAL now blocked his path.

"President Dean!" Sam called, standing face-to-face with the secretary sf State, "I'm afraid you're right, sir. What I gave you isn't even close to the correct code." The ex-SEAL took a step closer to the secretary as McWilliams unfolded his arms. "And neither is yours, Mr. President!"

The president did not catch the implication.

"Mr. Mason," he said, starting to lose patience, "what on Earth are you talking about!"

"You have a traitor on board, Mr. President!"

Sam continued to confront McWilliams as he called across the room to the president.

"We knew there was someone above Inspector Lee, someone very highly placed, we just didn't know who until a moment ago when Nicki recognized his voice from her time spent in capture up at Grass Mountain. The secretary of state is your traitor, sir. And your fail-safe code has been compromised!"

"This is goddamn preposterous!" McWilliams objected loudly. "General Blythe, have this man arrested immediately and held in restraint!"

"No, General," Nicki shouted, "Sam's telling the truth!"

General Blythe remained silent, his gaze hard on McWilliams.

"The Chinese headman needed a fail-safe of his own," Sam explained. "the secretary here was to be his last line of defense. He's switched the codes, Mr. President. The one you hold is useless. You couldn't have destroyed that rocket if you'd wanted to, sir. At least not with the code you have there."

"I will not stand for these outrageous accusations!" McWilliams shouted as he tried to brush Sam aside to move toward the control console, but the ex-SEAL stood his ground in front of the big man.

"Mr. President," the secretary pleaded, "I demand you remove this man from my sight!"

"General Blythe!" Sam warned, "the secretary is trying to get to the firing console! Probably to try to sabotage it somehow. May I suggest putting an armed guard on both of us, sir. Should either one of us make a sudden move for the console, shoot us both!"

"Mr. President, this is absurd!" Again, McWilliams was trying to move past Sam as he spoke, and again the ex-SEAL stepped in front of him.

From across the room, Sergeant Haggett called, "One minute!"

"Stay where you are, Hoof!"

The order came from the president.

"General Blythe," he said, "have one of your Marines train a weapon on the secretary and Mr. Mason."

The general gave the order, and one of the soldiers quickly dropped to his knee and pointed his M-16 at the two men.

Beads of sweat trickled down the secretary's brow as he appealed to the president. "Mathew, surely you can't believe any of this horseshit."

"General Blythe," Dean ordered, "if the secretary of state opens his mouth again, have him shot!"

McWilliams started to object but thought better of it.

"Mr. President," Sam asked in a softer voice, "who's the other man aboard with access to the fail-safe code?"

The president was staring at McWilliams.

"The secretary of state," he said.

"Who handed you the sealed packet at the last update?" Sam asked.

"Secretary McWilliams did."

"Is that the usual and correct procedure, sir?"

"No, it is not. And I'm afraid that's my fault."

"Mr. President," Sam said, "Secretary McWilliams switched packets. The real fail-safe is in his right-hand coat pocket, sir." Sam looked at the Marine, pointing the rifle at him. "General Blythe," he said. "With your permission, sir?"

"Go ahead, son," the general said.

Sam stepped in front of the secretary. Staring him in the eye the whole time, he reached into the secretary's coat pocket and removed the packet. Holding it away from McWilliams, Sam stepped back carefully and tossed it to Dean.

"Thirty seconds."

"There's still time, Mr. President!" Sam urged. "Compare the codes, sir. I promise you they're not the same."

The president broke the seal on McWilliams's packet and held the two cards up.

"Mr. President," Sam said, reading Dean's face, "the code I took from the secretary is the correct code, sir! Input it to the K-SATs! If I'm wrong, the system won't accept the code, and nothing will happen. But if I'm right."

"Fifteen seconds."

Dean looked to no one for input this time. It was his decision to make.

"General Blythe," he said, handing him the code card Sam had taken from McWilliams. "Blow it out of the sky!"

The general took the card and quickly laid it in front of the sergeant sitting at the firing console.

"Ten seconds."

The general placed a gentle hand on the young airman's shoulder. "Do it right the first time, son."

The airman took a deep breath, typed in the code, lifted the safety cover off the firing mechanism, and pressed the red button.

"General Blythe, sir!" Sergeant Haggett reported. "The target has attained minimal orbit."

"My good God!"

Captain Alosa was leaning over a screen on the next console. The first to know, he snapped up straight as a board, as if in shock. "The fail-safe code's been accepted," he reported to no one in particular, his face fraught with the realization of what must almost have happened. "Laser burst is confirmed, General. The target has been destroyed, sir!"

An excited murmur circled the COC as the rest of the room came quickly to their own grim conclusions. President Dean stood alone, silently staring at his secretary of state. After a moment, he stepped over to McWilliams.

"Why, Hoof?"

The secretary showed no sign of remorse.

"You fucking liberals have been running the country into the ground forever," he said sneering. "There was no hope for her, not as long as you were allowed to continue to weaken her as you did. I'd rather see her die a quick and painless death than to see her rot slowly from within."

Though he knew he could never fully comprehend the man's motive, Dean thought he understood in part.

"Like Katherine?" he said.

Put off by the suggestion, McWilliams just looked away. The secretary of state would have nothing more to say.

"General Blythe," the president said, stepping back from McWilliams. "Place the secretary under arrest and hold him in secure isolation until we reach the ground."

The general gave the necessary orders and then, as the president turned to consult with his national security adviser, Blythe picked the fail-safe card off the console and walked over to where Nicki stood, Sam's scribbled note still in her hand.

"May I?" he said, acting on a hunch.

Nicki handed him the piece of paper, and the general held it next to the code card Sam had taken from McWilliams. His face said nothing as he looked at Sam. He turned and walked to the president.

"Sir," he said, handing the president the two codes.

Dean looked questioningly at the general for a moment before looking down. The president's head jerked back almost instantly in disbelief. They were identical.

"Mr. President!" It was Bob Clancy, a phone held loosely to his ear. "White Plains ballistic missile complex, in Utah. They've got one, sir!"

The president shook his head in complete astonishment, turning with wonder to look at Sam and Nicki.

"All right," he said to General Blythe. "Let's find them all. You know what to do, Joe."

Still shaking his head in bewilderment, the president walked over to where Sam and Nicki stood. Forever gracious, Dean was not a man to speak in pretenses.

"It seems," he said, "the free world owes you two an immeasurable debt of gratitude." The president's famous smile revealed just the right amount of humility as he spoke. "For what it's worth, thank you both."

With that, the president shook both their hands as his national security adviser stood by patiently.

"Well, Bob," Dean said to Clancy as he released Sam's hand, "it seems I have a long-distance phone call to make."

The president turned back to Sam. "Tell me, Mr. Mason," he said, his smile still in place. "You wouldn't happen to speak Chinese, would you?"

Epilogue

Sipping drinks under a brilliant Bermuda sky, Sam and Nicki lay sprawled on a pair of hotel beach chairs, soaking up sun on their second day of a well-earned vacation, compliments of the US government.

The first few days following the destruction of the Chinese satellite had seen tensions run high between the two countries. President Dean had, with Sam's help, eventually managed to convince Chairman Lin of Wu Xun's thwarted plot. Following leads provided by the ex-SEAL, the Chinese military was easily able to confirm and quell the planned coup, hunting down and brutally executing anyone suspected of collaborating with General Wu.

At home, as in Russia, the military was engrossed in a massive and somewhat frantic weapons hunt while at the same time intelligence agencies in the US worked around the clock to track down the moles planted deep within government organizations—all with limited success. Help came, at no small cost, when Chinese intelligence delivered to US agents a disc they'd been able to retrieve from Wu Xun's computer system, duplicating the data contained on the original lost microchip. The search for hidden nuclear ordinance would continue, however, long after all the weapons listed on the disc were found, as it had been decided the possibility existed that the information provided by the Chinese might not be complete.

Through it all, Sam and Nicki spent much of their time enduring intense debriefing sessions and cross-examinations by a doubting military intelligence, until General Blythe finally put an end to it. President Dean himself then came to ask a personal favor of Sam to not publish the story. Sam agreed without reservation. Dean offered the getaway as a thank you from a grateful, if unknowing, American people.

"What do you say, Sam? One more margarita, a quick dip in the ocean, then we shower, dress, and you can buy me dinner downtown. How's that sound?"

Sam stole a peek at Nicki over the top of the newspaper he was reading. Her taut, lithe body damp with beads of sunny persperation was, he realized, a sight he could never grow tired of.

"Should we shower together to conserve water?" he asked.

"But of course, silly man!"

"Can I help you dress?"

"No, you'll slow me down. You can help me undress later."

"In that case, your proposal is accepted."

Sam waved for one of the cabana boys and ordered two of the tequila drinks on the rocks, one with salt for himself and one without for Nicki. As the young waiter ran off across the hot coral-colored sand, Sam returned to his copy of the *Times*, finishing an article explaining in more detail to the world, the previously reported explosion of a Chinese communications satellite seven days earlier.

The paper reported that after completing the analysis of all the available data, a team of Asian scientists had determined that a malfunction in the purging system of the main rocket engines, shortly after final stage separation, had triggered the explosion that destroyed the satellite. The article went on to say the design flaw would be corrected, and a second attempt was planned for the fall.

Sam tossed the folded paper onto Nicki's bare, sun-tanned belly.

"The Chinese have released their cover story," he said. "Made the front page."

"Any mention of McWilliam's suicide?"

"Nope."

"Anything more about Inspector Lee or Wu Xun?"

"Nothing."

"How about the seven hundred nuclear weapons General Blythe found?"

"Not a word."

Nicki sat up in her chair, pulling her legs to her chest. She wrapped her arms around them, hugging herself. "I know they had to cover it all up, Sam," she said, peering at him over the tops of her sunglasses. "It just scares me that they're so damn good at it."

"Does make you wonder," Sam said, stretching back out on his chair.

"Do you think they'll ever catch that Lo Fang character?"

"I doubt it. I talked to Bob Clancy just before we left Washington. He says the Chinese government probably won't even look for him."

"Why not?"

"The Tong is part of their culture. Has been for centuries. Clancy says the two governments are cooperating, and between them, they've identified most of Wu Xun's alliance. The Chinese aren't concerned about the Tong. It's an accepted presence over there."

"Aren't you worried that he might come after you? I mean, he must know about you, Sam. He must know that you spoiled their plans."

"Honestly? No. Lo Fang is a professional criminal. He's not the type to take things personally. He'll cut his losses and go back to business as usual. It's over, Nicki."

Turning to look out over the ocean, she let out a long sigh.

"I hope you're right, Sam," she said, lying back down. "Too bad about your book, though."

Later that night, long after dinner and Sam's consummation of his offer to help with Nicki's undressing and the obligatory duties that customarily accompany such a chore, the two lovers lay quietly entwined in each other's arms.

"Sam," Nicki whispered in the stillness, unable to sleep. "I've been trying not to think about it too much, but there's still something that bothers me."

Drifting near sleep, Sam merely mumbled his response. "Mmm-hummph?"

"The dreams, Sam. The scientist in me has a problem explaining them. It's just not logical. How do you explain being able to see the future, Sam?"

"I can't," he said, coming back awake. "But there's a great deal of phenomena in this world that go unexplained, Nicki. Similar stuff."

"But this was so weird, so…exactly on target. I mean, I know all the major police agencies use psychics to help solve crimes."

"Yes, they do," Sam agreed. "And military intelligence is heavy into them as well. Virtually every major agency in the world is experimenting with ESP to some degree. Your brother and I both tested very high."

"Really? He never told me that."

"Mickey was off the charts."

"Really! So you're thinking it was some kind of telepathy between you and Mickey? Some type of mind reading or thought reading?"

"More like thought projection. Nicki, what I am about to tell you is highly classified. It stays between you and me."

"My lips are sealed."

"And such cute lips they are."

"Sam, get to it!"

"Okay. After your brother and I showed some 'talent' for this kind of thing, we were both brought to one of those unnamed areas out in New Mexico. For three months, we participated in all kinds of experiments. A whole slew of egghead types had us jumping through hoops, day and night, basically studying us like lab rats. It was all sensory related stuff. Some of the guys there, like your brother, were unbelievable, some of the things they could do."

"Like what?"

"Well, one thing they'd learned over the years, they've been studying these phenomena since the forties."

"You're kidding!"

"Nope. Started with the code breakers in World War II. And the thing they'd learned is that people can get better at it. It is a 'skill' that can be developed. Mickey got very good, very fast."

"You know, he did always seem to know what I was thinking."

"No doubt. Anyway, one of the main thrusts of the research at this place was to determine the feasibility of thought projection. The ability to influence another mind telepathically. You can imagine what a weapon that could prove to be in the espionage field."

"I would think it would be huge."

"It is. One of the experiments involved some of us trying to project thoughts to a subject when asleep. It seems the waking mind, at least for now, is too muddled with function and task to be reached. A mind asleep, specifically in REM state, is far more receptive."

"And you had success at this?"

"Some more than others. We would sit in a dark room with the sleeping subject, who was monitored, and eight or ten times throughout the night when the subject went into REM, we would try to project a simple image to his subconscious. Easy things, like walking by a river or building a snowman. We'd write our images down each time, and when they woke the subject up, they'd ask him to remember whatever dreams he could, and then compare notes. Most of us scored about 50 percent, sending very simple images. But Mickey! He could get guys to dream about baseball games, and when they woke up, they could not only tell you who played and who won the game, but what the final score was and who the starting pitchers were!"

"Are you serious!"

"Completely. Mickey had the gift."

"Well, I suppose anything's possible."

"Nicki, the research they're doing now is just the tip of the iceberg. Imagine what they'll be able to do in a hundred years. Or two hundred!"

"But Sam, what about after Mickey died? I mean, you still seemed to be able to see things before they happened. Now I've read about some amazing police cases and I guess that's sort of the same thing, but holy Christ, Sam, I've never heard of anything quite like what happened to you!"

"Well, if you believe some of the great minds who've ventured opinions on this sort of thing—Deepak Chopra, for instance, or even Einstein for that matter—there is no future. Or past. Only present. Time doesn't really exist. It's just nature's way of making it seem as though everything's not happening all at once, which it really is. It's just happening someplace else."

"Is this like that bit about traveling in a rocket ship at the speed of light? Travel for twenty-five years out and twenty-five back, and while you've aged only fifty years, the Earth has aged one million?"

"If you believe in Einstein's theories, yeah. The faster one travels, the slower time passes. Time and space may be interchangeable. What exists now existed somewhere else before and will exist in still another place later. As beings, our true selves, our quantum selves, are nothing more than our thoughts. These bodies we reside in are nothing more than crude short-term housing for the soul, which is timeless. Thoughts are boundless, Nicki. Perhaps these people who can divine the future are just seeing 'other space' rather than 'other time.' Perhaps that space is very close to the space we are in now, and these precious few with the 'power' have the ability to see it. And," Sam offered, "perhaps I am one of them."

"Sam?"

"Yeah?"

"Perhaps you're just a fucking whack-job!"

"That is another possibility."

"Well, Mr. Mason," Nicki said, pulling the covers up snug, "all that's a little more than I care to think about right now, but at least the whole thing's over and those crazy dreams have stopped. Thank God!"

Sam said nothing.

"Sam?" Nicki said, an uneasy sense of forebode dawning with the prolonged silence. "Sam…the dreams have stopped, right?"

The ex-SEAL rolled onto his side to reach for the bedside lamp.

"Well, they had," he said, turning off the light, throwing the room into darkness. "Until last night."

Nikki could not let that go. She reached up to turn on her bedside lamp, "Sam, don't even fucking think about going to sleep! What dream? What did you see!"

Sam sat up a bit to face Nikki, leaning on an elbow. After a few seconds, he spoke very softly, and very slowly, as though trying to properly recall his dream from the night before. "It was actually more of a vision than a dream. From the future. Six feet, masks and soap."

"Six feet, masks and…and soap! Sam, what the hell are you talking about?"

"A pandemic, Nikki. They've developed a new weapon. A biological weapon. A virus!"

About the Author

L eon G. Chabot was born in Weymouth, Massachusetts, in 1951. He grew up in a village of Weymouth, surrounded by the waters of Fore River Bay called Idlewell, where he fostered a great love of the ocean, sports, and music. In his early teens, he became an avid reader and has remained so ever since. Chabot graduated from Weymouth High School in 1968 and went on to attend the University of Massachusetts in the fall. He left after only one year, however, to pursue a career in music. He worked full-time as a bass player in a rock band through the seventies. Chabot was married in 1971 and raised two wonderful children, a son and a daughter, Cory and Erin.

Having grown up in the fifties and sixties, through the beginnings of the Cold War turmoil, Chabot's thoughts on this most dangerous of times developed into a story that ultimately became *Made in China*. Semi-retired, he now lives on Cape Cod.

CPSIA information can be obtained
at www.ICGtesting.com
Printed in the USA
JSHW030508140121
10919JS00001B/1